BARBELO'S
BLOO

GW00633870

"In Mad Mick We Trust"

Joseph-Williams: Barbelo

Order this book online at Galway Print

Also available at all good book retailers and online stores

Contact: Capt. Joseph W. Barbelo on MySpace or

www.barbelosblood.com

Cover design: "Our Lovely Walkabout" by Capt. Barbelo

Interior Illustrations by Capt. Barbelo

All rights reserved. No part of this publication may be reproduced, stored in a retrieval system, or transmitted, in any form or by any means, electronic, mechanical, photocopying, recording, or otherwise, without the written prior permission of the author.

By accessing this book I state that I am in a fit and proper condition and will not make any claim against the author and the author's approved agents or managers in regards to this book or an individual's interpretation of it. Views and opinions presented in this book are for informational and recreational purposes only and may not necessarily be those of the author who may or may not support or advocate those views and may or may not have checked the accuracy thereof. Any similarity to person or persons living or dead is purely coincidental and insufficient grounds for legal prosecution. Or hysteria.

In fact by accessing this book I forfeit all rights to make any legal claims against the author and approved agents for any reason whatsoever. Instead, I will try to have a good time. Absolutely everything is purely coincidental but extreme caution is also necessary. This book may inspire people towards personal liberation and in some extreme cases has been known to cause feelings of sublime transcendence.

Please use your discretion.

ISBN 978-0-9559128-1-8
Published in 2008 by Galway Print Printed by Galway Print.

Website: www.galwayprint.ie Email: info@galwayprint.ie Distributed by Galway Print: Unit 16b, Liosban Business Park, Galway, Republic of Ireland

Conceived in the People's Free Republic of Brixton

To anyone who's ever gazed up at a starry sky, and wondered — what the fuck is all this about?

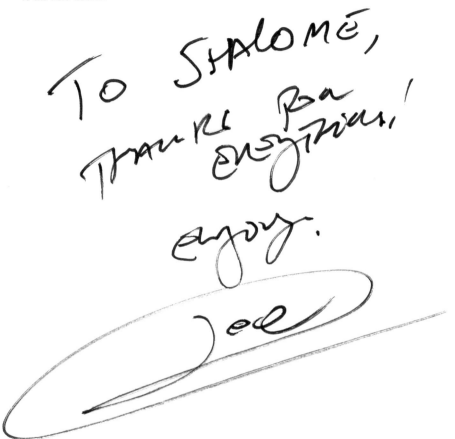

PART ONE
☠resurrection☠

"**Democracy** is two wolves and a lamb deciding what to have for lunch.

Liberty is a well armed lamb contesting the vote."

Benjamin Franklin

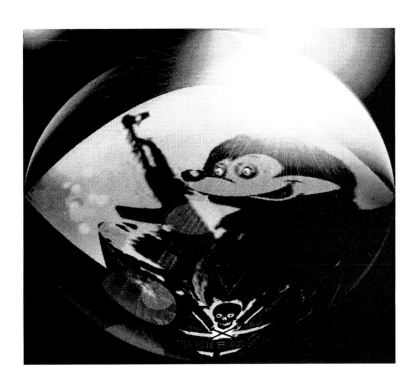

Chapter Zero

Rude Awakenings

The scent of ionised concrete; the underpass, dripping the evening rain, thundering a hundred regrets into my brain.

"Alright granddad?"

"Good evening young man, please stand aside – ach!"

His forearm pins my throat to the wall, his blade flashes under my nose.

"Stand aside? Oi oi, the old fool's losing his marbles; thinks he's fuckin' Charles Bronson!"

Cold laughter booms from the shadows, another two young'uns come into view.

Time slows, my senses quicken.

"Oh please," I rasp, "please don't hurt me, let me go home."

"Empty ya fucking pockets!"

I slipped my memorial pen out of my breast pocket, held up in front of his face.

"It's gold plated. It's all I have. Please, I'm too old for this, I'm not a well man."

"Let's have a butcher's then, ay?"

Reaching to grab my pen, his cutthroat razor slipped, slashing my hand – Blood!

My blood.

Everything has a price, we've all gotta pay tribute, we've all gotta pay our dues. Even me – and I'd not seen blood on my hands for over twenty years.

"Oopsy-daisy, sorry 'bout that, granddad, it was—"

It was the last thing this cunt said – my pen drives hard into his eye socket, my walking stick slaps into his groin.

Screaming onto his knees, dragging me down with him, again and again I drove my memorial pen into his eyes.

It was easy logic, a religious matter, my Gawd-given right!

It was over quicker than a blink.

Chapter 1

Easy Logic

Bloody hell, I was only going home from the pub, I was.

Fuck's sake.

Eighty-two years a scholar and a gent, I am. Scholar on account I talk a lot of sense, and gent on account I knows when to keep stum.

Mr Barbelo.

Just another old cunt, deep in his own private perdition down his Brixton local. Ever chance The Effra Tavern in the early 1980s?

You might recall I always did you the courtesy of a smile at the bar, or at least a nod on the way out. Think back. Geezer with the Trilby hat; three-pint man, always left around half nine before the gaff got mobbed with young'uns…?

Didn't think so.

Tap, tap, tap, went my misery cane, echoing through the underpass, drip, drip, splash, went the concrete roof, like it always did. And I thought about my tower block, the elevator, rattling the stink of urine up to my empty flat – and I thought, maybe one of these nights it won't stop, maybe it'll just keep going up, and up through the roof, into the starry sky, hurtling over the moon all the way to Happy Place, where people like me find peace at last, and shoot guns, riding on clouds…

The twentieth floor is the farthest you'll find anybody on my block, where the Dixons nest, burrow, and fester – nasty South London family the lot of them. And a floor below, Barbelo returns, and slumbers, dreaming my nightmares into the greasy-grey dawn.

Every night, except this night; the lamb returns as the lion, or doesn't return at all.

Self-educated, I am, always had the knack for easy logic, but three of them, one of me? And my memorial pen. Hardly rocket science, is it? Three of the gawky, brain-dead cunts, versus me.

I suppose I should be thankful for the wakeup call. Truth was, I'd been pegging the path of the walking dead a long time.

He bled, hard. He screamed even harder. Nah, no regrets. My pen was mightier than Excalibur when I struck his eyes again, and again.

The other two ran from the slaughter – splish, splash, huff through the underpass – but if they'd only paused to ponder… just how old I was, just how much my stiff little fingers ached, well, perhaps they could've helped their friend. If friend he was. Whatever this soggy bloody mess in my arms was to these junkies.

A true friend does not die alone. Never. I know, because friends I had, once…

So I left him where he lay. The underpass was his tomb, and my resurrection. Tapped my cane home, numb, nothing hurt; it never does at first, and so I sang,

"Raise the scarlet standard flying high, beneath its folds we'll live and die…"

Tap, tap, tap. I was covered in my scarlet flag alright. My pen was mighty, but his blade was sharp. I was cut, not as bad as he should have cut me, ay? Should've done the job in proper order, if he was gonna start. In for a penny, in for a pound – first rule of combat, first rule of any craft: follow through, always.

Silly bunny.

I don't recall getting home. I only knows that when I did, I felt – fuck me sideways, yeah – I felt *good!*

Chapter 2

A Reasonable Man I Am

"Alright granddad?"

"Please stand aside, young man – ach!"

His forearm pinned my throat to the wall, his blade flashed under my snooter, "Empty ya fucking pockets!"

I held up my memorial pen in front of his face.

"It's gold plated! This is all I have, this is all ya fuckin' getting!"

"What—"

My pen drives into his eye socket, but his blade runs across my throat, slashing, slicing – eighty-two years of life gushes from my carotid artery.

I drop to the ground, clawing at my neck. He leans down over me, spits in my face,

"My eye! My fucking eye, you old cunt!"

I awoke screaming, lying on my living room floor, cold and clammy with bitter sweat.

Quickly checked myself over, spied the clotted blood on my hands, and laughed, and laughed – thought I was still dreaming but nah, it was real alright, bloody and real. He was dead, I'd killed him, and it felt good.

Now, this you must understand, if nothing else, just this:

I awoke wanting to live.

Not just happy to be alive, but *wanting* to be alive.

Yep, guilty as charged. I make no apologies for what I am. Barbelo I am – you judging me, me laughing at you – dying in the street, dying on my knife, or, dare we say, withered on your stinking bed with cancer, with heart disease, with misery and contempt for all you did not do, for all you'll now never do, or become.

Better if I get to you first, ay?

Deep down you know I've got a point, because when death's shadow crosses your doorstep, you will say, "Please God, one more day."

That's what you'll croak on your last breath, "one more day," and no one will listen.

No one, except me. Standing over your deathbed, stroking your feverish brow, cooing kind words into your lughole,

"There, there, silly bunny, it's all alright! I'm dying too, fuck, what isn't? It's all fetid flesh, carcass, rotting worm-meat – you're free, don't you see?"

Nah, I didn't see neither – just another brain-dead cunt in the city of the damned – I had eyes but didn't see there was everything to do, and nothing to forgive. For twenty years little changed inside my brain. Outside my brain things changed alright, but inside it was all the same really.

I suppose you could say I was socially well-adjusted.

Crawling to the bog through an ocean of sweat, I puked my ring. Then I scrubbed down my memorial pen, cleaned the cuts on my hand and forearm – gummed them up with Super Glue, bandaged up, nice and tight.

That's the order it went that morning. Ah, the mighty pen, you might ask, what was it in memorial of?

Not yet, better start the morning on a good footing, I always say, and it didn't start there.

Where does anything start?

From a tiny little spark of awareness, here, right here in our hearts. Our conscience. The only God we ever need to listen to. I was never a religious man anyways, but I always knew what was righteous and good. And him dead, me alive?

Fucking righteous.

Shave, slowly, keep the whiskers – chin whiskers and moustache. Maybe shave my loaf too, the Genghis cut. There, all that's missing is the sword and horse!

Lovely job.

I was alive, I got my one more day, and more – a chance to turn everything back. We always have a second chance, but we'll only see it if we deserve it, and we'll deserve it only when we've *earned* it

And I'd fucking earned my second chance, alright. To make up for it all, to atone.

Stuffed my bloody clothes in a bin bag, brought out my best suit from the wardrobe, laid it on the bed. Hooked the gold chain of my timepiece to the buttonhole. Pukka. Better dress the part, the mortality trade respects a good dresser, I'd always found.

Needed a better weapon too, I mused, tucking my pen into the breast pocket. Needed to be ready for the next time.

Kitchen knives are passable, some, but mine were all cheapo—

"Fuck's sake," I mutters to myself, digging up my stash from under the floor, "Need a proper weapon, something *classy*."

Pegging out the door, I stuffed a wedge of notes into my wallet.

"Time to go shopping for a sword, if not a horse…"

The lift stank of piss, and it was good. My body ached, and it was good. The streets were greasy wet, the sky October grey, it was good.

All was good that morning.

Tap, tap, tap, around the corner and the underpass was cordoned off.

That was bad.

Old Bill everywhere, fucking everywhere, and that cunt-face PC Roger May, eyes all over me, up he plods,

"Mornin' Joseph," says he, "You're looking sprightly."

"Full of beans."

"Wouldn't be going this way. Been a murder."

"A murder," says I, "Better be off then."

"Wait…" he pauses, leans over close. "You don't happen to have heard anything? We think it could've been around nine or ten pm. Young lad, can't go into the details, but it was particularly horrific."

"Particular and horrific," keeping my eyes steady, "Last night? No officer, must've left the pub around that time myself, but no, didn't see nothing."

I frowns, mournful.

He frowns back, "What happened to your hand?"

"Oh, cut myself shaving, didn't I. Nerves were at me, dreamt of the Blitz again, woke up with the screaming abdabs. Shaking I was, bloody-well shaking and screaming I was—"

"Alright, alright, better have someone to look at it then," he says. But that's all he says, spins on his heels with a nod, and marches back to his car. I turned right and cut through the market.

Close call.

Nah. It was then I realised a second and very important fact. I was well-under the radar! Not in a month of Sundays could a Peeler suspect Little Barbelo of perpetrating any skulduggery, least of all murder particular and horrific.

Tap, tap, tap and down Electric Avenue, noise, cheapo clothes, foreign foods and full of Darkies. Not that I've got anything against Darkies and immigrants. On the contrary, the more the merrier says I – adds culture and intrigue to the place.

I mean, before they came, London was jammers with Whities, wall-to-wall – boring – a bit like being force-fed potato soup all your life, and then someone opens the cupboards and you suddenly discover Tandori chicken, Thai curry and chocolate pudding.

Never was one to have racial problems, me, always got on, even with the Irish.

Half past ten, timepiece declares. A pint? Why not, this was my new life now. Look for a sword after.

The Effra Tavern was empty. George the barman raises an eyebrow, "You're looking smart, off somewhere special?"

"Going to see my granddaughter," says I, "Thought I'd make the effort."

"The usual then?"

I nods, breathing deep the reek of last night's drink and fags, "Blimey it smells good!"

"What?" returning with my pint, "Smells like a cheap whore's arse in here."

"Did you see the sky this morning?"

"Can't say I noticed," says he. "What happened to your hand?"

"Hmmm, lovely steel-grey, strong sky that," I grins.

He tilts his head, all Bob Hoskins squints, "You alright mate?"

"Why do you ask? 'Course I'm alright," I nods over my pint.

"Nothing, just never seen you in here this early."

"Early bird catches the worm."

"Worms, and maggots," he whispers, leaning across the bar. "Bad business down the underpass, did you hear?"

"Yep, teeming with Old Bill. Some young'un. Found out who did it?"

Shakes his head. "Rumour has it as one of the Dixon Boys."

"Doubt it," says I, "Dixon's are all affiliated; any of them caught out of line… well."

"Fate worse than death," says he with a nod. "But whoever it was, if you ask me he did right by us. Cunt got his just deserts. He was obviously up to no good, lurking around with a cutthroat."

"A cutthroat?" I gasps.

"And heroin, so I hear."

"Deary me, must've come up against someone what wasn't having it, then. But what can we expect, ay? State London's in."

"It's that bloody Thatcher," grumbles George, "Have you seen her *eyes*? Fuck me, soulless, makes me wanna puke! Whole country's gone to the dogs since she's got into power. If I had my way, I'd round up Parliament in a field and fucking shoot them."

"Nah, put them to good use," says I, "Give 'em all an assault rifle and let them loose on each other, ship the survivors to the Falklands."

George laughs. "Better still, get them running this place on a Saturday night; that'll learn them some!"

I nodded, took a long swig of my pint.

"Learn them some respect for real people's lives," I says, and leave him to his cleaning and wot-not.

Needed to sit down, and take it all in.

One dead, or job's a good'un as I call it. I was buzzing; hadn't felt this perky since back in those days.

Work? Only fools and horses, mate. Don't get me wrong though, personally, I couldn't give a monkey's toss either way. What I did for a living was my calling, my nature, what I was born to do. But it's a well-known fact that there's people what want to work, but can't. And there's those what don't want to work, but are forced to.

I mean, there's those who go barmy without work, without something to do with their time, it's in their nature, see? Millions of the poor fuckers, rotting on settees, watching children's TV all day. They even top themselves because they can't find work.

Understandable.

And then there's those who don't want to work, and that's fine by me, why should they have to? They're not doing any harm, let them doss about and do whatever… philosophise, like the ancient Greeks.

Don't laugh! Why not? It's another well-known fact that the Greeks had a dole of sorts, and all those geniuses like Socrates and Plato? How do you think they got to be so clever in the first place? Well, they just let them doss about and argue, slag each other off all day – we wouldn't have philosophy without layabouts.

But, what you've got now is a whole bunch of cunts what don't want to work, forced to steal the jobs off the cunts what do want to work.

It's easy logic, therefore, that if the govermentals, as I call them, was to declare,

"Right! All who want to work, work, and all what don't, go on the dole." I bet you my good peg it would all level out sweet as – everybody would be happy.

And we probably wouldn't get cunts working at the dole what take it all personal, know what I mean?

It's like it was their own money they was dishing out. And why be like that? First thing what's gonna happen to that money is it'll get spent, meaning it'll go supporting someone's business – into a local shop to buy a bit of grub, or a caff, or a boozer and back into circulation – and sooner or later back into the exchequer's greedy mitts anyways. What's the fucking problem, then?

Draining my pint, I asked George for a fag. He didn't hear the first time.

"Said, have you got a spare cigarette please, mate?"

"I don't smoke anymore, sir."

Hear that? 'Sir,' always liked that about George, polite, old-school.

I pegged over to the cigarette machine by the door, pondered what brand – I hadn't smoked for nigh on twenty years neither – it felt odd, but finally settled on Camels.

Needed a light, spied a young'un over the road smoking a fag. Opened the door, "Oi! Young man, got a light please!"

He turns around, hesitates, and then bolts up the street. Took a moment for me too, but I never forget a face – he was one of the cunts from last night.

"Laters George, gotta go." And quickly tapping my way across the street, I knocked on the house he'd been standing outside.

Well, the door opened, and the other cunt got to see me there instead of his mate – fucking priceless, you should've been there.

"Yo-yo-you!" he stammers, all lanky-tremulous, eyes a-popping, "No, no—!"

Jamming my cane into the doorframe, I elbows my way inside.

"Yes it's me," I says, upfront, "Know where I can get a sword?"

"Wh-wh-what? Look, I don't want any trouble—"

"A sword."

"I didn't see nothing, right?

"Close the door!" I shove my way past him into the living room, slump down on the couch, and point to an armchair opposite.

"Sit over there!"

"Get out of—"

"Not going anywhere, need a sword."

"A what?"

"You deaf or something?"

"My mum's coming back any minute—"

"Put the kettle on then, love to meet her."

"Nah really, my mum's—"

"Said, put the kettle on then."

We eyed each other. Him pacing up and down, fidgeting with his adidas hoody. Me, smiling pleasantly. He reminded me a bit of that plonker, fucking hell, what's his name?

"Rodney! That's who you remind me of, from Only Fools and Horses. Bit of a coincidence that, I was just philosophising about work earlier – oi, I wouldn't bolt the fence early if I was you!"

Stalls in mid-stride towards the door.

"Come 'ere!"

Shuffles back a little closer, standing over the coffee table.

"Tried to kill me last night, why?"

"Didn't do nothing, we were just… were just…"

"After my money? Having a bubble? With me?"

"Ha-having a what?"

"Are you thick as well as deaf? A bubble bath, laugh."

Silence.

"Blimey! doesn't nobody speak Gawd's English no more?"

"Saw what you did," he mutters, "What you did to… it was…"

"I know. Horrific and particular. What was his name?"

"Dunno," he whispers, staring off into space – and I could almost hear his brain clanking, churning over, scheming, conniving – poor cunt.

"Well he was not from round here," I says, "Never seen him before, and not that it matters now," I winks, "Gone to Happy Place now, ay? So, get me a sword, there's a good lad, and we'll call it quits."

"A what?"

"Right, you deaf cunt! I'm upping your dues. Guns too, get me a gun and a sword, and then we'll call it quits, hmmm?"

He sat down himself after that.

"Look mister, I don't want any trouble."

"So you keep saying. Got a light?"

He points to a Zippo on the coffee table between us. I lit my cigarette, coughed, and smiled.

"Nice lighter this, can I keep it?"

He nods, brain does one last churn, and he tries to grin back,

"Okay, I'll do what you want."

"You'll get me the gear."

"I'll have it for you tomorrow."

I laughed. "No you won't, you're thinking Old Bill, grassing me up! Go on then, tell them what you saw me do, and I'll tell them what I saw you do but didn't. We'll see who they believe."

Well, thick he wasn't, I'll give him that.

"W-who are you?"

"I'm Mr Barbelo," says I, stretching out my hand. "Pleasure to make your acquaintance."

He shook my hand, firm handshake for someone shitting himself, I'll give him that too.

"Jake. I'm Jake."

"And how old are you Jake?"

"Sixteen."

"Well, now you see Jake."

"See what?"

"You see old cunts like me all the time, and you just think: what an old cunt. But you just don't know, ay?"

"Don't know?"

"You don't know who we are, what we've done, *what* we've been. You just think: oh, look at that old cunt, let's flash a blade under his snooter, let's have a bubble! But you don't think what you should be thinking: well suck my thorny cock, I bet that old cunt's *done* a lot! Bet that old cunt's had a fucking *interesting* life. Bet that old cunt's got to be that old 'cos he's hard as fuck!"

Nod, nod, nod, eyeballs like saucers.

"Young people nowadays, I dunno, time someone taught yous all some manners, bit of respect. So, a sword."

"And a gun, and then what? A tank?"

"Nice one," I chuckles, "a brave attempt at hilarity. Maybe I won't cut your throat after all; maybe I'll keep you for my pet monkey? We'll see, but first, a Luger."

"Where the fuck—"

"Oi, oi! Said manners! I want a Luger 'cos I liked them, from the War."

"You liked Lugers…"

"Don't much mind what sword you get me, so long as it's sharp."

"Sharp…"

"And classy, like a cutlass, like them East End boys used."

"The Krays?"

"Yeah, get me a cutlass, that'll do. Meet you over the road in an hour."

"An hour! Nah man, I'll need a week—"

"An hour for the blade."

I took out my wallet, pulled out a wedge.

"Okay, okay, an hour I can do the sword."

"Something classy, like—"

"Like the Krays, I know, I know. Fuck this," he mutters under his breath, and gets up. I gets up too, wrap my arm round his shoulder, and we head into the hallway.

"I'll get you the gear," he whispers, holding the front door open, "And then we're quits, right?"

"Of course," says I, stepping outside. "I'm a reasonable man, I am…"

Chapter 3

My Lovely Little Social Visit

Well, reasonably speaking, sometimes you just don't know people till they've chucked you off a flyover. Now, Jake was an obvious exception. Idiots like him go around giving it all that, making out they're hard, but they're all mummy's boys really. Normally, back in the days, I wouldn't have had nothing to do with the cunt, but I had the edge, and he knew it. And deserved it – well and truly fucked.

Once cunts like me get the edge on you, we don't let go. Not for any price. We can't help it, we're a force of nature, catch-madrift?

Bit like a Venus Flytrap, a great big giant one, closing in all sticky all over you. Not my fault he didn't have the nous to stay away.

Easy logic.

"Pint please George, and whatever this gentleman wants for himself."

Jake nods his head. "Whiskey, a double."

George shoots him a hesitant eye, "You old enough, son?"

"Eighteen, last week."

I nods. "Eighteen George, nice lad, helping him out with a little history lesson, for his college exams."

George shrugs, pours our drinks, and we make our way to a table by the door. I sat with my back to the wall, force of habit; he sat opposite, on what I call the 'lighthouse stool,' on account of having to keep spinning around like a lighthouse to see what might be coming at your back.

Had a lot to learn, our Jake, but he'd turned up trumps.

"You're late," I mutter.

"Sorry."

"Bloody lunchtime now, still, lovely cane," I says, well-chuffed. "Ivory handle, silver inlay… walnut?"

"Hickory, the bloke said."

"Hickory, hmmm… and the release catch's discretely fitted, here, you see… so what's inside?"

I flick the upper steel collar of the cane, slowly tip the blade out under the table. "Well I never! Fifteen-inch high carbon steel, ground to a needle point, and see?"

"See... what?"

"Fucking beautiful, that's what! Fuller groove running down each face, scalloped grinding on the upper edges..."

He nods.

".... spring tempered, pleasing to the eye."

The satisfying 'click' of the locking mechanism engaging made Jake flinch.

"Where did you find it?"

"Sorry, sorry I couldn't get what you asked for—"

Had to laugh. "Nah, this is the dog's bollocks! Couldn't have done better myself, very classy, haven't seen one of these in donkey's."

Nervously glancing behind at the crowded pub, he skulled his whisky in one.

"Mr Barbelo, can I go now? Please, you got—"

"Said, where did you get it?"

"Antiques dealer, Mile End."

"And the *other thing* we talked about?"

"On its way," he whispers, peering at the wall clock over the bar, and then grumbles, "Nearly two, I've gotta go down the Social."

"You going to sign on?"

Shakes his head. "Won't let me. Reckon I'm not eligible."

"Why?"

"Dunno, that's what I gotta go and find out."

"Fucking cunts," I says, "There's mothers with kids in their arms, little kids in their arms and they just goes, 'Fill in forms wot-not,' and then it's all, 'Nah, sorry madam, you're not eligible.' Sorry my arse, seen them smirk, one of them anyways – that cunt what runs the gaff, posh cunt with the pasty white mug. Wots-his-name."

"Christopher," Jake spits.

"That's him. Thinks he's lord of the manor, that one."

"He's the one I'm supposed to see today."

"Yeah? Well good luck! It's like squeezing blood from a stone. He's loving it. Family's fucking minted. Doesn't need to work in that shithole, does it for the power – knew his father, once, he was the same. Lord of the fucking manor."

I stood up. "Right Jake, I need you to stay here, keep my seat warm while I go to the bog. Here," I hand him a fiver, "Get us another round. And then we're done."

He reaches out a trembling hand. "Promise?"

"Promise. I'm beginning to see things a little clearer."

He glances up, "You are?"

"Jake, my young friend, I'm not a well man, I'd be the first to admit it. But I'm not *unreasonable*."

"Oh."

"Get us a pint then, go to the Social after. I won't be two ticks."

Passing by George at the bar, I made the point of clutching my stomach, grumbling about a bad curry I'd eaten the night before, and headed towards the toilets. I heard George mutter something about 'better out than in,' saw he was busy serving a punter, sidled round to the back bar and out into the street.

Time for *my* little Social visit first.

Picture a lunatic asylum, heaving on a full moon, suddenly let loose into another packed lunatic asylum just twenty foot by twenty – that's the dole office. Hell on Earth.

My swordstick didn't tap the same as my old misery cane did. It kind of thudded, on account of the fact it was heavier, I suspect, and had a lovely feel of impending malice to it as I jumped the queues and knocked on the protective glass.

"Christopher," says I, "Need a quick word."

The bloke next to me groaned. Christopher's mug cracks open with disdain, all blubbery white, spotty with chip-fat rash,

"Get in the queue. I'll see you in turn."

"It's important."

"It's always important."

"It's about Kate."

At the mention of his missus – poor deluded cow – he leans closer to the glass.

"Bad news," I says, "She's... she's..."

I made out I couldn't finish, and forced a tear squeezing the wounds on my arm. Christopher calls over to some other geezer round the back to take his place, and signals to me.

I thudded over to the side door, wait beside the cubicles.

He flings the door open, "What is it Barbelo? Be quick."

I squint into the swarming squalor behind us. Is that what I'd fought for?

"Is this what we fought for? Social welfare my arse!"

He sighs, "What do you want?"

"Want? Want? I want you to give these kids their money!"

"Hey?"

"Why do you think they need to go around mugging people, ay?"

"Okay, Barbelo, you obviously seem to be a little upset, go home and—"

"Upset! What are ya, some kind of Nazi? 'Course I'm upset! Look at this place, for Gawd's sake. You should be ashamed of yourself, treating decent people like this. You wouldn't, if you'd seen what I've seen."

"Oh not the war crap, I have—"

He stalls.

"War crap," I echoes darkly.

"I have work to do—"

I hold onto his sleeve, "Work, you call this work? Half a million British dead, good men and women all, fighting for your freedom – that's work! And for what, to have their kids degraded like this?"

And I was serious, but the cunt just shakes himself loose and starts laughing – fucking laughing at me.

There was that little voice what lives at the back of my mind screaming 'leave it!' – but bollocks to this. I stepped in closer.

"Outside," says I, squaring myself up. "We'll settle this on the field of honour, man to man."

"What?" he smirks.

"You heard, outside, now!"

"Are you... serious?" he chuckles.

"Deadly serious," I growls, turning on my battle-gaze – what just made him laugh even harder.

My shoulders sagged involuntarily, all vim drained from my eyes.

"Do you know what?" I mutters, "You're everything what's wrong was this Country."

And he was. At that precise moment with this cunt just standing there, laughing at me for saying what I did, I could see it all clearly, clearer than I'd never seen it before.

"If that's all, Barbelo, very funny, but I am busy, so get in the queue or go home—"

"No, wait!" I holds onto his sleeve again, and turns on my mournful long-face, "Oh mate, sorry, sorry about all that, I'm not well a man, see? And I wish it wasn't me what has to say it. *Kate*," I whispers.

He comes closer. I move in, arm over his shoulder,

"Listen to me, it's Kate, she's...she's..."

"She's what?"

Fifteen-inch carbon steel in his gut, up and under his sternum, giving his ticker a last little tickle.

Over quicker than a blink.

Now, you might be asking, how's this homicidal old cunt gonna get away with that, right in plain sight of everybody? You'd be surprised – people see what they *expect* to see – and ask anybody, immaculately togged-up old geezers do not gut dole officers with swordsticks.

I simply replaced the blade into my cane and sidled away into the crowded queues. The cunt swayed on his feet, and crumbled to his knees. Didn't even make a sound.

Lovely.

And it was. I was probably halfway up Coldharbour Lane before anyone sussed what had happened, and back in The Effra with young Jake, sipping my pint, when we heard the sirens.

"Oi, oi, sounds like trouble down the Social again," says I, "Looks like you might have to miss your appointment."

"Fucking 'ell..."

I'd not been gone fifteen minutes, but Jake was already swaying a fair bit beside me, wankered on whiskey.

"Easy on the booze there, son. George notices, he'll chuck you out quicker than flicking flies off a shit, and I need you to—"

"But – what else do ya want from me?"

"Told you, I want the *other thing* and then we're done."

"But you said you were reasonable—"

I grins, "People say a lot of things, don't mean it's true."

"Oh fucking hell!"

"Oh dear!"

"Please, *please*."

I had to laugh. He was all one-eyed squints.

"Please what? Calm down, tell you what, trade you the other thing for a word with your mate."

"Wha-who?"

"The other cunt with you last night, saw him earlier outside your gaff. What was he doing? You two gonna get your alibis straight?"

Doesn't reply.

"What's his name then?"

"Steven."

"So where's Steven now, do you reckon?"

Shrugs, "Dunno."

"Smart dresser, where's he work?"

"Dunno."

"Where's his local then?"

Shrugs again.

"You're a good kid," I sighs, "Always say nothing. But still, I thought we were mates." I glaze my eyes, fingering the release catch on my blade. "We are mates, aren't we...?"

Cringes, "Yeah, mates..."

"So, where's his local?"

"Please! Leave it out, ay? What do you want from me now? I didn't see nothing."

I give his hand a playful squeeze.

"I want us all to be mates," I winks, "The best of mates, after everything we've gone through, and I want to atone. The good over the evil, the strong over the weak, everything in nature seeks atonement. Even me. Look around, young Jake, life feeds on other life, doesn't matter how you dress it up. Whether it's chicken wings in a box from the chipper, or you've clubbed something over the head, pulled the wings off it yourself. To be alive, something's gotta die, and to make things good, you've gotta eliminate the evil. I didn't make the rules, I'm only a natural selector."

He mutters, "I don't understand..."

"Think of it like a gardener weeding your garden; can't have a good garden if it's fucked with weeds, can you?"

"... no?"

"Obviously not. And can we be mates if we can't *all* have a *friendly* drink together?"

"The Albert," he replies, after the appropriate pause what meant it was probably some other boozer entirely.

But The Albert would do.

The Prince Albert's a boozer down Coldharbour Lane, just up the road from the dole office in those days, where all our young and old social misfits went after they'd got their giros.

Packed, it was, and Old Bill plodding about everywhere – questioning, questioning – but nobody took any notice of us.

Jake was beside me at the bar, shitting gold bricks again.

Says Pat the barman, passing us our drinks,

"Someone got stabbed down the dole."

"Oh how awful!" says I. "Anybody see who did it?"

Shrugs, "One found in the underpass this morning, and now this!" Lowers his tone, flicking an eyeball to the Peelers, "And they're fuckin' useless!"

"Awful, Pat, truly awful."

"I tell ya, we should be organising ourselves into militias."

"Oh really?"

"What we need is the right to bear arms, we wouldn't be having these problems if everybody was armed. It's no good only some people being armed, dirty scumbags. And the rest of us?"

"Victims," I mutter, accepting my change. "You're a man after my own heart, Pat, never a truer word. But I dunno, I'm a little long in the tooth for all that malarkey, ay?"

"I'd protect ya," he nods.

"Thanks Pat," I grins, "Lovely thing to say, anybody ever tell you, you looks just like a young Marlon Brando?"

"Yeah, my wife, every Friday when I go home with the paycheque!" he laughs, "Enjoy your pint."

"Oh I will," I mutter, and squeezing our way to the tables, I whispers to Jake, "Cunt got his just deserts."

"Sorry?"

"You've got nothing to worry about."

"What?"

"Said behave normal and you'll be fine, you were with me down The Effra the whole time. The only time you wasn't, was when I went to the bogs. Bad curry *equals* good garden, got it?" I winks.

Jake finally gets it alright; puts two and two together and misses a step, spilling the top froth of his pint on my arm.

"It was you?"

"Well don't thank me all at once!" I whispers.

"Oh fucking hell."

"Oh what now? Did you a favour—"

"Get away from me you evil cunt!"

I quickly grab his arm before he bolts for the door, "Evil? That's an abstract concept given to personal interpretation. But gutted on the end of this lovely bit of kit *you* got for me," I flash my cane in front of his face, "That's universal fact. Catch-madrift?"

He nods.

"Not that he'd done nothing to me," I adds, "Don't get me wrong, wasn't personal, just natural selection. Alright?"

And I was well-rusty, that too, needed to sharpen up my edge and awaken my touch.

"Alright?" I whispers again, forcefully. "Or would you rather we have a word with the Old Bill?"

Jake breathes in deep, eyes flitting about the pub, "Alright, alright."

"Good lad!" I says, releasing his arm. "Now sit, relax, almost over."

Sat by the door, I scanned the crowded pub for Jake's mate anyway.

"What's Steven's name?"

"Who?"

"Your mate, Steven, what's his name?"

He groans, "Graham, it's Graham."

"Graham… looked a lot older than you, what, thirties?"

"Twenty-five, he's my older brother's mate, more than mine. Clever," he adds, biting his lower lip, "went to university."

"So what was he doing with you down the underpass?"

Turns on me, all wide-eyed, "Nothing."

"Nothing?"

"I mean alright, scoring some gear off us, then you came along and – oh fuck, here they come!"

Roger the Plod and side-kicks, but he only tipped his helmet at us on the way out of the pub.

"See that, my young accomplice? Respect. That's all we ever really need from anybody, just a bit of respect for who we are. But," I lifts my finger, pointing to his eyes, "you can't get respect if you don't respect yourself first. Nobody can *see* it, see?"

"Respect, yeah. Right."

"Respect is earned and *seen* to be earned," I whisper, leaning over the table. "How long you been on that shit?"

"Six months."

"Do you like being a smack-head?"

Shakes his head, "Can't do nothing about it."

"Got you by the balls, ay?"

Nods.

"Eat your own grandmother alive for a hit, ay?"

Nods.

"Well, I had a bit of a problem myself, as it goes, after I lost my leg."

"*You* were a smack-head?" he asks incredulously.

"Oh fuck yeah – up to the eyeballs in morphine I was, addicted quicker than you can spit! Lasted a lot longer than six months though. Blimey, not easy cleaning up, but can be done, can be done… if you know *how*."

"How long, I mean how did you do it?"

I rest back into my seat, and chuckles, "Oh, I was in the Army back then, a special unit, they had ways. Special ways."

"*Special* ways?"

"The Formula. It's amazing; works for all known addictive substances and more! I'd patent it and sell it off to the Yanks, make a bloody mint – except I can't. It's a secret and it's gotta stay that way."

Glances about, lowers his tone, "Can you get us this… *formula?*"

"I dunno," I sighs, "We're talking a very special procedure, I dunno know if you can keep a secret."

"I can, I can," he whispers. "Go on…"

I study his anxious face for a moment, take pity on the poor cunt, and puts my pint down.

"Very well then," I whispers, leaning over the table again, "This is what we're gonna do. The Formula gives everyone, and now you, obviously, exactly six months to get off any and all addictive substances. It don't care how you go about it, all it knows is if six months from now you haven't cleaned up, I'm coming after you."

"Wha-a—"

I grip his wrist painfully tight, turning on my battle-gaze,

"Look into my eyes, young Jake, and mark my words well.

I'm gonna see you earning your respect. Run for it, and make no mistake, I will find you. And when I do," I growls, clawing over the table, closer, "I will tie you to a chair in my kitchen, make a nice cup of tea and slowly, very slowly gouge out your eyes with a spoon. Do I make myself clear? Do not speak, just nod."

He nods.

"Then, taking my time, I will fry your eyeballs in the blood what had dripped, dripped, dripped from your eyeless sockets, and the resulting warm, soggy, and no doubt pungent slop, I will scoop from the pan and feed you, one spoonful at the time, until... it... is... all... gone! Do you understand?"

Nod, nod, nod!

"Then, after I've made myself another lovely cuppa, we will progress to your fingers, one by one, your toes, one by one, and other likewise suitable bodily *protuberances*. Do I make myself perfectly clear, young Jake?"

Nod, nod, nod, nod, nod!

"Do you promise to honour The Formula?"

Nod, nod.

"You can speak now, if you want."

"I promise, I promise!"

"Pukka! Glad we see eye to eye!"

I chuckles, clapping my hands with glee.

He mutters, massaging his wrist, "Why, why are you laughing."

"Well I could be wrong, and I hope I'm *not* wrong, but you don't stand a ghost's chance in hell of honouring that promise. Ah!" I raise my hand as he goes to interrupt, "Said I could be wrong. Me, on the other hand, I'm a gentleman through and through, and a gentleman always *follows through* – catch-madrift?"

Nods.

"Now, see that phone by the bar?" I points.

He turns around.

"Give your mate Graham a bell. We need to have some respectful words, him and I…"

Chapter 4

Silly Bunny

The pub was quieter now. Graham showed up about seven, well-after the Old Bill had gone and well-sussed to what'd been going on. Jake had been busy on the blower.

"Mr Barbelo," he began, all polite and upfront, smoothing down his beige cotton suit. "I want to assure you that the ermmm, *misunderstanding* which occurred last night, well, it won't happen again."

"Obviously," I confirms, and he sits with his back against the wall beside me.

I liked him at once, cut a fine trim. Hint of the auld Errol Flynn, only with a serious tan, and had potential – his inner killer bubbling just under the surface – shame he would have to go.

Well, there's lessons to be learnt here, what I do is a fine art. Oh, in the olden times it was par for the course, but nowadays you've gotta work at it, dig deep and root out the opportunities – it's a craft like any other craft – and as I say, I was well-rusty. Twenty-odd years of quiet retirement, and yeah, not proud to admit, but it had turned me into the walking dead.

Follow your nature, that's the first rule of natural law.

Graham was nodding agreement, "So," he says, "what I propose is we let bygones be bygones. We have prepared your compensation, a tidy sum, which I'm sure you'll find—"

"A pay off?"

He nods, puts three fingers up in the air, meaning three grand – well I hope that's what he meant – I shakes my head.

"Is that what I'm worth?"

"It's a lot of money," he frowns.

"Didn't ask that, asked is that what I'm *worth*?"

"I understand," he mutters, clears his throat, and nods his head understanding fuck-all. "We have a second proposal, something which could perhaps settle this to our mutual satisfaction. By that I mean we go into business. We could use a man of your experience and distinguished character in our, erm… *enterprise*."

"What enterprise, you mean a Firm?"

"S.L.H."

"Never heard of yous. What's it stand for anyway?"

"South London Hounds, a collective of mutual—"

I laughed, well, I had to.

"Poncy name! Where you from, Graham, bit of the Darkie in you, isn't there?"

"Dad's from Jamaica, mum's from Coventry," he says, and smiles.

"Ever killed anyone?"

He flinches, but doesn't reply, which is the correct etiquette, but I knew he hadn't. There's an air to someone whenever I'd popped that question in the past. Ask completely out of the blue like that, and it's unmistakable, if you know what to look for: a shadow, crossing ever so slight over the eyes, there and yet not there, if ya catch-madrift.

Well, he didn't have it – pity.

"Mr Barbelo, sir," Jake cuts in, "Graham's offering you a job."

"Only fools and horses, son, I don't work for no one, not no more, see?"

"I see," smiles Graham.

"Nah, you don't. And I certainly don't work with smack-heads. Fucking liability."

Flicks his eyes at my pint, "We all have our poisons–"

"Oi! Don't fucking try to lump us together, clearly there's a profound and irreconcilable difference between you and I. Alright, I've nothing against other drugs – and beer, the occasional fag, that's my prerogative – but I'm not going around hurting people to get money for beer. Fuck me, if I ruled this country I'd give yous all the drugs you want, for free!"

He chuckles.

"Yeah, give yous all enough rope, fucking hang yourselves." I sips my pint. "Getting bored, or vexed, I dunno which. So if you don't mind, tell us what I need to hear or kindly piss off."

"Then we have nothing further to discuss."

I nods, "True, meeting concluded."

Graham went to rise, Jake gets uppity, grabbing onto his arm.

"No, wait!" he whispers, "I can't go on like this! Fucking do something, get him off my back!"

"Chill out, S.L.H. will sort it," Graham whispers back, and then flashing a lovely ruthless grin, "We're gonna sort you out," he says to me, "It will be our pleasure."

"Pleasure's all mine," says I, raising my glass, "Bring it on, look forward to it."

Graham peels Jake's fingers off his suit, got up, and sits down again,

"Listen, I don't know who you think you are, but you don't know who you're messing with. Just take the money, stay away from him, us, and we'll stay away from you."

"Not what I need to hear, no deal."

Clucks his tongue. "You don't want money? Gal, pretty gals?"

"My young friend, you insult me – this is a religious matter!"

Flashes me a crooked grin, "A religious matter… what kind of nutter are you?"

Jake was nodding his head frantically, "Nutter, fuckin' nutter…"

I turns to Graham, "Did you know, way back, way back in the olden times, what I did was a holy profession?"

"A holy profession, is what?"

"What I did, and am now doing again."

"Murder," mumbles Jake, tight-lipped, "Geezer down the dole – I told ya – he's what done it."

I quickly leans over the table to Jake.

"No, no, what did I say earlier? I'm a natural selector, not a murderer! Gawd blimey, what do you take me for?"

Jake starts whimpering, eyes brimming with tears.

Understandable, I suppose it'd been a long day for him.

"Go home," I says, giving his shoulder a friendly squeeze it didn't want. "I'll call round tomorrow morning, first thing, and conclude our little agreement."

Jake bolts for the door. I turns to Graham again.

"Well," I says, "let me explain. I've been thinking, spent too long out of the Craft, see, and—"

"The craft," he scoffs, "so now you're an artist as well as a suicidal nutter. Listen to me—"

"Nah, you listen! My young friend, I am an artist, of sorts, always did like art, see? And if I could go back, do it all over, I'd be a painter, a proper painter mind, none of your modern bollocks, a proper gent like Caravaggio. Or a writer, now that's a worthy thing if ever there was one! None of that telly bollocks neither, a proper writer like Hardy or Marlowe—"

"Mr Barbelo, be reasonable; *what* is it you want?"

"Alright. I want to give you a chance, a reasonable chance all told, something yous all gave me last night. A chance to atone."

"Really."

"Otherwise, under the ancient laws of combat, I'm required to collect my dues on the field of honour."

"What laws?"

"Natural law. *Quid pro quo.* Tit for tat, this for that."

He sighs.

I sighs. "My young friend, I'll put it simply; you hang about dark alleyways, preying on the elderly and the weak; what do you expect an old-school gent like me to want?"

"Atonement."

I nods, "Go on then, atone."

"So you'll take the money. A wise decision. We wouldn't want you getting hurt, now would we—?"

Almost pissed myself laughing, tickled me pink that did!

"Oh, oh," I gasps, calming down, "Oh mate, seriously, listen to me," I whispers, wrapping my arm around his shoulder, drawing him near, "I've seen things you young'uns wouldn't believe. Cavalry attacks pounding through the sea fog at Beersheba. I've watched the dawn, blaze like a hundred suns on the wingtips of a Lancaster Bomber. My young Graham, I'm not gonna get hurt, and why? Because you're already dead. Run, I will cut you down. Hide, I will hunt you down. Now do you understand?"

He shrugs my arm off his shoulder.

"Nothing personal." I smiles. "I quite like you as it goes. Can I get you a pint?"

There followed a long pause.

He stands up, straightens his tie and shakes his head at me,

"You've got twenty-four hours to get out of South London."

"Come again?"

"You fucking heard," he grunts, glancing at his watch, "Madman!" And with that, he ups and leaves.

Madman?

Blimey! All he had to say was sorry and that he wouldn't do it again.

Silly bunny.

Interesting though, I'd swear I was getting younger by the minute. My step had a spring in it, and I'd found myself fancying the barmaid all night. But, the main thing was, I'd got myself past three pints without wanting to butcher every cunt in the gaff to the very last cunt, which is why I'm a three-pint man for nigh on two decades.

I don't know if you quite understand what that means, I suppose if you'd never felt it, no point trying to talk about it, but it was a fucking miracle to just drink till closing time.

A very promising prospect, I thought.

Got home, changed my bandages. Five more scars to add to the Barbelo collection, as if I need any more. Naked, I look like a rag doll stitched together by a retarded chimpanzee on absinth. I made a nice cup of tea, sat in my kitchen, staring happily out the window of my tower block till dawn.

London, my lovely London, twinkling across the land like an upside-down fucked up firmament – twenty-four hours to retreat, said Graham. Nah, it wasn't atonement by any stretch, but right enough, he'd followed the correct procedure. First, offer to buy them off. If that don't work, try to recruit them as well. And failing that: natural law.

Cause for concern? For the first time in more years than I can remember, I actually set my alarm clock and went to sleep with a smile.

Only thing missing was a bird. My bed was cold.

Chapter 5

Only One Bloody Nightmare

"Die! Die! Die! Kill the whole fucking lot-of-ya-cunts!"

The number two double-decker bus rumbles along Brixton High Street. Barbelo hugs himself, rocking back and forth.

"Did I say that out loud?" he asks himself in his mind.

His mind is strangely silent, and so is the crowded top deck, at least nobody appears to be looking in his direction.

Sighing with a curious detached relief, he braves a tentative one-eyed squint – immediately his mind screams,

"Kill 'em all, kill 'em all, kill 'em all!"

Hugging himself tighter, Barbelo whimpers, clawing his fingers into his arms,

"Oh what's wrong with me? I'm all fucking wrong! Nah, keep it together, breathe, deep, that's it, good, think happy thoughts, good, breathe, *happy thoughts* – KILL!"

The gentleman sitting next to Barbelo elbows him gently, saying,

"Please be quiet, I'm trying to read my newspaper."

Barbelo recoils against the window, shocked that this seemingly ordinary young fellow could read his mind.

"Can you read my mind?"

"I'm trying to read my newspaper," he mutters, disgruntled, but not unkindly. "You're ever so loud!"

"Loud?" Barbelo eyes the passenger up and down, "I'll give you fucking loud – hold on… don't I know you?"

"Of course," he grins a pasty white smirk, "It's me, Christopher, from the Social Welfare Office."

"Oh no you're fucking not!"

"Oh yes I am, you know."

"Well you're looking well, I killed you."

"Did you?"

"Didn't do nothing…"

"Didn't do nothing! Didn't do nothing!" scream all the passengers on the bus, turning around and staring at him.

"Oi, manners, keep your noses out of it!" yells Barbelo, and they turn away again, abashed.

"Oh alright, yeah," he whispers, "I had to. But do you know what? I haven't a monkey's why."

"Perhaps it was an on the spot ethical decision."

"Ethical decision. Nice turn of phrase, must remember that."

"Or maybe you have a special gift?"

"Maybe I suppose I do."

"But I'm not the worse, you know, there's some really nasty people out there who would, perhaps, merit the skill and attention you could provide."

He smiles.

Barbelo smiles, "Do you know what, that's beautiful what you just said, a capital idea!"

"I'm glad you think so."

"From now on, I swear I'll do better, if ya catch-madrift."

Christopher nods. "Well, thanks anyway, I'm much happier now."

"Glad to hear it, so it all worked out in the end."

"It did, and forgive me for those things I said, about the War."

"Well, you didn't actually say much, you just laughed."

"Forgive me for laughing, then."

"Fair enough. But what's—"

The passengers all turn again, "But it was the *way* he laughed!"

"Excuse me," replies Christopher, "I'm trying to vindicate myself."

"Oi you horrible lot, shut it! He's trying to vindicate himself!"

"Shut it, shut it, shut it!" they echo and begin to laugh, cackling wildly, "Haw! Haw! Haw!"

Christopher sighs, "I do have a terrible laugh."

Barbelo rises to his feet, smiles. "Excuse me a moment…"

A pickaxe materialises in his hands, and down it goes through the man sitting in front – a fountain of blood gushes from his neck.

"Slay them all! God will know His own!"

And down the pickaxe goes through another man's skull.

"Kill 'em all! Let God sort them out!"

Barbelo advances through the top deck, wading through a crimson ocean.

And down it goes through another man's chest.

"Slay yous all! God will know His own!"
And down it goes through another man's skull, piling up a giant
pyramid of butchery and blood

blood
blood blood
blood blood blood
blood blood **EYE** blood blood
blood blood blood blood blood blood
blood blood blood blood blood blood blood
blood blood blood blood blood blood blood blood
blood blood blood blood blood blood blood blood blood
blood blood blood blood blood blood blood blood blood blood

Chapter 6

Lady of the Road

Woke up screaming again, checked myself over, again.

Good, no blood, no bruises, and only one nightmare. I was approaching the edge, getting sharper. I'd lost my touch and was getting it back again – now the nightmares would be fewer and easier to forget.

Sat on the end of my bed, I strap on my wooden peg.

Twenty-four hours to retreat, said Graham, but that was bollocks. I'd made the point of saying I'd be calling round to Jake's in the morning. If they're smart, that's not where they'd do it.

If they're the wankers I was counting on, that's exactly where they'd do it.

Shave, shit, tog-up and tool-up.

Black suit, memorial pen, gloves, fishing wire, pool balls I'd half-inched from the pub, nylon sock, Jake's Zippo lighter and a Jif squeezy lemon – should be enough, don't want to overdo it. Improvise with whatever else lies handy on-site, leastways that used to be my speciality.

Bit more Super Glue, another wrap of fresh bandages and I was done – down the lift, out the estate, and before you can say 'Jack Robinson' I was marching and thudding up Coldharbour Lane.

Beautiful sky; all clear blue, crisp and blue.

Everything felt fresh, awake, alive and wanting.

Pukka little breakfast down the caff – two eggs, bacon and fried tomato with toast – three lovely cuppas after, and off to work we go.

"Good morning madam!"

"Good morning sir!"

Happy, happy, happy I am.

Needed lighter fuel and Vaseline, so I stopped off at the shops down Electric Avenue, before pegging up Kellett Road.

Pausing outside Jake's house, I primed my tools – filled the sock with the pool balls, emptied the Jif lemon, filled it with lighter fuel, added a small dollop of Vaseline, gave it a good shake – and carefully replacing my arsenal back into my jacket pockets, I knocked on the door with the Zippo.

"Oh, it's you, come in," says Jake, all pleasant, holding the door open, "I've got your gear upstairs, sir, please wait in the living room."

I pegged inside. "I'm impressed, thanks—"

Jake slams the door behind him and legs it upstairs.

Well, they were the wankers I'd counted on alright, two of them standing in the living room – a Darkie and a Whitie – big cunts, nylon stocking masks, baseball bats, no gloves.

Fucking idiots.

"Oh bloody hell," scoffs one, edging around the sofa towards me. "Said he was old, but that's fucking Alf Garnet!"

"Good morning granddad," says the other, peeling himself off the wall behind.

"Please, let's talk," I quivers, "I'm not a well man!"

"We're gonna have to teach you a lesson…"

"Please," grovel, grovel, whimper, "Oh, oh, I'm sorry!"

"A little late for sorry."

"… should know better at your age."

Still whimpering, I raised my Zippo, clutching it in front of my face like a crucifix. They were sniggering, coming in slow.

Now, if you ever find yourself in a pickle like this – Gawd forbid but who knows – what you want is chaos, the unexpected, there's never any point in talk unless it's to distract the eye.

Always distract the eye.

I chucked my cane at the cunt nearest, lit the end of the Lemon with my Zippo and squeezed.

Lovely little flamethrowers, Jif lemons, if you didn't know, live and learn.

Spinning around on my wooden peg, I showered their loaves in righteous firestorm. Their stocking masks lit up like Christmas. It was all burning and screams after that.

Cracked the knees off the Darkie with my the sock-mace, he went down, grabbed his baseball bat and mashed his loaf – heard a shot – cracked the knees off the Whitie, down he goes. Mashed his loaf.

Knees and loaf, that's how it went, all over in a Jify. Hehehe! Didn't even have to use the swordstick till after, for finishing.

Clean up, dispose? Unnecessary. I was still well-under the radar, so fuck it, tip the rest of the fuel on the sofa, the curtains, and open the windows. Let the gaff burn. Had nothing against Jake's mum, except she'd brought up a plonker, and two geezers in Happy Place is not a pretty sight to come home to after work.

House fires are more… respectable.

Checking to see the street was empty, I dragged Jake out the house by the ear.

"Two, only two? One shooter and one fucking bullet? What do they take me for, a fucking ballet dancer! Do they think I was born yesterday, just floated down the Thames in a bubble? Anyway, nice bit of kit," I says, calming down and letting go of his ear, "9mm, 17 series, brand-new."

Wrapping the Glock in a plastic bag, I shot him a warm smile.

"But how do wankers like that, get gear like this? Fucking disgrace!"

He trundled along beside me, gazing out into the street.

"Oh don't be like that! Chillsy out, I'm not *really* angry with you. Tell you what, forget the Luger, this is much the same anyways. Get me a full clip for this and we'll call it quits, ay?"

Jake wasn't listening. He was still on his feet alright, but that's about it. Seen that look before, poor bastard. Shock, or 'weak perspective,' as I call it. All his primal survival instincts scream get away from the homicidal cunt, but the homicidal cunt's all he knows.

I'm his entire world now – if I said Jake, rollover! rollover is what he'd do, leastways until a stronger perspective comes along.

"I'm sorry," I says, and almost meant it.

The Albert was quiet.

Pat grins. "Back again?"

"Thirsty work, is pensions and unemployment."

Personally, I've always liked pubs, and since my life changed for the better, I was happy as Larry to be inside one in the daytime. Something naughty about drinking in the day, like you're Lord Fuckface and don't have a care or nothing.

"Got the time?" I asks Pat, "My timepiece's on the blink."

Glances at the wall clock behind him. "Ten to eleven."

"What?"

"Ten to eleven."

"Cheers," I says, accepting our drinks, and Jake drifts his way to the table by the door. I gently steer him to a different table.

"Never the same place three times in a row," I whisper, "Too predictable. Always break up your tracks. Now, this table will do nicely, good line of sight to the entrances, see?"

I smile, he says nothing. We sit down.

"If you don't get me some ammo, you still owe me a proper Luger," I explain jovially. "Don't think just because I got this you're going to get away with not paying your dues."

His eyes glaze, staring at the plastic bag on the seat beside me.

"I suppose you're wondering what we're doing here? Nothing. Drinking beer. It's always good after a job to be seen somewhere else, even if you're a few minutes short of an alibi, it could still stand you good."

"What?" he mutters.

"It speaks!" I chuckles, "Good, good, what I mean is people don't synchronise their watches like in the movies. A minute here, a minute there. Cause for reasonable doubt, see?"

He nods.

"Now, don't get your knickers in a twist about our Graham. It's time to call it quits anyway. I'm too long in the tooth to be fucking about with wankers, and I reckon he's learnt his lesson. What do you reckon?"

He nods his head feverishly.

"So, drink your pint and chillsy out."

"Chill out," he mutters. "It's *chill out.*"

"Nice one, tell you what, hows about a nice story, help us both chillsy out, ay? A little history lesson, would you like that?"

I smile, he nods.

"Rats," I whispers, swigging my pint, "Amazing creatures. Resourceful, very nifty, I've seen rats grow to the size of a five-year old child! Bloody hell, where? You might ask, how's that even possible?

War.

Rats love war, human flesh," I winks, "Plenty of dead about, plenty of protein about. But these rats, they got so big these rats, I've seen them eat wounded men alive!

I shit you not.

They go for the eyes first, any exposed soft bits, and then burrow deep into your gut – gnashing, munching and guzzling through your innards, vanishing right into your body!

Awful. Nothing we could do about that in the trenches, fact of life – we're in trenches, the wounded are out there, fucked in No Man's Land.'

If they were unlucky, they had the strength to fight them off for a bit, prolong the inevitable. If they were lucky, they were in range and we could get a shot in; put them out of their predicament.

Now, you might think that was fucked up, and you'd be right, but, there was one memorable day when events turned truly surreal.

Mick, quiet geezer, never said much or mucked about? Well, out he climbs from our trench and just walks over, calm as you like to one of our wounded, kicks the rats away, throws him over his shoulder and brings him back – fucking amazing! There was a thousand snipers having a go, bullets zipping past him the whole time and not one did he cop.

Didn't end there neither, he pulled it off five or six times that day, and then the Germans stopped shooting – started coming out their trenches and picking up their wounded too.

Same thing the next day, out goes Mick, the snipers have a go and then stop. So out we all goes and bring back our wounded.

On the third day, our Brass Hats threatened to have Mick shot for disobeying orders – giving people ideas – so it was all over after that, but as you can imagine, we all thought Mick was divinely blessed! Like he had an Angel protecting him, or the 'luck of the Irish' or something.

And that might be, but I reckon the true reason he could get away with it was on account of Mick being Mick, fucking mental, off his rocker – when he set his sights on something, he'd follow through, no matter what. I think that in itself kind of 'blessed' him, if ya catch-madrift.

Stayed true to his nature, came out of all major conflicts without a scratch.

So, Mad Mick it was after that, and I can tell you, we'd get into some awful fights amongst ourselves just to be even near him when going over the top!" I laughed. "A true legend he was, all up and down the Western Front. But fuck me, these rats, Gawd blimey, they'd even try to eat you in your sleep! Cheeky buggers, ay? Rats…"

I pause, Jake had gone green, looked about to chuck.

"Don't worry son," I says, hand on shoulder, "That was then, this is now – just remember, we fought for cunts like you, that's what I'm saying, so you'd never have to. Says it all really, nobody should have to watch their mates scoffed alive by giant rats, catch-madrift?"

I hand him some coins, point to the telephone on the wall, by the side of the bar.

"Give Graham another bell, get him here, and get yourself some perspective back."

Jake zigzags to the phone, and I was just sat there, smiling to myself, looking at the old photo's of Brixton around the pub, when it happened – you'd think it shouldn't at my age, but it does.

If she had been a painting, she would've been a Caravaggio. An explosive fury hovered around her. She burst through the pub doors and stormed past, black raincoat flapping like a cloak, a rolled blanket strapped to her back with string; all young and crazy black ringlet hair – and filthy, alright, she obviously had the look of someone what lived on the streets, and by the way those giant violet eyes scanned Pat, the walls, the ceiling, and Pat again, she was not the full shilling neither.

But fuck me sideways, she cut a fine trim in those fishnet stockings and army surplus boots.

"He'll be here within the hour," says Jake, returning from his phone call. I didn't reply, couldn't. All I could do was pin my eyes on those two gorgeous dollies.

Pat was shaking his head at her, no deal on the beer, apparently, and then he grins. Don't know what she said to him, but he grins and pours her a pint anyway.

She only glances at my ogling, and sits down alone at the last table before the beer garden.

Odd, didn't see her pay.

"Within the hour," I affirms, and I gets up, goes to the bar.

"Pat," says I, "A discreet word, please."

"Mr Barbelo."

"Who's the young lady in black?"

"Lady? The lady's a tramp," he sniggers, affectionately, and yet for some reason I can't explain I want to skewer the cunt there and then.

"Lady," I reiterates. "Not tramp, Lady of the Road."

Pat takes an involuntary step back, looks suddenly abashed.

"Lady, right. I dunno. She claims she doesn't use money, 'cos a Celtic Warrior lost in time only uses Awen," he sniggers again. "And she's lost without her star chariot. But that's Paddy's for ya, imaginative."

"Irish?"

"And stoned off her tits, probably. Gave her a pint anyway, God loves a tryer, so He does."

"What's an Awen?" I glanced over my shoulder; she was talking to herself now, tilting her head from side to side.

"Not sure," says Pat. "I do remember it from the old Irish hymn books... the grace of God? Divine power or something."

I turns around. "Well Pat, she seems harmless enough. If she wants another pint, then by the grace of God the next's on me..." I pause. "What's a good Irish tune?"

Pat shrugs, "The Foggy Dew. No wait, Raglan Road, that's good."

I peg over to the Juke Box. Don't hardly recognise any of the songs, but find the one I was looking for.

Raglan Road moaned out the speakers, and I knew I was in the presence of superiority, nah, not the music – though it was quite nice – *her*, and I'm not talking bollocks, listen.

She just nodded, just nodded at me and shot me a look – and that's all she did – but her stare pummelled into my gut like a 50mm at point-blank.

Dunno what it was about those eyes, but for a moment I didn't know where I was, or who I was.

It was a prime cut beyond terror, almost beyond the screaming abdabs even – like my head was spinning one way, and my peg and leg the other, preparing to bolt for the door.

Breathing deep, focusing my mind to the business at hand, the reaction suddenly stopped, and I made it back to our table without embarrassing myself... too much.

Graham came within the hour, true to word, but this time he wasn't alone, of course.

I eyed up the two gorillas at his back, big fuckers, slow fuckers. Still, all togged-up in Armani's they looked well-pukka.

"Gentleman," says I, "Please, take a seat."

I placed the bag with the 9mm at my feet, and they sat down either side of me, with Graham and Jake opposite on the lighthouse stools.

"I suppose you know why I've asked you here."

Graham nods. "We need to talk, Mr Barbelo. This... this situation is getting out of hand."

"Well-out of hand," I agrees, "We needs to discuss matters, you and I, matters of great importance."

"You want us to back off. I understand."

"Gawd blimey, no! I want your unconditional surrender."

"I'm sorry?"

"Should've just said that the first time," I sighs to myself.

"Mr Barbelo," he squints, "What is this, what are you saying?"

"I'm saying that just now I was gonna calls it quits, but then thought fuck it. Change of heart. Decided I could do with a hobby, and I've never had a Firm of my own, see?"

"I don't understand."

"Ra, ra, ree, kick them in the knee!

Ra, ra, rollocks,

Kick them in the other knee!"

He glares, "And what's that supposed to mean?"

"Means I want your Firm."

"You want what? S.L.H?"

I chuckles, "We'd need to call us something else, that really is a poncy name!"

"Who the fuck are you?"

"Today? Just an old-school gent what needs a hobby. Tomorrow, who knows?"

"We're businessmen, not—"

"Well now you're my hobby." I give him my sincere nod.

Graham says to Jake, "Go home, this might take some time, you look terrible."

"Don't have a home, he burnt it down, dunno where mum is."

"Forgot. Go to my gaff then," he says, passing Jake a set of keys. "Wait for me there."

Jake shuffled away, poor bastard. Graham and his gorillas sat in silence for a bit, and then he pipes up,

"We did some checking, Mr Barbelo, you're nothing. Nobody. You live up that shit-hole on your own, no family, nothing, like a ghost."

"Oh I'm less than that!" I corrected happily. "I'm like the ghost of a flea, a phantom flea with a grudge on you – nip, nip, nip! Not a moment's peace, my young friend, it will never end. Can you imagine anything worse?"

Doesn't reply.

"I can, all the other Ghosts of a Flea I know. Do you think 'cos I live alone, I'm all alone? You don't get to my age without having friends, young Graham, and my friends don't run from the slaughter, catch-madrift?"

Rubbing his forehead, he pauses, trying to take in what I was saying, "Everybody knows you… you're a nobody who…"

"Who everybody knows?" I chuckles. "Thank you for the complement, glad to know I'm still under the radar."

"You're not going to back off, are you?"

"Depends."

"So what do you want?"

"Is it me, or is everybody deaf around here?"

"You want us to surrender."

"Everything you got. Unconditionally."

"Are you for real?"

He pauses again. I nods slowly, letting it sink in.

"Final offer, young Graham. Be reasonable. Let me run things for a bit, see how we all get on, ay?"

He clucks his tongue at me. "Madman!" And then says with a sigh, "Wasting my time, talking to a fucking madman…"

"Then prepare for battle. I'm collecting my dues on you, and all of yous. One by one." I swig my pint, and smile.

Well, I don't know if it was the way I smiled, or if he'd had a bad day at the Bookies, or what.

Looks me straight in the eyes,

"You are dead, Mr Barbelo," he whispers, "A dead madman," and that's all he says, rising to his feet. All three get up and leave without another word.

Cause for concern?

Yeah! Too bloody right this time, yeah – a shiver of profound apprehension shot right through my bones.

It was lovely.

Time slowed down, colours grew brighter. My beer suddenly tasted better than it'd ever tasted.

I glanced about the pub.

Pat, serving pints, joking with his punters at the bar. Two youg'uns beside me, grumbling on about the miner's strike and killing Margaret Thatcher. The lady in black muttering to herself in the corner, gorgeous, all-perfect and gorgeous and oh – cut my throat there and then – nothing feels sweeter than when your touch awakens!

I drained my glass in one, tipped my hat to Pat on the way out, and pegged home at full-peg.

Battle Stations.

Now, the thing to remember when someone picks up the gauntlet like that is, *there's no turning back*, even if he's a wanker, you have to follow through, always.

And no matter how much you're shitting it, the other thing to remember is that the other cunt, or cunts in this case, will be shitting it too. Don't matter how many, or how hard they are, a part of them deep down will be laying gold bricks at the thought.

It's not like the movies – all those mouthy 'I don't give a monkey's' whack-jobs – that's a Disneyland Delusion. Though I don't mean you don't come across them, the mortality trade attracts all sorts, but from experience I can tell you now they don't last long – nobody does without fear giving you the edge.

Fear cuts both ways and you've gotta learn how to use it. Total control. And nah, not by gritting your teeth and burying it – complete waste of effort. It'll cripple you. You've gotta dig deep, tap the power of your will and *relax into* your fears, gently, steer them into a meaningful expression.

Think of it like a team of wild horses on the rampage; they'll tear you to pieces if you let them. Harnessed and trained though, they'll pull a carriage and take you anywhere you want to go. And that's the onion, you've got to be the one holding the reins, at all times, directing your emotions to drive you towards your goal.

Master your fears, and you've mastered yourself and any cunt what gets in your way. And you'll be a happier person for it.

If you don't in this game, then you're liable to do something bloody stupid – which they were about to do – and I'd already proved I was well-up for it, and of course, done a pukka little job of it too.

Forgive me, I don't wanna sound like I'm blowing my own trumpet, bit early for that; truth be told I was just warming up. Though I will confess, taking over their Firm was an inspiration I'd had on the spot – just came to me when I saw the Lady in Black – and nah, don't know why. We'll see, the touch can be a tricky master but everything always turns up trumps if you follow through.

Can't stress that enough, always follow through.

So, not a bad day, I mused, making a nice cup of tea back at my gaff, not a bad day at all: sharpened my edge, fell in love with a tramp, and declared war on South London.

Chapter 7

Battle Stations

My front door isn't secure or nothing, but that's the point, no door ever is. False sense of security is a killer. Waste of money an' all – if someone wants to get in bad enough, they will find a way in. So turn the tables, let them.

It's one thing getting in, quite another getting out.

Woke up the instant before it happened. That familiar 'clunk' of the door-chain, splintering wood, and they were in. Six of them this time. Good. They were learning.

What followed is difficult, to do it justice I'd need a video camera or you'd have to have been there. But picture this: old cunt in bed, blade in one hand, lead-filled pipe in the other – always kept one of those under the pillow, force of habit – bedroom door swings open: thwack, thwack, thwack!

Six guns on silencers pumping away in the dark.

Old cunt's already leapt out of bed at that point, of course, rolling about the floor slashing and walloping knees – knees – can't stress the importance of knees enough neither. It's a main contributor to what keeps your body up, do the knees, and it don't matter how big they are or what they got in their hands, they're going down.

And eyes – a poke in the eye and it's game over. Eyes and knees, high and low, or visa versa. If you can't go high, go low.

I went low.

Didn't have to move about much, knees all around me, lovely it was, Barbelo's version of what the Yanks call a 'turkey shoot,' can't go wrong, in other words, not with a lead-pipe and blade.

Helps if you don't rush it, pick your targets, and have good Intelligence of your battlefield in the dark, that too, but anyways, in no time they were all pretty much screaming and crashing into each other and all that.

And by the way, if you don't know what it feels like to have your kneecap popped, your Cruciate ligament slashed, let me guarantee it hurts, fucking hurts – and it's psychologically debilitating as well.

So, it was all knees, groin when I could get it, and eyes – down they went. It's methodical, all told, it's a craft like any other.

The three in my bedroom were easy enough, one had shot another in the confusion anyway, but the other three were hobbling, crawling, screaming and backing away into the kitchen, still pumping away all over the gaff – thwack, thwack, thwack!

And finally click, click, click!

Music to my ears. I stood up, switched on the kitchen light, "Alright ladies? Fancy a nice cuppa cha then?"

They froze on the spot.

All told, I'd say the Craft is about ten percent physical, ninety psychological. Three good'uns in the bedroom helps a lot, but the sight of a naked one-legged geezer, with your mates' shooters in each hand, offering you a cuppa is a weighty percentage.

Pity it doesn't last, but what a picture, really wish I'd had a camera – all hobbled, bleeding, hopping on one leg around my kitchen table – and of course, all three making the same mistake, fumbling, trying to reload. Well, I suppose they were young, weak perspective?

Two head shots, job's a good'un.

"N-no-no!" the lucky one snivels, hands in the air.

"Better close the door then, ay? Awful draft in here."

Gun level to his head, I hop-shuffle along the wall towards him.

"Oh please!" whimper, whimper, "I'm sorry, please! Mummy!"

Mummy? What did I tell you?

I just gets to the door – pumping two shots in his mates' hearts for good measure on the way – when Nick, Daddy Dixon from upstairs, appears; pyjamas, string vest, shooter in hand all up for it.

"You alright, Mr Barbelo?" eyes up my gaff, "Blimey…"

"Sorry to wake you, Nick, just doing a bit of dusting."

He says nothing, of course, and immediately shuts the door.

I says, "Manners, please, take off the mask and sit down. Let's have a nice cup of tea."

Wanted one alive, tell you why. It's useless doing a pukka job like this without nobody to sing your praises after. You can bang on about it all you like, but what you need is a witness, specially a bleeding whimpering one – they'll blabber good and proper, sing your praises to high heaven.

"Pass me that, will you?" gesturing to my bathrobe hanging on the bog door behind him, "Cheers mate, what?"

Silence.

"Oh don't be like that! Said take off the mask and have a seat, ay, you're making me nervous."

He slumps down at the kitchen table.

Wasn't that surprised to see it was Graham, just that he would turn out such a plonker... somehow expected more from the cunt? I dunno, but it just goes to show, you can be educated but it don't necessarily mean you're very clever.

After making us a nice cup of tea, we both sat down at the table; me grinning happily, him groaning a fair bit on account he didn't have a kneecap anymore, but otherwise present and correct.

"Drink your tea, it'll go cold. Loads of sugar in it, good for weak perspective."

He sips his tea.

"Now young Graham, what were you playing at?"

I reach down to the corpse at my feet, pull off his mask. Blue lifeless eyes stare up at me, framed in a blond, shaggy-haired '70s cut.

"Who were they?"

"Soviet Block," Graham blabbers rapidly, "Lot of 'em hiding about lately, need work, do just about anything for next to nothing and I reckon it won't be long before Communism ends and—"

"Shut up please."

I turn the pistol over in my hands: Makarov PM, 9mm, eight-round detachable box magazine. "KGB?"

"They're Soviet Army," he whimpers.

"Interesting. Didn't drop their shooters when I asked though, did they?"

"Please, I'm sorry—"

"They should've known it was game over."

"W-what?"

"Said, I offered yous all a nice cuppa, didn't I?"

"Their English isn't very good, Mr Barbelo, please—"

"No! It's not Mr Barbelo to you! It's *sir*."

"Sir Barbelo, please sir, can we just—"

"No we can't," I grins. "Then why didn't *you* drop your shooter?"

Grimaces, "Because, because they didn't."

"And if they'd of jumped out that window, would you?"

"W-what?"

"Oh never mind," I sighs, glancing about. "Who's gonna clean up this mess, ay? Tell you who, you are. Nod."

He nods.

"You're gonna call up your associates, and they're gonna come round here and dispose your friends from Russia with love, all good and proper. Nod."

He nods.

"And they're gonna fix my door."

Nod, nod.

"And then you're gonna arrange a meet with your Firm's boss."

He stammers, "It–it–it's not what you think, we don't have bosses and—"

"Then what the fuck is this?"

"It's like I said, sir, we're business people, a collective of business people with mutual interests—"

"Shut it! A mutual fucking what? Collective? You said it was a Firm. Fuck it. There is no Firm, is there? South London Hounds, or bitches or whatever. You made it all up!"

"There is, there is…" he pauses, holding his busted leg. I almost felt sorry for the cunt.

"… but it's not what you think, it's not like the old days—"

"Blimey! I'd blame all that telly bollocks, but hats off to you! Had me going alright."

This was better than I could've hoped for.

"Kids nowadays, what imaginations you've got, phenomenal. Well, now you've got a real Firm, and a very real boss. What have you got?"

He groans, "A real Firm and a real boss."

"Can't have a business without a boss, need a top cunt, always. Dixons upstairs, they've got a boss, all the old crews had bosses, how else you gonna run things in proper order?"

He nods.

"Need to shuffle the pack, need to meet your… whatever, your business collective. Let's say tomorrow, down The Effra."

"The Effra Tavern?"

"Bring them down at four. Nice and quiet around then."

"I- I- I don't know who I can get together by then, I mean what will—"

"You mean you will, or I will."

He stares.

"Fuck it Graham, do you think I can't find out who's who? I've been around a long time, know a lot of people, an awful lot – more than even *I* would like to know, catch-madrift?"

He nods.

"So either you bring them down tomorrow, or I'll bring them down tomorrow, and the next day, and the next day after that till I got yous all. Do I make myself clear?"

Nod, nod, nod!

"You'll bring as many as you can who's important, and you can, can't you?"

"But don't, I mean you won't hurt—"

"Gawd blimey!" I slammed my fist on the table. "It's only a meet! Do I have to wave a fucking white flag? What do you take me for, a cunt?"

Shakes his head.

"Need a cab?"

"An ambulance, please."

"I'll call you a cab, where you go after is your business, right?"

He nods.

"That's settled then, be there at four, shake on it."

I shook his trembling hand, glancing at the kitchen clock.

"Right, what time is it, half five. I'm gonna have a nice bath, polish my peg, and then down the caff for breakfast. You don't mind if I don't see you out?"

I'd never seen anyone hop so fast from a slaughter in all my days, even me. But for wannabe gangsters they did a lovely job cleaning up, tell you that much.

Came back from the caff, and a nice peg around Brockwell Park at about ten, spotless, even left me some flowers and a card. Poor bastards, they were shitting it – best feeling ever, is turning the tables. I was still an x-factor in their calculations, a lovely weighty percentage, you can make yourself up as you go along.

Chapter 8

Barbelo's Blood

All was good, but I wasn't going nowhere without backup. Alright, their 'Firm' sounded well-Mickey Mouse, and it might end here, but it might not. I mean, what Graham had said about being alone works for giving you the x-factor effect, it's a lovely edge, but again it cuts both ways – a slug in the loaf from a passing car and it's job's a good'un for Barbelo – that's no way to live, always wondering when.

Have to settle it, final.

So at this stage in the game, you wanna play a hand what says it won't end with a bullet in the head or a hundred, it won't end ever – but that you can't bluff without backup, and I only had about four hours to get some of my auld acquaintances together for the meet.

Age don't mean nothing, what matters is the condition of your mind and body. You could be fucked at twenty-five, or fit as a fiddle at fifty, I knew some of my own would be up for it at eighty still, well-up for it. They just needed a wakeup call, like I had. Problem was, getting hold of them.

Leastways I knew where Sid would be, where I found him, down the docks in the East End, feeding the pigeons. Not 'cos he liked pigeons, he just liked to see the seagulls have a go when there was food about.

"See that!" he'd pipe up happily, watching the gulls batting out the pigeons in mid-air, "Natural law."

Couldn't agree more, and on the bus back to Brixton, I asked how he'd been and wot-not. Sid was never much of a talker, but he'd been a technical wizard in the Army, electronics, radios and all that malarkey, what made up for it. Well, nah, it didn't.

"How long's it been Sid, nine years?"

"Nineteen."

"Oh. How's the Home, then?"

"Like it, near the docks."

"Met any nice people?"

"Fucking walking dead."

"Oh? Why don't you go Royal Chelsea?"

"Why don't you?"

"Right. Walking dead."

Long pause.

"Seen any of the boys, then?"

"Ian, Easter time."

"Nice one! How's—"

"Nineteen years ago, topped himself."

"Oh… Reckon there's any of us still left in the pink?"

Long pause.

Shakes his head. "Doubtful."

"Must be."

Short pause.

"Nope. I don't think so…"

Very long pause.

"… What's this hobby about then?"

"You'll see, mate, you'll see."

"Wake us up when we get there."

Silence.

You get the picture. I'd got to explain earlier at the Home what'd been going on; he'd be game alright, he definitely needed a hobby too, but by the time I'd got him shaved and togged-up we was already running late. Still, better late than never and two's better than one.

And Sid more than made up for it on that score.

Six foot eight, still with his own teeth and hair, and gun-grey eyes what nailed you to the wall. But best of all, that polite, hostile disposition particular only to some of us English – a toff's smile, and suddenly that rolled up top lip.

If you saw that lip curl on Sid's ugly mug, Sid's ugly mug was the last thing you saw.

Thank fuck for Sid.

What was waiting for us down The Effra was, I have to admit, quite impressive in its own way. The pub was closed, sign on the door said something about gas leaks, closed for repairs and all that, but official, from the Council.

Sid and I stood outside for a moment.

"Oi, oi," says Sid, "Gas leaks my arse. Council's all on strike."

"I know. They've got a bit of clout, alright, closing the gaff down."

"What now?"

"Dunno Sid. Follow my lead, and just… just be yourself."

We shrugged at each other, and I knocked on the door.

Graham's soviet gorillas appear, taking my cane, dusting us down, and I lets my Jif lemon roll out onto the ground.

"Oopsy daisy," I says, "You can have that, souvenir of your visit to London." I grins. "Let's hope it's a *pleasant* one, ay?"

They didn't say nothing, but people have short memories; never does any harm reminding that old cunts always have something up their sleeves.

Inside the lounge bar, the tables had been cleared and arranged in rows, like a banquet table. Sitting around I counted a very classily dressed lady, and ten geezers of various racial denominations; a Chink, a big red-headed Paddy, two light-skinned Darkies what could pass for Daygos or Pakis, and a dark Darkie. The rest were ours, meaning English, but all very classy, all told, plus the two gorillas covering the doors what made a lovely picture.

Graham hops up to us on his crutches.

"Mr Barbelo, sir," he whispers, "This is the best I can do."

"Thank you," says I, "This is my friend, Sid the Yid."

"On account I'm a Yid," growls Sid, what gets a nervous laugh from Graham, as he leads us to our seats.

We sits down at the head of the table, they just stare, arms folded, looking menacing and some doing a pukka job of it too – there were at least three or four around that table what seemed well-up for it.

"Good afternoon," I says, "No point in hanging about then, I'm Mr Barbelo, and this is my friend Sid. Ordinarily, I'd say introduce yourselves at your leisure, but this ain't no ordinary meet – this is a straight takeover bid. To business then. I bid I take over, you shut up and listen. Now, who in our distinguished company is the eldest?"

They glance around at each other, whispering and frowning.

"I suppose I am," says a puzzled geezer in pinstripes and specs. "I'm thirty-two, why?"

I took out my notebook and pen.

"And your name?"

"Richard—"

"No, no, not your real name! Don't give a monkey's about that."

"Right, Mark, erm, Mitchell."

"Profession?"

"I'm only an accountant, but our company's been receiving contracts from The City, and soon we'll be—"

"Handles money and good with numbers, perfect," I draw a pyramid and jot down his name at the top, "And the eldest. Right, from now on you're our General—"

"Wait, wait," pipes up classy lady, "Richey, I'll handle this," she says to the specy, and then turns to me, all sly smiles,

"What do you think you're doing?"

"Putting our Firm together, of course."

"Of course, and what if I don't want to be in this, in your Firm, what then?"

"You have a choice?" I grins, "I'm an options connoisseur myself, as it goes, have to be in my line of work. Love to hear yours."

"Love to," says Sid.

Classy lady huffs, "Fine, what's in it for me, for us."

"Just said. Your life." I shrugs. "Look, what's your name young lady?"

"Rachel, and that's my real name."

"Rachel it is then. Listen, Rachel, you're fucked, you're all royally fucked. The biggest mistake you could've made was invading my privacy and security. Didn't nobody teach you, an Englishman's home is his castle—?"

"That had nothing to do with me or most of us around this table."

"No?"

"No. Graham was scared, Mr Barbelo, and when people get scared they make mistakes."

"Trying to kill me was a mistake, then."

She nods.

I laughed, "Oh don't go shifting the blame on young Graham here! Alright, he's an idiot, but you knew what he was up to or you wouldn't be here. All of yous were gonna profit by my... absence, lets call it. And that makes you all what?"

"I don't know, what does that make us?"

"Idiots and accomplices, 'accessories after the fact,' guilty as charged, in other words. But you're obviously a girl what enjoys money, and power, or you wouldn't be here neither."

"Graham explained you want revenge. We can offer you financial compensation, assure your security and—"

"Oh don't be like that! Gawd blimey, what do you all take me for? I'm a reasonable man, I am – I'm throwing in the benefits of my vast experience for free!" I nods my head, all smiles, switching on my battle-charm. "And tell you what, my Craft too, that's what I do best. As young Graham here will testify."

She says nothing to that, only folds her arms, leaning back into her seat with a quick librarian smile.

"So what do ya want?" asks the Paddy.

"A chance to cultivate my hobby, and my share. My fair dues; natural law, tit for tat, this for that. Call it Stress Tax, for all the stress you've caused me."

"Your *equal* share."

The emphasis he puts on 'equal' has Sid rising from his seat like black tidewater. I hold up my hand, he settles down again.

"Equal share," I agrees pleasantly. "Stitch us up, we'll find out."

"We have ways," growls Sid – which we didn't, but they didn't know that, and that's what counts.

I scrawls my old P.O. Box number on my notebook, and turns the page to Mark. "Memorise it."

"Got it," he says.

"For now, you all cut me in on everything, and then we'll work on expansion."

Classy Lady sniggers,

"Look, Mr Barbelo, we are a Firm already, or whatever you want to call it, we have it already." Everyone here, we do extremely well financially as we are. Extremely well," she reiterates, receiving nods from the others around the table. "We don't actually need you."

I'm shooting her twenty times in the head in my mind. But she went on,

"We're business people, we help each other out from time to time, that's all, and—"

"That's all? Help each other out? Too fucking right you do, and now you're gonna help me out an' all!"

I sighs, briefly turning to Graham,

"What on Gawd's Earth is this about, is she pulling the piss?"

"No-no," he stammers.

Classy lady snaps her fingers. "Boris! Igor!"

Boris, Igor? Had to bite my lower lip not to laugh, but the gorillas at the door stride forward, shooters in hand.

"Come on!" Sid, towering to his full height, gunning his machinegun glare at them all.

Graham gets frantic. "Rachel, please! Hear this guy out, for all our sakes!"

Sid's on red alert, seconds from bundling the gorillas. Three of the 'up for it' geezers had stood up, poised at the far end of the table, eyeing me with pure contempt. I'd already wrapped my fishing wire into a classic garrotte – I was taking someone down whatever happened.

Now, I suppose you're still asking, why don't they just bundle us to the ground and stick a bullet in our heads there and then? I mean, alright, I'd proved to be a hard cunt to do in, and Sid cut a fine vicious trim, but we'd stepped into the thick of it, as it where.

Answer is two reasons.

One, a righteous reputation. Graham had sung my praises to high heaven, and though do us in they could, between Sid and I we'd make it messy, very messy. Someone would be going down with us, that was realistic, but a Russian roulette with a couple of old psycho's wasn't.

Second reason was almost the same as the first: bog-standard business is business. Barbelo could be useful, and this lot had problems – namely, me, and now Sid and all the rest of the Ghost of the Flea lurking out there; who knows how many, ay? Leastways that was the impression I'd counted on.

And thank fuck first impressions last.

Rachel smoothes back her long brown hair, tying it into a bun.

"Fine," she says, clicks her fingers and the gorillas return to their posts.

I smile at that, giving into her display of power, it was classy enough.

"Options," she says, "If we accept your proposal, it will be only because we choose to, and not because we need to."

"Oh?"

"There are always *other* options."

"Always," I says, and we all sits down again.

"Rachel James. Twenty-nine and counting. Profession: lawyer."

Well suck my thorny cock, "You're our second General then!" I jot down her name alongside Mark's on the pyramid.

A bald, stocky bloke with a knurled brow puts up his hand.

"And you?" I says.

"Rob, twenty-seven, I'm a policeman."

"Lovely, a Peeler, what station?"

"Clapham."

"Put in a transfer for Brixton, even better. What rank?"

"I'm a sergeant."

"You're promoted to captain."

"Thank you," he mumbles, silly cunt.

"Rachel, I need two more captains and then we'll continue. Nominate them between yourselves, age first, while Sid and I have a swift half at the bar. Sid?"

Sid nods assent, and we gets up, leaving them to it.

"What you reckon, Sid?"

"Wankers," he growls, snatching a couple of bottles off the shelf.

I sits on a lighthouse stool at the bar, covering the gorillas at the door. Sid's covering the table.

"So young," I mutters, "So fucking young…"

"All gotta learn sometime."

"The Brief's a coke-head."

"Nasty piece of work," grumbles Sid.

"Reckon they're all fucked on one thing or another."

"Then can't we just shoot them all, go for a proper pint?"

"Sid, we don't have any guns."

"Not the point, they have," eyes the gorillas at the door, "Like taking brandy from a baby."

I sighs, "Yeah you're right…"

"I know I'm right. The Craft accommodates."

"Craft accommodates," I affirms, pondering, sipping my beer.

And then shakes my head. "Nah, give 'em a chance, wait and see what they does first, ay?"

"Affirmative," shrugs, glances at his watch, "Fifteen minutes."

I quickly lurch forward over the bar, "Fuck off Sid!" I whispers, "No fucking way – this is *my* hobby, alright? Bloody hell... thirty minutes."

"In twenty."

"Twenty-five..."

We lock eyes, Sid's upper lip twitches, I pick up my beer,

"Alright, alright – don't look at me like that, ay, you're giving me the abdabs."

Shrugs. "Well then, be civil. Battle stations in twenty."

We hear them arguing between themselves for a bit. It was all 'I'm not taking this' and 'who the fuck do they think they are,' and I'd just about made up my mind to release the wrath of Sid on the lot of them, when I noticed it was strangely... quiet.

Sid flashes his eyes at me, I felt a tap on my shoulder.

"Mr Barbelo."

The brief, Rachel, passing me my notebook.

"Here's your Firm."

To my surprise, they'd filled in the whole pyramid themselves – nominating the rest as 'sergeants,' what wasn't my intention, but still, hats off to them.

"We're in, until we're out," she says. "So a word of professional advice, even the *Magna Carta* offers a get-out clause, *options*, that's our get-out clause."

She smiles. I nods. I was well-chuffed.

Sid and I return, stand at the head of the table. I tear out the page with the pyramid, and scrawl BARBELO'S BLOOD over the top.

"Alright, listen up! This is the heart of our Firm, Barbelo's Blood. Memorise your positions on the chain of command, and remember – I am over yous all. From now on, I am your great grandfather in the sky, I am your emperor and god. In all matters of the Firm you do what I say, when I say it."

I took out my Zippo, and burnt the page, dropping the ashes onto the table.

"And like God, this Firm don't exist nowhere except our heads. Do you understand?"

They nod at once, like kids in a classroom.

"I want you to think of us all as a happy family. What are we?"

"A happy family."

"Nominate anybody else what's useful as 'honorary foot soldiers,' for now. No cunt has the authority to make a full member of our happy family except me – I am Top Cunt. Who am I?"

"Top Cunt."

"Pleasure doing business with yous all. Meeting concluded."

Boris the Gorilla gives me back my cane at the door. I nods to Sid, and we retreat.

Says Sid, outside on the street, "Good fun, that! What now?"

Had to laugh. "Did you get a butcher's at that list? Cut my throat, there's talent there! We got Old Bill, a brief, an accountant, council workers, three squadies fresh from the Falklands—"

"Liabilities," grumbles Sid.

"Up for it," I corrects. "Just need direction, something to focus on what isn't the normal shit, like any of us. Shuffle the pack and they'll turn up trumps. We all will. This is our second chance, Sid, our chance to atone, our chance for glory!"

Second chance for us, no fucking chance for any cunt what gets in my way.

Chapter 9

Those U-Turn Moments

Sid moved in to my gaff. All told, quiet, easy bloke to live with, leastways in a trench or a bunker, but we needed space, and there's something about Council Blocks what makes me want to chuck people off them, even Sid. And Sid was the same, so we got the Firm to procure us a proper house down Atlantic Road – massive – one of those typical Victorian 'Upstairs, Downstairs' jobs where you feel like Lord Fuckface one minute, and Tiny Tim the next, depending what floor you're on.

The basement was massive too, would've been the servant's quarters back in the days, so we turned it into our operation's room – that's where we spent most of our time, training – space enough for a firing range, a small workshop, Sid got the 'council' to dig us a fresh water well, plumbed in with a state of the art UV filtration system, and bit by bit, we got what we needed – rigged the whole gaff to blow if we got collared.

Getting mugged had upset me, considerably, and my visit to the Social Welfare had got me riled on a primal level – planted the auld proverbial seed. When we looks back on things it's easy to see how it all fits together – *Maktub*, like the Ragheads say, 'it is written.' And if you look real close at those times when your life did a major u-turn – for the better or worse – you'll notice there's always a moment when you saw it coming. Like you'd caught a fleeting glimpse of what was written for you, and in that split second, in that perfect *instant* it had already happened – *before* the thing had happened.

You have to be quick off the mark, though – most of us live our entire lives oblivious to the fact these u-turn moments even exist – but with age and a supreme effort of honesty, you can get good at catching them. After you do, even if just the once, you can't look at your life without taking responsibility for your part. You might still hear yourself saying things like, oh, I didn't see that car crash coming, or nah, I really didn't deserve to get the clap off that Latvian lapdancer, and so on, but deep down you know that's total bollocks.

You know it, if only for the simple fact that when something equally sudden but good happens, a warm glow of pride rushes into your chest and you go, yeah, I knew I was gonna get that promotion, or yeah, I just *knew* that lotto win was coming, I'm fucking great, I am!

Fair dues, not saying you're not. All I'm saying is I'm a skip and a hop short of a century; I've lived a life where sussing an impending u-turn was a matter of pure survival, and even on these early stages of our operation, I could feel something big was in the offing. A greater vision. A second chance.

A higher purpose.

Leastways money was the last of our concerns now. Problem was, getting our auld acquaintances together, somehow – those who weren't two pegs short or pushing up daisies.

Sid was easy to locate, but what we needed now was the likes of Tenstar Sally. Sally on account she was the finest mortality technician the Craft ever produced, and Tenstar on account of the ten stars tattooed on her nether regions. Long story – main thing was we were getting our edge back, and we had some bloody good talent behind us in the Firm, as I soon found out.

It was a couple of weeks after we'd moved into our new gaff. Rachel was driving us to Mile End, in search of that antique's shop where Jake had procured my swordstick – wanted one for Sid. I was chuffed with how our Firm was shaping up, but London reeked of misery and blocked drainage that day. The winter homeless crammed the doorways of closed shops, while the rest shuffle along, aimless, grey and worn. My lovely London. Bins full of rubbish, spilling onto the pavement; plastic bags fluttering in the cold rain.

"Bloody disgrace," I mutters, "what happened, why doesn't anybody sort this?"

"Banks, corruption, and Thatcher," she spits, "The usual suspects. Fortunately, however, there is a remedy to the recession, and I have plenty of it," she grins, pulls the car over into the bus lane, and sitting up all prim and proper, cuts a line of coke on the dashboard.

Snorts it in one.

Chucks her head back, "Oh my God that's incredible!" sniff, sniff, turns to me, "Would you like some?"

"Ermmm, not sure, what's in it?"

"Nothing but pure euphoria," says she, retying her hair in a bun, brushing down her business suit, "I've been doing this batch for six days straight and it's just the sexiest and most empowering, conversational and elucidatory coke there is. Clean, no chemical heart-racing paranoiac edge in the slightest. Good coke doesn't do that to you. Difficult to accept, but it's true. Why do you think it's so trendy?"

Fair point, fuck it, and in for penny? I rolled up a tenner. She cuts me a line, I snorts, and we pulls away again onto the main drag.

"Shop's a couple of streets round the back of here," I sniffs.

"Where?" peering through rain-spattered windscreen, "I can barely see the road."

I points to an alleyway on our left. She almost takes the turn, and continues on, "Bugger, one way street."

"Alright, take the next left, maybe we can circle round."

"You were saying?" sniff, sniff. "The jungle?"

"I was saying getting into physical shape's crucial."

"That's not easy these days, people just don't have the lifestyle conducive to fitness, we're not hunter-gathers anymore."

"Wrong, deep down we haven't left the jungle, and at eighteen or eighty, it's not as hard as all that. Oh, govermentals make it sound hard, 'cos they want to sell us stuff, pills and shit – people nowadays would buy bottled dysentery if they thought it would get them trim."

She laughs, nods a couple of times, "It's all about growing a source of profit and fuck the rest."

"Exactly," sniff, snort, "They need everybody chronically sick with something – matters not whether that's mild rheumatism, or crippling heart disease – a chemicalised 'health' industry depends on sick people to buy their chemicals. Catch-madrift?"

She nods, "Supply and demand; a world full of healthy people spells financial oblivion for the medical industry."

"The entire Firm down the plughole, yeah, and they know it. Give you a small example. Cancer. Philippines it was, poor country, can't afford modern medicine, most people, what isn't a bad thing as it turns out. Saw a doctor there, back in '53, curing cancer with baking powder."

Sniff, sniff, "You *saw* that, in actual fact?"

"I shit you not," I affirms, "Cancer is a fungus, or better said, what causes cells to go cancerous is a fungus, otherwise known as Candida. Ph levels in the blood go out of whack, go too acidic, and Candida grows well-out of hand. Immune system can't handle it, cells freak out, literally, and go what we call 'cancerous' – replicating like mad, trying to fight off the Candida attack, but they can't."

"Okay, fine, but why?"

"Just said, acidic blood's a breeding ground for fungal infection. So, baking powder – one of the best anti-fungals known to man – cut them open, squirt a solution of baking powder on cancerous cells, job's a good'un. End of fungus, end of cancer. On the other hand, no need for surgery. Simply eating a few drops of raw hemp oil, the cannabis sativa strain, twice a day should do the trick. Filipinos, ay, any excuse for a blood-fest! But the point is, I've come across dozens of cures on my travels, I could go on and it only tallies up to the same conclusion: govermentals *need* us sick," I tap her on the shoulder, "Take the next left, here," I says.

"One way too," sniff, sniff.

"Alright, keep going. Anyways, avoid their medical scams like the plagues they are. They even contaminate our water with toxic waste – aluminium, chlorine, fluoride, and try to pass it off as healthy—"

"Ah, no, I disagree. Fluoride's good for our teeth."

"And I'm Willy Wonka."

"My dentist is one of the best in London, he would never lie—"

Had to laugh at that, "Where's my straightjacket? Nurse! Wheel me to the garden!" I snortles, "Rachel, I've been around, seen things. Calcium fluoride's good for teeth, up to about the age of twelve or so, and it comes from the Earth, it's natural, but that's NEVER been put into our drinking water. *Sodium* fluoride's what we're force-medicated with, daily, the chemical the Nazis developed to keep prisoners docile."

"Nazis."

"Ask Sid, if you don't believe me, he did a stint in a POW camp during the last War. Either way though, you've gotta ask: *why* is chemical fluoridation of drinking water compulsory by law?"

"Hmmm… that's something I have questioned too, though it's not law, not strictly – an act or statute is only a rule, given the *force* of law, yes, but only through mutual consent."

"Mutual consent?"

"The highest law of the land is Common Law," she says, "Only three basic principles: do not harm anybody or any thing; do not steal; and do not make false contracts. That's it. The rest are rules of commerce, Admiralty Law, the law of the sea. Two very different things, we're on land, not on a ship at sea. Nobody can make you do anything outside Common Law."

"Alright, but how—"

"They need to gain your consent."

"Blimey, well how, seeing as nobody knows it's not compulsory?"

Sly grin, "Precisely. 'He that would be deceived, let him.' People give their consent through silent acquiescence. None of these rules are enforceable otherwise, except if you're a member of the Law Society. We create the rules, so we are bound by them. You are not."

"Yeah right," I mutters to myself, "try saying that when they're kicking your door down at four in the morning... Still," I says, "it's gotta be illegal to force-medicate people."

"Correct, it is," nod, sniff, nod, "Unless they're incapacitated in some way, like in cases where severe mental illness might inhibit a patient's ability to help themselves, to reason, to think clearly, yes."

"So hold on – when did the Minister for Health declare us a nation of whack-jobs?" sniff, sniff.

She chuckles. "They don't need to. All they need to do is pass the act through Parliament, and you *believe* you must comply. In legalese, 'must' means *may*, it's an offer. Even a court's summons is an offer, an invitation to put yourself in 'the dock' – you're technically a ship under Admiralty Law, sailing through commerce, and not human—"

"A what? Nah, seriously, are we so daft we can't even *choose* how to take care of our own teeth? Can't we get fluoride in the fucking chemist – it's called toothpaste! And doesn't it come with a printed health warning: *do not swallow*," I sighs, "And alright, what's aluminium about then? We *don't* need that in our water."

Nods, "Aluminium, I can't see any reason for – it's an established cause of degenerative brain diseases."

"Right, Alzheimer's, I suppose that's good our teeth too. They're trying to kill us, mate. Left turn, here."

Swerves the car in, dead end. "Bugger. Cul-de-sac. Check behind."

I looks round, check the traffic, "You're clear," I says. "Reverse.

And isn't chlorine a well-known cause of heart disease?"

"And cancer."

"Alright, so how are these doses regulated? Is it good for a newborn baby to drink the same chemical dose as an adult? Hmmm, perhaps it's better to force-feed children more aluminium on Fridays, and a little less fluoride on Tuesdays – you get the picture. Medical industry is an *industry*, and the last thing govermentals want is fit fuckers getting uppity, specially old cunts with experience and know-how. And fitness at any age starts in the head, persistence and patience. Airborne not Chairborne, that's what we used to say in the mob. Try this one, quick, caff on the corner."

"I think that's a one way too."

"Nah, go for it."

"It's a little tight—"

"Go, go, GO!"

Just as Rachel tears the car into the laneway, I leans against her wiper switch, turning it off – the windscreen instantly mists over with rain – and we hear this sickening crunch of steel.

Screeching to a stop, "Oh bugger…"

"Sorry, leant on it."

We looks out our windows.

"Nothing my side," she says.

"Motorbike," says I, "Fucking Old Bill's bike…"

"And here he comes," says she, peering into the wing mirror, as this lanky Plod in leathers runs out of the caff, just behind. He slows his pace, and begins swaggering up to Rachel's window.

"Great," she whispers to herself, "And the boot's full of coke."

And I've got a small armoury in my cellar—

"You're doing a fucking delivery?"

"Fifteen Ks of the good batch," nod, sniff, "Oh here he comes—"

"Not good!" I whispers back, fingering the 9mm under my suit jacket, "Not fucking good!"

Turns and pouts, "It's in the boot—"

"Don't give a fuck if it's up your arse! You tell me these things *first*, right?"

"Fine, but this is your fault, not mine. And it was a one way—"

"No buts. *Never* do that again. Do I make myself clear?"

He comes over, glances at his bike again, and takes out his book.

"Okay," she sighs, "I'll handle this."

"Too bloody right you will."

"Hello officer," sniff, sniff, winding the window up halfway, "What seems to be the problem?"

"I think you know, madam," he grumbles, jotting down details, "Can I see your licence please."

"Is your bike okay? My insurance—"

"Your licence and registration please."

"Look, I *will* pay for any damage—"

"Step out of the vehicle, please."

Sexy librarian smile, "It's raining, officer, do you want me to get *wet?* I'm very susceptible to colds—"

"Step out of the vehicle, now!"

"Okay, fine, on the understanding that you're giving me an order," sniff, sniff, climbing out, "I conditionally accept."

And on it went, the twenty questions routine, I supposed, because a few minutes later the Plod's picked up his bike, and he's all fidgety, speaking into his radio. Rachel swans over to my window,

"I don't think he likes the look of us."

"You've cocaine all over you're blouse."

"He wants a warrant to search the car."

"I can see he's radioing in. Sort this, or I will, catch-madrift?"

"No, he's not calling home about that."

"Oh?"

"Won't be long now. Sit tight," says she, and saunters off again. He returns her driving licence, they exchange a couple of words, and then he's marching back into his caff, glancing behind at us.

"Let's go," she says, reversing out.

"What happened there, that was… odd. He was bricking it."

Shrugs, "He gave me an order, I gave him my bill."

"Come again?"

"He contracted me the moment I stepped out of the car, and I'm not standing around in the rain for free, not for anybody, who does he think I am?"

"Ay?"

"Have a look in the glove compartment."

I took out a stack of business cards, turning one over. It read:

I, Rachael-Susan: James claim my FEE SCHEDULE for any transgressions by police officers, government principals or agents or justice system participants is no less than TWO HUNDRED AND FIFTY POUNDS STERLING PER HOUR (£250) or portion thereof if being questioned, interrogated, transported, incarcerated, or in any way detained, harassed or otherwise regulated without my express and freely-given written and notarised consent.

Had to tip my hat to that, "Clever. How does this work, then?"

"Exactly the same way as picking up a bill in a restaurant. Any government agent orders me to do anything I don't want to do, I hand them my fee schedule. If they choose to go through with it, then they're agreeing to become personally liable for my fees."

"That's why he was bricking it."

"Once I explained what had happened, yes, he became more than a little concerned!" she laughs, "And called home to check with daddy. They usually do."

"Can anybody do this?"

"If they know what they're doing. Years ago, when I was still in college, I drafted an extremely long list of bizarre claims, and filed them as notice of claim of right using a Notary Public. I was on a compound drugs orgy at the time, and it was originally intended as a prank, but I sent a copy to the Police Commissioner, posted copies on courts' notice boards, and so forth – clearly stating that any affected parties had twenty-one days to register their dispute. Failure to do so would result in an automatic default judgment, securing forevermore all rights therein claimed, and establishing permanent and irrevocable estoppel by acquiescence."

She chuckles, "I didn't hear a peep, not even a counter-claim, so everything I wrote stands. I don't think anybody even bothered reading all the way through, it ran on for pages."

"Blimey, very clever, so you can charge them to hell and back for even talking to you?"

"I haven't tested it in court, I haven't needed to so far but I claimed the right, yes. Along with the right to wear frilly pink knickers on my head in public places, whilst singing the national anthem and dancing the Cancan."

Woman after my own heart. "Could've still arrested you, though."

"Of course, I wasn't stopping him, that's entirely his choice. Instead he chose to give me a verbal warning."

"Blimey, Top Brass can't be happy about it."

"Actually they are okay with it. They operate under the same policies too, commerce, everything does – the UK's been a registered company since the 1930s – and the police force act as their *policy* enforcers, collecting revenue. But I'm only a small fish that slipped through net, they're not losing a great deal of revenue here. Have you looked into our law system, Mr Barbelo?"

"Can't say I have, not much. I've got my own system though, what I call natural law, based it on Darwin's theories of natural selection. Works for me, end of the day."

"The Constitution and the Bill of Rights, that's natural law. The *Magna Carta.*"

"Never read it."

"I'll get you a copy, if you're interested. I think you'll find Article 61 extremely explicative. At last, here!" She starts turning into another street.

I shakes my head. "No, leave it, I'm inspired, Sid's present can wait for another day. Just cut us another line and keep explaining all this. Drop us home after…"

Wasn't the point anyway. Point of the manoeuvre was to get to know my Generals, test their mettle. Specially that one, after her little 'classy' display of power in The Effra. The Plod was always in that caff lunchtimes, and his bike was always parked on the corner – obviously didn't know she'd packed the boot – but passed with flying colours, she did.

As for Mark, I gave him the task of tracking down our war acquaintances, and let him get on with the rest. Anybody who works finances in The City doesn't need their mettle tested, they're already a Class A cunt and bound to turn up trumps.

Rachel did a u-turn home, and so did I. Read the *Magna Carta* and the Bill of Rights, cover to cover, and by the end of that winter the auld proverbial seed had sprouted with conviction – my country was going to the dogs! It wasn't even a country anymore, it was a fucking limited liability company?

And as if I didn't have enough problems, I find out I'm a fucking ship. Something had to be done. Natural selection's all about conviction, even small adjustments will have effects for the higher good – if kept up long enough.

For Sid and I that consisted of a punch bag, an assortment of bladed weapons – katanas, nagamakis, tantos and so on – and a skipping rope. Simple.

As a one-legged student of every martial discipline under the sun, I'd almost say fuck the blades, and even the punch bag, a good session on the rope's invaluable, build up that good peg first, get a spring back in it – it'll make up for the lack of the other and some.

No weight lifting or machines and all that malarkey, that's for plonkers. Got to chuck your body about, move the blood, but in ways what are going to be constructive after – engage the mind.

Working on a knockout punch is useful. A fast sidestep and knife thrust is useful. But lifting lumps of iron in the air for hours isn't useful, except for lifting lumps of iron in the air.

Easy logic.

And it was easy, almost too easy. On those frosty winter nights, I stalked the streets of London with precision, awakening my touch, sharpening my edge on the field of honour.

"Do you have a light, young man?"

He pauses, turns around.

Fumbling for my fags, I drops my wallet on the ground.

"Oopsy daisy, can you pick that up for me, please?"

He eyes the wallet, eyes me. The streetlamp casts sickly yellow shadows across his greedy mug.

"Please? There's a good lad. Back isn't what it was, you see?"

He sees alright – Barbelo the Lamb, lost, old and helpless – he sees the choice. And in that perfect instant I see it too, I see it all – my senses heighten, my mind is still, my breathing, balanced.

Shuffle, scuffle, gurgle, gurgle. They dropped like flies.

Chapter 10

Merry Chris-mash!

Oh shiny sleek and shiny 9mm Glock
Perched on my windowsill
The winter morning sun.
Oh mighty two-inch mortar
Brixton stirs
What bliss!
Alive. Wanting wanting wanting

Not exactly Shakespeare, true, but I was cheerful when I wrote that poem; Christmas Eve, the day I got my first monthly rattle – my special list of particular and horrific psycho-bad'uns, what Rob down the cop-shop provides for me once a month.

I mean, all told, what I do is a community service, free of charge, and hanging about street corners getting yourself mugged is all very well, serves its use – and as I've already explained, if they're gonna start, then in for a penny, in for a pound.

Line them up, I'll knock them down.

But there's nothing quite like a job's a good'un on true evil – and before yous all get all moralising and uppity, let me just say one thing:

VERMIN.

End of.

We're talking about true evil here – psychos what enjoy torturing children are on another level entirely. There's scum out there what are in a class of their own, and they gets away with it time, and time again; a clever lawyer, a fat wedge into the right pocket, and they're out stalking the streets again.

Your street. The street your mother lives on.

You know the Old Bill don't protect you, obviously, because if they did, there wouldn't be no vermin left out there. And you can bang on all you like about how these people are sick and need help, rehabilitation and all that bollocks, but deep down you know I'm right – it doesn't fucking work.

So what does work?

You know fucking what.

It's not rocket science, think about it for a minute. For every one of these vermin I send to Happy Place, I save ten innocent men, women and children – meaning you, your kids, your loved ones.

What gives me the right to do what I do?

Because I can, that's what gives me the right.

But more importantly, because I can and *I do*.

And if only more of yous who also can, but don't   and I know you're out there – got off your fucking knees and served your community proper, well, enough said.

And for those of you who think you can't, I tell you now, you can. Give you an example: Animal Control Officers – where would we be without them, ay?

I'll tell you where, dinners for Rover's food bowl…

Three in the morning it was, and I was taking a lovely stroll up Brixton Hill when I heard all this commotion up ahead; growling and breaking bottles and all that, sounded like a riot was kicking off, so I slowed my pace, crept forward.

Up on the brow of the hill appears this massive pack of wild dogs, hundreds of them, taking over the entire street, all swarming down the hill like a ravenous furry ocean towards me.

You see, the Council had downed tools, on and off for months, what meant there was bin-fulls of rubbish everywhere, and it also meant the dog catchers must've been on strike too, 'cos I'm squeezed into this doorway watching Alsatians, Poodles, Labradors, all kinds of dogs hurtling past, tearing into rubbish bags, all gone wild again.

And I say 'wild' because more than several of them looked at me funny, if ya catch-madrift – any sudden moves and I was a good'un – but I'm watching this rabble of gnashing fangs, thinking my Gawd, just a matter of months ago they were all unassuming, obedient specimens of human domestication, and fuck me sideways, just look at Little Fido now! Beautiful. All of them back to being the perfect killing machine nature had intended them to be.

And what's more, they looked happy.

Luckily there was still food about in the streets, otherwise they would've had a go for sure, and that's alright, a dog is in actual fact a wolf – the inner killer is barely under the surface – you'd be a right cunt for judging a wolf for doing what a wolf does best.

And the human?

Self-explanatory. Top Cunt of the food-chain and not for nothing; every single one of us fucking gifted, mate, unrivalled exterminators – Da Vinci himself couldn't have designed us better for mortality trade. Killers the likes of which even the mighty wolf had to bow his head, and tip his snout in the presence of outstanding brilliance.

Think about that whenever you feel you're not successful in life.

Proof's in the pudding, mate, we earned our slice, and maybe all I'm doing here is preaching to the choir, but let me just offer one bit of universal truth, you think you can't but you *can*.

Not saying you have to if you don't need to, just saying be proud when you do.

After the first time it gets easier, and easier, effortless. You realise it's innate, comes on a natural level; it's what our ancestors did to live and continue the family line, all through the ages – and we're all the living testament of just how well they did it, their inheritors, the *only* reason why yous and I are here, right now.

But, and this is the onion, there are some cunts out there what are *different* – different to the natural – True Evil. Going after them is a religious duty, places you a cut above the primal level and into the Spiritual.

Helps if you've got an insider, a Peeler like Rob to point you in the right direction, but if you haven't, go out and get yourself one.

Get it right, and you won't regret it.

The first day I got my monthly rattle it was like all my horses had come in at once – though there were only three names on the list, so it was more of a 'daily' than a monthly, catch-madrift, but he was turning up trumps, was our Rob.

"Christmas present, Mr Barbelo," he whispers, scanning the cop-shop, leaning across the front desk.

"Oh how lovely," says I, slipping the envelope he passes me under my coat. "Mug-shots?"

He nods.

"And profiles?"

He nods.

"Oh lovely, lovely…"

"They're all local, but I'll have more for you next time," he whispers, "And about time."

"Oh how lovely…" was about all I could say, floating out the door on cloud nine, and ripping open the envelope in the street, I hailed a black cab.

"Where to?" asks the cabbie.

"Crystal Palace," says I, reading the addresses on the list, getting them in proper order, randomising the route. "Drop me off at the bus station, please."

The first was a serial paedophile, and a bit disappointing, nothing special – except he no longer has any balls, on account they're nailed to his living room wall.

The second was another nonce and another cab ride, up Norwood this time – neutered him in the alleyway round the back of his house. Had to wait over an hour for the cunt to get back from work, traffic warden – your proverbial 'two birds with one stone' – but much the same as the first, all told, nothing to write home about.

But the third was a rare auld piece of work.

"Streatham High Street, please," I says to the cabbie, and settled back, studying the scum's profile – paedophilia, murder, arson, fucking necrophilia an' all – in a class of his own, this one was.

Turned my stomach.

Had to stop reading at the part where he breaks into this old lady's house, ties her to a chair and cuts off her eyelids, and then her lips – and I said I was going to try to keep my personal life short, so I won't go into what this cunt does next, join up the dots…

I knocked on the door, I wasn't going to, but I'd done a little reconnaissance around his house and the cunt wasn't alone – sounded like he was having a fucking Christmas party.

This geezer the spit of a mature Jonathan Ross – if you can picture that – dressed in red dungarees and Santa Hat, answers the door.

"Merry Christmas!" I declare, over the Carol singing coming from inside, "Mr Christopher Sandmount?"

He squints down at me, ringing his hands, "Are you—?"

"I'm Gerry Redman," I interrupt happily, "And this is the address the Agency gave me, you've won!"

I wave my brown envelope in front of his face, "Says here a family member entered you for our lottery."

"I'm sorry, what agency?"

I grins. "S.L.H. Insurances. What did you win? First prize! Just need you to sign a couple of forms, I'll explain everything inside, won't take a minute."

He takes a step back, nods, all serious, "Come in Gerry, please."

I followed the cunt inside, nice gaff – in a wannabe Lord Fuckface kinda way – and into his living room.

Not a pretty sight.

What at first I thought were people sitting around, were all these inflatable wank-dolls dressed up in Santa gear and tinsel – he'd sat them around on the couch, the armchairs, under the tree, everywhere.

"I'll just get my glasses," he says, nervously rooting around the bookcase by the window. "We're having a little family reunion."

"Oh how lovely," says I, creeping up behind him.

"Family's important this time of year."

"Isn't it just," flicking the release catch on my cane.

He leans over to his record player and turns it off.

"You have come!" he whispers, "I know who you are."

He spins around. I stalls in my tracks.

"They said he would come tonight. They said he would come with a gift!"

The hairs on the back of my neck stood on end, and I froze, like a statue. Can happen to the best of us in the presence of true evil, I assure you, particularly when they use their special powers like that.

Squints, nodding slowly, "They said he would call me by name."

I gasp under my breath – "Who said?"

"My family."

I chance another glance at the inflatable lunacy around the room.

"And my name is Mr Sandmount!"

"I know…"

"Why don't you sit down, we could have a little Christmas drink while we go through the paperwork." He grins, gesturing to the dinning table; two glasses and a bottle of sherry.

I grins back, my pegs were working again,

"Very well then, a nice drink with the paperwork" – gives me a chance to regroup before I rip your liver out – "Why not."

I sits down at the table, with him on the lighthouse seat, opposite.

"Well now, let's see," he says, pouring us a glass each, "What gifts do you bear?"

"Oh, two weeks in the Bahamas, for two, or the cash prize," I fidget with the envelope, "Oh! Silly me, I didn't bring the right forms—"

"Excuse me," turns around briefly to the inflatable Doris on the settee behind, "What did you say Rubert?" Tilts his head, smiles at me, "You must forgive Rubert. He doesn't trust strangers. He thinks everyone new is the Angel of Death."

I offered a nervous chuckle, "Oh that's alright."

"Don't let him upset you, he's the timid one of our family," nods a few times, lowers his tone, "He's terrified of dying. Quite a common mistake. People say they're afraid of death but that's not really what scares them. They're only afraid when they think they're going to die. Death itself is quite a liberating experience, once you know you're going to die, in that moment you are free. There is no choice. Nothing to decide. Only, surrender…"

I perks up at that, my blade sliding out of my cane under the table.

"Very true Mr Sandmount," I says, accepting the glass he passes me, "I found the very same thing myself in the Wars. Many times. Where did you serve?"

"Fourteenth Army," he replies, tight-lipped, and then sighs, "Burma. That's where I realised there's only one thing worse than thinking you're going to die, and that's not knowing why you're alive in the first place, who you are, what is your purpose," flicks his eyes to his bookshelf at my back, "Do you read?"

"I do as it goes, a fair bit."

"Take Edmond Dantes, the Count of Monte Cristo."

"Read it too, Mr Sandmount."

"What a fantastic archetypal principle, fundamentally flawed. Yes, flawed. Did Edmond know why he was alive until he found his purpose? Taking revenge for his suffering became his entire life, but, once accomplished, where does he go from there, what was left of his purpose, was he any the wiser as to who he was?"

"Good point," I says, eyeing him suspiciously.

"The book doesn't tell us what happens to our noble hero after he'd taken revenge, and there is a skilful motive for this. Mediocrity. That was the true villain of the story. Edmond's life is merely an ode to the primal urge to gratify ourselves; in essence he doesn't even right the wrongs which were done to him."

"I suppose what is done, is done, regardless, Mr Sandmount."

Smiles, "What was done cannot be undone, and in taking revenge a man is but equal with his enemy; but in passing it over, he is superior. Even after the skilful execution of his vengeance, we are still left with a certain unfulfilled emptiness at the end. His purpose over, he reverts from exemplifying the extra-ordinary, to the ordinary: Self-gratified, mundane and humdrum, sacrificed to the demons of mediocrity."

"Demons," I echoes.

Sips his sherry, "Mediocrity, that is the true enemy of mankind. Where is the sanity in living a life of monotony."

I nods, "Put like that, you've got an excellent point. Seems to me that Edmond merely traded one prison cell for another—"

"Excuse me," he interrupts, glancing behind him again. "Oh, yes, good idea Rubert, we had better double-check," turns to me, "What do think Gerry; does God play dice with the universe?"

"Dice?"

"The Uncertainty Principle."

"Nah, He plays cards," I says, getting vexed, "Deals out some fucking rough hands an' all. The only certainty is a plot in the boneyard—"

"Wait!"

I stalls, halfway out of my seat.

"Is your sword sharp, is your purpose honed?"

It was the way he said it, calm, off-hand, and yet with profound confidence – at that precise moment I knew that he knew.

"My sword is sharp," I replied. "My purpose, honed."

Smiles, "We are not the mediocre types, you and I," drains his sherry, "Come then, Jack Robinson, before we change our minds."

He stands up, pacing into the centre of the room.

I rose to my feet, and pegged over, standing before him,

"How did you know?"

"They said you would come. They said the Angel of Death would bring me a present. They said he would take me home, tonight, and that it would be… quick."

I nods. He kneels down.

"Take me home."

And I did, except I'm no angel, so nah, it wasn't fucking quick…

Chapter 11

Happy Days

I'd say the first three months living with Sid were almost the happiest of my life. I returned the lion every night, Sid tinkered with his TV sets and electronic wizardry – don't ask me what he was working on, well-over my head – but we'd shaped up, and shaped up our Firm, what was turning up trumps; loads of funds coming in.

Didn't much care what skulduggery they got up to, so long as they weren't mugging old ladies doing it, told them that from the off – fraud, weapon's smuggling, transnational money laundering, extortion of celebrity sport figures? Why not.

Insurance scams, medical scams, export-import, counterfeiting, credit card forgery and please, 'trash and cash' all the stocks you like – just divvy up fair and square with Barbelo and keep it rolling in.

Respectfully settled our tributes to the bigger Firms first, namely the Old Bill and the Irish, and pretty soon one or two smaller Firms were paying tribute to us – meaning 'tax,' depending who was doing what and in who's turf. Any cunt got uppity, Sid and I would job's a good'un – settled a few scores along the way too, nothing worth talking about – main thing is business is business. It's not like the movies, soon settles down if you're reasonable, and we was.

We was all happy, one big happy family getting bigger and richer by the day. Best hobby I ever had – I shit you not.

And then it got complicated.

Remember the lady with the legs, in The Albert that day? Right. I will confess I had my eyes peeled for her an' all; even dreamt about her and everything. Nice dreams, some, really, really nice – and that's fucking rare and special for me, all I have is bloody nightmares.

And then there I was, three in the afternoon in Brixton Library, at a meeting with Mark, our General and Accountant – I'd got him on the case trying to track down Sally, nothing yet, as he explained,

"Nothing yet on Sally," he whispers, as I sits down at his table.

"Quiet here, isn't it?"

He nods, takes off his specs, puts them down next to a book.

"Banks," he whispers, giving the book a pat, "Specifically the gold standard. Do you want to have a look?"

"Nah, I know all about them – biggest skulduggery of all time. Govermentals, banks, different shit, same arse…"

I pause, studying his mischievous grin, as he takes out a twenty pound note from his wallet.

"Mr Barbelo," he says, "Do you know what this is?"

"Money."

Shakes his head, all sincere and Clark Kent, "It's a contract."

I sighs, "What do you have in mind this time?"

"Banks print money, lend it to governments, and nations worldwide pay back both the capital and the interest. Endless cycle of ever-increasing debt. Owning a bank has to be the most profitable business on Earth!" He chuckles. "Wars, lending money for wars, all governments have to borrow massively from the banks."

"Catch-yadrift, Mark, my good man, and the people are forced to pay it off. It's called a perpetual war economy."

"Exactly, we're still bailing them out for the last war, and as long as banks coin money at interest, there will always be war, but *what* is money?"

I chuckled, "You're not suggesting we start up a bank, are you?"

Rubbing his eyes, he slips his specs back on.

"This note," he says, "was worth twenty pounds weight of gold, once, and yet it is still *legal tender.*"

Holds up the note again,

"Next to the Queen's head, it clearly states, 'I promise to pay the bearer on demand the sum of twenty pounds.' It is signed by Andrew Bailey, the chief cashier of the company: The Bank of England. *The company,*" he stresses forcefully. "Technically, with this you could've gone into any bank and cashed it in for *your* twenty pounds of gold."

"Alright…"

"This note is an IOU slip. It has to be honoured *on demand*, like it says, or it is not legal tender. And if it's not legal tender, then this particular bank is committing a criminal offence."

I shrugs, "Particular or not, they're all a shower of crooks anyways. What's your point?"

"I suggest we do just that."

"Ay?"

"I was at an office party the other day, a girl there went over the road to her bank and tried it."

"She cashed in her bank note?"

"God no, they called the police and arrested her! She was out of her mind on champagne, 'disturbing the peace,' or some such nonsense, but she gave me the idea."

"Give us a quick butcher's at that." I turns the note over a few times. "Mark, it doesn't say gold."

"Not specifically, but the *intent* to pay is clearly stated."

"Alright… but I dunno… you could go in with a million pounds and they could give you a million pounds of horse shit!"

"And I'd sell it off for fertiliser," he chuckles, "Good rates for organic fertiliser these days."

"You're serious, aren't you."

"I am. Rachel and I have already mulled it over, and we're confident we could pull it off. Money is a legally binding contract. They're required to give us, pound for pound, of *something* on demand. If they do not comply, and they won't," he shrugs, "breach of contract. At the very least."

"At the very least…"

My brain rattled with the vicious delight, pondering the pros and cons of suing The Bank of England – way too high profile considering our likewise nefarious activities – but I had to tip my hat to the cunt, "My Gawd Mark, you really are a nasty piece of work!"

"Thank you sir," he smiles, "We could sue for everything from false advertising to usury, and fail of course, but the beauty is it won't come to that; what company isn't terrified of negative exposure?"

I raised an eyebrow at that,

"You mean *blackmail* The Bank of England."

He coughs. "In a manner of speaking. It's no more or less what they do to us, the world over – debt is the essence of economic blackmail. Inflation: The bankers say 'pay up your debt,' a nation can't because the banks have cut off their money supply, so the bankers say, 'oh dear, no money, can't pay up, hmmm… we'll let you off some of your debt if you give us your home, or your business, or the Amazon Basin, the Brazilian Rainforest—'"

"Or your Aunt Fanny's wedding ring," I raise my hand, "Alright, alright, but no, I can't approve this particular little caper."

"And I understand," he sighs, stuffing his twenty back into his wallet. "You're not interested, are you?"

"Mark, me auld china, it's a pukka idea, but we can't publicly expose the whole banking industry as a swindle, and we simply don't have the clout to blackmail the Queen," I shrugs, "We'd be wiped out at the drop of a hat."

"Money," he reiterates. "You're not interested in money, not really…"

"Come again?"

"Mr Barbelo, I mean, I love money, the feel of it, the smell of it. I've been like that ever since I can recall; my first wage packet, do you know what? I couldn't even bring myself to spend it! I laid out all those beautiful notes on my bed, and just, just, mmm, money!"

"Alright, you love money."

"And I'm a good judge of people, Mr Barbelo, I know when someone else is likewise enamoured." He stifles a nervous chuckle. "I mean, what could you possibly want with the *Magna Carta?*"

"The original copy of Article 61, yes, very explicative."

"But… what, *what* are you really up to?" he says, and shrugs, all upfront.

I shrugs back. "Cultivating our little hobby, what else?"

"And yet neither you nor Sid display the attitude of… of…" He smiles. "Forgive me."

"Gangsters? Is that the word you're looking for?"

Glances about the library, and then nods.

"And what are we supposed to *display?*"

"Well, I've been hired before now – nothing spectacular, bookkeeping, that sort of thing, and well," he nods his head a few times, "You, Mr Barbelo… you and Sid."

He smiles again.

I smile back.

"Tell me Mark, are you happy with our little arrangement?"

"Oh yes!" he whispers. "Extremely."

"Then what, on Gawd's Earth, do you mean – *display the attitude?*"

"Nothing," he mutters, tight-lipped. "I meant nothing."

"Very well, then put your fancy ideas in a box and wrap them up with a pink ribbon. What else have you got for me?"

"There's a major conference coming up, in The City, soon, our company's working on the MOD's defence budget. This is a big contract for us…" he pauses, leans over the table, "Shortly followed by the annual arms show and—"

"Hold it. You'll be there too, hands on, doing their books?"

"Projections mostly, yes, financial estimates for the run-up to the Millennium. I'm not entirely sure of our brief yet, but—"

"Can you get me these figures?"

"I could, maybe… but why, what for?"

He eyes me suspiciously again.

"Been having these *funny* dreams lately," I says, and turn on my gentlemanly 'don't ask if you value your kneecaps' gaze.

"I'll see what I can do," he says.

"Thank you," I says. "Annual arms show, go on."

"There might be some *scope* there, it's not entirely out of our league," he whispers with a wink.

I winks in return, "I approve."

He settles back into his seat, "Nevertheless, our investments are all coming along tickity-boo. But no sign of your wife, and I've tried everything, tax records the lot; she's vanished off every registrar."

I sigh. "Well, she was one of our best at precisely that. Keep at it though, ay."

"Of course."

"I mean, our marriage wasn't exactly above-board, well, not recognisably – unless you live up an oak tree in Brittany – Gawd, I wouldn't know where to begin explaining, mate, but she's the nearest thing I ever had to a nearest and dearest…"

"That's okay. If she's left any trail, we'll pick it up," he smiles.

"Thank you," I says, reaching out a hand and rising to my feet, "Pleasure, as always."

"Pleasure's all mine," he says, shaking my hand.

I made a mental note of letting Mark in on a couple of the subtler aspects of the operation, but I had to get out, now, right there and then. I'd got the touch – if you've still got yours, you know exactly what that means.

And sure as spit, no sooner out the library and on Effra Road, when Irish Lady legs it past with two geezers, proper Darkies dressed in army combat gear, waving machetes over their heads, right behind her.

Believe me, Darkies in combat gear swinging machetes wasn't an unusual sight in Brixton at the time, a lot of them were coming over again from the Caribbean – a new crew, Yardies, they were called – and understandably, they needed to get their territories sorted.

Business is business, and all that.

What was obviously unusual was them needing to butcher lovely young girls in the street, unusual and highly disturbing to my sensibilities, now heightened to a keen edge on account of all the workouts Sid and I were doing.

Without a second thought, my cane tripped the first sprawling into the road, my blade skewered the other in the gut. I turns around, see the girl standing there, watching.

The cunt in the road gets up – traffic swerving and beeping – sees his mate fall, clutching his gut, but then comes for me! Why? Could never understand some cunts, it was fair game, one on one, why be like that?

His blade misses my head by an inch, as I sidestep in slashing under his armpit. Drops the blade, eyes me for a split second and legs it, heading down Coldharbour Lane.

The other cunt's dazed, trying to get up. I give him a helping hand, discreetly severing the artery between his legs – force of habit – but people everywhere now, and one or two had seen what'd happened, kind of – standing there shocked and frozen. I needed to put on a good show. Standard psyops, 'strategic perception management,' blanket over their weak perspective with a stronger one, namely a memory they can understand:

It's just an old gentleman helping a poor Darkie what had tripped, running for a bus.

The old gentleman's trying to get him up, dusting him down, cooing kind words into his lughole,

"My dear friend, oh please don't die! I wanna take you home, cut out your heart, have it for supper…"

All that happened in a blink.

The rest was the usual, 'Get this man a doctor, he's bleeding!' and all that malarkey. So I sidles away, casual as you like, played out to the wailing of an ambulance with Irish Lady on tow.

Once safely down Saltoun Road and away from the main drag, I hear,

"Hey mister, mind if I join ya?"

Without waiting for a reply, she'd hooked her arm into mine and we were heading towards The Effra Tavern.

Chapter 12

Dirty Old Man, hehehe!

"People," she says in that hypnotic Irish lilt, all smiling violet eyes over her pint, "Not Darkies or Whities, *people*, don't be racist!"

"What's the difference? Look, young lady —"

"Brid! Told ya, my name is Brid. And you're Mr Barbelo the boring old Racist."

"Brid, I'm a lot of things, but I was never a racialist," I reiterated patiently – we'd been over this a hundred times, seemed like – "It's just the way I was taught to talk, see? Some people are darker than others, so's they're Darkies. Some are whiter than others, so's they're Whities. Some are from Pakistan, so they're Pakis. China, Chinks; Arabs are Ragheads 'cos they really do wear rags on their heads – I've seen them – and so on, and so on."

She nods, scoops a mass of raven curls from her brow, and tilts her head to one side,

"Gotch ya," she drawls, "But why?"

"Why what?"

"Why is some skin darker?"

"Ahhh, right. Melanin, that's the chemical what makes darker skin, protects you from harmful sunrays, see?"

"Sooo… it's because people need Melanin to survive outside."

"Exactly, it's a survival thing, protection from the sun."

"So yer saying 'Darkies' are superior?"

"Nah, I'm just saying darker skin's better… for… I mean the *production*, the production of melanin, that's why they're Darkies, and we're Whities—"

"Gotch ya the first time. Yer saying that sunlight harms the skin without melanin, so it's a survival mechanism, yeah?"

"That's right."

"And the production of Melanin is crucial to protect the body, so in terms of survival, yer saying 'Darkies' are of a higher order of importance."

"Exactly."

"I agree, nature wants them around a lot more us—"

"I mean no, I'm not saying that—"

"Yes you are! Us 'Whities' need creams and artificial chemicals to protect us from the sun, or we have to skulk around in the shadows; we get burnt to a crisp, even die from overexposure. 'Darkies,' however, already have protection, naturally. So naturally the darker the skin the better."

"Gawd blimey…"

"Better, superior, and if nature herself intended the production of melanin as a survival mechanism?" She grins, sipping her pint. "Then naturally, people whose melanin production is higher, are of a higher order of importance than those whose skin is not."

"Gawd blimey…"

"Easy logic," she winks. "Anyhow, you can't call me a *Whitie*, not when I'm actually more of a Pinkie, a magnolia-pinkie with blotchy bits, and so are ye!" she laughs, "We're all just people, Mr Barbelo, one huge race of multi-coloured people."

"True enough," I mutter, turning my hands over, "And I can go pretty dark an' all. After a couple of months in a trench I can pass for a Darkie myself, or a Daygo leastways…"

I pause, massaging my temples, take her in over my pint. Beautiful, mad as a hatter, but fucking gorgeous. And dangerous. All my nerves were on red alert. Halfway through our second pint, and not a word about what I know she'd seen me do, not a peep.

She read my mind, some of it leastways.

"But don't listen to me," she says, "I don't know who I am, ya know?" she taps her head, "I'm escaped, nearly six years to the day! I'm a good escaper. I escape often."

"Oh?"

"Broadmoor was the last place, genetic experiments, Neanderthal gods and infiltration of Inner Orders, that's why the other Inner Orders won't take me in. They could, but they won't give me Sanctuary, not until the Protocol says it's time."

"Protocol."

"Seven years, then they take you in, Sanctuary, if you can prove to them you're free of the Illuminati." She drains her pint, quick smile. "Not a simple task, proving that. Jesus! No, no, no, very *demanding*…" she pauses, serious frown etched across her brow.

"… Mr Barbelo, why did you really save my life just now? Do ya wanna fuck me?"

"I-I-I…" I stuttered. I think, more than anything, at that precise moment I wanted to tie her up and throw rocks at her.

And then fuck her.

"You didn't actually kill him," she mutters to herself. "They can't be killed, unless you know how…"

Her eyes glaze over, ever so slightly, like a fleeting shadow passing by, there and yet not there.

I was in love.

"What did you just say?" I asks.

"If you want," she replies, faking well, "If you want to take me home and look after me, then yes, you can. I'm sick of the streets, I need *quality*…" she pauses again, shakes her head. "But, it will be dangerous for you; they are looking for me, ya know?"

"Who's after you? Yardies?"

"No, no," she whispers, leaning closer over the table, eyes flitting around the pub. "*Feharchrove!*"

I nods, even though I don't have a clue what she's on about.

"Those two you saw weren't *people*. They were people who are not people. Beings from another *vibration*, another world. They're here, all around us. Shhh! But there's one, there's one really powerful *feharchrove*; that's the one they sent to retrieve me. The Wrenhunter!"

I find myself entranced by her melodic voice, glancing into the shadowy corners of the empty lounge. She holds my hand. I let her.

"Mr Barbelo, I am the Wren, and the Wrenhunter is *my* feharchrove. The other two were other people's feharchrove, right?"

I nods.

"Everybody has a feharchrove."

"Everybody…"

"And if you are serious about protecting me, the best thing to do is you hide me, somewhere dark, underground, and we can play a game, together…"

"What game?" I ask, even though I know I shouldn't.

"A lovely game! You could be my granddaddy, hmmm? And I'll be your naughty little girl. What do you say, Mr Barbelo, my saviour, my knight, will you look after me, will ya? Will ya fuck your naughty little girl?"

90

"Ah! The auld shamper-floot? Thanks, but no thanks—"

"I beg your pardon?"

I sighs, "A Champagne Flute: prosti—"

"A prostitute? What!" she flares up, "No!" And then she giggles, twirling her hair, "Although I'm a great little horizontal refreshment, when I need the Awen. And I nearly always do… so?"

"Another pint, says I," getting up, "And then I think you should meet my mate Sid."

At the bar, George wasn't happy.

"Mr Barbelo, it's none of my business, but we've got to have a word."

"Oh?"

"Her, that girl," his eyes flick to our table – she was talking to herself again.

"Yeees," I says slowly.

"She's not, not *right*, and we've got standards, if you catch my drift."

"I catch-yadrift, George. We always had a bit of a problem with the poor girl, ever since she was born."

Surprised eyebrow shoots up, "That's her?"

"My granddaughter," I whisper. "And I'd appreciate it if you kept stum."

"Of course, but you always said…"

"She was in university, yeah, cover story," says I, "Though hospitals of those types are a kind of university, catch-madrift."

"Oh poor girl. I am sorry."

"Don't be. She's loads better now, I'm looking after her, see?"

"I see," passing us our pints, "But should she be out?"

I shrugs, "Thatcher's fucking 'Care in the Community.' They just chuck 'em out onto the streets to fend for themselves, like stray dogs! I'm not letting *that* happen to one of my own."

"Thatcher," he spits, "But I mean, in pubs an' all…"

"Doctor's orders, part of her so-called re-socialisation program."

"Oh, better have these on me then. So sorry…"

I felt her before I saw her, she had her hand on my crotch, miracle I didn't spill our pints.

"Who's this, granddaddy?" she flashes her lovely smile. George's face lights up like Christmas. I put our pints down, wrapping my arm around her shoulders, pressed up against the bar.

"George, this is my granddaughter, Brid."

"Thought it was Sharon."

"It's *Brid*," I winks.

"Pleasure to meet you, Brid," says he, holding out his hand.

Big mistake. The dirty cow's got one hand inside my trousers, stroking away, and now she's holding George's, sucking on his fingers.

George pulls back, quick, a little too quickly and knocks over one of our pints, splashed onto the bar. I step back and it was game over.

Old cunt, standing there with young trollop holding his wanger.

I think there's a law against that, but I suppose wanking off granddad in public is what nutters do – nowt queerer than folk, as they say, and never a truer word.

And George, bless his heart, didn't say a word. Just turned away, got a cloth, wiping the bar casual as you like.

I put my wanger away.

Trying to resume my seat by the door, she jumps in first. I sat on her lap, then shifted beside her, snarling,

"Now, young lady—"

"They say I have a pussy like a silk purse!"

"Do that again in here I'll stick you like a pig!"

"Hmmm, sounds nice," she whispers back.

"Fucking mean it!"

"Oink, oink! Will ya stick me, mister, will ya? Stick me like a pig?"

Infectious laugh, that too, had me doubled up.

"You don't scare me, Mr Barbelo," she says, calming down. "I've seen it all, I walked with the gods! And I'm serious, I'm happy to oblige. I like you. You like me too, yes?"

"Listen, Brid, I don't know you well-enough to—"

"Shhh! And which Brid do ya wanna know? I'm a multi-dimensional being of great power! I'm a check-in girl," she pouts.

"Right," I says, "That's where you worked, then? Loads down Heathrow Airport have been laid off—"

Shakes her head. "I said, *I am* a check-in girl: Sister Samantha."

"Who?"

"One of me, we *dream* together. But, she and I need to wake up."

"Dreams," I sighs, "All I have is bloody nightmares."

Narrows her eyes, "Then isn't it about time you checked-in too, Mr Barbelo?" she asks, in a voice like steel. I flinched.

Alright, the poor girl needs help, considerably, but I didn't like the way she said that, not one bit.

Then she whispers, snuggling up, "Every dreamer needs his Muse, so he does. And when I saw what you did to those feharchrove, oh yes, they were scared! And I've never seen them scared, never. They can't, it's not in their nature; they're made of fear itself and yet they were terrified of you, of your Awen, your awareness and power! Oh please, fuck me now," she croons on, sinking her head into my lap, "fuck me now, my knight," she looks up briefly, tears in her eyes, "take me to the Earth Dream…"

I chance a quick glance-about.

George was serving round the back bar, and the lounge was empty, save for another couple at the far end who'd just come in, and with pretty much the same idea she had, snogging away and all that, and well, it'd been more years than I'd dare to count – I had a stiffy King Kong would be proud of.

Rude not to oblige a lady in my hour of need.

She was light as a feather, her sitting astride me, and it was only for a few minutes, but if I was King Kong, she was Niagara Falls – I shit you not – but it was then I realised I had another problem on my hands. A very, very complicated problem, because all that she'd said earlier… well, how do I say this without sounding like a fruitcake too?

I can't. Only that cut my throat, I felt I'd known her all my life, a part of my brain believed her! Not the part talking now, but that other part – the touch – the part what has you sitting bolt-upright in the dead of night, lead pipe in hand, all up for it just before some cunt breaks into your house.

That part knows stuff the other parts don't, and when we left the pub, we went home the long way round, via the High Street like she insisted; something about needing to 'complete a circle of initiation.' Yeah, right, tell me about it.

Outside the tube station entrance, we had to pause, it's always tricky navigating through Maggie's Miserables – chocker block with winos and dossers, sprawled on the road, slumped down the stairs – and now there's a dozen 'care in the communities' dancing around some cunt wrapped in a blanket, screaming down a loudhailer about the Antichrist ruling the world. And just as we caught an opening, one of them, a woman, hurtles past and shoves something into my coat pocket. And fucking well-done an' all, totally under my radar.

I looks around. She's vanished into the crowded street.

Reaching into my pocket, I pulls out a funny-looking playing card.

"Tarot!" gasps Brid, "And that's the zero card, The Fool."

"Oh," I says, about to chuck the thing away.

"Not that kind of fool," she says, "not always, it can be lucky, like a Joker in an ordinary pack. Means new beginnings, total carefree innocence."

"Well, we could all do with some of that alright. Do you want it?"

She smiles. "No, keep it," she says, "I know the woman who gave it to you, and she works in mysterious ways."

"No doubt."

"She's from the Earth Dream."

"What, I mean where is that, then?"

"That's where we do our recruiting."

"For what?"

"For the Inner Order. See him," she points at this huge Rastafarian, leaning on a lamppost over the road, "That's Brother Ignatius, a Dream Master."

"A what?"

"Come," she smiles, hooking her arm into mine. "He'll be Initiating a young Dream Warrior from Locale 5, tonight, and I have to be on call."

"Ay?"

"Take me home, I'll tell ya all about it…"

And she did, all day and half the bloody night! And blimey, by the time we'd got to bed I was dizzy with her weirdo prattle. So yeah, hold onto your hats, events are gonna take a brief turn into the surreal…

Chapter 13

A Different Kind of Nightmare

Samantha at the check-in desk was nervous.

"Brother Ignatius," she explains, again, "Forgive me sir, we really do not have any record of you in our database. You don't appear to... *exist*—"

A massive fist crashed down on the desk in front of her.

"Listen! I an' I hafta be in Dub-Lin in Iry-land tonight!" screamed the giant, his thick black dreadlocks shaking with indignation as if with a life of their own. His enormous eyes beamed at her from his great height, and again she felt compelled to hide behind her computer screen; nobody in Nazi Britain dresses with a leopard skin cloak and army combat fatigues.

"Likkel gal," the giant implored, more gently this time, "De Creator lives in Iry-land!"

"The... Creator?"

"Yes! I an' I hafta fight de dark malignant forces trettening de entire ex-histance of reality, do ya overstand? Where's my ticket?"

Sighing deeply, trying to regain composure, her fingers worked frantically on the keyboard, searching, searching, searching...

DNA record: negative. Biometric identity: negative. RFID tracker chip implant: negative. Behavioural control chip implant: negative.

Brother Ignatius growled impatiently, threw back his bearded chin and began to roar,

"Reality, vitality an' integrity! By the power invested in I an' I by the Most High, WAKE UP!"

Brother Joseph stood in line behind his Dream Master. He had spotted two British SS Guards, one on each side of their desk, watching proceedings at first with malevolent suspicion, but now, with the kind of predatory instinct more commonly found in pack animals, they simultaneously decided that the 'mad black bastard' needed a corrective session in the detention cubicles, around the back of the Terminal.

They began to squeeze through the mass of businessmen and Nazi Party dignitaries queued up at the check-in desks. Of course, Brother Ignatius had seen them too, but they were on a recruiting mission, and these were particularly the kind of theatrics he was known to relish. It was always a profound joy to see a Dream Master at work, so his young acolyte stood back, allowing the first guard to get close.

The guard snarled, trying to reach a restraining grip on the huge man's shoulder.

"No officer," Samantha ventured, desperately, and immediately looked down, averting her eyes. She wanted to say it's okay, that she thought the man harmless, but the microchip in her brain instantly scrambled her protest into a placid smile of compliance.

The giant was far from happy. He spins around to face his assailant, "Whooodahht! Babylon come run me down? Come test I an' I with de powers of darkness? Malignity! Barbarity! Time to get stoned…"

He only whispered his last words and the guard became frozen, his hand resting lightly on his gun holster. Everywhere in the Terminal, people solidified, poised between one instant and the next, midway between then and eternity.

Midway between now and nowhere.

Brother Ignatius turns to his apprentice, and momentarily losing all trace of his Caribbean patois, he quietly asked,

"Well, Brother Joseph, how would you proceed from here?"

His young acolyte pulled the hood of his monk's habit over his head, and wrestled with the increasing uncertainty in his mind. An image of his country home on Locale 5 flashed before his eyes; the snow-capped mountains, the cool stream flowing past the Monastery, and into gentle green valleys below.

Brother Ignatius shook him by the shoulder, "Well?"

"Follow protocol," he replied, eyeing the security guards. "Provide these vipers with identification, anchor our recruit, and be gone from this Locale immediately. But…"

"But?"

"I am sensing that she is lying with an old man in Locale 32, he has a leg missing and often resides within terrible, terrible nightmares…" he paused, looking around. "Do you know what Sid, this place looks exactly like Dresden!"

Brother Ignatius chuckled, "Who is Sid?"

"Don't piss me about, why have you turned into a psychotic Yardie? And come to think of it, why was I talking like a knob?"

"Hmmm, I believe you are merging with him," he explained patiently, "When travelling the Realms of the Earth Dream, it often happens that we draw our awareness from others."

"Blimey, then why hasn't my leg grown back?" I mutters, patting myself down – real enough.

"Because we are running dangerously low on Awen."

"What's that then?"

"Acute awareness, the means by which we navigate the Realms."

"Alright, but it's one thing talking like a knob, and quite another *being* a knob. And I'm definitely a knob – look at me, and fucking sandals? But…" I pause, looking around again, "Sid, what's Brid doing here?"

"Sister Samantha and you need further instruction—"

"Sister who? Nah, that's Brid, *my* nymphomaniac fit-bird from The Awake. She walked with the gods, so keep your hands to yourself when you meet her, alright? She's not the full ticket."

He shoots me a concerned eye, "We are in Heathrow Airport, on Locale 22, recruiting a Dream Warrior for the Order—"

"Fuck off, this is Dresden Train Station… Gawd. I was detained here in the War… oh shit! I think I know what's happening… I'm living inside someone else's head! Sid?"

Brother Ignatius wasn't listening; he'd begun pacing up and down the aisle formed by the statuesque forms of motionless people, waiting in their queues.

Despite the 'Death Penalty' signs plastered everywhere, trails of solidified marijuana smoke rose in grey columns from a group of British Nazi Party officials behind them. He stopped there, drew a long puff from a marijuana cigarette, and knotting his fingers into his sprawling mass of dreadlocks, his eyes locked on a point six inches from his boots,

"She's not responding… and yet… 'Psychotic Yardie…' Perhaps…"

He resumed walking at a hectic pace, and Brother Joseph couldn't help but marvel at the way he moved his immense frame, weaving a graceful path all around the crowded Terminal without knocking anything – or indeed anyone – over.

Not that they would know, all would be exactly as we left it when we returned.

"She has a behavioural microchip!" yelled Brother Joseph, his words sounding hollow within the deafening silence of the Inbetween, or 'the stoned,' as his Dream Master affectionately called this state. Regardless of the countless times they had shifted here, he'd never managed to get used to it.

"Woy Rasta! We are chant down Babylon tonight!" came the ranting reply, and Brother Joseph feared he was losing him, or rather, he was losing himself. Between the Worlds the mind has great difficulty concentrating. Many of the Order go astray here; wandering eternity, seduced by silence, and it was beginning to take its toll.

With a monumental effort of will, I recalled my training and finally managed to break my cerebral fix on the eerie stillness,

"Shut the fuck up, Sid! She's fucking microchiped to high heaven, that's why she's not responding."

The Dream Master glided effortlessly back towards the desk.

"Hey, simmer down, I an' I know dat," his face breaking into a concerned grimace, "But man, dis place is dangerous! Ya have some interesting scars growing on ya face, here and here…"

And Locale 22 was also dangerous, judging by the disposition of those guards.

"Scars?" I jabbed wildly with my finger, "Her, her, her!" I growled with clenched teeth, "Let's just Anchor her and shift out of here!"

"Ya mean Samantha?" he murmured, bent down almost double to peer intently into the woman's face. "Ya man, dis gal's cute!"

"Not telling you a third time, Sid! Hands off the fit-bird."

Thrusting his lower lip forward, Brother Ignatius scrunched his forehead. "She needs shock tactics," he grinned, "Just a likkel wakey-wakey," reverently shaking his giant head up and down, "We're going back in a psycho-stylee!"

Brother Joseph was unimpressed.

"It is not the position of a Novice to question his Dream Master, but I believe this approach is unwise. The Protocols for recruitment clearly state non-interference, else we risk becoming Anchored here ourselves."

Ignoring the pleas of his acolyte, Brother Ignatius placed himself next to the SS Guard, and immediately roared into his ear,

"Likkel bwoy come test I? Boom! Armalite a let off!"

The scene around us became reanimated once more. The SS guard had just enough time to realise that an Armalite assault rifle was planted squarely and firmly against his armoured vest, before the 'mad black bastard' proceeded to let off the entire contents of the magazine, sending him hurtling backwards into the crowd.

Quickly vaulting over the desk, Brother Joseph wrestled the now suitably shocked Samantha to the ground. She lay there, paralysed with fear, as people scattered in every direction, away from the gunfire and his Dream Master's crazed laughter.

Armed guards swarmed all over the building like cockroaches. Brother Joseph was trying to reassure Samantha over the rattle of gunfire, when Sid leapt back behind our check-in desk.

He raised his eyebrows to the confusion,

"Do we 'ave 'er yet?" he hollers, lobbing grenades in high arcs at a the escalators, and another group of guards closing in to our right.

"Not quite, her Awen's waning! We need an Anchor!"

"Coming right up!"

Something the recruit could take back to the Awake in full consciousness, and in a lull between volleys of gunfire, Brother Joseph bent down over Samantha and sang along with the reggae song now booming through the Terminal's tannoy system,

"One looove, one heart, one destination…" were her last words before she passed out.

She was Anchored.

The rapid fire of two Uzi resumed blasting from our check-in desk, followed by more screams and breaking glass.

Sid vaulted away again, and Brother Joseph comforted me with the knowledge that Samantha could be picked up at a later date by someone in the Order.

An instant later, I was distracted and filled with dread.

Sid was crawling towards me from underneath the check-in desks, dragging a monstrously large metal chest on a chain.

He smiles, passing me one of his Uzis, and with the calculated grace of the truly insane, slowly opened the lid of the box,

"Wanna 'ave some fun, likkel Joe?"

Reading the worry etched all over my face, he laughs.

"Trust me," he says, "We haven't the energy to shift anywhere right now."

I nodded, "I still appear to be drawing my awareness from the one-legged man on Locale 32."

"So let's have some fun, enjoy yourself!"

"I am practically out of Awen."

"Continue to use his. Unless you want to try and shift Between the Worlds," he adds, "Wait it out till morning, but I seriously doubt we can even do that…"

I shuddered at the prospect of the Inbetween again. It was too close to the Shadow Realm, and Brother Joseph nodded assent; best stay with his Dream Master, even if he was clearly out of control.

"Hey, look, I made us a little present. This'll cheer you up."

Peering first into the box, and then slowly turning to look at Sid's proud smile, I was far from cheerful.

"Bazookas! You used the last of our fucking Awen on bazookas?"

"No, I used the last of yours," he grins.

A volley of bullets ploughed into the check-in desk, and my mind began racing. This was Locale 22, a barbaric world ruled by a ruthless corporate elite, and with the exception of one or two twists, it conformed to the basic laws of consensus reality in the Awake–

"These bullets are fucking real!"

"Oi, don't get narky," grumbles Sid, pouting his lips, "Mission accomplished and time for a likkel fun, right?" He pitched another deranged grin from behind the box, and strangely comforted by his now confirmed madness, Brother Joseph started to warm to the idea,

"Where's the fucking magazine for this thing?"

Sid passes me a handful of cartridges, but craning my neck above the desk, I could see we were clearly fucked. All around us, to the left and to the right, up along the balcony and all over the escalators, dark-clad uniformed figures prepared for action with trained precision.

"Woy! likkel Joe! Dere's a tousand Babylon a coming fe I an' I!" he cried gleefully.

"And 'me and me' too, you fucking mad cunt," I mutters.

"Good! Draw on de power of de one-legged-man!"

"I'm fucking trying mate… oh no… here it comes!"

A hail of canisters bounced rhythmically off the desk, spewing grey toxic fumes. Nausea gripped my insides, accompanied by searing pain shooting from my nasal passages and into my lungs.

"Cunt! There's too many of them!" I rasps, as the first spasms of retching began. Sid was searching frantically in his metal box,

"Go out dere and tell 'em we're really sorry," he suggests, trying to giggle and gasp at the same time. "I 'ave gas masks… somewhere. What time're ya due back in De Awake?"

I stole a nervous glance at my watch, which told the 'real time' back in Locale 1. Half four in the morning.

"Oh no, no, we've got hours of this!"

It was too horrible for words. Brother Joseph's alarm was set for nine. He always set his alarm late for a recruitment, with the intention of giving his body a good night's rest.

"Aha!" Sid triumphs, thrusting a Mickey Mouse mask into my arms. I quickly slipped it over my head, inhaling the purified air.

"Mine doesn't have any ears," I couldn't help but notice, as Sid donned his Dumbo the Elephant mask. "Have you completely run out of Awen too?"

"Nah, dat's because evil Babylon 'ave de copyright," he explains helpfully, "But don't worry, it'll work all de same."

"But your Dumbo mask has ears," I mumbles.

Shrugs, "An' who says it's Dumbo? Prove it! Could be any elephant, dis… could be Dimbo De Elephant."

It was a hideous sight anyway.

Sat on its haunches, a gigantic Dimbo the Elephant in leopard skins primed rocket launchers for action, and Earless Mickey wept with confusion, loading weapons, fighting back the rising bile of panic.

Brother Joseph and I briefly considered inducing an awakening in Locale 1 on our own. But he was so low on Awen he was running the risk of having my awareness fixated in this Locale, permanently, or at least until someone pulled us out.

We still needed the presence of a Dream Master for that kind of manoeuvre, and ours wasn't going anywhere yet.

Hopelessly resigned, I finished loading all the weapons we had, and stared into Sid's eyes through his mask.

Dimbo's head bobbed rhythmically up and down, his demented grin seemingly understanding the predicament we were in. We stood a chance if we could just hold out till morning.

Peering over the check-in desk, Sid raised three fingers.

On the count of three we leapt up as one, and laid down a field of fire across the escalators and the balcony above – dark shapes fell through the tear gas.

Temporarily infected equally with the one-legged-man and Sid's mania, Brother Joseph lobbed handfuls of grenades wildly into the air, Sid switched his Uzis for an old WWII Bren gun, and for a good while it appeared Dimbo and Earless Mickey might just hold out – until the return fire rained down on us from everywhere at once.

We were vastly out numbered. Our check-in desk barricade rapidly disintegrated into a carcass of splintered wood. We dived for cover behind Sid's massive metal box and pulled it up against the wall; Sid and I screaming with laughter, Brother Joseph just screaming, and all the while the murderous rattle of gunfire.

Then it stopped.

"Likkel Joe, gotta go! See ya on de other side!" Sid, shaking my shoulder. At that precise moment, I was down on all fours, half-deaf, hurt, fumbling desperately for more grenades, then I found myself staring into the darkness, sick with disbelief.

He's shifting out!

Trying his best to suppress his laughter and evident delight, Sid gave me no time for argument. He kicked the metal box away from us, and hurled himself onto the remains of the check-in desk.

"Rasta Unity levels all scores, fe true!" he hollered, and stretching himself to his full height, he hoisted both rocket launchers onto his powerful shoulders.

Beneath a rain of lead, I scrambled back under the box, just seconds before the building's central support columns exploded into blinding white heat, bringing down the entire floor above crumbling to dust.

A few moments later, I dug myself out of the rubble, and staggering onto my feet, scanned the devastation through a veil of smoke and fire.

Sid was gone, as was most of the Terminal. Someone somewhere was laughing, raucously – at me? It seemed. Voices on loud hailers were making indecipherable demands. I hobbled forwards and immediately took another bullet.

As Locale 22 spun into oblivion, my body falling to the ground, my mind had a brief moment to pause,

'Where are you gonna end up now, who are you going to be?'

Then, through the roaring din in my ears I heard the laughter again, and finally realised, it was her…

Chapter 14

Supper with Sid

"Cunnnnt!"

   "Mr Barbelo—"

"Dimbo set me up! Just fucking left me there!"

"Everything's okay, I'll put the light on."

"No! Leave it off… oh Gawd… stop laughing!"

"You're very funny!"

"Nah, it's not funny, Brid… Dresden, I was captured."

"Is that what you were just dreaming?"

"I dunno… yes, no, it was like I was somebody else. There was this giant leopard-man shooting Nazi cockroaches with his wanger, and—"

"Is that nice?"

"Hmmm, yeah, but… again?"

Sanity is a complicated subject, I know. There's been situations where I must've lost it and found it a hundred times a day, and in almost as many years.

Most of the times you don't even know you've lost it, it's the world's quickest vanishing act, you don't have a monkey's unless something happens what shouldn't – like some cunt isn't dead what should be, in my case, or you've sodomised your Alsatian and thrown your wife off the balcony – point is, everybody loses it to varying degrees of horrific circumstance, pertinent to their natures.

Insanity, therefore, is nothing less than the part of you squeezed out, trying to get back in to join the rest of you – back *in sanity*, complete, sane in other words, catch-madrift?

Follow your nature, let it in. If it wasn't meant to be a part of you in the first place, you wouldn't be you.

Easy logic.

My nature for the next two days was poling Brid cross-eyed. And the more I did, the more I got affected by her weirdo stories. Affected? Nah, infected, more like. I felt I was living them; I was in her world of reincarnation, astral realms and Inner Orders, right in there. But, as always, all good things come to end and in our case it was around three in the morning, when Sid finally came home from one of his random gambling spells. Casinos mostly, West End, classy joints was always his nature, and horses – then again who knows what he got up to, but still, we had more than enough cash floating about to accommodate.

Wankered on brandy, he staggers in on Brid in the kitchen, bottle under one arm, AK 47 wrapped in a bin liner under the other. For the arsenal, in case you're asking.

Cause for concern?

Ordinarily no, except what Sid can't accommodate is nutters, never could, never will. Irony is, the cunt's worth a hundred Brids on the nutter-scale when he gets going – but that's not the kind of nutter I mean, not the run of the mill kind, I mean the 'other kind,' what Sid calls 'clinical.'

I'd got there a split second too late; he was onto her before I could explain why there was a naked fit-bird stewing bacon and cabbage in our kitchen.

"Who's the fuck are yous?!"

"Who the fuck are you?"

Pause.

"Sid."

"Brid."

"Why're yous in my house?"

"Dream Warrior, fighting *T, H, E, M.*"

"T, H, who?"

"The Hierarchy Enslaving Me: *them.* And who are *they?* The Hierarchy Enslaving You. The Illuminati! Who else?"

That's the exact moment I hopped in, the moment Brid yells 'Illuminati!' and Sid knows something's loose in the house what shouldn't be.

Even without her weirdo chatter, he knows. It was in her eyes – The Screaming Abdabs! Passes almost as quick as it comes on, but now she's singing some Darkie song at him – it was familiar somehow – and Sid's backing away against the sink, and I know what he's gonna do, 'cos if I'd had an AK under my arm in The Albert ...

Lock and load – ask questions after.

Only difference was, Sid did have an AK under his arm, what's now primed and hoisted menacingly on his shoulder. I was bollock-naked, hopping through the doorway, strapping on my wooden peg.

"Sid! Fuck, no!"

"Gonna only ask one more time. What're ya doing in my house?"

"Ooone love," she croons on, "One heart, one destination…" pause, quick smile, "Cooking in the Realm of Shadows."

Sid's top lip curls.

Brid steps up, casual-quick, and sticks her finger in the barrel.

"Squeeze the trigger, big boy, and ka-boom! Blow the barrel apart and your face with it."

Nah, it wouldn't, that's a civvy urban myth, seen it done before, we both had, very, very messy, but that's not the point – point was the bottle involved, and it was so classily done, completely under Sid's radar. Fuck me sideways, I know I was in lust, but at that precise moment I'd of given her my good peg if she'd asked for it, just to see the eyes popping out on Sid's ugly mug again.

He squints at me, "Is this yours?"

I nods, buckling up my peg.

"Where did you get her?"

"Stole her from some Yardies."

"Saved me from the Illuminati," Brid corrects.

Sid smiles, and breaks into a full belly laugh – what sounds like the Jolly Green Giant eating a bowl of gravel – and lowers his rifle, very, very gently.

Took half a pound of butter to pop Brid's thumb back out, and well, we were all the best of mates after that. Cut your teeth on the end of an AK like that, who wouldn't want to be your mate?

Sitting around the kitchen table, eating her gorgeous stew,

"Sid, where did you get the Kalashnikov?"

"Won it," says he, in-between mouthfuls.

"Oh? Where?"

"West End."

"Off who?"

"Ishmael."

"Nice name," says Brid. "I knew an Ishmael once. Friend of Jesus, well, he was one of his lovers actually."

"Oh really, my dear?"

Twirls her hair, all coy, "Actually, we were both his lovers, although back then we didn't have sexuality as you have it today—"

"Wait a minute," I turns to Sid, "Off who?"

"Said won it off Ishmael. Says he can get us all we like," munches into his bowl, "Everything we want for the arsenal."

"What arsenal?"

"Sorry my love," giving her hand a warm squeeze, "What the fuck were you doing with those mad cunts?"

"Poker. Winning mostly, then got drunk with his nephew down Stringfellows, wots-his-name. Found myself in Bradford anyway. Ishmael, what a laugh, didn't know I was still in the pink! Bit of a shock to see me."

"Bit of a shock for Jesus too, when—"

"Sorry dear – Out of bounds! Do you hear me, Sid? Out of fucking bounds."

"So now you're Mother fucking Theresa, that's all I need."

"I don't want you going up there again."

"Up yours!"

"You know what happened last time!"

"Forty years ago, that was. Nobody remembers False Flags."

"We remember, they remember."

"What False Flags are you talking about?"

"Military term," says I, "It's when you're ordered to attack, say, your own troops, and then blame it on someone else."

"For an excuse to then attack that someone else," mutters Sid, munch, munch, "That's one way to start a war. Pukka stew, this."

"Another way is to rope in the assistance of an ally. Israel versus the SS Liberty, that's a good example. Blamed that on the Gypos."

"Didn't work though," munch, munch, "Israelis got caught. Better still is to allow the enemy to attack you: The Japs versus Pearl Harbour. That's a False Flag."

"Or even better," I adds, "just make it up! The Gulf of Tonkin incident, now *that's* a False Flag."

Shakes his head, "Doesn't count. Got the Yanks their Vietnam war but they stole the idea off Hitler – his fake Gleiwitz invasion. Operation Northwoods is far superior."

"What on Gawd's Earth are you on? The Yanks nicked that off Hitler too! He's not well," I whispers to Brid. "What's your point?"

"Point is, got to admit it's by far superior in principle. Terror attacks on your own citizens, works without fail."

"That's not *a point,* Sid, that's just reiterating what we're already bloody-well discussing—"

Brid gently interrupts, "So where were you two?"

"Did a stint everywhere, didn't we Sid? Palestine, Lebanon—"

Slams his fork down, "Drop it Joe! Alright?"

"Alright, alright," I says, "Lovely stew, this, ay?" Sid rarely calls me Joe lest he's seriously pissed off or seriously guilty about something. He wasn't sulking, so it's the former.

"Do you prefer being called Joe, or Mr Barbelo?"

"Sid, just be careful, that's all I was saying. Ragheads say they forget, but they don't. They're like us."

"Deserved it. Said it was all forgiven anyway, we'd paid our dues."

"Who deserved what—?"

"Nothing dear, you were saying?"

"Hmmm, that I like both but I think I prefer Joe, like Jumping Joe," she giggles, "Now he really was a very funny man."

"Who?" Sid and I says at once.

"Jumping Joe. Caught a packet the first day after Christmas, back in the Great War? Remember? Nice guy and very nice looking. I missed his jokes in the trenches, we all did… what's wrong?"

The way Sid gripped his bread knife, I thought he was going to cut her throat on the spot.

"Jumping Joe was a clown," I explains, "He was a clown, and—"

"A Comedy Technician," corrects Sid.

"Yes, I know," she says, "What's wrong?"

"Well… nothing dear…" I chance a glance at Sid, pale as a sheet, "It's just that he'd come a cropper alright, exactly as you says."

Sid nods. "He was my brother."

"Oh then you must be Little Sidney! Talked a lot about you, all the time!"

She leans over the table, grabs his hand, grinning like they'd known each other forever. Sid drops his knife, I snatch it discreetly.

She goes on, "It's okay Sidney, he loves you, loves you all so much; Auntie Marge, Helen, they're all on the Otherside now, all happy." And then she smiles at him, so fucking sweetly he's turned on the waterworks.

That was the moment it got truly surreal, like when your girlfriend suddenly declares she's off to fight in the Spanish Civil War, and does – well it happened to me – but fit-birds personally knowing very dead First World War geezers doesn't happen. Or leastways it's not meant to, specially not to Sid.

She's moved round the table now, sitting next to him, cradling him in her arms like a giant baby. It was horrible, almost gave him his knife back.

Better leave them to it, I thought, picking up the AK by the door; not my business, at least they're getting on.

But truth was, that part of me what had always believed her, the part in the dark with the lead pipe in my hands? Well, that part was now moving in the door to the bigger part. The part talking now. I was sane, and now that I was going in, I was going insane.

We all were, all three of us at that moment – suddenly insanely complicated to fuck.

Left it a couple of hours, thoroughly cleaning Sid's AK in the operation's room, musing about the advantages religious fruitcakes have for building up large arsenals, and finally thought fuck it; what was all that about anyway?

I had to go back.

Nah, I wasn't jealous, don't get me wrong, but I had to go back; you would've done the same.

I crept up the stairs, and paused at the kitchen door. I was gonna knock, private conversation and all that, and I know I should have, but I listened at the door instead.

Odd though, all trace of her Irish-ness had vanished, and never, never, never heard Sid talk like that in all my days…

"Immortal," he was saying, "We're all immortal, then."

"Our continued existence on the Otherside is assured."

"By God?"

"Guaranteed by the One," Brid affirms. "The Otherside was never anything to be feared. What are you worried about?"

Uncomfortable sigh, "The Devil, Hell… I've done some terrible things, Brid… and I might do so again…"

"Spare the rod, spoil the child," she says.

"What do you mean?"

"Hell, demons and the soul being consumed in the Shadow Realm, the soul cannot be destroyed."

"But it can become trapped, in what do you call it?"

"Lower Astral realms."

"Right. So you're saying it's like being trapped in a frequency, like a radio tuned into a radio station."

"Or a television, yes, but here and elsewhere, freewill is freewill."

"I dunno, but you say we can't be influenced against our will."

"We can be attacked and herded into this Realm; anywhere we choose to let ourselves be caught. And the soul *can* be consumed in lower vibrational concerns, fear, greed, misery and pain and so on. Through ignorance, yes, and yet it cannot be destroyed…"

Long pause, sound of kettle boiling.

"Many people misunderstood this issue of Lower Astral entities and the 'consuming of the soul' – they were supposed to. The idea stems from teachings specific to training purposes in Mystery Schools; Inner Orders such as ours use many subterfuges to keep Initiates focused away from materialism and destructive behaviour."

"Like fear of the Devil and Hell and so on."

"And which later became dogma to the uninitiated, whether through misinterpretation or conscious intent, by those wishing to maintain power by the rule of fear. Or both."

Pause. Quick sigh, "Okay Sidney, okay, you're right. Many traditions maintain the literal reality of these beings, and they *are* real in one sense."

"And hellish realms… where a hapless soul might come a cropper?"

"Yes, but that's just an allegory for the self-judgment, or self-examination of our temporal deeds, which happens on the Otherside anyway."

"The Otherside, you're serious, you've been there, you've been… dead."

"Being dead is not much different to being alive, my love. The human body – including our thoughts, emotions, unconscious intentions – generates a frequency field, a force the ancients called 'Awen' and recognised as being present in all things."

"And Awen is indestructible, alright, so you keep saying. So depending on how we've behaved in this life, we could create a hell in the next."

"Everyone answers for their own sins, you judge yourself…"

Pause. Heavy sigh.

"I'm doomed then!"

"Completely!"

Laughter.

"No, you're not Sidney, no. Depends. The Otherside is a higher vibrational Realm, far more flexible; there you manifest your intent very easily, your thoughts, feelings become your world – literally. Yes, it can be hell, or paradise, depending. Like attracts like. Birds of a feather flock together. Harmonic resonance…"

Pause.

"…You're an engineer, so… yes, maybe think of the Otherside as a movie broadcast, a super-real movie and your soul, your awareness is a vibrational field within it. You will tend to vibrate with similar frequencies, countless other souls, and together co-create what you will. Hell? Heaven? Freewill is freewill—"

"I understood that part, it's basically how TVs work: frequencies, so we're talking about a difference in wave characteristic."

"Basically. The Otherside vibrates at a different speed."

"Right, but why would people on the Otherside want to mess things up for us, here, in this life? I don't understand that part."

"Okay, there are souls who seek to inspire people, in this Realm, toward materialism or religious dogma, to reject spiritual growth, but only because they don't know better."

"Ignorance."

"That's their vibrational field."

"Then it makes sense to be careful."

"Well, yes, especially if you're involved with practices which might be quite difficult at first; renouncing material wealth, dealing with fear and greed and so on, and which at the same time open you up to other realms of existence. Nuish Bash'swan hates losing its host."

"Nuish Bash'swan?"

"That's the entity's Aramaic name. The literal translation is the Double Mind, it's a Lower Astral being, an immensely powerful parasitical entity which has infected humanity's consciousness."

"Another subterfuge, then."

"Hmmm, it can be used as such, yes, as a device to spur the Initiate on, to question your reality, to question who you are, where you are."

"So it's not real."

"Yes and no, depends on how much Awen you give it. That voice living in your head, your internal speech, you think it's you."

"My thoughts, yes."

"But is it you? What proof do you actually have of *what* it is?"

Pause. Slurping tea.

"Good point, I speak to myself in my head all the time."

"We all do."

"Never really asked myself with what, though."

"Asking with *what* is the first stage to finding out *who* you are."

"So it's some kind of… it's alive?"

"Oh yes! It's a parasite; a mirror of yourself, but it is not your *self*. The Double Mind is the source of all division and conflict – 'them and us, up and down, black, white' – and it expresses itself as duality because we are its retainer, its means of expression."

"So this entity."

"Nuish Bash'swan."

"It's not actually real, physically."

"For now, let's just say these beings are real enough, as experienced within specific vibrational densities. Don't worry, you'll be just fine, sometimes we all need a big stick to keep us on the path."

"Spare the rod, spoil the child."

"Yes…" Short pause. Scraping chair along the floorboards.

"… Mr Barbelo, is that you?"

Heard the door open, I was halfway down the stairs.

Didn't know how to handle that, truthfully, seriously lost my perspective. Thank Gawd it didn't last. I went out for a little stroll around the park, and by the time I got back home, I'd thought up a dozen rational explanations for how she could have known about Jumping Joe and all that.

Sid, however, was completely sold on her.

Chapter 15

Happy Stick And I

"Bit late for a stroll in the park, isn't it?"

"It is, young man, or early, depending on how you looks at it."

"Bit nippy an' all."

"Yep, but spring will be with us soon, a new start, lovely skies. Do you have a light please?"

"Said, it's a bit *nippy*…"

Scuffle, scuffle.

"Oh, oh, please! You're hurting me——!"

"Fucking shut it!"

"Please, I'm not a well man."

"Shut it! Give us all yer money, NOW!"

"Oh please, oh, oh, put the knife away!"

"Shit!"

Shuffle, scuffle.

"Let me go."

"Bit late, is it?"

"Oh no, don't, don't."

"Say hello to Happy Stick!"

"Aaaah!"

"Sorry, did I nip you?"

"Aaaaaaaaaaaaaaaaaaaah!"

"Oopsy-daisy, did it again, must be 'cos it's a bit *nippy*, ay?"

"No, please," whine, whimper, "Please, I won't, I won't——"

"I know you won't."

Chapter 16

Trapped in Infinity

Do old cunts get jealous? 'Course we fucking do! Nothing much changes inside just 'cos of age, unless you make it change, unless you want it to. That's the key fact young'uns never grasp, leastways not early enough to do any good. Nothing changes except your face in the mirror, as it's meant to, before everything rots into the ground and you're pushing up daises. No? Tell me about it when you get there, see if I'm wrong.

I'd come home feeling pretty chirpy after my lovely stroll, and was still in the basement – on the firing range testing Sid's AK – when he comes down. I smiles, take off my earmuffs,
    "What did you say?"
    "Said good morning Joe," he sulks.
    He's poled her. Cuuunt!
    "Get a good kip?" I says.
    He shrugs, and then it gets worse – she appears from behind the stairwell wearing his shirt.
    They stare at me.
    "Oh fucking hell! What's she doing down here?"
    "Sidney told me everything," striding up, bold as you like, "You are a genius, Joe, a genius!"
    "Oh for the love of Christ – get her out of here!"
    Sid shrugs.
    "Don't be angry," she says, "I can help. I want to help, it will help me too." Stalking around the stacked steel cases, "How many guns? Is this it?"
    Sid declares, proud as you like,
    "Nine AKs, seven M-16's, seven Glocks, twenty-six Makarovs, 4,500 rounds, hollowpoint, another case of grenades due in Friday, what makes eighty total, then RPG's we've only two…"
    "Three," I correct, force of habit. "That's enough Sid."
    "Three, surface-to-air we're still working on, but—"

"That's ENOUGH!"

My AK trained itself on Sid's head, the trigger squeezed by itself—*Click!*

It all happened by itself. I'd never trained a weapon on Sid, never.

Spying the empty cartridge on the desk beside us, all vim drains from his eyes, his shoulders sag, walking back up the stairs.

I sits down heavily at the command desk. She sits too.

"I can help, it's a good plan. Let me help."

"Where you been?"

"Oh, my knight, don't be angry."

I peeled her arm off my shoulder. "I meant how many times you been down here?"

"I haven't, the door was always locked."

"What exactly did he tell you?" I says, gripping her arm tight.

"Well now," she goes on, all happily, "Sidney said that this is not to be the only operation's room, oh, by the way, we've started calling them command centres, better term, don't you think?"

"Don't give a monkey's."

"Anyway, he said there will be hundreds like this in London alone. That on a Friday the Thirteenth, you are going to storm Parliament and 'go out in a blaze of glory!' Brilliant. What else…" She gazes down at her hands, and then shoots me a smile. "Oh yes, that Operation is strictly an over 70's affair, non-affiliated to any political agenda, well, that's not what he said, just how I understood it. Total freedom, he said. That's what you and he had always dreamed of, freedom, before you lost your touch, before the Craft was retired." She stalled, gauging my reaction; I'd already garrotted the slut a hundred times in my mind.

"Well anyway, he went on, and on, but finally he said that 'Barbelo's Blood would grow all up for it, getting well-out of hand!'"

"Told you everything, then," I sighed to myself, "Fuck it Sid, dip your end away and sing away, why fucking not?"

She shakes her head. "No, he didn't."

"Oh?"

"Told me everything except the Dream."

"Oh."

I let go of her arm, and she peers at me, her eyes peeling my head open like a can of sardines.

"I'm sorry," I says, "I wanted to show you all this myself, I got the touch when we first met; I knew you would understand, somehow, I dunno why I says that, but I just know. So fucking tired, Brid... nightmares... and they're different since I met you."

"I know, but how different?"

"I dunno, *different.* Can't remember them much, but they're not like the ones I used to have. It was all like wading through mud before, thick, thick mud and blood, and then I'd job's a good'un someone – usually my mates – but these new ones arc... it's like I'm somebody else, don't ask. Christ, I dunno..."

Shrugs, "Maybe you're checking in with another one of you."

"What do you mean?"

She gave my hand a gentle squeeze, "Happens all the time, don't worry about it. But the Dream was not a nightmare, was it?"

"No, the Dream was the loveliest dream I've ever had..."

"Relax then, relax my love. Come." She sidles up, sits on my lap, resting my head on her shoulder. "Tell me."

"This world belong to the young, Brid. But we can see what's coming, we've been around. We all returned from the Wars thinking that was it, no more. Millions of us with all the high hopes for a free world, a world of equality, justice, honour and all those other words we hardly even use anymore, and then the real fight started, at home, specially after the last War – had to fight tooth and nail to get even the promise of social welfare."

"Welfare, to fare well," she affirms, "You need to be free to create the social and spiritual conditions in order to live satisfactorily."

"Gawd-given right! Your freedom, freedom to create your world as you want. It's natural law."

She winks. "Do what thou will, harm none. That's natural law."

"Dunno about that, more like 'do what thou will, get out of my bloody way,' I'd say," I chuckles to myself, "But our freedom on any level's the last thing the govermentals want. I woke up from twenty years of sleepwalking nightmare straight into another nightmare – nothing's changed! Same old same old."

"Granted, something needs to be done. Tell me about your good dream then, what did you see?"

"Oh I dunno... you'll think it's stupid."

"I will not," she croons. "Tell me. When did it start?"

"There's three dreams, one after the other. The first on that night, the night I first saw you in the pub. Sid and I and Sally, we were all in that one, all my auld acquaintances from the Wars. And my dear, we've fought in all major conflicts, just about everywhere you can think of till '69, and we've seen every hope of a free world sold down the fucking Swaney! Bloody hypocrites.

Commies, anarchists, socialists – marched behind a hundred flags and in as many countries, not worth wiping your arse with, your shit's worth a hundred flags. A million Firms, one govermental Top Firm at the top. Wars, revolutions, it's all like Disneyland, spinning us a fucking Disneyland Delusion – the goodies and the baddies, the red flags against blue flags, blue flags against black – just one fuck-off giant pyramid of blood, paid for by the same purse."

"Pyramids," she perks up, "30,000 years ago, when the gods still walked the earth, I was given a vision of Nuish Bash'swan. It was an eye, at first, set within a giant pyramid. The Inner Order—"

"Come again? Nishbash what?"

"The Double Mind," she whispers, her eyes a pair of blue light bulbs floating in a saucer of milk, "A disincarnate being, fleeing from the lower realms. For aeons it drifted across cold depths of space, searching for a species to provide it with a home. The birth of human consciousness was a beacon, shining bright across eternity, and so, from the immensity of the darkness out there, it sensed our light – and struck!" taps her head, "*Infected.*"

"Blimey, I don't know about all that!" I says, nervously, I will admit, "But… what do you mean?"

Shrugs, "Nuish Bash'swan, it's like, like the king of the feharchrove – it *controls* them – they are its slaves."

"Kings, ay? In the olden days he'd be swinging from the highest lamppost in the land! Sooner or later. Seriously, it's about time we realised again we don't need the cunts."

"We used to build giant wooden effigies of Nuish Bash'swan, and fill them with straw dolls. That's what *feharchrove* means in the Old Language, 'the straw people,' and then we'd set light to them and dance around, and around the ritual fire, around and—"

"Interesting," I cuts in forcefully, "but communities is what matters now, I reckons."

"True, true," she nods, settling back down again, "Very true."

"And I'd never seen anything like what I saw in these dreams, not just the hope, the commitment – that couldn't be betrayed, do you understand? It doesn't have a name, it doesn't have a flag, can't be bought or sold at any price. Commitment.

We were an army, thousands, millions strong, and not one of us was under the age of seventy. Old and fucked, but up for it – scared me shitless, and that's not easy, seriously. It was the anger, pure venomous hatred but without purpose, at first; the cunts in this dream didn't give a fuck. At our age, you know you're a good'un already. That's what can turn inwards, make you asleep, make you give up, or it can push you outwards to the world, wake you up and fire you up! Catch-madrift?"

"I understand."

"And that's what these old cunts were doing, waking up and tooling up to high heaven, ready to hit Parliament and take over. They had the commitment, and now they had the purpose too, see?"

"I see."

"Special Forces nowadays are good, not saying they're not, but these old cunts were the originators, they were there at the beginning, they *were* the beginning – just one of these with purpose was worth twenty of them nowadays, well, leastways that was the first dream. Truth was about that, we didn't even know how many we was, or even what we was, in the proper sense.

Oh we were all there alright, well up for it, saw it clear as day in the second dream. The Operation had grown and spread, not just in England, but to Ireland, France, Spain, all over the gaff. I could see us all from this huge flying boat I was on, beautiful it was, a flying galleon, sailing over the world.

I had x-ray eyes, I could spy into houses, basements, full of old cunts like us, planning, tooling up, organising. And I could see it was well-out of our hands by then. It was an operation with no name, following no leaders, no flags, just old cunts and easy logic; knowing what had to be done, and how to do it.

The last dream was all about the last day, the thirteenth, midnight – hit the parliaments, govermental buildings worldwide, and take over. And that's all I remember from that one, sure there's more to it, but I didn't even know which thirteenth of what month, or how it would all get so big. But the very last bit was…"

"Go one my love."

"The very last bit was just a glimpse, more of a feeling than anything. But I saw a dawn, a sunrise over a world I can't... describe, but it was fucking beautiful, this world, a clean world, with great forests, trees as far as the eye can see – but there were no countries, no borders, no religions or hunger. Didn't even know how it would happen neither, only that it could, if it could grow... with commitment, with purpose... sad, so sad."

"What's sad, my champion?"

"I saw our second chance for justice, for a world at peace, and yet I can't describe it – isn't that fucking sad or what?"

Don't know what she does with those eyes, but the waterworks started and couldn't stop. She wiped at my tears. I let her. Truth was, I wanted to top myself. Sounds fucked, I know – never had the courage to take 'the coward's way out' – but if she wasn't there, Sid would've come home to Barbelo Brain Stew. I shit you not.

"Dreams are seeds," she was saying, stalking around the ammo cases in the far corner, "We never know what they could grow into. Don't worry if you can't describe it, the point is to make a start."

I glance up from my desk, "I suppose it all started with you, and yeah... a conversation I once had, Count of Monte Cristo, it was..."

"Good book."

"Got me thinking about purpose. Fair dues, he wipes all the cunts out, but all that treasure he nicked from the island, all that good he could've done after and didn't. Or does he? Maybe he does. That's why we're not told, see? Mediocrity—"

"Mr Barbelo, I too see what is coming, as do all in my Inner Order. Slavery and war. War without end."

"No doubt," I sighs.

"So what would be the first thing you'd do in your dream world?"

"First thing?"

"As a government."

"That's easy. Cease to exist."

She nods. "Sid mentioned a constitution, giving power back to the Nation."

"And a bill of human rights."

"Based on the *Magna Carta*?"

"Based on the law of the land, our unalienable rights," I says, getting vexed, "And yeah, every constitution we've looked at offers a get-out clause, a pledge that first and foremost is your liberty. Democracy, the rule of the 'majority?' Bollocks! The majority vote *against* a government—"

"They vote for someone else," she cuts in, "if they bother to vote at all. It's precisely the government the majority didn't want which is voted in. I understand that," she smiles. "Yes, it's a con-trick."

"Right, the puppet with the blue tie, or the puppet with the red, take your pick. Fucking insult to humanity. Communities, Brid, fuck centralised government. People form small regional authorities, if needed, and they look after their own patch. You need resources to fix a road, you don't have to beg for it off some snot-nose toff sipping champagne five hundred miles away."

"May I see this constitution?"

"I'll give you a butcher's later – it's simple and gives everybody a chance."

"How?"

"That's easy too, worked this out with our accountant. Simply put, coin interest free money, and you wipe out national debt. Imagine that, you wake up one morning, you don't owe a penny any more and your money's worth ten times what it was. Gets rid of surplus too, so we wouldn't need to work fuck-all 'cos we're no longer forced to produce ten times what we need. Then, dismantle the social security system, and all the resources wasted on the chain of command goes to the people what need it. When you come of age, you get a basic wage income, for life; any money from work goes on top of that, but everybody gets enough to have their own gaff, food and all the rest."

"How?"

"Easy, banish all private banks from the land."

"How?"

"Fucking hell, Brid, what's up with all this 'how' business – how do you fucking think?"

"Boom!" she chuckles, stroking a case of grenades.

"Yes, boom fucking boom till we get them all! Listen, and come over here, ay, your making me nervous. Listen, the key to all of it is economic freedom. So, first, the militias, us, wipe out every last one of the cunts to the very last cunt."

"Okay," she says, "But why? Money's only a symbol."

"Well it's hardy rocket science, my dear. Money's a symbol, true, and what's that? A symbol is only as good or bad as the thing it represents. As long as we let private banks coin our money at interest, money represents an ever-increasing spiral of national debt. Do the maths. *Our* money's created out of thin air and *loaned* back at us, at interest. So where's the money to cover the interest on the fucking loan? Eventually they'll own everything."

"Okay…"

"Interest creates debt, debt creates enslavement – doesn't matter how you dress it up. So we'll immediately start coining *interest free* money, returning it to a symbolic tool at our *service*, rather than a source of profit for those creating the interest and consequent debt.

How? Because every private banker's been skinned alive, strung up by the bollocks off Blackfriars Bridge."

"I know, run them down with ice-creams vans!"

"Ay?"

"On telly," she shrugs, "Let them loose in a big field, and just when they think they're getting away, out comes a deadly fleet of Mr Softies!" she laughs, "Can you think of anything more… embarrassing?"

My good Gawd, and I thought I wasn't well…

Sighs, peering at the Bren Gun on the wall behind me, "In a world run by money, you can't be free without economic freedom…"

"That's what I'm saying, money will be interest free and controlled by the Nation, us, the people. Not by private banking elites. Fucking hell, Brid, people can't pay off debt using IOUs. What're you paying with, more debt? Nah, they pay with their labour, their homes, their businesses – real wealth in the form of foreclosures."

"But, can we coin interest free money?"

"That's the onion, there's no reason why not. It's only these parasites poncing off us what do. But get rid of them, our wealth stays at home, in Britain. That's the first target, a resource-based economy without parasites."

"A good start," she says, stopping to stand in front of our desk. "But you'd need to hit fast, not just take over Parliament, that's only another symbol; you need to inform people, take control of communications – specifically the television networks."

"We know."

"And how will this be accomplished with only two of you."

"There's plenty out there what are up for it."

"Oh for sure there is!"

"Ultimately, this is about justice—"

"No, justice is a blind bitch! Her sword is reckless and indiscriminate; she never gives us we want, or even what we need. But…" Leans over the desk, looks me in the eye, "Let me in," she whispers, "and perhaps, we might just get what we deserve…"

Keep friends close, and enemies closer, so the saying goes. Or in my case, keep enemies close, gutted on sharp pointy stick – but fuck it, what do you do with a fit-bird who likes eyeing up guns?

Shuffle the pack.

"Need to know your age, "I says, "to know your rank."

"Only a matter of time!" she delights.

"You're in the Firm, *not* the Operation. Can't lower the age group, Brid, gotta stick to what I saw in the Dream. You know that."

"I know," she says, going all serious, sitting down opposite me. "I understand dreams. There are forces, here, all around us which guide, uplift and influence, and also forces of a lower nature. Both we must respect, to fully understand. If you're going to defeat the government, then you must know your enemy, at least as well as they themselves. But the real enemy isn't 'out there,' but *within*," she taps her head. "The first battlefield is always within—"

"Chicken and egg, Brid, outside or inside makes no difference in our case. We take them out, and it's job done."

"No, it makes all the difference in the world to a permanent victory. Take the root words *govern*, 'to control' and *mente*, 'the mind,' and put the two together, only then do you uncover their true objective: 'mindcontroller.' This is a religious matter, as you say, and there are forces beyond our ordinary sense and comprehension—"

"Religion, let me tell you about religion—"

She holds up her hand. "Please, Mr Barbelo, my turn now, no interruptions."

"Very well then, what?"

"Silence…"

The Lemon Tree

"In the beginning there was no beginning, only silence.

In the silence, the sound of all things in harmony.

And the sound of all things in harmony was the song that we shared with the Goddess.

The Earth Dream.

We, the First People, sang with Her and dreamed the First World into being. The Earth Dream is the source of all initiatory power. All things that are, are dreamed, and in turn dream with Her. The past, the present and the future act simultaneously, the part containing the whole and the whole, infinite.

To sing the song of silence was to dream with the Goddess, and all things that have been or are yet to be, are held there, in silence.

As it is now, in this age, music comes close you to the wisdom of the Goddess. By music I do not mean the notes or chords or even the sound of it, but the silence that the notes and chords punctuate. The manner in which that is achieved will dictate the surface aesthetics of the piece, but it is in the silence that its power is contained. It is this that will make you weep, cry out in ecstasy, or march you to war. Those that know the art of punctuating the silence, with words, music, or images and ideas, know well of what I speak.

And they control you.

If you believe me not, try to listen to *your* silence. Try to think of nothing. Try to listen to the space between your thoughts, your words and actions. Thinking about the silence is not the same. Listen to the silence.

You cannot, I know. But how can this be so? Is not your mind your own? Then why can you not command it what to do?

So who does command it? Whose mind is it?

It is mine, oh yes, and I will show you how easy it is to control you.

It is easy for me, because under the surface of my words runs a river of silence. Its current drives my words, and squeezes them into a bitter juice.

Bitter like the lemon fruit.

Imagine a rich, golden sun-ripe lemon you squeeze against your open lips, exploding into your dry mouth. Its juices run sharp, cascading, the acid collecting alive under your tongue. Drink it and squeeze more of the fresh juice into your mouth.

Now stop, and close your eyes… Do you see the lemon?

Does saliva gush from the glands beneath your tongue into your mouth? Think then, where is the lemon?

There is no lemon, and yet the saliva is real. Your reaction is real. And yet the lemon exists only in concept, punctuating the silence of all there is. This is the power I speak of; the conditioned domestication of our species.

If you still think that you are not controlled, think again. If Amaya can invade the intimacy of the interior of your mouth to the extent that it salivates, with just a few words, just think what governments and institutions could do with more ingenious machinations.

If I sound harsh, it is only because there exists a simple truth in what I say, a truth you need to know, and one day ultimately face.

Was that thought my own? Shush, listen.

Lemon, I whisper, yellow lemon…

What do you see?

Watch out! Scan! You are living under siege! It's me, Amaya, running around laughing inside your head.

The same forces at work now are the same that ever were…"

When I opened my eyes, Brid was staring at me across the desk.

Cut my throat, that was good – "Who's Amaya?" I asks, licking my lips.

"Indeed, by all means ask who I am, but a more pertinent question might be where did I learn what I know?"

"Where did you learn all that… Psyops?" I ventures in a whisper.

"From a book," she replies, all casual, "*Lucifer's Mirror*, a book which has not been written yet. A book I'll write in the future. But now, I'd like to apply for a secretarial position in the Operation."

She raises her eyebrows, beckoning me to speak, and fuck me, she looked and felt completely normal.

Alright, her prattle wasn't normal, but she was. The poor girl was in reverse gear. Like, get her onto weird-shit she's normal as. And visa-versa, normal-shit, she's weird as fuck.

"Who are you?"

"Just another fool on a fool's journey," she smiles, "I don't know who I am."

"That makes two of us then."

"My earliest memories, in this life, are of hospitals which aren't hospitals, doctors and nurses who aren't doctors and nurses."

"What did they… do there?"

"Experiments. I am not permitted to divulge further, I'm sorry."

"Alright then, go on, just tell us what you can then."

"They, the Illuminati, opened the door, a doorway into the inconceivable. I remembered everything. All my incarnations on this Locale, on the Earth plane."

"Past lives?"

"Past, future and beyond. Beyond time, beyond the mortal shell of the flesh. And from that perspective, I am old enough to be included in the Operation. I am *immortal*. I have no way of proving this to you, and yet I know you do believe me, you know I'm *different*."

She pauses, letting it sink in, and smiles. I get a shiver crawling up and down my spine.

"I believe in your dream, Mr Barbelo, I truly believe your dream could grow; it would be their nemesis if it did. But permit me, if I may?" She reaches over, holding my hand.

"Permit me to offer you some friendly advice. Nobody owns anybody, least of all me. And without love, we are nothing – love is freedom. Do you understand?"

"I understand."

"As you say, fate deals the hand, but how we play it? That choice is entirely ours, Mr Barbelo; listen to your heart, the mind is too easily deceived."

"Catch-yadrift," I muttered, "Lemons."

"Good," she narrows her eyes at me. "Can we, can your new secretary, hmmm," pauses, glancing around.

I perks up, "What, in here, now?"

Eyes settle on the Bren Gun hanging on the wall behind,

"Can I have a go on that?"

I laughed. "Ehmmm, no my dear, you can't."

"Okay, what about an AK?"

"No, I don't think—"

"One of these Glocks, then, just a couple of rounds—"

"What part of 'no' don't you fucking understand?"

"Okay," she sighs, letting go of my hand. "Okay, I suppose you need to draw the line somewhere. Shame, I could have shown you a thing or two."

"I very much doubt that."

"Justice," she says, and gets up, heading for the stairs, "If this is about justice, then I, at least, won't be in doubt when the hour arrives. *My* conscience will balance the scales, oh yes, but will yours?"

"What do you mean by that?"

But with that, she goes up the stairs. Calm as you like.

Well, I didn't doubt I felt fucking awful, really, I wasn't well. Hung around the command centre all morning, polishing my boots, the fax machine, the RPG's, my boots again, cleaned the whole gaff spotless and some.

Tried hitting the punch bag, imagining a particularly brutal killing spree up the West End to calm me down, but my heart wasn't in it – no, my conscience wasn't clean; I make no apologies for what I did in the Wars, nor the Firm's business and all that, never have, never will, but I did have an awful regret about that Chris down the dole office. Why him?

I dunno either. He was a spineless wanker, no sense of honour, the ancient laws of combat don't apply. But all told, maybe a job's a good'un wasn't his just deserts – then again, who was I to judge? I'm a natural selector, not Mystic Meg, he might have been a child-murdering monster in his spare time, or was going to turn into one, for all we know.

Nah, nah, hear me out before you go making no judgments too. All I did was follow my nature, at that precise moment, at that precise time. It might not be everybody's nature, it was mine.

And I'm open to change, 'course I am, but can you truly change anything till you let yourself off the hook? Alright, I'll briefly let yous in on what I learnt that day, it's important. This isn't just about sussing impending u-turns or taking responsibility, we can all get good at that. Brid was hinting at the total opposite.

What I saw in my soul-searching was that all our lives, 'cos I reckon it's true for all of us, all through our lives there is this force what leads us – I'm not talking about no bible-bashing bollocks, you know me better than that by now – I'm talking about how events are strung together, and the laws *binding* them to each other.

Thousands of events, millions, untold numbers of stuff happening all the time, everywhere in the world, in the universe; planets crashing into each other like pool balls; suns exploding; black holes sucking up entire galaxies – or even just the skulduggery going on in your street – how are we ever gonna get our heads around all that?

It's massive. We're in it, lost in events up to our necks. Infinite events, all influencing each other. We say, 'I chose to do this,' or 'that cunt decided to do that.' We do things all the time and can we ever really know where the decision came from?

Can't make a proper decision unless you're in full possession of all the facts. And we can't be in full possession of the facts unless we know all that's happening in the universe, or ever happened *ever.*

Therefore we can't make a proper decision.

Easy logic.

So what's a right thing to do, or a wrong thing to do?

Example. Our mate, Mad Mick, loveliest geezer on Earth, pushed a burglar off his car – and by that I mean all he did was push the cunt – cunt turned on him, tripped, split his loaf on the wing mirror.

One shove – job's a good'un.

Alright, Mick thought he was doing the right thing, or maybe he didn't think at all, I dunno, but what he ended up doing was the wrong thing. Leastways that's how the Judge saw it. Twelve years, served nine, missus left him, took the kids.

Topped himself the week after he got out.

Fucking ironic, gets through both Wars without a scratch, and well, says it all really.

Some other geezer might have shat themselves, let the cunt drive off with his car. Or pushed him slightly to the left, or to the right, missed the wing mirror altogether – who fucking knows?

The law saw it one way, we all saw it the other; Mick was only following his nature.

Now, you could argue that Mick's *thinking* wasn't to do the cunt in, whereas mine with the Doley was. But that's irrelevant. Neither Mick nor the cunt nicking his car could've done anything else but what happened, at that precise moment in time – *including* their thinking, or lack of. Catch-madrift?

All the events of their lives, all their loves, their fears; all the galaxies and suns exploding; the sinking of the Armada; Uncle Jack swinging on the gallows two hundred years ago – everything what had ever happened *ever* led to that precise moment.

It couldn't have been no different.

So, me and that cunt in the dole office?

Same as.

Mad Mick took a split-second decision, whereas I gave it a little more thought, not much more thought, all told, and in the grand scheme of things what's the difference? Both me and Mick were following our natures, trapped in all the events of our lives what had led to our decisions.

That's what I realised in the command centre that day. We're all Trapped in Infinity. Ambushed by events, connected, influencing – me here writing these words, you there reading them – everything, countless events all strung together.

Strung together like a huge pearl necklace, bouncing about on some giant fit-bird's tits – tits too fucking big to see…

Lovely.

And my point? Brid was right, justice is a blind bitch! Let yourself off the hook. I did… well, I gave it a good shot.

Gave Mark our accountant a bell, and sent him round to that poor cunt's missus' gaff. Settle any financial loose ends – offer discreet but appropriate compensation, in other words – and then thought, better get her some flowers too, it's only civil, and a nice card. The personal touch. Treat her like one of our own.

Fancy coming then, go for a mosey round the flower shops up town?

With renewed vigour and a spring in my peg, I marched out the house and hailed a cab for the West End.

Chapter 17

Our Lovely Stroll Up Town

Thud, thud, thud, "My young man, do you have a light please?"
"Fuck off!"
"Oh deary me, what language – hold on, wait!"
Thud, thud, thud…
"Stop following me!"
… thud, thud, and thud.
"Hold on—"
"Let go of my arm, alright?"
"Fair dues son, sorry, but what seems to be the bother?"
"Nothing. After I've cut Thatcher into pieces and stuck her head on a pole. Nothing."
"Like your style… Falklands? West Belfast? What regiment?"
"Just go away."
"Oh, very well then. Look after yourself, ay."
Thud, thud, thud…
"You there! Do *you* have a light please?"

Alright, I know we're meant to be sourcing flowers for the dead cunt's missus, not hanging about stinking alleyways, sorry, I suppose I am easily distracted by vermin but I mean, what is it about the West End, ay? Doesn't matter how many times I've hunted up here, brimming with scum it was, day or night – came from far and wide for the Soho nookie shops too, which is where we're heading now.

Why? 'Cos one of the cunts just got away from us and that's the direction he was heading. Come on, quick, on the double!

I don't know about you, thud, thud, thud, but I fucking loves it when they gets away. Fact of the trade though, they do sometimes, leastways they try.

Right turn, here!

Pegged through Chinatown, following the trail of blood, twisted right, and then left up Charring Cross Road for a bit, and before we knows it we're in Bloomsbury, standing outside the British Museum.

Thought we were gonna see some nookie? Nah. Climb the stone steps to the entrance, and that's where the trail ends. Determined little cunt to make it this far, though, I do likes that.

Scanned about, and pegged inside one of the greatest acts of piracy known to man, the British Museum, except what's British about it? Fuck all, apart from the sheer magnitude of priceless skulduggery, of everything and everywhere – from the Amazonian rainforest to Mesopotamia and ancient Greece – and you've gotta admit we are bloody good at it – when suddenly I'm shoved, sprawled under a giant statue of dog boy.

(Anubis, circa 1,500 BC Egypt, according to the label).

Back on my feet, I catch a glimpse of the cunt hurtling towards the entrance.

"Well done," I mutter, brushing myself down, and it was. Didn't break the skin, but look: Three puncture holes in my overcoat, a neat little grouping around the kidney area, nice and tight.

Out on the busy street again, I spots him leaning against the window of the bookshop opposite – clutching his gut, gasping for breath – and please, let's just pause in the delicious thorny moment:

Scumfuck, flick-knife in hand, the pavement drinking the blood drip, dripping from his left trouser leg, and passers-by just passing on by, and by, and by… hmmm, don't you just love London sometimes?

I do.

Waving Happy Stick at the traffic, a leisurely peg across the road – serenaded to beeping horns and cabbie-mouthed curses – and we makes eye contact, him and I.

And oh, how delightful his wide-eyed terror! And see that? How sincere, equitable, how perfect and compelling as with trembling hands he offers up my wallet.

I slows my pace, and flick the release catch of my blade.

"Thank you," I whispers, but my battle-gaze yells RUN!

He chucks my wallet, I picks it up, we resume the hunt.

Taking our time, he's in our sights, staggering around Russell Square, and then up Guilford Street, where his knife finally slips from his fingers and where I seriously steps up the peg!

Whoa! Close, ay? Caught him just before he collapsed in front of the hospital. Clever cunt.

Arm around his shoulder, I helps him regain his footing,

"Nice try," I says, "Gonna give you a chance for that," I nods, "You've earned it."

Told you I was reasonable.

"Can you speak, young man?"

Gurgle, gurgle...

"Good, just answer yes or no. Is it nice hurting elderly people?"

Gurgle, "No."

"You've been a very silly bunny, haven't you?"

Gurgle, "Yes," gurgle.

"Does silly bunny wanna go to Happy Place?"

Gurgle? Gurgle, moan...?

"Or does silly bunny wanna go doctors?"

Gurgle!

"Good. You promise you won't do nothing again, not to no one, never?"

Moan, groan, "Sure, promise—"

I plunged my steel home; silence, my kind of silence, clean through his heart.

Time to get that cunt's missus her flowers and go down the docks. Sort it with Sid before everything goes to custard, the moody old cunt.

Chapter 18

SNAFU

Found Sid late evening by the docks, feeding his pigeons, or better said, feeding his pigeons to the seagulls.

Sat on the end of his bench, I pass him half a loaf, "Got you this."

"Thanks, just leave it there," he says, chucking slices of bread into the feathered melee. "Are you… alright?"

"Yeah! Had a nice stroll up West, sent some flowers… yeah."

"She alright?"

"Home, won't go out, says she can't. Inner Order's after her."

Squints at me, "Reckon it's true then?"

"What you on? Some cunt's after her, definitely, but Yardies? I checked with Errol and his crew, they swear she's nothing to do with them. But… I dunno Sid, I really don't, I'm stumped."

"No, it's not the Yardies," roots into his pockets, and opens me up a pocket encyclopaedia, "Read this," he says. It read:

The Illuminati (Latin, 'enlightened') refers to several historical and modern groups, both real and fictitious.

Historically, the Bavarian Illuminati was a secret society founded on May 1st, 1776, by Jesuit-educated Adam Weishaupt; the first lay professor of canon law at the University of Ingolstadt.

The society was made up of freethinkers, which many historians claim were committed to the systematic conquest of nations by stealth and secrecy, and ultimately the entire world.

In recent times too, Illuminati refers to an alleged organisation which acts as a 'shadow government' manipulating world affairs through key politicians and corporations, with the aim to establish a totalitarian world government, commonly referred to as the New World Order.

Illuminati also refers to a Gnostic spiritual group who oppose the Bavarian Illuminati's agenda of world domination, but like the former, believe that they are uniquely empowered by a mystical Buddhist-like enlightenment.

Many secret societies and mystical traditions seek the attainment of this kind of illumination or enlightenment via occult practices, keeping the secrets of their alleged superior knowledge of the universe to themselves and their initiates.

Recently declassified SIS (Secret Intelligence Service) reports confirm that Weishaupt's Illuminati group never posed a threat to world security or even survived into the 19th century."

Closing the book, I pass it back to Sid. "Those pesky Jesuits, ay?"

"Something about her story rings true," he says, "And if she's involved in something paranormal, it probably means SIS are involved too: MI13 or even MI18."

"Rumours, Sid, cobblers, those departments always were."

"She was bang on about my... brother..."

Long pause.

I nods. "Very odd that, gave me the abdabs, I will confess."

"Feels like... there's something uncanny about her, familiar."

"Yep, I get that too, Sid."

"Notice how her voice changes? Prattles like a Paddy one moment, a fucking toff the next?"

"Yep."

"And what are the basics of BAP?"

"Tomato and bacon mate! Good point, I'm starving—"

"No, no. I meant the Behavioural Adaptation Program."

"Blend in," I says, after a moment's pause. "Blend in, blend in, blend in."

"Precisely. The basics."

"What you getting at?"

"Rapid Accent Modulation Adjustment – RAMA – and one of the first infiltration techniques they taught us—"

"Fuck me, what was that cunt's name, 'blend in, blend in, blend in,' remember? What a wanker."

"Roberts," mutters Sid, "But where did she learn the tricks of the trade?"

"Roberts, that was him, and then it was all languages – French, Spanish, German, who was... oh yeah, Corporal Smyth, with a Y – Y for *why* don't you fuck off!" I laughs. "Nah, that wasn't it, Y for... what was it again?"

"Listen! Have you tried her on languages? I have, and she knows her onions, she'd wipe the floor with us—"

"Y for what—?"

He growls, upper lip twitching, "Know what your problem is Joe? You don't know how to fucking listen you cunt!"

"Alright, steady on! BAP, the basics. I catch-yadrift—"

"You have to listen to people, could never get a fucking word in edgeways!"

I shift along the bench. "Said alright, continue, fucking hell…"

"I'm telling you she's *different*. She knows things she shouldn't."

"Yeah, but just 'cos she runs rings around you at French doesn't make her James fucking Bond, does it. I'll put her on the firing range, first thing tomorrow, she seems to like guns—"

"No, no, not just that," he sighs. "Technical knowledge, background data for devices I didn't even think possible! We spent the whole night talking, gave me loads of ideas. Look at this!" he declares, and rolls up his sleeve. On his wrist he's taped a matchbox.

"It's a matchbox," I says.

Shakes his head. "It's a 'Zapper,' she calls it. Inside is a 9volt battery. Two copper washers pass a small electrical current through the skin, and into the blood. Has to be a positive offset, mind you, but a very low voltage, from about five to ten volts is enough to cure everything."

"Really? Even cancer?"

"I dunno if it works better than cannabis oil, but the principle's sound: Alkalise the blood. At a pH of 7.4 cancer cells become dormant and at pH 8.5 cancer cells die. Parasites, bacteria, viruses, fungus – all known pathogens die in an alkaline environment."

"Are you…?"

"Gawd no, no, I felt a cold coming on, so I thought I'd give it a go. Worked," nod, nod, "I made it last night, easy as pie, a child could do it. But do you see what I mean, she's *different*."

I shrugs. "Give us a go then."

Rolls down his sleeve. "Wouldn't recommend it here, not without a bog nearby – first thing that happened, almost cacked myself!" He laughs. "Seriously, biggest shit in a month of army rations, and full of little dead worms, it was, all floating about—"

"Worms," I cuts in, "The lurgies."

"Yep, parasites, cleans you right out, but I'm going to start working on something else," he lowers his tone, "Been after this for decades, almost cracked it, I'm bloody *close*, I can feel it." Shakes his head. "I can't tell you yet, you'll only take the piss, but when I do get it up and running I want you to be the first to see it."

He grins. I nods, and then he goes all grim again, so we sat in silence for a bit, chucking bread, and watching the birds doing a pretty good re-enactment of the Battle of Britain, if you ask me.

"I'm fucking sick of all of this!" Sid pipes up, scowling around the grey docks, "I don't want to be here anymore."

"Alright then, let's go—"

"No, no I mean *here*, I mean look at all this, look at these birds even. All this death. All this killing."

"Alright…"

"Look at them."

I looked.

"We chuck in the bread, they peck each other to pieces!"

"True," I says. "Not a bad little hobby this, all told."

He sighs, "Self-forgiveness. I come here because it helps. She reckons the higher in the Realms you go, the less you need, but the Earth plane's smack in the middle of the Lower Astral, and so to be alive, to exist, we need bodies – eating-shitting-pissing tubes!" he chuckles, "We're all eating-shitting-pissing tubes. Constantly on the lookout for other eating-shitting-pissing tubes to eat, and shit, and reproduce; and make *little* eating-shitting-pissing tubes which grow up to eat more—"

"What about vegetarians?"

"Doesn't matter, the *hunger's* still there. The innate fear of hunger and starvation, of never having enough." Lifts up a finger. "That's what makes us all cunts, underneath."

"I suppose, doesn't matter how you dress it up, ay? The inner killer's not gonna let you starve."

"That's what I mean; given the circumstances St Francis of Assisi would eat his own grandmother alive."

"Natural law."

He squints at me, "So what's the point?"

I shrug. "Freedom – freedom to eat, shit and fuck."

"Bit primitive though, bit argie-bargie."

"Egg and sperm race, mate, bit like… bit like football."

"What?"

"Our father's sperm," I says, "we're all the winning goal, that's why football's so popular."

"I suppose life's a game of two halves."

"The first and the last," I chuckles, "Balls in the back of the net, last whistle blows – game over!"

We both laughed at that.

"Yeah, but what else?" he asks.

"I dunno mate," I says, "All I know is what we've got, now. All we've got is this moment, this bloody miracle we've made it this far."

"Bloody miracle," confirms Sid with a nod, "So do some good then, while we're here, no?"

"Yep, like Mad Mick used to say, 'be all you that can be; the good and the better will follow,' that's what."

"Well, on the Otherside all that's not necessary, there we *are* good, all is good. Because on the Otherside feeding bodies aren't necessary, hunger's unheard off, so nobody's going around killing, to eat, to survive."

"To defend ourselves," I adds.

"Right, and to defend ourselves. The Earth's a battlefield between two forces – food and shit…"

We paused again, watching the Battle of Britain for a bit. And then Sid's eyes flitter restlessly around the docks again,

"Do you know what I want more than anything right now?"

"What, Sid?"

"To be able to drink water out of a cool, clean stream. Just that. Says it all to me right now, if we could just do that whenever we wanted, we'd have it all."

"I know what you mean, mate. Me? I'd love to see the world twenty years from now, cleaned up of all vermin."

"Shame we won't be around…"

"Canada," I offer, "Plenty of clean rivers up there, so I hear, and loads of space with no people, and there's skies from horizon to horizon – great big giant skies."

He looks straight at me, raises his eyebrows.

"What, Canada?" I asks.

Shrugs. "Are you game or what?"

"Very well," I says, "We do what we got to do here, and we scarper, why not. Vanish into the woods."

"Drink clean water all day long."

"Watch the skies..."

Very, very long pause.

"... Sorry for almost shooting you, Sid."

"Sorry for poling your bird."

"Not my bird."

"Oh... then..."

"Two's up? Pole her all you like. The female hold all the cards, mate, always have, always will. By the way, I made her our secretary."

"Pukka... situation normal, then?" he grins.

"All fucked up," I grins.

"Bored."

"Me too."

Chucks the rest of the bread in the water. "The pigeons always lose. Let's go home."

"You go," I says, "It's a lovely evening for a stroll."

Frowns, "Again, why?"

"Why, good question. I suppose... I suppose it's a bit like what you said earlier; you come here 'cos it helps your process of self-forgiveness. Me, it's more a question of not knowing who I am to actually know who or what to blame, to then forgive. If that makes sense..."

"I understand," he says, "It's a bit like the Australians; when they've had enough of it all, they just drop everything and go walkabout."

"Come again?"

"Walkabout, spiritual practice. They go into the wilds for a long walk with nothing but a knife, months, years, whatever it takes, and when they come back, if they come back, they feel loads better."

"Right, spiritual, but mate, I really, *really* don't know who I am."

"Nor I," he shrugs, "Craft accommodates, we can be whoever we like."

"True," I sighs, "It's a lovely evening for a stroll, then..."

Chapter 19

Like a Lamb to the Slaughter

Under a gorgeous crescent moon, the lamb went walkabout one lovely London evening – I love skies, I do. Many a times the sky was the only thing what kept me going in the trenches, the only thing we had left.

We'd just stand there, shivering with the morning, knee deep in sludge, the lice crawling under our great coats, and then I'd look up into that bright rosy dawn, imagine I'd grown wings and gone!

I was flying into the heavens.

I'd look up, and for a small time nothing mattered.

For a small time, life was a sky of golden dreams…

And then the orders would come, and the pounding roar of drumfire, and screams.

The screams.

But I love skies, I do.

"Good evening young man, do you have a light please?"

"No, sorry, I don't smoke—"

"Oopsy-daisy, can you pick that up for me? It's my back, see?"

"Sure, here you go."

"Thank you."

Must've said 'thank you' twenty times that night, no fish were biting, then again I had to laugh – I'd completely over-fished these waters yonks ago – not a bad'un to be had from the Isle of Dogs to the Mile End Road.

So there you go, just goes to prove – had to let the supply regenerate or cast a wider net.

The bigger the net, the bigger the catch.

I did think about leaving it at that and going home, but then I thought nah – can't start a walkabout empty-handed – and I was just hailing a cab for West Kensington when I got the touch.

I remembered.

There was still one left in the previous month's rattle.

Another doctor, standard child-murdering nonce again, except this one had been a Catholic priest; resigned back in '62 for 'unspecified health reasons', so said the profile, which added to the fact he'd been a cleric made him a fascinating venture for me – mysterious, befitting the spiritual qualities of what Sid had said earlier as regards walkabout – definitely a prime cut above the others.

Problem was, I'd not been able to catch the cunt. Seemed like he was either abroad, or Rob down the Station had got it wrong – and Rob insisted he hadn't, and at gunpoint, so the cunt was definitely still in town.

Oh yes, mate, make no mistake about it; I take what I do very seriously, but then again, I was notorious in the Firm for asking people things at gunpoint anyways. It really is the most efficient manner to get a straight answer.

I hailed a cab and spun up the posh end of North London to have another go. Muswell Hill, not far from Cranley Gardens, as it goes, where David Nilsen finally got collared the year previous. Not surprisingly. Killed sixteen innocent people between '78 and '83. And then boiling their heads, their hands and feet, he'd strip the flesh – chopping up the entrails into small bits – and flush them all down the bog!

What a plonker.

Well he was bound to get caught, wasn't he – he'd stuffed so much human flesh down his bog he'd blocked all the drains in the entire street! Place stank to high heaven, he even had bin bags full of human organs in his cupboards, his wardrobe, all over the gaff.

Wish I'd got to him first.

Anyway, I must confess that this Dr Cob – that's the cunt's name in the rattle – had got my goat, pissed me off to high heaven; I couldn't fucking find the cunt and I felt like a right plonker too, but I'd obviously pushed him to the back of my mind long enough 'cos I'd got the touch, and when you get the touch it's always for good reason.

Profile said he was fucking loaded. The Old Bill had fingered him over a dozen times, and he'd always got off scot-free on some technicality or another – friends in high places, more like.

Stood by the corner of his gaff, like I always do, smoking my fag, taking my time – spring was in the air, clammy with pollen. People milling about, taking an evening stroll; a work crew was piling into their council vans, another day's graft over – I watched as the street slowly emptied. That's the way it goes in the mortality trade, waiting, absorbing what's around you to the last detail, like you're a sculptor on the definitive strokes of your *magnum opus*, the one what will be the measure of your years – I must've been pacing about for hours, my timepiece declared it was half twelve, when this car pulls up outside his door. A fucking Porsche.

Oi, oi, thinks I, and sure enough, out he comes; all togged-up in Armani with a butler and a classy fit-bird on tow.

Snuffing out my fag, I let them go inside and peg into the phone box opposite, calling the speaking clock for cover.

A light went on upstairs, and then it went out. I advanced.

All was quiet. But I must've sensed something wasn't right 'cos I hesitated at the door, holding the brass knocker in my fist.

And fucking odd that thing was too, gave me the abdabs, looked like a goat's head; grinning like it *knew* – it knew this cunt had got my goat – I retreat back to my corner. Regroup.

Good thing 'an all.

Shaking myself down, Happy Stick in hand, I watched as another car pulled up, a BMW, and then a Merc, and another, and another; a whole fleet of posh motors pulled up outside his house – seven in total. The butler opens the front door, and all these togged-up toffs file inside the gaff.

And then it gets truly surreal.

This battered old bread van pulls up. A couple of hefty geezers in overalls gets out, open the back doors, and slides out a coffin.

Hefting it onto their shoulders, they quickly vanish into the alleyway round the side of the house.

A minute later and they're back in their van, haring off up the street. Bollocks to this, I thought, and I still don't know what made me do it, but ups I goes, and whacked three times on the door with that grinning brass knocker.

Eyeing the butler up and down, I switch on the RAMA in my poshest flawless tones,

"Good evening, my good man, I'm Dr Goater," I boldly declare, "Is Dr Cob home?"

He eyes me up and down too.

"The Master is entertaining this evening."

The Master? Fuck me, what century does this cunt think we're in?

"It's a personal matter," I interrupt gently, "I have some rather *personal* news for him, you do understand?"

I nods, all solemn. He takes a step forward, and snarling menacingly, opens his jacket – a gun holster pops out.

"Oh, it appears I've come at an inconvenient moment?" – fucking cunt – "Tomorrow, perhaps?"

"Tomorrow," he growls, and pegging back to the main drag, I slipped down a couple of side streets, gave it another fag-break. So now what, turn heel and go home? Invoke the wrath of Sid and come back with a two-inch mortar?

Fuck off – sweated conkers for a pop at this cunt – I finished me fag and snuck around the back of the house.

The garden was massive, totally overgrown with those long stalky weeds what look like bamboo but aren't, and I creeps up to the giant bay window at the other end.

Grey curtain all but covers the murky interior – they're all there, kneeling, dressed in red robes with hoods. At the far end of the room's a twelve foot owl, and an altar with two large candles.

Between the candles lies a naked girl, no more than ten years old, tied up and gagged – can't see her face 'cos it's wrapped in red and white bandages. I shudder. An impression, just a flash of my orphanage crashes into my head – *focus*, I tell myself.

The girl must've been in the coffin, leastways it was gonna be used for her, because up gets Dr Cob, a fucking cutthroat razor in hand.

Taking out my Glock, I crouch down, leaning on the window ledge, and I'd just got a good line of sight through the gap in the curtain, when this fucking cat jumps up beside me.

Heard a twig crack behind—

All went black.

PART TWO

☠defeat☠

A priest once asked the Buddha,
"Are you a god?"
"No," said the Buddha.
"Are you a saint?
"No," said the Buddha.
"Are you a magician?"
"No," said the Buddha.
"What are you then?"
"I am awake."

Chapter 20

Astral Gretel

I drifted weightless, high above a great ocean, heaving the texture of warm honey. In the far distance lay woodlands, glacial rivers and snow-capped mountains peaks festooned with alpine forests; everything emanated life, and crooned directly into my heart, waiting expectantly for me to join it.

"Gorgeous, is it not?" Amaya's voice whispered from all around me. "The Old World. I saved some of it for you, here; a dream within a dream. Alas, it is but a tiny part of its former glory, and in its own way, a grotesque parody of what could have been the Awake. No, it does not delight my being as it will yours. To me it is a place of sorrows, a dead thing..."

The dusky, azure canopy began to brighten into the pre-dawn sky of a world that felt to be entirely comprised of hope. For a long time I could do nothing but glide on my back, and look up at the stars, scattered into infinity. The slightest movement contained an almost unbearable bliss; the currents of warm air gently caressed my skin.

With each breath I trembled with ecstasy.

"Go," I heard her say. "It is my gift to you, I will return for you after. You have one day and night in the world, as it was, undefiled, before the War in Heaven, before the Fall of Man..."

Concentrating on the mid-section of my body, I soared through the clouds, as a golden sunrise slashed the last of the night into pink and blue ribbons across the horizon. The scents of pine, wild jasmine and clean sea spray shattered my understanding of the sensuous, until, unable to bear it a moment longer, I dived into the valley below.

With my entire being I devoured this realm, and in turn, it consumed me. I allowed it to. I was no longer merely within it, something separate from it. My existence permeated the fabric of its Awen until I was this world, and this world was me.

I flew with cormorants, skimming along clear crystal rivers as they whispered their secrets to me.

I dived into the oceans, leaping in great arcs with a thousand dolphins, and ran the great plains with bison, fought, caroused, and lay with the wolves and the deer of the forest.

And I drank from the waters of life, communed with the giant oaks of the Sacred Grove, and learnt their secret joy also: simply, to be, to be, to be…

I rolled on the soft moss of the forest floor, crying tears of happiness amongst the wild bluebells, daffodils; completely intoxicated with pleasure.

I felt Amaya draw near.

Walking up to me, she leant down to where I lay with the flowers, whispering, "Come, my love, I have one more concern to show you."

Husky, yet delicate, her voice registered as small, electric shivers on the surface of my skin. She laughed, reading my thoughts.

"After, my sweet, after we will have time for that. But now, follow me," she gently commanded.

Holding my hand lightly in hers, she led me along a river, and up a gentle slope until we rounded the ridge of a hill. Below, another richly forested land extended as far as my eyes could see. Within the folds of undulating valleys, settlements could be seen, but only just, for these dwellings were constructed in such a way as to almost fool the eye into believing that they were part of the land itself.

"This was my home," I whispered in recognition.

A sad smile played on her lips, "Use your Awen, and see."

Focusing my vision on the nearest of these green, dome-like dwellings, I was aware of people, sitting around an open fire in the darkening evening light. They wore no clothes, and were completely engrossed in the animated story that a dark-skinned woman, with copper-grey hair, was chanting in a melodic drone.

I listened, and understood the strange language.

"She is singing about the future," I said.

"What is she saying?"

"That in great battles soon to come, these great forests will die, and with them, all hope for the people of these lands also."

Amaya nodded slowly. "Your Awen is getting stronger, and the longer you spend here, the more you will be capable of remembering. And yet this place is but a chimera of the Earth Dream; an unfathomable wonder lies beyond." She pointed towards the skyline.

"For when you near the end of Initiation, this is how we shall come for you. See…"

At first I could not understand what I was supposed to be looking at. Then, in a flash of rainbow coloured light, another forest appeared, hovering low over the trees. I smiled with inner comprehension.

As it slowly shaped itself into a giant galleon, the entire sky lit up in multicoloured bursts, and a vast fleet sailed majestically over us. Some, I noted, were constructed of finely sculptured sheets of ice. Their hulls glowed an incandescent blue, lit from the inside by a miniature sun, and on close inspection, all were as different to the next. I wanted more than anything to be with them.

"They are Dream Warriors. And your time will come, perhaps, if you succeed and cross the Realm of Shadows, and there complete the circle of your Initiation. The two need to be as One, for any of this to come to pass."

Gently, she turned my head away, and leant down to stroke the lush green grass between my feet.

"Your purpose is unfinished in the Awake. You must dive into my Healing Pool, and imbue your Awen with its waters and of all you recollect of here. Until your Initiation is over, you will retain no memory of me, and little of this vision; yet enough will remain for you to return when in need."

The instant she focused her intent, the ground in front of us rumbled, peeling back on itself, sending clods of earth into the air. I shielded my eyes and when I looked, a calm blue lake now lay on the brow of the hill.

Leaning her body against mine, Amaya wrapped my arm around her waist, and held me tight against her. I returned the embrace as if it would be the last act of my existence. We kissed, lightly at first, and again the sensation was experienced throughout my entire body at once. Slowly, we began to caress, all the while rising weightless into the warm night sky, stalled, and plunged deep into her Healing Pool…

The early morning sun danced on the backs of my eyelids. A warm, golden glow of relief invaded my bones, and mid-way between sleep and glorious awakening, I truly believed myself home.

But, as my Dream Master avows, when we face eternity with our last vital sigh, the only truth is that in death, as in life, we are as good as our hearts.

Or as stupid as our heads.

Held to my hospital bed by a retention harness, a black cat lay as a Sphinx on my chest. In the far corner, I could discern the huddled figure of a uniformed SS Guard, snoring on his chair. A pneumatic drill pounds in the streets below, the ceiling's barred window casts a lifeless light on my situation; evidently this was still Locale 22.

The cat stretched, yawned wide, and began preening itself. Something in the lithe quality of its movement both repulsed and fascinated me, but when it locked its glowing yellow eyes onto mine I retched, and almost vomited over myself.

A feline voice sang into my mind,

"Oh dearrr, does my power unsettle you? Aaaah yes, my love, all those nasty bullets, what a frrrightful mess! Multiple compound frrractures, mmmm, verrry, verrry painful when the anaesthetic wears off... What? Do I mean you harrrm? Nooo, I only mean to see you torturrred into complete annihilation, like the pathetic shit-worrrm you are!"

She rolled over languorously onto my stomach, arched her back and began to sharpen her claws on the straps holding me down.

I calmed myself with a series of deep breaths. The important thing in these situations is to regroup your thoughts, and above all, stay focussed on your intent. So the Order teaches us. I tried yelling to wake the guard but my lips clamped shut—

"Ah! I would not do that, my puppet, you don't rrrealise just how much trrrouble you're in... Please don't frrret, only minutes to go before you return to the Awake... If, of courrrse, I let you go."

Whatever this being was, it had power enough to control my dreaming body, but it could not prevent my natural awakening—

"Oh rrrealy!" laughed the cat, "Would you stake yourr soul on it? Then rememberrr I can read your thoughts; be sweet to little Gretel, be rrrespectful and when I have what I want, I will release you. Or, perrrhaps... I will not. Oh hush now! Never mind what Order I may, or may not belong to. Consider your prrredicament, my sweet, if your awareness became ensnared in this brrrutal Locale..."

The cat released a torrent of newspaper headlines into my vision:

'Hundreds Dead In Airport Attack!'
'Sisterhood Of Light and Redemption Destroy Terminal Building!'
'SOLAR Terrorists Strike Again!'

On all the front pages, was the same photograph of me lying amongst the rubble.

"Do you understand now, my puppet? They believe you Solar's leader, afterrr a little mind trickery of my own… Of courrrse you are not a woman! But the authorities here have long suspected the head to be a man, stupid humans… You're rrresponsible for a variety of sorrrdid assassinations and industrial sabotages… oh yes you arrre!" she cackled, flashing her yellow eyes over to the sleeping guard.

I only had minutes to go before I awoke, but she persisted with her torment, as beings of this nature often do.

"Later today, you will be taken to the interrogation cubicles beneath this verrry building, and well, frankly my love, I do worry, considering the frrrightfull state you're in. *Brrritish* Nazis employ methods which are somewhat, mmm, *barbarrric*, wouldn't you say?"

Although creatures like these can grow immensely powerful, years of travelling the Realms had taught me not to trust their claims. Often they only wanted to vampirise your Awen, and scaring you witless is an effective way of doing that.

Sex, of course, is another tactic. And yet I sensed something else with this one, the stress she'd placed on her last words, a veiled agenda set apart from the expected parasitical struggles for energy.

She jeered, slowly shuffling up my chest, "And are you not frrrrightened, my only one, that the attention of your petty everrryday life might become fixated here? While your body, lying in a coma, slowly rots into putrid stink-flesh, like everything else in your purrrecious Awake!"

Her paws came to rest on my throat, our noses all but touching. Recalling my training, I resolved to set up my resistance; reciting lines of Shakespeare over, and over. The words themselves were irrelevant, what matters here is Awen, full awareness, focused intent, at least enough to get her out of my head for the remaining few minutes before I awoke.

"We are such stuff as drrreams are made of," Gretel sang along with me in my mind, "and our little life rrrounded with sleep… How delightful!"

Two sets of razor-sharp claws dug into my temples. I felt her soft breath on my lips, her mind searching, penetrating deep,

"Indeed, think then, what could one such as I, an all-powerful transdimensional being, possibly want from one of the Orrrder's Dream fucking Warriorssss!" She hissed with contempt, barring her white fangs inches from my face. "A mere foot soldier, a puny single-dimensional rot-bag, rrriddled with self-importance, fear and self-pity! You disgust usss! Buffoons! Like all your species... the collapse of the Shadow Rrrealm... Evolution of Consciousness... the Awakening of the Earth Drrream into the One... Peace? Ha, ha! Peace! Oh how typically fucking human!"

As she continued, I invoked in my mind's eye the memory of the Inner Sanctum on Locale 64. A gigantic fleet of Lyraquai Galleons fanned out across the horizon, sailing majestically through the heavens in a resplendent golden dawn. Their translucent sails, rippling like a gentle tide on the shoreline, shimmered a bluish hue in the light of the twin moons.

A thousand bright stars glistened with eternal hope—

"How verrry quaint: The fucking Angelic Realms!" she scoffed, but then sat bolt upright in surprise, "*Non Serviam*, says he... Purrrpose, says he... I'm blocked out?"

Glancing around the cell, rapidly, as if following the erratic path of flies, she then rested her head to one side and listened, communing with her other selves.

Eventually she returned my petrified stare.

"Congratulations, my sweet! Your purrrecious body stirs from its slumber, and yet the trrrue Dreamer has yet to awaken. Who am I?"

Narrowing her eyes into minuscule slits, she peeled reels of merciless feline laughter.

"Wrong question! When in search for the Truth, there arrre only ever two things worth asking: Who are you? And wherrre are you? The answer to both will set you frrree. The answer to both is the opposite of what you arrre thinking..."

Once again plunged into darkness, my soul shuddered with foreboding, heeding her distant cries,

"Thus brrring *him* here, to me, bring me that relic of the ancient law, and perrrhaps, we shall both be released... you and I... you and I...you and I... you and I...you and I..."

Chapter 21

Non Serviam!

'The part contains the whole,' my mind whispered softly, 'and the whole is infinite...'

I wake up in this massive wine cellar; head-splitting headache, sick as a dog. Last thing I remember, Dr Cob's got a cutthroat in his hand, and then it all went black. For child-murdering owl-worshipers they weren't very good at this abduction lark. I mean, they hadn't even tied me up! They'd even bandaged my head and put a blanket over me...

Odd.

Turned on the light, saw my timepiece was broken, and briefly taking off my gloves, I checked myself over – judging by the stubble on my face it must've been no more than thirty-six hours – sore ankle but otherwise present and correct.

Staggered to the wine wrack, slide a bottle out and let it smash on the floor. And froze – heard footsteps outside.

Switch off the light, grab the broken bottle neck and pin myself beside the doorframe.

The door opens, light goes on – and Sid's got the good sense to sidestep before I slash his throat.

"For Gawd's sake Joe!" he growls, peeling off his balaclava, "Give me that!" Snatching the bottleneck from my fingers, he looks me up and down, "Is this your idea of a night out?" he chuckles, "Bloody hell mate, you do need help!"

"Oh very droll..."

Well, what had happened was that when I didn't go home, Sid had got worried – as you would considering my nocturnal vocations – and called Rob down the Station, who'd said I'd been royally pissed off about this Dr Cob cunt I couldn't find, and Sid had put two and two together.

"This cuts deep," he whispers, glancing outside the door.

"Govermentals?"

"Cuts deep."

"Interesting. My weapons, please."

Passes my cane and a 9mm Glock.

"Saw a giant owl," I says, checking the silencer. "They had a girl, I think they were gonna kill her."

He nods. "Well she's not here now, but the butler is."

"What time is it?"

"0:300 hours. Are you alright?"

I nods. "Feel like shit. Are you alright, there's… blood… fuck me, it's all over you…"

"Not mine. Had a go on Happy Stick, got caught up in lower astral frequencies—"

I raise my hand. "Please, no more of *her* prattle. Butler's alive?"

"In a manner of speaking."

"Better have a word then."

So upstairs we trundle, and sure enough, there's the butler passed out on the sofa – Louis XIV silk upholstered Chaise Longue – in fact the entire gaff's a miniature fucking palace.

Bohemian eighteenth century crystal chandelier, wall-to-wall paintings of inbred toffs with funny bandy legs, posing next to inbred dogs with stupid haircuts, but no altars or anything suspicious, except for the blood, everywhere, splattered up the walls, ceiling, fucking everywhere, and taking pride of place in the centre of the room: three good'uns crucified on the grand piano.

"Oh… my… Gawd. Sid, *what* did you do to them?"

"I dunno what came over me," he sighs, "I found you hanging upside-down from the rafters, by the ankle, trussed up like a Christmas turkey and I flipped." Shakes his head. "It was Burma all over again."

"I suppose you always were a messy cunt. Been here a while, then?"

Nods, "Cleaned you up, thought a little kip would do you good."

"Thanks mate, appreciate it," I mutters, as we peg over to the piano, "But from now on, try to keep proceedings strictly professional, ay? How did you know they were govermentals?"

Looks at me funny, "Two reasons, but mainly because they told me, didn't they."

"Ah."

"Butler though, different story," glances behind at the cunt on the sofa, "Copped one in the knee, knocked seven bells out of him, quiet as a dormouse. But that's a Lord there, from the House of Commons; barrister and a doctor either side."

"Really?" I gazed at the carnage on the piano, and stifled a yelp—

"Bastard! Sid, you got my Dr Cob as well?"

"Had to."

"Oh why, why, why—"

"He had a gun."

"Not the point! That was *my* job's a good'un."

"Sorry—"

"And if my mother had a gun, would you shoot her an' all?"

"Probably."

I round on him, "Alright then, if *your* mum was here with a gun, would you shoot her an' all?"

"Bloody hell, you're worse than a child sometimes."

"*See*, clearly you wouldn't—"

"Here," passing me a grenade, "this'll make up for it, suck on that!"

"Not funny Sid! Sweated conkers for a pop at this cunt, been after him for donkey's—"

Throws his arms up in the air, "Left you the butler, didn't I?"

"Don't care, not the point..."

Sighs, "What's your point then?"

I jab my finger at his chest, "My point is universally obvious, Sid, this is my walkabout, *my* spiritual voyage of self-discovery; I don't need to discover you're a miserable old cunt, I already know you're a miserable old cunt – he was my *priest*, I needed to give him my *confession*."

"That's bollocks, we've already got a confessor, Uncle Pete, down the Hope & Anchor—"

"Irrelevant, Pete's only a landlord—"

"Leastways we always tell him everything."

"That's not the kind of confession I *meant*! Dr Cob was a proper priest, spiritual and *mysterious*."

"Oh, right, well now he's mysteriously disembowelled on a—"

"Exactly! Now look at him; you've gone and ruined it all."

"Give us another butcher's at your head," he mutters, peering round to the back of my head, gently redoing my bandages, "Nasty that, concussed, hey, dizzy?"

"Feel like I'm floating in a giant goldfish bowl… your fault."

"We'll find you another priest, I promise, come on," he says, making his way over to the butler on the sofa. "We can't hang about here all night, I'm not sure I got them all."

"Glad to hear you've still got some restraint, for fuck's sake, we'll wait for them here then, and—"

"No, we won't," waves his hand in the air, "Come and have a butcher's at this."

I pegs over to the sofa. "Looks like Noel Edmonds."

"Does a bit," whispers Sid, rolling up the cunt's sleeve. "He's branded, like us. *'Non Serviam.'*"

I squint closely at the cunt's tattoo. "And the other three an' all?"

"No, just him."

"Coincidence?"

"Must be," murmurs Sid with a shrug.

And that's as far as it always went on that score. Partly on account the Craft 'discouraged' recruits from getting personal – constructing false identities was our prime directive – but mainly because neither of us could rightly remember where we'd got it done.

Sounds odd, I know, a brand like that must've hurt some, and between the two of us we had dozens more we couldn't account for. Then again, war does funny things to your head. *Non Serviam* was what Lucifer had said to God, means kiss my hairy arse in Latin,

'I Will Not Serve.'

Sid slaps the cunt around the face, "Wakey, wakey, rise and shine!"

The cunt groans, and I leans over, pressing the tip of my memorial pen on his upper lip, just under his snooter – there's a pressure point there what revives people in his condition, in case you're asking.

He perks up quick-smart, jerking on the sofa. I pop a cap in his other kneecap for good measure.

He screams. Sid slaps the cunt round the face again,

"This is my mate, he wants a word. Do you hear?"

The cunt spits out a tooth. I advance,

"Where's the girl?"

"Sacrificed to Lord Moloch," he grunts.

"Who?"

Sid nods. "I think he means the giant owl you saw."

"Oh?"

"Read about it in a magazine; Satanists sacrifice children to giant owls. Did you know, in Britain alone, over thirty thousand children go missing every year, *never* to be seen again—"

The cunt laughs. I pressed the barrel of my 9mm into his forehead, "You had the chance, why am I still alive?"

"Already asked the others that," grumbles Sid.

Cunt whispers, "Welcome home, Brother," and grins.

"See? Cunt thinks you're one of them."

"Come again?"

Sid's upper lip starts to curl, "Your tattoo."

I shudder, compose myself, and whisper in the cunt's ear,

"There's two ways we can get to know each other better. One's gonna hurt like hell, and the other's gonna hurt like hell – tell us where she is."

He chuckles, "Or what?"

"Well, do you see this big ugly cunt over here, he's gonna cut off all your fingers—"

"You mean your girlfriend?"

Grins up from his sofa. I grins down, shake my head.

"Girlfriend? What fucking girlfriend – that's my wife!"

Thwack!

"Aaaaaaaaaaaaaaaaaah!"

"And that was your fucking ankle!"

"Didn't know you cared," swoons Sid.

"Token of my undying afflictions, I mean affections."

"Do the other one."

"Will do, darling, wedding gift—"

"No, no," whimper, whimper, "don't, don't!"

I smiles. "Who else is involved; names, addresses, numbers."

"Didn't ask them that," mutters Sid.

"That's 'cos you don't think," I grumbles, "First time on walkabout and it all goes to your head—"

"Didn't get the chance, did I."

I straightens up, "Why, 'cos they had *guns?*"

"Oh don't start! How was I supposed to know they were only child-murdering devil-worshipers?"

"Child-murdering *owl-worshipe*rs, actually."

"Same fucking thing, *actually!*"

"Alright, alright, tone it down, please, I've got a headache."

"Sorry."

"You ask, Sid, that's how you know. These are *precisely* the things you've got to ask when you go walkabout. There's an etiquette to—"

"He's passing out again."

"Oh, looks a bit peaky an' all, wake him up again."

"Oi! Wakey, wakey!" slap, slap, "You're gonna tell us, aren't you?"

"Or what?" the cunt smirks up at us, "Chisel out my teeth with a screwdriver?"

Sid shrugs, I nods.

Cunt mutters, "Maybe cut off my nose and ram it down my bleeding gums?"

"If you want."

"I tell you what I want," Sid pipes up, "I want my wedding gift."

Thwack!

"Aaaaaaaaaaaaaaaaaaah!"

"There you go dear."

"Thank you darling, can I have his elbows as well?"

"Hmmm, what do you reckon," I ask the cunt, leaning over, "Can my wife have your elbows?"

Cunt nods, "Do it," he rasps, "And then gut me open… hang me up… from the chandelier."

And fuck me, almost couldn't believe it, he starts laughing again! One minute he's all imaginative and amiable, the next he's all clever-cunt. Very disconcerting, I was impressed.

Straightened up again, I turns to Sid,

"We've got ourselves a hardboiled. This'll take time. We'll call the boys, take him with us and—"

Thwack! Thwack! One between the eyes, one in the heart.

"No Sid!"

"Strictly professional?" Thwack! Another in the heart.

"Oh no, no… what did you do that for?"

Shrugs, "Couldn't help it."

"Couldn't help it?"

"Reason enough."

"But he was useful!"

"Not taking that piece of shit anywhere."

"Can't take *you* anywhere, more like," I sighs, "Bloody hell…"

Puts on his long coat, carefully buttoning up to the top, "Let's go home. This place is giving me the screaming abdabs."

"Alright Sid, you sure though; don't fancy waiting for the others."

"Positive," scanning the room, "Why? Two reasons."

"Can't help it and you can't help it."

"I'm serious, Joe! I've not been right since I got here… something about this gaff's not right… no phones, no TV, no radio even…"

"I dunno, it's quite nice here, I think. Except for the mess…"

"*Feels* derelict, abandoned, crawling with lower astral frequencies, I think it's used specifically for ritual purposes—"

"Alright Mystic Meg, second reason?"

"Same reason I knew they were govermentals. Use your loaf."

I glance about, "Well, for govermentals there's a distinct lack of tactical response, I was expecting a firearms unit, minimum…"

Nods, "Look outside the window."

I pegs to the window, and gently pull the curtain.

Scanning the quiet, well-lit street, it slowly became evident that the citizens sitting inside their cars did not appear to be moving, at all, almost as if they had mysteriously frozen to death overnight, and yet they still managed to retain a remarkable lifelike quality in the variety of their postures—

"Sid, could the distinct lack of tactical response be due to the fact you've wiped out the entire fucking street?"

"You're so melodramatic," he laughs, coming up beside me.

"Oh please, tell me I'm not looking at what think I'm looking at; there's council workers, gasmen and everything."

"Council's on strike again, that was their security team."

"Oh how embarrassing…"

"Had the gaff covered for two blocks. Standard govermental procedure."

"Gawd, I'm not gonna hear the end of this am I…?"

"My lips are sealed," he gloats, "*That* says it all loud and clear. But, what would Sally say?"

"Happens to the best of us?"

"Hows about – 'If I havta save your sorry arse one more time, Barbelo, I'll skull-fuck you to death with a donkey in front of your mother.'"

"Yep, sounds about right, Gawd I miss her…"

"As do I, shall we go now darling?" he smiles, closing the curtain, and we starts pegging towards the hallway.

"Nerves are at me Sid, seriously, feel like I'm gonna puke—"

"Give us the grenade then."

"Why?"

"I wanna lob it at the chandelier on the way out."

"Oh no fucking way."

"It'll calm your 'nerves,'" he chuckles.

"If you think I'm letting you anywhere near my grenade you've got another thing coming – you've got problems Sid, *serious* control issues, you have. And blimey, alright, *maybe* I was a bit reckless, but that's because I was eager to give my confession; I don't think a little enthusiasm reflects negatively on my overall Craftsmanship and integrity… Sid?"

I stalls in the hallway, about turns. Sid's pacing back into the gaff, rooting around in his coat pockets. Bollocks! I peg after him.

Leaning against the mantelpiece, grinning like a cunt, "Aha!" he holds up a grenade. I slowly creeps up towards him.

"Sid, use your loaf, is that a good idea in here, posh area an' all?"

Shrugs, "Under the Radar."

"Not the point, we're Craftsmen," I mutter, squinting at him, head spinning, "Gawd, never noticed before, Sid, you're like a big kid, you are…"

Grins up at the chandelier, pulls the pin, "On three?"

I take out my grenade, pull the pin, "On three then. One!"

"One!" he echoes.

"Two!"

"Nah, three!" And fucking cunt, lobs the grenade legging it past me into the hallway like an Olympian,

"Last one out's a dead cunt!"

Chapter 22

Confessions of a Top Cunt

"Stop over there please," I asks the cabdriver.

"Don't stop there," says Sid.

"Stop over there please."

"Don't stop anywhere, he's concussed—"

"You'll be fuckin' concussed, you will—"

"Last warning!" yells the cabbie, "Shut your cake-holes or you're both out!"

"Please, stop here," I says.

"Don't stop," says Sid.

"Stop here—"

"No!"

"You fuckin' promised me a priest—"

"Right you two, out!"

"Lovely job, cheers mate." I stuff some notes into his paw, we gets out, cabbie hares off.

"Well done," grumbles Sid. "Now what?"

"Hail another cab, wait for me outside Victoria Underground; I won't be two ticks. Give us your balaclava. Thanks."

Without more ado, I peg across the square and climbs the steps into Westminster Cathedral.

Gloomy, miserable places, churches, I fucking hates them. What am I doing here then?

Giving my confession. Nah, not that kind, *my* kind. I'm not a mug, last thing I'm gonna do is confess nothing about myself. Had dealings with the SVS back in the Wars; Vatican's got the classiest Intelligence Service on Earth *precisely* because people grass themselves up all day long.

Locate a booth, slip on my mask, and sit inside.

"Good morning," I whispers, "This is, well, this might be a little difficult for you; I had a notion on the cab ride home just now, what I need to confess. Immediately. You there?"

"I am here, my son."

"Please don't call me that, this partition's wafer thin, and there's a fully-automatic 9mm Glock aimed at the vicinity of your gonads. Pardon my French."

I flash my gun past the grill. He recoils into seat, but keeps stum.

"You've seen one of these before, haven't ya?"

"I know the harm they cause, and it's not necessary to——"

"Shhh! Guns are always necessary... Missionary?"

"Yes."

"Where?"

"I worked six years in Sierra Leone, and then the Sudan."

"Come a bit closer; let's have a look at ya."

Edges forward; lean face, clean, short brown curls, mid-thirties – and yep, eyes had that weary air of having seen a thing or two.

"Very well," I whispers, "Listen, I don't want us starting off on the wrong foot, but I'm twice your age and calling me that's not... *natural*, alright?"

"Yes sir."

"Just hear what I've got to say, respectfully and in proper order, and all will be well between us. By the way, if you touch that panic button under your seat, I'll *know*. Catch-madrift?"

"No sir, I won't..."

"I know you won't, priests are brainy and mysterious, but tell you what, please don't speak. Head injury," I taps my head, "Spent the night with child-murdering owl-worshipers; feel a bit woozy. Just nod when I say nod."

He nods.

"Had an awful night of it, mate, seriously. I'll spare you the details, but I didn't get a chance to talk with the priest I wanted to talk with, and I'm upset. Considerably. Do I make myself clear?"

He nods.

"Tell me something, is God good?"

He nods.

"You can speak if you want, is God good?"

"Yes."

"And you lot, you do serve God."

"We try to emulate the good works of our Lord and Saviour Jesus Christ. Now please, this is the House of God, put the——"

"Sorry, it's not what you *try* what counts, it's what you do. Other people might be forgiven for not *doing*, they don't have the clout, but even so, a lot of them still have a go, regardless. You and me though, we do have the clout and no excuse, *no* excuse is good enough!"

"Sir, please, what is it you need? Let me get you someone to—"

"Right! Well here's the onion. One of my Generals sent me a fax a couple of days ago, told him never to fax to HQ from work, the young fool thinks he's James Bond or something. I know, I know – I *will* have another word with him. But I want to read it to you, if that's alright," I says, and paraphrased the gist of Mark's message. It's first-rate, I'll give you the straight version. It read:

General M to Mr T.C.

US Military are back swarming all over The City. I have to be quick. We're working on finance projection charts for the next 20 years. You were right, different shit, same arse.

The purpose of the military is to ensure that government have access to resources, especially oil. The military drives the banks, and the banks return the favour by funding the military.

Here are the figures you asked for:

The official US defence budget for the year 2007 will be $462.7 billion.

To educate everyone in the developing countries will require only $6 billion.

Water and sanitation for every person will require only $9 billion.

Reproductive health for women will require only $12 billion.

Providing basic health and nutrition for the poor around the world will require only $13 billion.

For $40 billion dollars, the US alone could transform the entire world from poverty and misery to comfort and health. That's less than 10% of their proposed 2007 defence budget.

As you say, Mr T.C. same old, same old. Something has to change.

General M

P.S. Still nothing on T.S.S.

"Says it all," I sighs, folding the memo back into my pocket. "Problem is, can we assign the Yanks the logistics to end world poverty. My thoughts exactly; they're useless, mate, bloody useless – wouldn't trust them to do an on-target bombing raid on the Grand Canyon, and in broad daylight. Now, you lot though, different story. Your Firm's been in the saviour trade for what, nigh on two thousand years – helping people is your entire purpose. Tell me something; do you think God plays dice with universe?"

"I'm sorry?"

"Or does He play cards? Sure deals some rough hands, ay?"

"The Lord's methods are beyond the scope of mortal understanding, but sir, I think—"

"I'll ask you again, is God good and do you serve Him?"

"Of course, but I think you need—"

"Shhh! I know I need help," I grins, "that's why you've gotta be so *quiet*, like a little mouse. Here's what you're going to do. Oh, wait, do you have a pen and paper, you might wanna take some notes."

Roots around his booth, holds up a pen and notebook.

"You're going to write up my confession later, and pass it on to your boss. Nod."

Nods.

"Start with, let's see… Dear Mr Pontificus. You have a bank, The Vatican Bank, richest institution on Earth."

Nod, nod. Scribble, scribble.

"Well, me auld china, open the coffers and end world hunger, or I'm coming after yous all, one by one, starting with you."

Wide-eyed glare. Scribble, scribble

"I will personally finance and unleash wave, after wave of natural selectors; thousands upon thousands will descend upon yous until yous have all been wiped-out to the very last priest, nun and nonce.

This is not personal.

This is natural law… Does that sound alright? The bit about natural selectors, will he know what that is, or does top-notch assassins sound better?"

Nod, nod.

"Top-notch assassins, then. And you're gonna tell his Pontificus I don't care how he does it, pawn the altar gold, sell the Sistine Chapel – but he's gonna *do* it, right?"

Scribble, scribble.

"If he needs a hand with the logistics, I'll be happy to offer any assistance my Firm can provide – nah, scratch that bit out."

Scratch, scratch.

"The logistics are hardly rocket science anyway, not for a Top Firm like yours, is it?"

Nods.

"Alright, continue. And you also know, as well as I, that it could be *done* in no time, but I'm a little busy with plans to overthrow Parliament, and I'm not in the habit of making idle threats. Therefore, tell your Pontificus one year, as from today, or all-out war. Non-negotiable. Do I make myself clear?"

Nod, scribble, nod, scribble.

"Reckon he'll get the pun? 'Not in the habit?'"

Groan…

"Fair dues mate, bad joke – but!"

Wide-eyed glare!

"But, I am a reasonable man, so we'll give him a get-out clause."

Nods.

"Get-out clause. If anyone can find that bit in the Bible where Jesus says, 'Go forth and hoard the world's wealth while billions suffer in abject misery before starving to death' – then we'll call it quits. Alright? But only then."

Nod, scribble, scribble, nod.

"That's settled then. Sign it Mr T.C. afterwards."

Scribble.

"I'm so glad we understand each other; saving humanity is your Firm's entire purpose. And if the Yanks could do it with just a fraction of their resources, you lot could do it standing on your heads! *And* you'd still get to be Top Firm in the yard."

Nods.

Sighing heavily, I glance into the gloom outside, and rest my head back against the wooden wall.

"I'm tired mate, so tired – tired of all of it, tired of the greed, the hypocrisy, tired of threatening people an' all! Why is this the only way to get through?" I whisper, flashing my gun past the grill, "It's much nicer to be nice, ay, why can't we all just be *nice* to one another?"

Nods.

"Your Jesus Christ was a nice geezer. A diamond, he was… and he was… loveliest geezer ever, just like my mate Mad Mick. Alright, Mick didn't have superman powers, he couldn't rise from the dead or nothing, he just *helped* people, just a lovely geezer to be around… and yeah, I wish he was still around…"

Burying my head in my hands, I closed my eyes, cradling my gun on my lap. Something about the haunting silence of the place, or the smell maybe, that melancholic frankincense stench, I dunno what, but something threw me back to childhood – it wasn't the orphanage this time, no visuals at all, just an overwhelming desire to cry. But whenever I try to squeeze a tear, I can't – what sounds a bit like a squirrel being fucked by a jackhammer – so I takes a deep breath, shakes myself down,

"Very well," I whispers, "better go, I'm worried about my mate waiting for me – he's afflicted with control issues – but don't you worry an' all, your boss will do the right thing. Because there is no excuse good enough otherwise, is there. I mean, yous can't *all* be child-murdering owl-worshipers, can you?" I chuckles, getting up, and then a deathly chill invaded my bones, "Unless yous are… oh bloody hell, because thinking on it now, why haven't you done something about all this before? Oh my good Gawd!"

Wide-eyed glare!

"Could it be that bloody obvious? Speak! *Are you all child-murdering owl-worshipers?* Speak!"

"No sir, we are Christians and—"

"You sure? Why not then, why haven't you done all this before?"

Long pause.

"Mate, listen to me. I'm moments away from being rendered unconscious due to head injury and *extreme* Lower Ashtray Dentistry. This gun is fully automatic. My last reflex action will be to squeeze the trigger and dice your gonads into Gonad Stew – please speak."

"I really don't know how to answer why. There is a great deal of poverty in the world, my – sir, and it worsens every day. But we have charities and projects which do improve people's lives, and in very significant ways."

"Significantly murdering children and—?"

"No, that's not true! In Africa we have—"

"Ha! And where do these funds come from?"

"From donations and—"

"Right. So on top of owning half the world, you ponce off other people. Marvellous. And why does your Ponce-ificus need all that charity codswallop in the first place?"

"Because people like to give to people in need, and The Church tries to help by coordinating these projects, but we do provide funding too."

"That's not what I asked. For example. If you were starving to death, and I had the last chocolate pudding on Earth, just throwing you crumbs every now and then, hoarding the rest for myself in a bank surrounded with armed guards, what would happen?"

Pause.

"My gun-arm is aching."

"Sir, I'm sure what you say is right. The Church, we probably could end world poverty, if we—"

"I know you could, we just said, open the coffers."

"But... I... but all the other Churches are wealthy too."

"Wealthy beyond all reckoning, we just said. And your purpose is to help people, we just said. I just need to know if you're a child-murdering owl-worshiper or not, that's all."

"We worship our Lord and Saviour, Jesus Christ—"

"Oh spare me! We know who you *think* you're worshiping!" I groans with frustration, "Bloody chain of command, again. Alright, sorry. Let me ponder this... yep... dunno... was she right? Speak."

"Who?"

"My wife, she always said you lot are evil. So, are you?"

"I don't, I mean no, no, of course not."

"Well, you would say that, but how can we be sure? Fortunately, using the threat of imminent violence, coupled with my fail-safe method of logical deduction, appropriately called easy logic, we can easily deduce whether or not you are a child-murdering owl-worshiper. At the very least, yeah?"

Nods.

"Would a lovely geezer like Mad Mick and Jesus, or any lovely geezer who's concerned about the poverty and the injustices in the world, care about helpless starving children too?."

"Yes, of course."

"And if this lovely geezer was minted, what would he do?"

"I... I imagine he would proportion a large amount of his wealth to helping those in need. But—"

"No buts, simple question. Now, would a child-murdering owl-worshiper care about the billions of starving children in the world?"

"No."

"And having vast, unimaginable wealth in his banks, what would he do with it – all that money and priceless arts and riches; tons upon tons of pilfered Inca gold, silver and jewels? What?"

Shifty sideways look... quick sigh...

"Well? We're not talking rocket science here, speak!"

"He would hoard it for himself..."

"Yeees, and then?"

"... And then, what?"

"Hunger, minus money, equals?"

Long pause.

I tap on the grill. "Getting vexed here, me auld china. Equals, what?"

"I don't know..."

"You don't know? Damn-it! And just when I was just starting to like you, an' all. Alright, sorry for this, I really am. Prepare for Happy Place, on three," raising my gun level, "One, two—"

"And he'd let them starve!" throwing his hands up in front of his face, "He'd hoard everything and let everybody die!"

"Correct answer! So, you're saying that child-murdering owl-worshipers murder children by starving them to death. Yep, makes perfect sense. And so, by logical deduction: having the clout to end their suffering, your Ponce-ificus, and his entire chain of command, obviously, are all child-murdering owl-worshipers."

"But the other Churches, the other denominations—"

"You just said, murderers all, accessories after the fact – it doesn't matter how you dress it up – you're allowing countless of innocent people and little kids to die, when you could easily save them. Easily!" I growls. "Right, now I'd better go. You just pass on my confession, and..."

I stalls again, halfway from standing; another chill shot right through me.

"Nah, nah, this ain't quite finished."

"Sir, please, I'm going to find you someone who—"

"Move, and you die. We can conclusively prove yous are child-murdering, but are yous *devil-worshiping*? Presuming my afflicted mate's right and the owl's a symbol for the Devil. Is it?"

Nods.

"Because if you are worshipping the Devil, it gives you a motive for all your murdering and crimes and wot-not. Do you know the difference between good and evil?"

"Yes."

"Alright then, is dishing out vast riches to save lives good."

"Yes."

"Is hoarding vast riches to destroy lives good?"

"No."

"What is it then?"

"It is evil."

"Say it again."

"Hoarding vast riches to destroy lives is evil."

"Is God good."

"Yes."

"And the Devil?"

"The Devil is... evil." Leans back, shakes his head, "Perhaps we have strayed from the path, but we are *not* devil-worshipers—"

"Didn't say you were, you did."

"But that's what you believe."

"All I'm saying is you've got a year to pull your holy finger out, before I make your lives Hell on Earth. Have I made myself perfectly clear?"

Nod, nod.

"Very well, really have to go now. I'm a man of my word, and my word is my bond. Got work to do, busy with regime change. Anyways," I says, and gets up, "Been a pleasure; I still think you're quite a nice geezer underneath, just a bit confused—"

"No, wait," he whispers, eyeing me through the grill, "Don't go, yet."

"Blimey," I chuckles, "Are you alright? Thought you couldn't wait to get shot of me."

Heavy sigh, "Africa... I was there."

I sits down again, "You said, six years. Seen a thing or two, ay? Been there myself, horrific and particular, it was."

"… You are right. The Church is not doing enough."

"I know I'm right. Seen what poverty does, son, not pretty."

Nods, "I arrived at a similar conclusion when I was there. Money, everything came down to money – a dollar *was* the difference between life and death. But there's the mortal flesh, and then there's the soul, your *immortal* soul. Our focus is on saving people's souls—"

"Cobblers! Mate, watching your children starve to death does not make you St Francis of Assisi. You've got it all arse-over-tit. As it is in Heaven, so shall it be on Earth – that's what you lot say, isn't it?"

Nods, "And what have we actually *done?*" rubs his forehead, intense stare, "Could the solution be that… *simple?*"

"Don't make me explain it all over again, please, I've got an awful headache. Listen, I'll come back another day, swap horror stories—"

"But I do have faith, sir, I love God with all my heart—"

"Well I love my shiny knives."

"—and I became a priest because I wanted to do all the things you say. I would have taken my vows from the cradle if I could because that's all I ever wanted, to serve God."

"No, no! That's the bit you don't get – you only *think* you serve Him. Have a look around this place, 'House of God?' It's a bloody palace! How much do you think all this is worth, in sterling? Fifty, sixty million?"

Shakes his head, "More, much more."

"And you, *you* personally, given the chance to use these resources, how many villages could you have sorted? Imagine it now, go on. Think back, how many people could you have lifted out of that poverty – the pain, disease and squalor?"

"I'd use the money. Definitely. There were hospital projects I was involved with, which—"

"Yeah, yeah, I'm sure they could've done with the cash," I sighs, "You're still missing the point. Point is, you're supposedly a man of God, you *wouldn't* keep it for yourself."

"No."

"Then lord it about in these cathedrals all you like, but you know full-well that if God is good, He sure as spit wouldn't want yous to keep it either. So, what *does* God want you to do?"

"God wants us to serve Him."

"And that means what, in practice?"

"Following the example of His only son, our Lord and Saviour, Jesus—"

"Being good people, *doing* good, yeah?"

Nod, nod.

"So question is, who wants you to do evil?"

Gulps a couple of times.

I nods, "Get the answer to that, and you've got the answer to who it is you're serving."

"The Devil," he whispers. "We're worshiping the Devil, but… we don't realise…"

"Dunno about that, I'm not a religious man either way. But I do know a chronic case of cognitive dissonance when I see one. Bog standard psyops."

"A what did you say?"

"How do you feel?"

"Terrible… I can't see any reason why we let this go on."

"Unless somebody *wants* it to, ay?" I shrugs, "Don't blame yourself, mate, you're a good kid, I can se that. Just mind yourself. You're on the verge of realising you've wasted your life practicing the total opposite of what you believe, what's gonna lead to fear, guilt, and then anger, or at best all three followed by denial – total denial of what a stupid cunt you've been. Catch-madrift?"

Nods.

"Mate, seriously, it happens to the best of us. So my advice to you is to get out of this nuthouse at the earliest, procure yourself a good gun, and go out there and do something positive for your community of choice. You won't regret it. Alright," I concludes, getting up. "You have one year. Open the coffers."

Chapter 23

The Plot Thickens…

I awoke in bed, screaming, thrashing about like a sweaty fish,

"Grrrretel! Cunt! I know what she wants, his legs! It's not his fault! Gotta tell him, gotta tell him she wants his legs and—"

Red-hot nails hammered deep into my brain. A pair of golden cat's eyes glared at me from the face of my alarm clock. I chucked the fucking thing across the room, and curled up into a ball.

"Are you okay my champion?"

Brid, snuggling up beside me.

"Nah, not okay! No more weird-shit, alright?"

She giggles. "What weird shit?"

"You know what I mean, all your transdimensional reincarnational astral claptrap! It's driving me fucking bananas. Seriously."

"Another nightmare, hmmm… Do you recall any of it?"

"Trapped in this horrible place… it felt like Dresden, back in the War… but it wasn't… it was here, but like the Nazis had won…"

"No owl-worshiping Satanists, then."

"Nah, just a talking cat… and that young knob again… and this huge fleet of flying boats! It was like a film; they were beautiful, they were…"

"Beautiful, I know, for aeons they have defended the border-realms of our locale from the shadow realms beyond. Of course, the Lyraquai Nations have warred with the Lords of Shadow too—"

"Codswallop," I snap, "I don't wanna hear it. But, wait… suck my thorny cock!"

"Okay—"

"Almost forgot! I saw that world again, the clean world from the Dream! Forests, Brid, it's so simple, we *need* to grow them all back!"

"They grow themselves, my love—"

"That's what I *mean*, we've gotta *let* them all grow back to normal! It's vital, they'll provide everything we need!"

"Shhh, go back to sleep," she croons, "You are right, when the great forests return, all will be, as it was meant to be. Take comfort, for that which can still be imagined, may never be truly lost." And running her hand over my shaven head, for a long time I was content to simply lie there; relishing the realness of the sheets on my body, staring at the ceiling, slowly drifting into a sky of golden dreams...

Sorry you had to find out about our plans for regime change like that, I mean with us turning on the waterworks in front of Brid, and a fit-bird an' all – probably all sounds a bit naff now, coming in on the first stage of operations; just a couple of old codgers stockpiling weapons down a basement in South London. Would have told you earlier, but I'd kind of planned on cutting you in with a bit more, I dunno... flair.

Then again, overthrowing governments' big skulduggery; you were gonna find out one way or another.

Now, listen up. Devil-worship and personal issues aside, it must be confessed here that as the weeks rolled on, the emphasis was subtly shifting away from our noble intentions to save the Nation, to an equally noble objective of saving our woman. Problem was, we didn't know what we was up against.

The Illuminati, according to Brid, and all that Satanist malarkey was only the tip of the iceberg – their foot soldiers, as I understood it, which isn't saying much.

Sid's an electrical engineer, a right genius all told, and even he didn't know what to make of half her blather. And I'm self-educated, as I said – what the Craft didn't teach us, the Craft taught us to teach ourselves – but all that religious codswallop had always got my goat. They all need their heads testing, I'm serious. Think about it.

Go tell a shrink there's an invisible man living in the sky watching your every move; you'll be on the happy-pills quicker than shit off a shovel.

Fair enough.

But call this invisible man 'God,' tog-up with a purple dress and a shepherd's crook – even though you've got no sheep – and what happens?

People fall at your feet and give you money!

Fucking hilarious...

Except I don't get it, mate, I really don't – these people can't be well, and we're surrounded by the fruitcakes.

We rub shoulders with them in shops, on buses, fuck me, we even let them *drive* buses! Isn't there a law against that? They even take children to school, serve food, and a lot of them have *guns*. Yeah, right, wandering about the streets armed to the fucking teeth!

People what believe invisible men live in the sky, I shudder too, mate, I really do. I remember when the Chaplains used to come out to the Port of London and consecrate the ships – they'd bless boats, tanks, cannons, landmines, you name it – and one time I did ask, had to, made me nervous; they were stalking around these 40mm two-pounders waiting to be shipped, making a rare auld racket with their incantations and holy water.

"Gentlemen," I says, "Please, careful around all this equipment, they're not toys."

About turns, and the cunt goes, "Oh there's no need to worry, my son, the good Lord knows his own."

"Never a truer word," I affirms, respectfully, "Just be careful anyways, that's all I'm saying..." and then I paused for a ponder, glancing at the ammo cases piled up all over.

I ventures, "May I ask why... I mean what, exactly, are you doing?"

"Blessing these cannons," he says, impatiently, so I thought fuck it, leave them to it, I suppose.

"Right," I says, "Carry on, just be sure God doesn't stop them working, ay!" I chuckles – bit cheeky, I know, just slipped out.

"Oh no," he declares, "These are the Lord's cannons now."

And then he nods, all solemn, and goes back to his incantations – I froze on the spot.

The Lord's Cannons?

Alright, I was not a well man even back then, first to admit it, and neither was that the first time I'd seen them consecrating our weaponry – just the first time I'd actually stopped to consider the 'whats and whys' – but I still knew the difference between something virtuous and holy, and an instrument of butchery and torment.

Blimey, doesn't matter how you dress it up. God is on one side of the fence, all-loving and good. A 40mm two-pounder is way, waaaaaay on the other side, giving you a whopping headache, at best, and it did – the Lord's Cannons pounded the truth straight between my eyes:

We are on our own.

You see, I hadn't rightly known it until then, but, deep down, a part of me had always believed in some kind of divine presence; something what was all-powerful and all-good, what looks out for us and *cares*. But I knew it then alright. I knew because I felt that part of me being snuffed out, instantly, annulled into the barren stupidity of what that cunt had just said.

Never looked back after that, seventh of September 1940, that was – the day the 'good Lord' did a pukka job sanctifying our cannons and Gerry's bombers an' all – the day the Blitz started, and the day I finally realised that even if there was a God, and it was suddenly a big IF, then He's sure as spit one fuck of an almighty evil cunt.

Sid was right though, it was different with Brid. She was classy, clever and upfront. And hiding in the basement, what worried Sid and me no end. It kind of made her story seem truer, and yet made her seem crazier than she already was.

Though we didn't know what, we were both convinced somebody was after her; she was scared and that part was real. The two cunts what nearly did a hatchet job on her in the street were real enough too, well, only one was now, if ya catch-madrift. And he was still out there, and had copped a good eyeful of me finishing off his mate to boot. Along with half the Satanists in North London, no doubt.

Cause for concern?

Nah, not really. Most the effort's in looking for the cunts, so if they want you, let them come to you – was always my motto – just be ready for when they do.

I always was.

In other regards, all our efforts were now on expanding our two operations. The Firm was growing, it was well-out of hand, neither Sid nor I knew how many we had in our 'honorary infantry,' nor did we particularly care.

The funds continued to pour in beyond our greatest expectations; we continued to pay our dues to the bigger Firms, smaller Firms paid their dues to us. Didn't even know who anymore, the boys now dealt with the uppity cunts – Boris and Igor, turned up trumps.

Everything was growing and coming together nicely.

Sid and I go down into the command centre that evening, and fuck me sideways; you could kit out the Congo with what we had. Only problem was, there was still nobody over seventy in the Operation except us. All our auld acquaintances had either vanished from the face of the Earth, two pegs short, or were pushing up daisies.

Or most likely working for Military Intelligence, much the same, all told – and that's where our little genius comes in,

"Finished editing the first draft of the Constitution," she pipes up over the typewriter, "It's done like a chain-letter, but grew into more of a handbook, than what we first had in mind. I hope that's okay with you, but I felt we need to provide information as well; home-made explosives, where and how to appropriate ammo, equipment and so on, just in case it gets passed to people who need the info. What do you think?"

Truthfully, all this 'we' business was a bit unsettling, specially from a bird openly admitting to have escaped from the Funny Farm, but she was in now, and yeah, hats off to her, doing a lovely job too.

Sid peers over her shoulder at the booklet, "What now then?"

"We need to distribute them, selectively at first, that's the next step, and then let it spread."

"You did write up the Dream, though," I asks.

"Of course," she passes me her booklet. "All there in the first section, Easy Logic, everything we've been talking about; following your nature, trapped in infinity, changing yourself through self-forgiveness and direct action. So I reserved the sociological infrastructure of decentralised communities for the next section.

No flags, no leaders," she smiles. "Natural law. There's a section on reforestation, the *Magna Carta*, Zappers, interest free money, SIS black ops and psyops – everything nice and simple, 'no poncy bollocks,' like you said."

"I'm impressed, good work," I muttered, flicking through the pages, and then stalled. "'The Earth's A Battlefield Between Two Forces: Food And Shit'…" I looks up, "Sid?"

Sid nods, "My personal contribution. A section on cleaning up landfill sites and capitalising on their methane emissions, combined with converting sewage treatment plants into methane digesters."

"Like the ones we used for the tractors, in the last war."

"Same principle, only bigger. Methane gas, a hundred percent ecological and one hundred percent free. Within a year, every household will be self-sufficient with a never-ending supply of free energy and," flourish of hand, stage bow, "organic fertiliser."

I smiles at that, "Good rates for organic fertiliser, these days."

"And easily done."

"Easily done," affirms Brid, "Oh, and another fax came in from The City, what shall I do with it?" Reaches into the filing cabinet beside her, hands me a memo. Mark again, some kind of Brazilian Rainforest acquisition thing, with loads of graphs. I'll give you the short version this time:

In order for humans to maintain normal health and bodily function, we need to breathe an atmosphere with a minimum 15% oxygen content.

Oxygen levels for the last 50 million years were relatively constant at between 30-38%.

As recently as 2,000 years ago, the oxygen content of the Earth's atmosphere was still between 30-38%.

Any less than 6-8% oxygen and life can no longer be sustained. It is a fundamental and immutable fact of our physiology. With increasing deforestation, the oxygen level in our atmosphere has now been reduced to less than 16% and as little as 11% in the most impacted areas.

At these reduced levels, the body cannot function at full efficiency. Oxygen starvation causes hormonal imbalance and genetic mutations; cells, bodily organs and the immune system is compromised – cancers and degenerative diseases increase; natural brain function and hormone production is impaired.

Greatest cause of deforestation: Livestock.

According to the UN IPCC report 'Livestock's Long Shadow,' livestock production is the main contributor to global warming, more than all the transportation in the world.

With industrial waste pollutants reducing oxygen production levels in our oceans too – discharged sewage, landfill run-off, etc – and at the current rate (exponentially) of deforestation, we have LESS THAN 60 YEARS OF OXYGEN LEFT.

Regards, M.M.

"It's good," I replies, "But if he sends us another fax here, I swear on my eyes, he'll be running out of air with my mitts around his jugular! But it's good, this. Trim it down, put it with the reforestation section. Dead right, for fuck's sake, *trees*, it's not rocket science—"

"And this too," she sighs, handing me another memo, "It's related."

Industrial Hemp and Biofuels. In 1892, Rudolph Diesel invented the diesel engine, which he designed to run on 'a variety of fuels, especially vegetable and seed oils.' And Henry Ford built the first cars using a robust plastic made from wheat straw, hemp and sisal, stronger than steel—

"I'll give this a proper look later," I says, folding the memo into my pocket, "After I've opened his throat with a spoon—"

"Joe," Sid cuts in, "I do know my onions, mate, our phone line's scrambled." Turns to Brid, "So how do we get these distributed?"

"By Post," says Brid. "We search service records, find veterans over seventy, and post it to them, direct."

Sid groans, "What, to any old Tom, Dick and Harry?"

"What's wrong, my love," she asks.

Sid begins pacing, rubbing his forehead.

"I don't know… I expect some will be up for it, we'll see, but what if somebody goes to the Old Bill?"

Stops in front of me, glares, all serious.

I laughed, "And what are they gonna do? Bang up some old cunt for possession of a pamphlet—"

"Not just any old pamphlet, that's a call to arms!"

"Right enough," I muttered, rereading the front cover. "'The Trusty Terrorist's Illuminati Handbook For Lawful Rebellion And Armed Uprising.' Hmmm! Change the title there, Brid. Something a little less hectic—"

"But I thought we were going after Craftsmen first."

"Sid, our lot would be the first on my list, but if they're not brown bread, they're most likely working for SIS."

"And so?"

"Are you off your tits—?"

"Shitfaced."

"Ay?"

"Whacky-backy. Pukka hash, this."

Reaches into his breast pocket, lights up a joint.

Brid shrugs guiltily, "Helps with concentration."

They giggle.

Oh bloody hell…

"Nah, listen you two, cunts like MI7 and all that, wipe your tracks clean off."

Sid nods. "And who's in charge of propaganda and censorship?"

I pause. "MI7. Catch-yadrift… joint ay, good shit?"

"*Unbelievably* good shit."

"Smells good. Can I have some?"

"Not in here. You know what happens."

"Oh go on, it's been a long time, I won't get antisocial—"

"Antisocial? Hows about hostile, cruel and despotic—?"

"That's not true, don't listen to him! I had some coke with Rachael that time and it was totally inspirational. Nothing happened, *nothing.*"

Huffs, "Inspired to do what, exactly?"

Walkabout – "Nothing."

"Admit it, you go fucking bananas on drugs."

"Do you dear?"

"And he loves it," says Sid, exhaling a plume of smoke. "Even the happy-pills the army shrinks sometimes gave us would send him barmy. Remember?"

"Alright, yeah, but I used to love a joint, I did, especially after a recce—"

"Yeah, right, especially just after you've—"

"Either way," Brid gently interrupts, "at the very least it will ring a bell or two," she smiles. "I agree with Joe – fire them out to as many Veterans as we can; it's done like a chain-letter anyway. We'll get our army, you'll see. All good things come to those who wait."

"Alright," says Sid. "It's like feeding pigeons then. We let the plot thicken, wait and see which of the big gulls bite."

Chapter 24

The Peeler Always Rings Twice

And that's exactly what we did; printed, posted, and waited – well, exactly what we got the Firm to do – and a week later, an ex-serviceman called Russell is sitting on a bench in Regents Park, feeding the ducks with another ex-serviceman called Marcus.

I looks Marcus up and down again, not a bad looking bloke; would've still cut a fine vicious trim if he weren't in all that Royal Chelsea clobber. I continue to explain,

"You can't," I says, "Get you and your boys out of that shit-hole and into a proper gaff."

"By the sea then."

"Anywhere you like."

"Fancy Portsmouth myself, always did like it by the sea. But I can't vouch for my mates – they're game on principle, but a little stayed in their ways."

"I catch-yadrift. Just need a wakeup call. Pass on my offer, see how they feel."

Lowers his tone, "And you'll finance us, get us all the equipment we need to get started as well."

"Everything you like." I throws the last of my bread into the lake, dust my hands, turns to him, "Both wars? Don't look old enough."

He laughs, "Nor you! But cheers; everybody says that. Took the King's Shilling at sixteen, just caught the tail end of the First; Artillery." Lowers his tone again, "Never spill your seed unless it's for procreation."

"Oh?" says I – first thing they taught us in the Craft – "Who told you that, then?"

"Indian chap, Bombay. Does the trick, fit as fiddle, me," he winks.

"Must give it a go then."

"India," he sighs, "Seems like five minutes ago now."

I nods. "All said and done, mate, I reckon it's all going to seem like five minutes."

"Never a truer word." Chucks his bread into the lake.

"What regiment were you in for the Second?" I asks.

"Regiment? SBS, my friend."

"Proper order."

"Well they didn't give us much of a choice."

"Never do."

"Go where you're told."

"Do as you're told."

Raises a bushy grey eyebrow.

"SAS," I half-lied.

"Thought so. Blimey, but they've got it good these days," nod, nod, "First-rate training; glow in the dark compasses, waterproof kit."

"Doesn't mean diddlysquat; can't beat experience."

"Tell me about it. First time I'd ever even been on a plane was the first time I had to jump out of it! A week they gave us, before our first jump."

"Us too. A week leaping off barrage balloons, and that's it, all aboard."

"A Whitley, it was, noisy thing."

"And cold, yeah, hated them," I says, "Flying rust buckets."

"Froze your bollocks off; drunk a gallon of tea laced with rum on my first recce."

"As you do."

"As you do. Bursting, we were, all the way to the coast. Norway."

"Wet jumps, blimey, I dunno how you boys did it."

"Didn't that time, miles off the drop-point. Straight over the ruddy harbour, swept by artillery and machinegun fire, across the beach and behind enemy lines! Dunno how I got out of that one."

"Never do."

"Improvise, adapt, overcome," he chuckles, "Leg it! What did you do after the War?"

"Moved onto greater things," I winks.

He winks back, "Very well, I better be off then, pass this on to the boys. T-Day has knocked years off them too—"

"Come again? Tea what?"

"T-Day, 'T' for Thirteenth," says he, "That's what one of the boys started calling it, and it caught on."

"Hold on," I says, "Who else in Royal Chelsea know about this?"

Shrugs. "Everybody."

Fuck me…

"Although not everybody's game, unfortunately, and a lot who say they are, aren't, not really. Oh they'll swear and shake their fists at Thatcher on the telly – and I keep telling them, blimey, we're heroes; what can they do to do to us?"

"Plenty, mate, and pray that they do," I mutter, "pray they're that thick."

Nods, "They'd have the whole Country up in arms! Blimey, but some are game, oh yes. Some. Men like us, we know there was never anything to lose, and everything to gain by trying."

"Never a truer word."

"As you say, Russell, all they need is a wakeup call. I have mine…"

I raise an eyebrow.

He replies, "How long do we have left, ten, fifteen years at most and to do what? Rot in front of the telly, feed these daft buggers?" He chucks the last of his bread at the ducks, and nods at me, "It's regrettable how you got yours, it is, but wake up call? Every time I look in a mirror, that's my wake up call."

We sat in silence for a bit, him staring at his hands, me gazing at the thick, sombre clouds gathering for a summer storm. The Organisation was growing! Blimey. What had I done? Then I saw ourselves sitting there, two old codgers like countless others, sitting on their lonely benches, wrapped in their private revelry, reminiscing their lives over, and over and suddenly I felt so small, mate, so fucking insignificant…

No, not insignificant, worse, *forgotten.*

"Purpose," he mutters to himself, standing up.

I gets up too, shake his hand, "Alright, you look after yourself, Marcus, we'll be in touch."

"Pleasure to meet you sir," he beams.

"Pleasure's all mine, sir."

And that's how it went. Met with Marcus and his crew a couple of times after that – well-up for it, didn't give monkey's win or lose, point was having a go – did wonders to dispel any doubts. That's the best thing about dealing with our lot; they know their onions and follow orders. The impossible is possible, always, don't need telling twice.

Did a fair bit of travelling about in the following months, up to various Homes up and all over the Land – from Glasgow to the Isle of Wight – it was amazing the interest, I was well-chuffed.

Feeling invincible.

They came round early, half-six. We was already up, all three of us, though it was Sid's turn on Brid Patrol that week so they were poling upstairs when the bell rings, and the knock came. Why do they always do that, you'd think one or the other would do.

Silly cunts.

"Good morning Mr Barbelo," says Roger the Plod.

"Good morning PC May," says I, scanning the car outside. One in the back, one in the front, not a good sign.

"I hope we're not disturbing you?"

Well I pay you enough so ya fucking don't!

"Not at all officer."

"Would you mind accompanying us to the Station?"

"Not at all. What's it about?"

"Just routine, nothing to worry about."

Routine? It was something to worry about then.

"I'll just throw something on, bit nippy out here, ay?"

He nods. "Taters."

I shut the door, peg it upstairs, and bang on Sid's door.

"Come in!"

Brid, poised behind the net curtain, grenade launcher over her shoulder, grinning like a cat.

Sid at the window beside her, bollock-naked, joint hanging out of his gob, grinning like a cunt,

"Not yet, my lovely, hold… easy… let the feharchrove move closer to their car, that's it, we'll get the lot, hold…"

"For the love of Christ!"

"What's that mate?" asks Sid, concentrating on their slaughter.

"Put that down!"

"She can't, nearly got them… hold… FIRE!"

I throw my hands over my ears – force of habit.

Click!

He laughs. "What's wrong? We're only eliminating feharchrove." He taps his head. "In our *minds*."

She lowers the RPG, "Forgive me, Joe, we were only—"

"Need you to call Rachel. I'm being taken down the Station."

"The brief," echoes Sid. "Alright. Why though, everything's in proper order – just tell them to go away."

"You sure Mark's memos aren't being intercepted—"

"For the hundredth time, Joe, the phone line's scrambled!"

"Right enough, all's well," I mutter, except I should never have sent Chris' missus those flowers. Who's stupid idea was that? And fuck me, that card, that card – I Am Really Sorry For What I did. It Was An Ethical Decision—

Stupid, stupid, stupid cunt! Leastways I couldn't think of anything else what wasn't in proper order – everybody was either brown bread or on the payroll – and child-murdering owl-worshipers aren't likely to go moaning to the Old Bill, are they?

Fucking conscience.

I nods back to Sid, "Go easy on the whacky-backy, I think I know what this is about; serious situation."

Grins, holding up his joint, "Telling you too, *serious* hash this. Reminds me of '47."

"Palestine?"

"Can't remember."

"Never mind, just call Rachel, she'll know what to do." I turn, pause, and about-turn. "Oh bollocks, pass us that Joint then."

Looks at me funny, "Promise you're really going out."

"Give me it…"

I togged-up in a jiffy, all pukka; suit, overcoat, memorial pen, glasses – never needed them but it's always good for official occasions. The 'intellectual look.' Statically, the odds of a specy going down are ridiculously low compared to the fully-sighted.

And one-legged geezers are practically unheard of in Nick, ask anybody.

So nah, I don't know what I was worried about, but I was. I stood in front of the mirror, smoking my joint, thinking take your time, Joe, let the cunts wait outside freezing their bollocks off, why not? What do we pay them for anyways?

And then the root of my feverish fretting hit me in a smoky nebula of narcotic comprehension.

Time!

Those Peelers outside had all the time in the world to freeze their bollocks off, but I didn't have a moment to spare.

Prison?

Until that point I didn't give a monkey's, even with all the skulduggery we was up to, I mean, what's the worse they could do to a couple of old geezers like us? All the tea we want and let us doss about all day?

Lovely.

Well, that's what I'd thought, but at that precise moment I realised I didn't just not want to go down, specially not like that, not for some spotty cunt in a dole office, conscience or no – and by the way, apart from the Monthlies, I'd hardly good'uned at all, not since all my soul-searching the day I nearly shot Sid – no, I had the purpose now, I didn't want to go down for any reason.

Couldn't afford one minute off my life doing or being anywhere I didn't want. Fucking wasted half of it doing exactly that. Wasn't going out in no Nick, not for all the tea in China. If I was going out, I was going out in a blaze of glory!

Until then, I wanted to live, and that meant I needed time, *my time* – for shooting AKs, poling Brid and eating chocolate pudding or whatever. And alright, yeah, a job's a good'un now and then, if the cunt deserved it.

Love is Freedom?

Time is Freedom, time for following your nature – that seemed the whole key to natural law now.

Pukka gear alright…

Sid was at the top of the landing. I signed him with my hands to burn the gaff and scarper if I wasn't heard of within the hour. Up north, if you're asking, we'd appropriated loads of kitted out bunkers since just after the War days. He signed back for Canada, paranoid cunt, what I okayed with a simple nod.

Much the same, all told. The point was not to get caught poling an escaped nut-job with an armoury the size of Africa in your cellar.

I opened the door to the frost and the Peelers waiting outside…

Chapter 25

Shitfaced Down the Cop-shop

The room they took us into was requisitioned from the Gestapo; stone green walls, low ceiling, light bulb on the blink.

The blond cunt sitting at the desk *was* Gestapo – leastways I'd bet my good peg that he was – never shat myself so much around Old Bill in all my days! It was truly horrible, threw me back forty years. I just stood there, swaying, I was in Dresden again, cyanide capsule on my tongue.

Pukka gear alright.

"Captain Joseph Williams Barbelo," he mutters, without taking his eyes off the file on his desk. "Hmmm, my goodness… interesting… ahhh, very interesting. Forgive me," he declares, looking up, "I'm Inspector Philips, from the Yard. Please, take a seat."

Scotland Yard? Dammit, not on the payroll then, not ours leastways.

I sits down. Roger the Plod stands against the wall behind, making me the cunt on the lighthouse stool – it doesn't get worse.

"This won't take long, we hope," Gestapo Geezer jokes, flashing me that smile what means it could take fucking months. "As you are probably aware, we've been investigating a particularly nasty series of violent crime of late. Heard anything?"

"Bitte geehrter Herr?"

"I'm sorry?"

"I mean, forgive me officer, but no, I wasn't aware" – fuck only knows what Boris and Igor get up to – "Probably them new Darkies," I declare. "I don't get out much, wooden peg, see?"

"Yes, so I see, Dresden," he says, and goes back to the file.

I try to read it upside-down. Can't, all the letters swim about, though I'd kill for an apple crumble with chocolate pudding–

"Nice cane," Roger the Plod, stepping up, "Can I have a quick look?"

Are you out of your fucking mind – *defile* Happy Stick?

"Yes, of course Roger."

"Walnut?"

"Chocolate."

Hickory!

"I mean Hickory; can I have my last cigarette please?"

Placing Happy Stick by my chair again, he passes me a fag with a puzzled eye, and resumes his post at the wall.

Gestapo Geezer triumphs, "Right, I think we have everything here! P.C. May, you can bring them in now."

"Yes sir," plodding out the door.

We sat in silence, him reading all about my life of slaughter and mayhem; me, head spinning from here to Mars, sweating like a pig.

My left eye was twitching, it never does that. I was fucking losing my perspective, and I knew it.

Nothing feels worse than knowing it.

"Inspector Philips, what's all this about, exactly? I can explain about the flowers, 'ethical decision,' you see, Kate was a friend of mine, no! I mean an *acquaintance*—"

He glances up briefly, "Really? I do a bit of gardening too, as it goes, roses mostly."

"Gardening? Ha! We've got loads in common then; I'm growing forests, yep, great big giant forests and industrial hemp; everything was made of hemp back in the days. Listen to this!" I declares, taking out a Mark Memo, going full-peg into my narcotic chatter,

"Arguably the most versatile plant known to man, hemp can be used to produce paper, medicine, textiles, clothes, food, biofuel, biodegradable plastics – it is extremely fast growing and requires little to no pesticides, no herbicides, controls topsoil erosion *and* produces oxygen. *Oxygen*, see?

In addition, hemp can replace a multitude of harmful materials, such as petroleum-based plastics and cosmetics – which do not decompose easily – and tree paper, which uses chlorine bleaches and other toxic chemicals, *and* contributes heavily to deforestation.

Deforestation, Inspector Tulips, Spectra *Phillips*, this is *serious!* We needs oxygen! Luckily, trees *do* make oxygen, and breathe in carbon dioxide. Therefore, *therefore*, chop them down and we're all up shit creek without a paddle!"

Glances up from my file again, "Ahem… remarkable…"

"Yeah, that's what I thought. And luckily we've got a lot of shit too, ay! We're full of it," I chuckles. "So, more trees, make everything from hemp again. And *methane* gas – that's nature's paddle for our shit creek. I mean, think of all that discharged sewage; running into the sea, the rivers, our *water supply!* Wasted, when it can be *used.*"

"Fascinating…"

"We'll run every home, automobile, and power station in the Land on methane and hemp biofuel. Sorted. Stuff petrol, diesel and all that codswallop – *total* self-sufficiency – get everybody off that national grid rip-off with their *own* methane digesters. Never have to pay a fuel bill again!" I tap impatiently on the table. "Can I go now?"

"Hmmm?" grins, "Oh, don't worry about all this, I'm sure it's nothing to worry about. Light?"

I nods, fumbling conspicuously with my specs, take a good long pull on my fag, sizing up the cunt through a veil of smoke. Here I am, out of the goodness of my own *heart,* explaining how to save the entire fucking planet – and nothing, fluoridated to high heaven, lobotomised, attention span of a fruit fly. Why even bother?

Nah, to gut him or not to gut him; that is the question—

"Interesting file?" I asks.

"Never seen anything quite like it in all my years!" he beams. "You must be very proud, Mr Barbelo, very proud."

"So you don't know what this is about."

"'Fraid not." Raises his eyes to the ceiling, standard code for govermentals. "There's some kind of conference with the Americans," he whispers, "In The City, orders came from there."

Shrugs, concern etching across his brow,

"Are you alright, Mr Barbelo? I'm sure this is just routine for a man with your distinguished service record. Can I get you a cuppa?"

I smiles at that, "If you make it with spring water, yeah, thanks."

"What's wrong with the tap?" he chuckles.

Definitely, last fucking straw; gut the stupid cunt, go home and compost his innards – put him to good use.

"What's wrong with tap water? I'll tell you what's fu—"

Half way out my chair, Happy Stick in hand, Gestapo Geezer suddenly stands up and fucking salutes! I spins around, two suits wearing shades stride in, and bloody hell, they was all saluting…

At me?

Chapter 26

Dying For Chocolate Pudding…

Nah, nah, of course they weren't saluting me! Had me going too though. No, they were saluting the geezer what came in immediately after the two suits. A fucking Yank, a General, Air Force, I shit you not, a real one.

I stood up and saluted the cunt – slashing his throat in my mind. His CIA spooks, or whatever they was, file out leaving us both alone.

"Captain Barbelo, call me George," he grins, settling down at the desk with my file and a briefcase.

"Pleasure to meet you, John, I mean… are you sure?"

Fuck me sideways if the cunt isn't the spit of John Wayne!

"George, George, *George* – call me Mr Barbelo."

I smiles.

He frowns, "You're a man who likes to do things the straight way, I can see that, so I will be straight with you. Please, take a seat."

I do, glancing at the wall clock above him. I'd not been here long; forty minutes before Sid torches the gaff. There was time. He would still be packing or poling, either way, I was safe now – shitfaced, serious munchies but otherwise present and correct – leastways none of this was about gutting the Doley.

Opens his briefcase, takes out a file. Aerial photos of Railton Road spill out onto the desk.

"That's my street," I mutter.

Nods, all serious, "AKA the Frontline; drugs, murders, yes, I know what you are thinking, we do indeed think alike. Something must be done, and your house, Mr Barbelo, is situated on prime location for surveillance of these vile, drug-fuelled crimes of violence, would you agree?"

Agree? I couldn't understand a fucking word this nut was on about. What crimes of violence?

Truth was, the Frontline was probably the most laidback areas in South London, had been for as long as. Self-policed by the Firms what lived local, never a Copper in sight, which is why Sid and I chose the spot – and drugs? The only drugs you could get was weed and hash, very good hash as I'd just found out, what made good business sense an' all, if you wanted your customers to come back.

Any cunt caught selling smack there got their kneecaps popped.

"The time has come," he prattles on, "The time to serve your Country once again, Mr Barbelo, the time to stand up, and with the Lord's help, make a difference…"

He pauses.

"You need me to do what, exactly, sir."

"We need your expert knowledge of the local area and its indigenous population." He grins. "We're finally going to clean up this town."

Fuck me, I suddenly sussed on. CIA? Drugs? My fucking Country? Does he think I floated down the Thames in a bubble?

Alright, let me explain. I was one of theirs, that's how they look at you, forever; sign on the dotted line and you never get out, same as any Firm.

So, what this cunt sees isn't just a model citizen, he sees a good bit of kit: a Vet what never gave cause to have his loyalty questioned, was a brilliant killing machine in his time, lived in South London since the start of the century and now smack in the epicentre of their intended territory to boot. I was perfect for the job! Catch-madrift?

No?

Blimey. If you really want to know what's going in the world around you, you've really gotta start learning to think like a cunt. It's run by cunts, govermentals – English, Yank or fucking Chinese, all a shower of cunts.

So whatever they say, turn it on its head 'cos it means the reverse.

All that drivel about nasty drugs and cleaning up the streets, nah, nah, nah, it means the opposite – keep the drugs coming in, the more the merrier, but take full control of the trade. By trade I mean all street drugs, specially highly addictive ones like heroin and cocaine.

And by full control I mean take full control of everything, from production to supply – everything from invading all those Raghead countries where the crops are grown, to sales and distribution, what means making your Firm on the streets Top Firm; in this case, the Secret Service – sounds fucked at first glance, but it isn't.

Black ops money, you see? Dirty money, funds for the world domination game, and I should know. I make no apologies, of course, but free-lancing (mercenary) was my game for a while too. And I can tell you now, continually destabilising all those Darkie countries costs a bomb, pardon the pun. What, with paying off militias, buying weapons and putting our Top Cunts into power?

Where do you think all that money comes from?

Dictatorships don't grow on trees, they are bought. And govermentals were going full-peg into world domination since what?

1941, I reckon; the United Nations was already a done deal.

We all knew back then the Yank's were financing both sides of the War, leastways until '41, until joining the side most likely to win. So it makes sense that's when Europe's Top Cunts got together for their meet, amalgamated their Firms, sorting out who was going to get what territories – meaning 'Countries.'

All told, World War II was a giant turf war. The decider, in my opinion, after that they all clubbed together and made one giant govermental Firm, which is pretty much what we've got now.

By the way, some of this I learnt from the horse's mouth (Churchill) back in '47, some I sussed out by and by, so when I talk about govermentals and Firms, keep bearing in mind I mean pretty much the same thing. All told it's only words, only difference is one's supposedly legal, the other's not – and it's the Firms with the biggest clout what lay down the law anyways, so what's the difference?

What works on the big end of the scale, works on the small end of the scale. And obviously, you can't go around declaring the funds used to fuck up other countries, fucking up other countries isn't nice. And surely not if you're meant to be the 'good guys.'

And yet the money for black ops has to come from somewhere, hence the illegal drugs trade, and hence why govermentals *need* to keep street drugs illegal – funds to do the illegal stuff they need to stay Top Firm.

Yeah, I know, it's hard to get your head around it at first. Specially 'cos it doesn't end there, why should it?

Imagine. You're a top cunt in Top Firm – the govermentals. You have a finger in every pie, everything with the illegal tag you put on it – spoils of war, *you* get to decide from prostitution to gunrunning what's legal and what isn't – all other Firms have to pay their dues.

The legal funds you put on the books, declared and public, the illegal funds you don't – you use that to fund more skulduggery.

So, next time you watch the News, think of it like any Firm would and it'll all be clear as a bell. Though it's even easier if you're Top Cunt; you don't need a dodgy car lot to launder your dirty money, you can laugh all the way to the bank, straight to the bank you own anyways.

"George," I says, "I need to make a phone call, please."

"Can't it wait?"

"No."

"Oh I am sure it can wait. We have another issue here that you, I know, a man of your calibre will appreciate."

I was appreciating the 9mm Makarov materialising in my paw – I check the clock on the wall again; half an hour left, well, five minutes here, five minutes there... and then I double-check with mine and it boldly declares I've just nineteen minutes.

Nineteen minutes before Sid torches the gaff, vanishing into darkest Canada with my fit-bird and our dreams of saving humanity. Sorry, *our* fit-bird.

"George, this is a very important call."

I hear something drop.

"What's more important than serving one's Country?"

"Fucking cunt," I pick up Happy Stick, "I mean nothing sir. Just got to call my girlfriend."

He eyes me suspiciously.

"I mean my granddaughter."

He stares.

"They are very alike," I says.

"Your granddaughter's girlfriend?"

"What? No! I mean my granddaughter's *like* my girlfriend, no! I mean same *age*, see? Gawd blimey, *what* do you take me for—?"

"Are you okay Mr Barbelo? There's no mention of a granddaughter on your file."

That's 'cos I made her up, you cunt! And that's 'cos I needed some kinda proper thing to stop me going fucking *insane,* you cunt, 'cos I've never had a fucking proper life, you cunt – 'cos cunts like you were always making me do things what weren't fucking proper!

"Blimey," I mutter, "Did I say all that out loud?"

Looks at me funny, "Is this a test?"

"What? Please, I just need to make one phone call, sir."

"There are no phones in this room."

"I'll use the one upstairs then."

"I don't understand—"

"Just two ticks, *the one at the Sergeant's desk.*"

"Ahhh," he sighs, "Now I understand. You *are* testing me, as a man of your integrity must! Impeccable. I cannot permit your request, Mr Barbelo, we have not concluded. In the interest of national security, you cannot leave this room without the authorisation of a British Officer. Ours is not to reason why, these rules exist to protect our great nations' welfare—"

Bastards! They're always moving the goalposts, I swear they make it all up as they go along – I shut my ears, listening to my conscience. Was this situation worth a job's a good'un?

I dunno. Never got messy with a US General before. Breathe deep. Restraint.

"—and the other issue concerns the creation of a little *disturbance.*"

I perks up at that, "A disturbance."

"For God and Country?"

I shook my head, at first, and then I saw what this cunt was driving at, "You need another riot, the last one wasn't enough."

Chuckles, "We need many more to consolidate our position, *Ordo ab Chao*, my good Captain, 'Order out of Chaos.'"

"I understand."

"And we need solid Intel," he adds with a sly grin, "You will be leading a team working to determine who best to take out first, and when: maximum impact, combined arrests, nothing you haven't accomplished before but I suggest…" pauses, flips out a file from his case, and flops it with a thud in front of me. "Read this file, diligently, it outlines your remit within the current political climate."

Diligently? File? That's not a file, that's the fucking Yellow Pages!

My heart sunk into my gut. I pick up the tome:

TOP SECRET

"Sir, I formally request authorisation to conclude this briefing."

"All in due course, when you read that, we will proceed to discuss the importance of this Operation—"

"It is a matter of life and death, SIR!"

He stalls. We glare. He gets up from his desk, slowly, all tight-lipped and in a huff.

"Wait a moment."

And he ups and goes, locking the door behind him. I flick through the file anyway.

Actually, it did read a bit like a phone book; names mostly on the middle pages, recognised a few from some of the local Firms, then maps of London carved up into territories, the usual shit, the last part was a standard homeland black ops manual; splitting up communities where racial integration was happening, leastways on any creative level; a section on the promotion of addictive substances, opiates and all that, and something classed 'crack cocaine,' what sounded nasty as fuck from what I read.

I glance at my watch. Ten minutes.

Visions of Sid and Brid sailing away on an old-fashioned steamer pummelled into my brain. By the time I heard the door being unlocked, they were both in First Class, sipping Champagne after an extremely vicious poling session.

Cunt!

The door opens, the Yank swaggers back in, slowly settles into his chair opposite me, and smiles.

"There's been a delay," he triumphs. "The Officer in question has been held up in traffic—"

Traffic?

If you've never seen John Wayne skewered by the throat to a chair in a cop-shop, don't worry, neither had I until now.

It was over. I'm not saying it didn't feel good, but I'd completely muffed it.

Well, almost, but not quite… not if I stopped Sid, and did the right thing – time for chocolate pudding after.

Chapter 27

Friendly Fire

"SNAFU!"

"Joe…?"

"Oh fuck Sid, what've you gone and done now?"

Guilty pause. "Nothing."

"Never mind, listen carefully. SNAFU!"

"SNAFU. Roger and out."

I replace the receiver. The Sergeant at the front desk glances up from his football magazine,

"Anything else, Mr Barbelo."

"Can't remember… chocolate pudding, I think, more than anything…"

Smiles, "I've something better." Slides a brown envelope across the desk. "Your 'Christmas' present."

"Oh lovely. How many this time?"

"Eleven of the worst of the worst."

"Got any priests?"

"I don't think so."

"Pity. Thanks Rob," I says, and I goes over to the front door, scan the street outside, one last time considering doing a runner, but headed back downstairs to the Gestapo Room instead. It was pissing it rain anyway.

Was pegging the last flight of stairs, when Rachel, our General and Brief, was climbing up.

"Joseph, there you are!"

"Here I am," says I, thrusting the dead Yank's briefcase into her arms. "Take this, please give it to Sid."

"What's going on here?" sniff, sniff, "I tried, but they actually refused to—"

"No time to explain, I've done something I know I shouldn't have, but I did. Was gonna scarper, but," I raise my finger to make the point. "I think it's all gonna be alright now. Laters."

"I don't think that's a good idea, there's something fishy—"

"Said go, that's an order! And don't even think about billing me for it," I jests, but without another word, she ups the stairs and goes. Turning up trumps, was our Rachel.

I continue down to my carnage.

As you know, sidling away calm as you like from the slaughter is one of my specialities. And I suppose you're asking, why? Why not shuffle the pack again, let Sid blow the gaff and disappear into the sunset with my, our lovely fit-bird? After all, I'd muffed it up good and proper.

Yes, no, and maybe; but scarper now and it's game over. Staying put, I stood a minimal chance of saving myself and our entire operation. I know it might not look like it, but appearances are almost always deceiving in this game; I still had the edge. And why?

Because I couldn't technically leave until authorised by a British Officer. And that means what?

Use you loaf – *chain of command.*

So you go back, sit tight, stoned off your tits thinking up jokes, in my case, and wait for whoever the fuck's in charge.

(Here's a good one:

Where do you find a US General with a spike in his head?

Where you left him!)

Nah, seriously, I was just sat there, pondering who the devil would reactivate me for this low-down dastardly black ops skulduggery, when who pops his head round the door?

None other than our auld CO from the War. Brigadier Francis Moon, 'Frank the Finger,' on account he always had a finger in every pie, meaning an 'insider' – and Moon on account you wouldn't wanna get on his dark side – fucking diamond in all other respects. Hadn't seen each other in donkey's.

Aged a fair bit, like you're meant to at our age, but I immediately recognise his quick feral grin and David Niven easy manner.

"Morning Joe, sorry I'm late, damn awful traffic."

"Blimey, well I never… Frank?"

He strides in, stalls at the sight of dead cunt, and rolls his eyes,

"Don't bother getting up."

He locks the door. We shake hands.

"I was just pondering who'd be behind this."

Smiles. "Always need a good man on the inside."

"Still in service then?"

"Retired."

(MI5, in other words).

"Oh? What Branch?"

"F Branch."

(Counter-subversion, in other words).

"Shower of cunts."

"Shower of cunts." Glances over to dead cunt. "Still got the nightmares?"

I nods. "You?"

He nods. "Looks like one more to chalk up here," he mutters to himself, and then pipes up, "So Captain, anything to report?"

"Friendly fire," says I, sitting up straight, "Enthusiastic ex-serviceman, decorated to high heaven, eliminates US General in British Police Station."

Nodding his head slowly, Frank folds his arms, leans up against the door, "And our current mission status?"

"Mission status: Captain Barbelo and Dead Cunt; affirmative and expedient resolution thereof."

"Modus Operandi."

"Modus Operandi: Standard MI7 media disinformation package, inquiry and trial. Result: Humiliating loss of confidence in national security, and a fucking Class A international incident. Nobody's happy. Frank looks like a cunt."

He chuckles. "Options."

"Option one: Drive the homicidal maniac to the New Forest and dispose. Result: Fucking Class A in-house international incident. Humiliating loss of confidence in national security, and—"

"And nobody's happy, Frank looks like a cunt." He nods. "Option two?"

I shakes my head. "Negative: Mum's the word, because the moment you copped an eyeful and said nothing, sir, 'option one' was already a car crash up the M1 later this evening."

Frank flashes me his satisfied smile – I wasn't *totally* barmy it seems – but he still says nothing. Whichever way you look at it, this was still a royal pain in the arse for both Firms. But, the thing to always remember about the mortality trade is? It's always rife with mortality – shit happens – and kit goes skewy on you all the time, specially old kit like me; like your proverbial rifle what jams and blows your head off, that kind of thing. Tough titty.

Frank and I stare at each other for a moment, then he turns around and unlocks the door.

"Situation normal then," he sighs, "The Craft accommodates."

"Craft accommodates," I reply, getting up, "Thank you sir, I expect we'll be in touch."

"I expect we will."

We shake hands.

"Oh, before I forget, did you get *something* in the Post?"

He grins. "'Lawful Rebellion?' Came this morning."

So there you go, live and learn. Of course it goes in your favour if a fellow Craftsman's burying your shit, but past credentials aside, much the same goes for anyone who applies the golden rule: always do high profile targets in restricted areas. Give SIS a way out, and the worse they'll do if you get collared is offer you the job… well, probably, but either way it'll be an offer you can't refuse.

What nobody could refuse after all that malarkey was a hearty plate of Bubble, chocolate pudding and a nice cuppa after. Last thing I wanted was going home just yet. I'd caught Sid's sulk on the blower earlier and he'd used my sacred name. He was guilty about something, and Gawd only knows what those two had got up to while I was away. Last thing I saw they were bollock-naked playing with a grenade launcher – practicing jobs a good'uns on disincarnate beings in their minds, or whatever – not going near that on an empty stomach, would you?

Fuck that for a game of soldiers.

It was a little after eight in the morning by the time I left the cop-shop, and there was a good choice of caffs in Brixton in those days, proper jobs – did three course roasts on an equal footing to Bubble and Thai curry – and one of my favourites was on Brixton Hill, appropriately called, The Café on the Hill.

First munchies in decades, this had to be done in proper order, and I could do with a bit of fresh air, so I heads up there full-peg in the pelting rain, my head spinning on about our Peelers, seeing as I wasted half the morning with the cunts and almost killed one.

Nothing against Peelers in the personal sense, don't get me wrong, but you've gotta admit, their entire Firm's a bit naff, isn't it? A bit Mickey Mouse, ay? To Serve and Protect? When's the last time you saw a Peeler, I dunno, leaping out a jam sandwich and bravely fighting off a mugger? Or saving a damsel in distress and all that.

I never have, not once, except on cop shows. And Crime Watch? What on Gawd's Earth is all that about anyways? Can't do their jobs without *us* grassing up crimbos for *them*? Bloody hell, put us all on the payroll then! Personally, I'll happily watch crime for them all day.

I'm not saying they're not brave, people are people, it takes all sorts and there's bound to be loads what's got the bottle. I'm just asking; when was the last time you saw, or even heard of them *actually* protecting anybody? Precisely. Do the maths: we're under siege by psychos of every variety possible, and yet we've hundreds of thousand of Peelers too, all well-trained, paid-up and tooled-up.

We should be hearing about their protecting all day!

Rachael was bang on, the Old Bill are policy enforcers, the heavies collecting revenue for some giant company called the UK. After all, that's what a Firm is, but I reckons there's an additional motive.

Mad Mick went down for twelve years, a child molester gets just three to five – and let back out on the perv in eighteen months. Why? 'Cos Mick served and protected himself.

Can't do that, oh no, had to be taught a lesson, made an example of. Gives people ideas otherwise, namely: *communities*. Right. Last thing the govermental wants, people in charge of their own lives – makes the whole reasoning for the govermental defunct.

Not that your average Peeler's in on the whole game, nah, he's on the bottom rung of this huge ladder, looking up, being told what's supposedly what, and what to do about it, by another cunt above him. And he only knows what he gets told by the cunt above him, who only knows what he gets told by the cunt above him, and so it goes, all the way up to Top Cunt.

Works the same in any Firm, be it police, banks or traffic wardens – chain of command – those on the bottom rung don't have a monkey's of what's really going on at the top. Even though there might be thousands looking up, they'll never suss without the proper Intel. And simply put, that's how those at the top get to stay on top. Even though there's only a handful.

So where's the Peeler when you need them? Auditioning for Starsky and Hutch? Worse, down the Station filing supposed crime reports, hours and hours of ticking boxes and filling out forms when they could've been out on patrol serving their community.

Top Cunt's not a plonker. He knows the difference between crime *prevention* and crime *detection*. Gawd forbid they prevent any true crime, that's the side his bread's buttered! Crime detection's what the average Peeler's forced into – fulfil a quota of arrests, anything will do, it's all about statistics.

Nick a few young'uns for smoking cannabis at the end of the week and it's job done. Peeler's satisfied his quota, and govermentals can waffle on about how much we supposedly need them; scaring people shitless with rising crime waves. Namely all the true crime and misery addiction to street drugs cause – prostitution, muggings, murders and all the rest we have to put up with daily. But, and here's the onion, make all drugs legal and available on the NHS, at no cost for addicts, with quality control and the proper medical attention?

Just for starters; free up some time, money, and resources. Think about it. No cunt's gonna knife you for your pension then, for what? To score some dodgy gear off some idiot down the underpass? Don't be silly! Why they gonna do that, knowing there's pukka gear over the counter at their local chemist? But nah, Top Cunt's making a packet from all the levies on the smaller Firms below, illegal or otherwise – and he's not going to rock the boat, is he?

'Course not, wouldn't be Top Cunt for long if he did.

You've got to remember the Old Bill's a govermental Firm, just another Branch of the Armed Forces, all told, and every Firm needs a good front – and the best fronts of all are the ones what claim you do the reverse of what you're really doing – To Serve and Protect?

Serve and protect who exactly? You, me?

Pull the other one, it's made of wood!

Them, of course, the govermentals. The Old Bill's there to protect them from us, come the day we get sick of being on our knees and fucked up the arse – more on that later.

I pegged it into The Café on the Hill and for the second time in as many hours fucking shat it.

The gaff was packed full of leather-clad warrior lezzies.

Chapter 28

My Only Flaw

Face slashed, three broken fingers, two cracked ribs – fucking miracle I still had my dentures.

Assessing the damage, I pegged, limped, wheezed away from The Café on the Hill, heading full-pelt for the local estate pub round the corner on Water Lane. Knew the landlord well, knew he'd open up for me, and he did.

Crashed through the door.

"Uncle Pete! Uncle Pete!" I was feverish, pushing past. "Lezzies! Lezzies! Nice cup of tea!"

"Mr Barbelo—?"

"Oh for the love of Christ…"

"What happened to you?"

"Oh what a fucking long morning…"

Guides me gently to a seat by the window, "Mr Barbelo, you're bleeding! Sit down and I will—"

"Sit down too with us a moment, ay?"

"You need a doctor—"

"Need Super Glue. Sit down, please."

He pulls up the lighthouse seat. "Who did this?"

"You'll never believe it, mate… never!"

Now, in case you don't recall, Uncle Pete's a *confessor*, as Sid calls these types of people.

The spit of Ray Charles, and with the patience of a saint, Pete doesn't say much, unless asked, but pays attention and is up for any kind of good yarn – laps them up like a little kid. Not in a gullible sense, just up for it. If you're gonna release your inner killer and you haven't got a confessor, get one.

Highly recommended.

I mean, like Sid, I can tell him just about anything and he won't grass, but unlike Sid, he won't judge me neither. Partly 'cos he's a diamond, and partly 'cos civvies don't have a bloody clue what I'm on about anyway, but mostly it's because…

197

Because fuck it, mostly nobody believes me anyway – a good edge, and a curse sometimes: the curse of being under the radar.

"… Blimey, I'm still hungry, what time you opening up?"

"About one hour," he says, and calls over to the back bar, "Jake! Get this gentleman a steak and kidney pie!"

"A nice cuppa, five sugars."

"Go to the café and—"

"No! Don't go round there, there's evil there! I mean there's women there…"

"Evil?"

"Never mind, got any Iodine?"

"No—"

"Detol?"

Shakes his head.

"Detol then, three icepops, Super Glue, forget the grub, and a roll of Sellotape."

"And Sellotape," echoes Jake, and freezes at the door.

"Alright mate," I wheeze, tapping my finger under my eyes, "Good to *see* you again, earning your *respect* I hope? Quick as you like, please, there's a good lad."

Jake scarpers without a word, and I turns to Pete.

"Got any bandages?"

Shakes his head.

"Never mind, Sid'll strap me up later. Need to talk, now, right now! Oh Gawd…"

"Talk, what does this have to do with… women? Evil?"

"Root of, mate, root of…"

"Now then, Pete, listen up," I says, scoffing down the third icepop, "Better let you in on this one too. Wait, that's it, strap it up nice and tight."

Pete tapes the icepop stick onto my last broken finger.

"It was horrible, horrible – the caff was heaving with leather-clad warrior bull-dykes – I shit you not! *Heaving*. There was a hundred if there was one. Alright, at least a dozen. I knows people what throw right wobblers around nut-jobs, who doesn't? Me, same as, only it's lezzies – I fear them beyond mortal terror, Pete, beyond the screaming abdabs even. And I don't scare easy, I really don't.

The lezzy. Not saying they all want to chop off your balls and feed them to their budgie, a lot of them are really nice, but without a doubt a lot do. We've all heard the stories. There's lezzy out there what are capable of all sorts of dark malevolencies against a geezer.

And I'm not saying that some geezers don't deserve it neither, I've been doing a little of the auld natural selection myself, as it goes, but I've never laid a hand on a woman in all my days, and the reason I'm in mortal terror is highly emotive for me."

Pete nods, "You cannot hurt a woman."

"How did you suss it? Never mind, bang on. It's my Achilles heel, my kryptonite, I start retching at the thought, no, the prospect of having to do it, blacking out and all sorts.

Of course, they did everything they could to cure me of this deficiency in the Craft. The shrinks all said it was only a minor psychological defect, something to do with all that 'kill your dad and fuck your mum' malarkey. And I would be alright, they said, the training was the best in the world, they said, and it was; they had us doing in all sorts, even puppies at one point, and I love puppies – no problem, job's a good'un, Barbelo Puppy Stew. But fuck it, Pete, I wasn't alright, nothing worked. Therapies, drugs? Nothing."

"How terrible for you."

"Terrible, right, almost come a cropper over it, Dresden, and at the hands of a particular and horrific lezzy called Gretel – how do you think I lost my leg? Fighting in action?

Nah, that's my cover story, can't go spreading about what really happened, but that's how I know what the 'gentle sex' are capable of. Still got the nightmares, fucking hell, don't get me started. And don't get me wrong, but don't think females are all 'sugar and spice' neither, no, no! Give 'em a grudge and a geezer tied to a bedframe, a hatchet and a blowtorch?

Standing room only.

Luckily these handicaps level out in other ways; the shrinks also reckoned it could be the reason why I was so good at what I did, and so I was in – the Craft accommodates. Though my condition, let's call it, was always a bit of a liability, specially in the line of work they primed me for.

And nah, never found out what was wrong with me neither. Army shrinks never tell you nothing, though I can tell you now, I was under siege by the lezzy at the caff and I knew I wouldn't be able to lift a finger if they turned nasty. But what's almost worse, they've fucking invaded my favourite caff of all time…

I'm the only geezer in there, except the Chink serving at the counter. He smiles at me as I stalls in mid-peg, seeming to understand the perfect horror we're in. His once beautiful establishment of culinary delights is a sea of creaking black leather jackets and bald heads.

They're sizing me up for the slaughter, and these lezzies were… I dunno what, but I can tell they were something 'cos no civvy polishes steel-toecaps like that – force of habit – but it's too late, I'm in now, creeping down the isle, and at the counter,

'Good morning young man. Bubble and Squeak, chocolate pudding, a nice cuppa made with mineral water, please, and another chocolate pudding. Please.'

I turns around, spy an empty table just behind me. Avoid eye contact, *do not* make any sudden moves.

Pealing off my raincoat, I slowly sits down, slowly takes off my hat, when Brid – that's a fit-bird me and Sid are banging – bursts into the gaff and swaggers past. Completely ignores me. Odd, and then again, I remind myself, not odd for an escaped nut-job.

I don't dare move, just sits there, and I swear, all the lezzies are staring at me, every fucking one with pure hatred and malevolence; like I shouldn't be there, like I was an aberration in their world what needed to be rubbed out, cancelled, annulled – and then I realised they were actually staring at Brid, standing at the counter behind me.

Alright, I was shitfaced, been a long morning and all that, but I mean it Pete! I wasn't imagining it – they wanted her good'uned.

I overhear the Chink, 'Go down to the under,' he whispers.

Even odder.

She disappears into a doorway round the back of the counter.

Now, the lezzies at this point go back to their watch, by that I mean they all turn their heads and stare at the door. They're expecting someone, or something to happen. Synchronised behaviour like that is not normal otherwise, well, nothing about them was normal but either way, not one is looking in my direction.

Curiosity killed the cat, but fuck it, I needed to know what this was about, specially after all her weird-shit earache about Insider

Orders and the Nish Bash-wots-its and so forth – it was unbearable, inevitable, destiny – had to get round the back, somehow, problem was, how.

Well, as you know, I've been in some tight spots in my time, but there was no way of getting round that counter without an assault rifle. Patience, I says to myself, I'll just wait and collar her when she comes out. Has to at some point.

'Thank you, young man,' I says, as the proprietor puts down my Bubble and chocolate cakes. I tuck in, and gets settled into my waiting, and waiting…

Fucking waited an hour, must have skulled a dozen cups of tea, needed a bog or it was going to be Barbelo Bladder Stew all over the gaff. Chanced a furtive glance, just the lezzies covering the door, no bog, never was in this gaff as far back as – always used the pub over the road.

Give it a go anyway.

'My young man,' I says, slowly getting up, 'You don't appear to have a toilet, but, do you have a backdoor somewhere?' I grimace. 'I mean, bursting see? It's my age, happens to the best of us—'

'No backdoor sir, new toilet is through door on left.'

Typical.

Anyway, I squeezed round the counter, find the bog where he said it was, do the business and sneak out. In the gloom, I spy a stairway, bags of cement lying about, a hawk and mixing tray, and the sign says 'Danger! No Entry.' I peg it down quick-smart, step by step.

First thing to assail my senses was opium, and fucking strong it was too, wafting up thick from the darkness, but I continued down, going down, down further into the murky depths to the end of the stairs.

Flipped my Zippo, looks around.

I'm on a large stairwell with a door on my left. Store room, thinks I, and creeps up, slowly, slowly push the door open ajar.

On my right is this huge burning brier, a ton of opium smoke swirling into the spacious, candlelit storeroom, and at the shadowy far end is Brid, kneeling down in front of a giant statue of a one-legged lezzy, what's standing on human skulls, six arms holding spears, knives and all types of lovely kit. I stifle a scream—

Brid's a lezzie Satanist!

I take a step forward and stall – through the veil of smoke stalks into view another giant lezzy, a real flesh and blood one, though my brain screams 'No, no, it can't be real!' And by that I mean she's so fucking big, this lezzy, her head's almost touching the ceiling.

Brid's on her knees, muttering something, a prayer, some kind of incantation to the goddess of malicious one-legged femininity, I dunno, but the one behind her's tooled-up to high heaven. I catch a glint of a zigzagged blade in her paw, a Filipino Kris, she's standing over my, our lovely fit-bird, sword over her head and – fuck it!

She's seen me, just a flick of the eye but she's seen!

With my balls in my throat, pegging it upstairs, I wrestle with the turmoil in my conscience – the cunt's gonna job's a good'un and there's nothing I can do, nothing except scarper – oh damn this affliction!

Damn, damn, damn it all!

Scurry past the counter, snatch my coat and hat off the table, and chuck myself out the door to the sound of scraping chairs and creaking leather – they was all piling out after me!

Pegging it up the street, I staggered to a halt – the Yardie I'd sent to Happy Place a while back was walking, calm as you like, straight towards us – and fuck me he was looking well!

But it gets worse, odder, besides him's this woman, a girl, fuck it Pete, besides him a woman the spit of Brid, fucking identical, dressed the same – black raincoat, stockings, boots and everything.

Well it could be her, you're asking? She could've somehow got up there by some secret passages? Don't be silly – no, it wasn't her, it looked like her but it wasn't her, and I can't explain how I knows it… her eyes, her feel, *cold*, like she could suck your soul out in one breath. I dunno mate, but I've never shat it like that ever, not even at Ypres – teenager I was then, with shells and men exploding into bits showered in guts, mud and gore – and nah, doesn't even come close.

The lezzies behind me don't move.

We all just watch as the Yardie and the Brid look-alike walk up and stop, about ten feet from us, with me piggy-in-the-middle. People are all milling about, going to work, doing this and that, but normal, like they didn't see us, like we was all invisible.

It was a stand off. I could feel the energy, electric, like when two bare-knuckle bruisers are sizing each other up before a bout and they both realise, with equal dread, that they're well-matched, too well-matched, catch-madrift.

I feel a hand on my shoulder, and one of the lezzy's pulling me back behind their line, like they're protecting me or something. Protecting me? Christ! I looks round and some of the lezzies are surrounding the Brid look-alike in a circle. Suddenly she opens her mouth, and howls – she howls this horrible ear-piercing continuous howl and her eyes go all black and there's this crushing pain in my chest, crushing, crushing and—

She vanishes!

Gone, Pete, I swear I am *not* making this up! She vanishes right before my eyes, gone. Like switching off the telly or something; one moment she's there, the next she's not.

Feharchrove, people what aren't people, Brid called them, and she was right, fucking bang on! She reckons they're around us all the time; in the street, on buses, walking about supermarkets, fucking everywhere and we don't notice them, see? *They look just like us.* Oh mate, I pegged away frantic and the Yardie followed…"

Pete's gently shaking my shoulder, "Mr Barbelo, here's your Super Glue. I lost you there for a moment. You were very quiet."

"I'm alright, cheers. You gonna open up yet?"

"What happened next? Did he do this to you?"

"Oh, what, the Yardie? Nah, he bottled it too, legged it right past me towards the park!" I tried laughing, but my cracked ribs wouldn't let me. "Nah, nah, I got hit by a bus, didn't I, wasn't looking where I was going, silly cunt—"

"Is that all?" Uncle Pete roared with laughter, "Then we must look on the bright side; at least it was not an ice-cream van!"

"Bloody hell, you too?" I shudder under my breath. "Seriously," I says, looking into his eyes, "I can't live like this. I can't go on – I feel at a crossroads in my plans, I've got too much on my plate as it is, and now this… this… *weird-shit.*"

"I understand…" Pauses, nods a few times. "You need to take stock," he says in a soft tone, "When life piles up on you, throw out what is absolutely non-essential."

"It's piling up alright," I says. "Just spent the morning down the cop-shop; SIS wanna reactivate me for another treasonous black ops, first in decades – needless to say I've got no intention of doing nothing."

Eyes widen in dismay.

"Nah, might not have to anyway, not after what I did to that Yank, then again, it all depends how my CO deals with it," I sighs, "Stuff 'em either way. But if that's not bad enough, I've got my two Generals at me the whole time to sue The Bank of England."

"Imprudent."

I nods. "Right, my thoughts exactly, this is not the time to take on the big guns… not yet. It's gotta be done in proper order. First, we need to send an emissary to Buckingham Palace, and serve Queeny with an affidavit invoking Article 61 of the *Magna Carta*.

We simply request the removal from Parliament of all traitors – namely Margate Thatcher *et al* – and if our grievance doesn't receive redress within the lawful time period of forty days, *then* we're entitled to enter into Lawful Rebellion. Has to be done right, we're gentlemen, after all.

But fuck me, shit in my mouth and call me your mother! Almost forgot! On no, oh no…"

I buried my head in my hands.

"It cannot be that bad—"

"Nah, it is, it is! Sent a death threat to the Pope, didn't I?"

"Hmmm, yes, a very foolish thing to do."

I looks up at him, and nods. "Got a feeling I'm gonna seriously regret that, I dunno what came over me that day, Pete, I must've been off my head. He's got a year to pull his holy finger out and end world hunger, or we go to war on them all. Non-negotiable. We'd be no match against the Vatican Army in all-out war…"

"Imprudent, and yet," he scratches his head, "There is still a chance he will 'pull his holy finger out.'"

"Do you reckon? I don't make idle threats Pete, you know that, My word is my bond. But this time…" I shakes my head.

Nods, "Either way, concentrate on what is absolutely vital now."

"Overthrow of regime, get our Country back first, that's vital. After that, yeah, maybe, we might have the clout to take on his Pontificus – wave, after wave of trained top-notch assassins…

And Brid, she's important to us, very important. Nah, I dunno if she's alright, I'll have to send Sid round to the caff. Or maybe just leave her there, I dunno, she's fucking bananas sometimes; thinks she's some kinda secret agent from another dimension or something, and after what happened earlier… Gawd, I dunno what to think anymore, I swear, Pete, I feel like I'm cracking up!"

"It is enough to give anyone 'the screaming abdabs,'" he smiles, "I suggest you focus only on the essentials."

"Lawful Rebellion."

"Like you say, stuff the rest."

"Stuff the rest! Oh mate, thanks again, ay."

"I'm glad. Now, attend to your wounds, I will call you a taxi home."

"Please, thanks… but wait, Uncle Pete, I hope I haven't shocked you or nothing but—"

He throws his head back and laughs again, "I am African, nothing you say shocks me!"

"No, I meant about all that feharchrove business… do you believe me, do you think they're… real?"

He lowers his tone, "Our ancestral history is defined by colonial genocide, our own chiefs sold us into slavery – I do not think demons are real, Mr Barbelo, I *know* demons are real; the Ajogun, as they are called, and their opposite, the Orisha, who are also real.

And yet these are only inherited forces, merely a part of a continuing journey, that journey which we call life, leading to a deeper understanding of the product of who we are, and ultimately, the realisation of what we may yet become."

I nods.

"In the end it is a personal choice, Mr Barbelo, a potential. Violence, brutalisation, love and justice – in Orisha, all things merely define parts of a greater whole, that which we call 'Ashe,' the undying totality of all that is the One."

"Undying," I mutter. "The One…"

"Life and death, all is Ashe, within which is presented the choice to be either a divided fraction, merely a product of our inherited experiences, or something far greater – a vessel for the spirit of humanity itself, Ashe, as expressed within the heart of our communal existence."

"And have you," I ventures, "Have you had experiences of this undying Asashy then? You see, Brid and Sid, they prattle on all the time about all this and... oh Gawd, I dunno."

Nods, "Oh yes, many, but I think you should go home and–"

"Nah, nah, go on me auld china, I'll bear up for a bit. Tell me."

He smiles, leaning over, elbows the table,

"Once, as a small boy, I was with my older sisters coming home from the market and we stopped at the well for water. I was young and adventurous and always getting into trouble, and that morning, feeling very spirited, I climbed onto the edge of the well and began to dance along the rim, like the Moko Jumbies dancing in the Carnival.

My sisters were shouting, 'get down, get down!' and came to grab me, and I slipped, falling backwards into the well. My arms spread out to hold on but I hit the rim, hard, bouncing inside like a pinball!

And so down and down I go, a long, looooong way," he chuckles, shaking his head. "I was terrified, Mr Barbelo; my right arm had become dislocated, and clawing and thrashing into the water with only my left arm I could not stay afloat. I went under more and more, and before long, the water entered my lungs and I gave up.

It was not that I gave up because of anguish, although I knew there was no hope and I had drowned, it was that I gave up and surrendered into peace, a peace I had never known, but which I now understand to be merely the union with Ashe; the cessation of all division."

"Peace," I whispers, "Blimey."

"Yes, Mr Barbelo, peace. It was a darkness, at first, and then a golden light shone all around me, and in this light I saw an angel, an angel made of pure sunshine who called to me by my childhood name. She held my hand and spoke these words,

'Kwame Diabaté, choose! Return with me and I will take you to your spirit home, or go back to your home on the Earth, and learn the way of the Orisha.'

I was not frightened in any way, I was happier than I had ever been, but I did feel some sadness to leave my mother and my sisters behind. I asked the angel,

'Can I bring my mother and my sisters?'

The angel smiled, and answered,

'They cannot come now, but they will come after.'

And so, I asked the angel to please take me to my Earth home, and I promised to learn the way of the Orisha.

To this day I do not know how or who or what got me out of that well – my sisters also have no recollection – but Mr Barbelo, I can tell you with all honesty, I have never been more alive than when I was dead!"

I gets up, shakes his hand. "And I really don't know what I'd do without you, Uncle Pete – a proper gentleman, you are, seriously. I mean it, you should do this for a living…"

Sorry to cut Uncle Pete short like that, I hope I'm not being rude, he's an interesting geezer, fucking interesting, and if I didn't have to check on killer-lezzies and glue up my face, I could've sat there all day.

So I left Pete's establishment in a cab, fucked, home to Sid, an icepack and bandages.

Didn't ask him what he's guilty about, I knew he was, but no more, just couldn't take any more. Sent him round the caff to investigate, and lay there on the sofa until I passed out…

Chapter 29

Hot Awen In The Lower Astral

The house was deathly silent, the living room dark. I hauled myself out of my sofa, and crept forward through the gloom, Makarov PM in hand.

I'd felt the touch as a light blow in my mid-section, an all-prevailing 'knowing' – someone, *something* was coming to the house.

Training my awareness through the walls, I scanned the street up to Coldharbour Lane, until my mind captured the scene: a giant woman, black leather, AK47 over her shoulder.

I braced myself behind the front door.

A key rattled in the lock.

The door opened.

I squeezed the trigger—

Thwack, thwack, thwack!

Staggering, clutching his stomach, Sid crashed through the hallway.

"Sid, what the fuck happened? You're… shot!"

"That's 'cos you shot me!" he coughed, breathless, and collapsed against the wall.

I rushed to steady him before he fell to the ground.

"I shot you?" I muttered to myself, working fast to inspect his body for more wounds.

"Oi, stop trying to feel me up! I'm fine," he chuckles, "I'm an accomplished Dream Master." He coughed again, spitting out blood, pushing me away gently.

Stepping back to let him through into the living room, our bodies momentarily jerked in stilted robotic movements. Inexplicably, I was not in the least concerned.

However,

"Despite your ghastly condition, for which I appear culpable, my thoughts have vaulted into self-preservation. The Order's Protocols are flexible on many counts, but justifiably stringent concerning contact with Initiates in the Awake."

"You are correct," he juddered, "It is the first time we have acknowledged our rank and status in this Locale."

I followed him inside; he stalled, twitched, and turned around,

"The Inner Order has mastered the art of staying hidden from those that stalk, and continuously hunt us down, should we surface and make our presence felt for too long."

I confirmed,

"The Illuminati trade our Awen with the Lords of Shadow for technologies of Power! T, H, E and Y scan tirelessly for signs of dissent! Appropriate countermeasures must be engaged, and our objectives concealed within the mundane tasks of the profane."

He nodded furiously, and we continued into the living room, where I tried to take control of this dire situation,

"You were that giant lezzy what killed Brid! I saw her with my Awen, it wasn't you!"

Easing himself down onto the couch, Sid lurched forward and grabbed me by the wrist,

"You can't job's a good'un women, therefore, I couldn't have been a giant lezzy. Betrayal!" he rasped, "Babylon cut Brid down!"

"Why you speaking like a Darkie?" reaching for the phone on the coffee table, "Switch off the RAMA, ay? I'm gonna call the Boys and sort this—"

Spitting blood onto his sleeve, Sid pulled me down close,

"There's a war your mind!" he wretched, and drops his voice to barely a whisper, "Your mind is infected with parasites!"

"And I fucking shot you!"

He dragged me closer.

"They are legion, suckling on our awareness of life; equally on our joys, and fears... Our recruitment, Brid is *consumed*... in Shadow..."

"That's because she didn't fucking hide her objectives in the profanities, silly cow, but, and this is the onion Sid, she's not our recruitment. Brid was a high Initiate of the Inner Order, she was the one recruiting us!"

"Ahhh," he sighs, clawing at my trouser leg.

"Oi, stop doing that, it's disgusting—"

"And... and how did you know... who she was?"

He grinned, I stalled – I didn't have a fucking clue – the room began to spin.

Someone somewhere was pounding a pneumatic drill. It was loud, painfully loud!

Small bat-like creatures flapped around the walls.

This is madness!

I breathed deep, tried to compose myself,

"Sid, where are we, who are we? What did they do to us, mate, what did the Craft fucking do to us!"

Sid cracked a crooked smile, "They divide the psyche for the pestilence of the great parasite, Nuish Bash'swan! Thus free your mind by any means necessary; shatter the mirror of self-reflection. The Craft psycomotrates."

"Yes! Of course! The Craft psycomotrates!"

"Else the war in the mind will mirror in the Realms; will mirror the war in the Awake... and all will be harvested for Awen... All will become sustenance for the Realm of Shadows..."

I returned his anxious gaze, rapidly calculating the disastrous impact a Dream War of that magnitude would have on the Awake.

"Impossible," I gasped, "The Gates to the Shadow Realm are barred to this Locale – the Lyraquai Nations have defended our borders for aeons – and nothing gets past the Ashe, for it is the undying totality of all that is the One!"

"The confessor is in error..."

"Impossible! The confessor is never in error, the confessor is an *interesting* geezer!"

"The gates shall open... they will enter... and the Awake shall be forfeit to eternal sorrow..."

Licking his lips, Sid opened his eyes wide, swallowed hard, working his ugly mug into a grimace, "Eternal Lower Astraaal..."

"I'm gonna call," I mutters, picking up the phone, and yelling at the bat-things, "Fucking stop that fucking drilling!"

The bat-things fled into the hallway.

Frantically pressing the keys on my phone, I listened with great sadness to Sid's incoherent rant,

"Why kill me on The Fool's Journey... oh why now Joe... after everything we've been through... and yet, all begins in Nothing, ends in Nothing... thus... perhaps... it is all... *Maktub.*"

He winked one blood-shot eye, and dropped his head to one side.

The drilling stopped.

My phone slid from my palm onto the tabletop.

I checked his breathing and felt for a pulse.

Nothing.

Staring down in shocked silence, I swayed on my feet with the crushing reality of what had happened. I'd killed Sid?

"Nah, nah, nah," I mutters, "I'm dreaming, I'm dreaming, I *must* be bloody dreaming..." And quickly pegging into the hallway, I checked for the bat-things.

What, no bats-things?

Where did they go?

I spun around and around looking for the bat-things and finally realised – it had happened – at long fucking last I'd completely cracked up!

Shuffled back to the living room, crumpled to my knees, my chest heaving with guilt and despair,

"Oh no, Sid," I whimpers, "I'm sorry, I am..."

Outside, youg'uns returned from the pubs, their laughter mocking my madness as I leant over, mustering myself to close his eyes.

"Goodbye, my friend," I sighs, "See you in Happy Place."

"If they let you in!"

His eyes snapped open, two golden feline orbs drilled into my brain, pinning my heart to my gut.

"Oh my darrrling, my only one!" mocked the sing-song voice from Sid's lips, "How touching! Thank you for all those juicy morrrsels of raw emotion, hmmm, I do love my Awen hot in the morrrning!"

Cascading into sadistic laughter, echoing around the walls, the living room melted; colours bled and ran into one another, spinning into flickering black shadows.

My awareness resided in total darkness. A pneumatic drill started up from the streets below, excruciating pain shot through my chest and legs, and once again I found myself strapped to my hospital bed on Locale 22.

"Oh deary me, we arrrn't as well-trained as we thought, my little puppet, arrre we? Very, verrry sloppy! Never mind, you'rrre with me now, and I'm well-fed, that's the important thing..."

She lay draped across my throat, pawing my nose affectionately.

"There, therrre, my love, don't cry, it was just a little demonstration of my talents, just a little cat and mouse game, it's my naturrre, shall we say… what my darrrling? I prrromise, yes, when I have what I want. But no, no, no! Not before I give you something in rrreturn for your… Present."

I glimpsed the SS Guard, still snoring on his chair in the corner, and yelled for help – my lips locked shut, instantly gripped in a vice of nausea.

"I told you it is most foolish to do that!" she screeched, and then cooed, "Poor little human, oh hush now my sweet, indulge me. You're becoming trrrapped in an extrrremely unpleasant Locale. Yourrr individual signature, cast within the Earth Drrream, will change shape, and then yourrr body changes shape. Slowly, all your memorrries will fade, rrreplaced by whoever, or indeed whateverrr the pressures of my Awen dictate…"

Craning my neck as far as it could stretch, I stole a glance at the glowing digits of my watch.

"Half ten in your prrrecious Awake, yourrr time is up! Your time has come to frrret, my only one, frrret and turmoil! Now we are trrruly Anchored togetherrr, at last! At last! At last!"

In utter desperation, I tried something I had never accomplished on my own; mustering the little Awen still available to me, I attempted a shift to another Locale. Anywhere, as long as it wasn't here.

Nothing happened, at first, I sensed only a curious mix of emotional disconnection and ardent resolve, welling up within me.

The creature's eyes danced with expectation, as she sniffed around my face, "Arrre you… there?"

I lunged forward, my teeth at its throat – razor claws swiped my head away, and then sank deep into my temples.

"Fuck you!" I spat, "If it's me ya want, yeah, go on—"

"Verrry good," she purred, gripping my head tighter, "Finally! Welcome to the Shadow Realm, Captain."

"Come on! Do it—"

"Shhh! Oh yes, Gretel will do it, Grrretel is pleased! So which leg firrrst, hmmm? Eenie meenie minie mo!"

My left leg vanished, replaced by a gory stump and a leather tourniquet.

"We can't have you bleeding to death, can we? But… it does look rrrather tasty there, shall I have a little nibble before we continue?"

She disappears from view. I feel her crawling about, and I breathe, calming my mind, relaxing into the pain – and then she's sitting on my chest again, slurping, licking her paws,

"Mmmm, tasty yum-yums! Now, if I rrrecall, I was going to rrrequisition your other leg, and your arms, and your eyes—"

"Said fuckin' do it, go on, take my thorny cock an' all!"

"Verrry well, whatever you say, my love, let's go to Dresden then. Let's do it properrrly…"

Suddenly the air raid sirens wail and the bombs begin to drop, shaking the underground bunker. The SS Guard jumps to his feet.

Crumbling masonry and dust pours down around us, as he rushes over to where I lay, tied to a bedframe. He hesitates, wide-eyed with apprehension. I reassure him again: his life will be spared if he helps me escape, he would be looked after – the War was nearly ended.

The cat leaps out of his way, he quickly undoes my bonds.

"Thank Bomber Harris!" she hissed, "The mass murderrring little cunt! Undeniably my sweet, but no, no, no! This forrr that?" she cackled. "No, I do not have what I want, our books arrre not yet balanced. What, did I? Well 'I beg your parrrdon,'" she sang, "'I never promised you a rrrose garden!'"

Without warning the bed swallowed me whole. Plummeting through an infinite starry space, for an instant, I was looking out through a young girl's terrified eyes, straight into a boy's face.

A cutthroat razor, in his hands, covered in her blood.

"Do you not recognise them?" her voice asked in my mind, "She is me… One of me, and also one of you. Is she not beautiful? And that there, heaving on top of herrr, is actually one of you too… How can this be? Oh yes, my puppet, the parrrt contains the whole… what you do to one, you do to all… *Non Serviam?* Ha! Ha! Ha! Don't trrry your pathetic games here, you know where we arrre…"

Beneath me, a long silver bridge grew in size as I continued to fall, its two ends stretched out in the darkness, vanishing into a vale of stars.

"Will you set yourself frrree? Then submit to us, *quid pro quo*, acrrross the Bridge of Penitence."

"Fuck you, fuck you, fuck you, fuck you, fuck you…"

Chapter 29

Sid Goes All Brainy

My awareness resided in total darkness, content to simply listen to the rain drumming on my living room window.

"Joe, wake up…"

A soft sigh, followed by a familiar giggle, and I opened one eye.

Brid stood over my sofa, peering at me with narrowed slits,

"…I must go, tonight!"

"Fuck you, you're alive!" I screams, sitting upright, checking myself over. "Oh no, where's Sid? I killed Sid!"

"In your dreams!" Sid's laughter rumbled through the hallway.

Brid shoots me a quizzical eye, "Can you recall why?"

"You must hide in the profanities!"

"Okay!" she chuckles.

I squints at her, my heart racing. Is she real?

"She was fine, mate," says Sid, sitting down beside me.

"Sid, did you find any bats in the hallway?"

"No, but I found her down the caff, drinking tea. The Inner Order weren't there anymore. They've shifted out of our Locale, back into the Realms of the Earth Dream."

"My exile is over," she smiles, delighted, "I'm going home!"

Luckily she was going that night; I couldn't take much more. I was fucking losing my mind, and I knew it. Sid was sold from the start and yep, now me too. Leastways I gave it a good shot, went along with everything – adapt – seemed the only way to keep it together. Told her about the lezzies. She explained it wasn't lezzies, or even Satanists, but an elite corps of an Inner Order – SOLAR – Sisterhood Of Light And Redemption. Made complete sense.

The Yardie I'd good'uned the day I'd saved her was a feharchrove, and the Brid look-alike was a Wrenhunter, a type of feharchrove the Illuminati use to track down their dissidents – very powerful, they can shift between the Realms at a drop of a hat, what explains how she vanished before my eyes in the street.

This means, of course, that Brid was originally Illuminati too; leastways that's where she cut her teeth, initiated into all sorts of martial disciplines and esoteric powers.

Why not? Who the fuck was I to say otherwise?

I'd been run over by a bus.

"You can say what you like, Joe, but I don't need back up…" she pauses over her cup of tea, tucks her legs under her, nestles into her armchair. Sid's all steely-gazed and serious on the armchair opposite, and then she's shaking her head at us,

"Listen, the reason I ignored you in the café earlier was because if I hadn't, you'd be a dead man. I had to cast a glamour on you as I walked past."

"A glamour?"

"A psychic cloak," explains Sid, "If they'd received even an inkling that you knew each other, they would've—"

"Brown bread. Got that the first time, tarred with the same brush, and all that. So what? That was then, this is now, you've convinced them of your loyalty and you're safe now… no?"

"My apprehension is complicated," she says, looking at both of us in turn, "If I succeed, then yes, we may yet be the greatest allies your Operation could ever hope for, the Sisterhood is ensconced within every institution on Earth…"

Closing her eyes briefly, she tilts her head to one side, and the living room falls eerily quiet; for a moment I can almost imagine I can hear whoever it is she speaks to in her mind.

"Many lifetimes ago, when the last of the Inanuquae Gods were vanquished from the Earth, we made our home on the banks of the river Danube."

She stops there, frozen, eyes wide open.

"What?"

Sid lurches over the coffee table, "She means the Neanderthals," he whispers, "Humans believed they were gods, before we wiped them all out, all except one. Go on Brid," he says, "It's a good story, this."

"Not sure I'm in the mood for stories, Sid. Been a long day, and you and I need to have words—"

"Shhh, later, let her talk…"

"Our tribes were being decimated by war, with horse warriors, those who later came to be known as the Kurgans. We had driven them back into the mountains for another year, but at a terrible price. What for us were great battles were but mere scraps to their lion-hearts, lusting for fertile lands and slaves. Now their feharchrove would hunger evermore for suffering defeat, and they would return in ever-increasing numbers. Peace with the Horse Warriors had to be found, we would not survive another onslaught.

Our shamans decreed we must journey to the East, and there consult with the last of the living goddesses. She who knew all things would provide us with counsel. That task fell upon Rahanna, my sister, and together we made the long journey to the edges of the great forest, where the land fell away into the ocean.

The ascent to the Sacred Cave took us high along a cliff wall. The evening sun had dipped below the mountains, the crashing surf on the rocks below became but a distant murmur, when reaching the cave entrance we crept forward into a labyrinth of musty tunnels. Guided by a violet light, pulsing in long bursts from its dark interior, at last we came upon the lair of the Goddess deep within.

Squatting on her haunches, mounds of her flesh gathered around her feet, her white matted hair fell in a cascade of elflocks on the ground. Lightning crackled around the chamber walls; a ferocious storm striking out from her outstretched vulva which she pulled ever wider apart. Her face all but covered, one luminous eye pierced the surging gloom like a polished mirror, and there, I beheld the Kurgan hordes marauding across the entire world – I touched the heart of that which compelled them, and how they would shape all that our people would suffer and later become.

Time seemed to fold over itself, forever repeating. I witnessed the departure of the Creators at the dawning of the ages; their star chariots blazed into the heavens, their great cities of light vanished beneath the waves, and how the Inanuquae took on their mantle, chosen to be our gentle guardians and teachers, until the gods returned. And I witnessed their demise, when the Kurgans let loose their treachery, and demanded to be worshiped as gods themselves.

Grotesque parodies of all the Inanuquae had been, their souls became misshapen with power; enslaved, the peoples of the world fell under the dominion of priest kings and gold.

The free spirit of the land was crushed into submission. Forged in the fires of war, the shape of the Kurgan Soul was to run amok in the hearts and minds of all men. From father to son I witnessed this ceaseless process. Armies of slaves endlessly clashed, their masters craving the gold stacked high within stone fortresses, and above these battlefields was at all times an eye, set within a giant pyramid; it beheld their savagery weeping tears of blood and shameless pleasure.

This symbol was far and wide, as leaves scattered to autumn winds, the measure of life in this age of destruction and torment. It held the people hard and fast, beyond the reach of the Earth Dream's wisdom, entranced, bewitched, the wild bittersweet taste of freedom entirely forgotten.

The beauty of the land no longer touched them. Now the Sacred Groves were cut down. The last of the great forests and all life therein, decimated. Only the docile grazing of deformed animals was permitted, feeding the gluttony of a misshapen multitude, herded into grey stone boxes. Fearing the food they harvested, afraid to bathe in the rivers, to breathe the air too deeply into their lungs, or to even feel the gentle caress of the sun on their skin – all these things could now bring death as readily as they had once brought life – they feared all that was once abundant and freely given, and they feared their children, and each other.

To be deceived had become their greatest achievement, their ultimate joy and happiness, their greed.

At last the heavens blackened. The moon turned blood red, and the Kurgan priest kings unleashed the devastating force of the sun upon their slaves. The entire world was set ablaze, oceans burned; enormous cities vanished in the turning of a single day. And yet the departed never journeyed beyond this realm, their souls forfeit to an entity spawned of their own avarice, picked off one by one, as morsels by carrion birds. Over and over, the same entity regurgitated them back onto the barren plains that is now the Earth. Devoid of all meaning, forlorn, they crawled and scavenged amongst the scorched dust, festering beneath perpetual winter skies.

All the while, this being grew strong. Its danced before my vision, first as the Eye within the Pyramid, then as a mad puppet-clown, cackling, feasting upon our cold flesh – it whispered its name,

'I am you, you am I...'"

Blimey, and I thought I had nightmares. "How do you do that, with your voice? Brid? Is she alright Sid?"

"She's in deep meditation," says Sid, leaning over and waving a hand in front of her face, "It takes her a few minutes to come back. But yeah, feels like you're there, doesn't it?"

"Did they make peace with the horse warriors?"

"Obviously not, judging by the state of things. Humans killed off the Neanderthals, who we saw as gods, and then we turned on each other. It's been like a scratched record ever since."

"Why did we think they were gods, then."

"They were a superior species, in every way. Your average Neanderthal could pick up a small family car, and throw it across the street. As a result, they didn't really have any natural predators, they were a very gentle lot at heart. Last thing they banked on was our bloody-mindedness. One on one, no contest. But when humans band together and start scheming, different story."

I nods at that, "We're a bunch of evil cunts, alright. So who were the other gods, the ones who fucked off in the star chariots?"

"*Very* interesting, the Creators never returned. They came to our planet from another star system, and genetically modified our—"

"On second thoughts Sid, nah, leave it. Gonna make us a nice cuppa, we've gotta talk."

"Talk about what?" Brid yawns, stretching her arms in the air.

Sid cuts in, "Why didn't you describe the part where Rahanna kills the Goddess, and then becomes one herself? That's the best part."

"You tell him the full version, Sidney," she smiles, "I need to go downstairs and ready myself."

"I understand," he winks, tapping his ears.

"Very droll, Sid," I mutters. "Good story that," I says, "but I still can't see why we can't come with you tonight."

"The Rule of our Inner Order," she affirms solemnly, "demands that we dedicate our efforts to chaos, anarchy, and toppling existing regimes until we wrest control of the world's institutions from the Illuminati."

"Very well, that's something we agree on."

"I have something instrumental to its accomplishment, something from that cave… It would tear our organisation apart," she groans, "You would not understand what you'd be up against if I fail."

"Fail, what?"

"I can't go into it, please, it's for your own protection."

"We can protect ourselves," grumbles Sid. "Well-enough."

"Please."

"I still think it can't do any harm if we come along and—"

"Please!" She glares at me.

"No problem," I shrugs. "We'll wait for you here, then."

"I am begging you, *do not* involve yourselves further!"

"Bloody hell, said we won't! Will we Sid?"

"Nope."

"Thank you," she says, and with a warm smile, she gets up, gives us both a peck on the cheek, and goes down to the command centre. I went into the kitchen, made us a nice cuppa, and went back to our business at hand.

"Sid, put the file down a moment."

He peers over the pages.

"Sid, earlier on, on the blower you were, I mean, what..."

I pause, easing myself back down into the sofa, gauging his mood. Hard to tell these days, since hanging about with Brid he kept shifting under different covers, almost like he was back in the Craft.

"We've got a problem," I says, "The Yanks are taking over, everything, London, the entire Country."

"So what's new?"

"Good question."

"We pay our dues, don't we?"

I nods.

"Well then, business as usual," he says, and goes back to reading the Yank's file.

"Business as usual. Until T-Day anyways, but Sid—"

"Alright, alright, you mean what happened when you were down the cop-shop," he grumbles, taking another file from the table, "It says it here. Control key people, control the city; legal services, planning, local police and all the other Firms; and then create civil disturbances; clamp down martial law, or at least strip away people's liberties under the guise of 'it's for their own protection,' and—"

"And hold your position, yeah, I got the auld 'Order out of Chaos' routine down the Station. Cunts. Thought I was born yesterday."

"And *how* are these key people controlled? Bribes, blackmail, in the past they were all toffs anyway, but now it's gone a step further. Now they're being *created*, from scratch, from the lower and middle classes too: brainwashing members in 'charities' like Common Purpose."

"Brainwashing."

"Right. And it's not just Common Purpose, there's a whole heap of these new organisations churning out 'leaders,' and it cuts deep. It's what Brid was saying earlier, we all have the concept of hierarchy ingrained as an archetype, from the Neanderthal times. For over a hundred and fifty thousand years, we lived side by side with a superior humanoid species, they were like gods to us. Then, around forty thousand years ago, our populations grew and we start wiping them out. Who's our top cunts then?"

"Whoever's good at killing Neanderthals, obviously," I says.

"And with no Neanderthal left to kill, the top cunts turn on each other. It's pathological. Doesn't have to be like that, human beings are not like other animals, we have self-awareness, we've a choice; the last call is ours. Should be, but the brainwashing works because it triggers that primeval pathological response, climb to the top, to the top of the pyramid and rule like a god."

"Alright, standard psyops, so what you getting at?"

"I'm saying take out as many of these bastards as we like, there's always gonna be hundreds waiting to take their place…"

"So what?" I says, "We get them too."

"We'll never get them all, that's what I'm saying," he mutters, rooting around the Yank's briefcase for another file, and turns on his professor tone of voice,

"A neurone is a cell, the largest in the human body, and ten billion neurones minimum comprise our brains, making connections, firing trillions of synapses in a blink of an eye. So, ten billion's a very significant number for humans. We need that many neurones, *minimum*, to sustain self-awareness. Any less won't do it," pulls out a file, looks up, "And with ten billion brains in the world?"

"You're losing me here a bit, Sid."

"A rat has four to five square centimetres of cortex, and therefore roughly sixty-five million neurones. A chimp has about five hundred square centimetres of cortex and therefore seven to eight billion neurones, the gorilla about the same—"

"Alright, get the picture. En masse, we're like some giant animal."

"Collectively, yes, we behave like an animal, in a cage, performing conditioned tasks for rewards, jumping through hoops, gets your bananas. Sometimes we have a flash of what life could be like beyond the cage. We get angry then, rise up against our masters, rattle the bars and if we carried on, who knows? Maybe we would eventually break free. But we don't, we're too domesticated. We soon get fearful and hungry again, and lulled by a lifetime's monotony of conditioned tasks, we're again jumping through hoops for bananas.

However, if the population of our species were to ever rise to ten billion? Perhaps our collective consciousness would also rise and achieve self-awareness. Connected, psychically fused, functioning as one and yet still individuals within the collective whole."

"Never get there anyway," I grumbles, "We'll trash this planet long before that."

Shrugs, "Of course, ten billion under our present economic system is not sustainable. Though actually, it's relatively few people, they could all still fit on the Isle of Wight. But… yes, just as we've domesticated other animals, it's almost like something in our distant past *knew* to do this to us; installing those hierarchical archetypes that we see reflected in the societies we build – something that *needs* our species stunted, to never reach its highest potential."

"If you're gonna start talking about star chariots and aliens I'm gonna call the police. I mean it. Conclude."

Chuckles, "I'm afraid it gets far worse than that," opens up the file on his lap, "This is highly technical, it's decades ahead of anything I know, but all those new transmitter masts going up?"

I nods. "Saw one on the cop-shop even; they're all over the gaff, something to do with British Telecom."

"Right, and it says here… all sorts about the length of insect antennae, the length of wavelengths that can control them, and well, the human spinal cord works the same, it's basically an organic flux antenna, an extension of the brain."

"Come again?"

"Our spinal cord, works like an aerial for a two-way radio, sends and receives signals directly to our nervous systems. What we see, everything in the world is a frequency, a brainwave range, so pump out a different signal and the world changes."

"Oh fucking hell, here we go… is this relevant?"

"This is bloody serious, Joe! It states here, mobile phones, cordless phones, GPS, Wi-Fi routers and modems, Bluetooth, and more, they have all this new technology waiting on the sidelines and all of it operates at brainwave ranges. That's the plan. In the future we'll be blasted with artificial frequencies, and our nervous systems will convert these neural signals into thoughts, feelings, whatever sensory input they want us to experience."

"Blimey… and we won't know?"

"And that's the beauty of it," flashes his wry grin, "Nobody will be able to tell which thought or feeling is theirs from the others – the brain believes it's completely normal – because in reality, our minds are *not* inside our heads…"

"Nah, but the brain is."

"Two separate issues – the brain is physical, the Mind is psychological. Scientists still haven't located the physical seat of the Mind in the brain, and we won't, ever, because we've been looking in the wrong place. We're not a mind inside a body, walking around and so on, we're a body walking around inside the Mind! The brain, all of us, our entire physical body is an organic flux antenna, and the Mind is *outside* of us."

Normally, this is the point where I take the piss, but I went all wobbly; seemed for an instant like the room was turning inside out…

"Please Sid, don't, I think I'm losing my mind as it is—"

"Won't be losing much," he chuckles, and then nods at me, slowly, "Never yours to begin with. You are little more than a walking-talking aerial, receiving signals from *out there*," waves his hands around his head, "Translating those signals into sensory experience, into what you call 'reality.' Other animals have different realities. Why? Because they're differently shaped, they have different aerials so they tune in slightly different frequencies, and interpret their realities accordingly."

"Slightly different… how do you mean?"

"Well, depending. Like an ant's world must be vastly different from ours, that's why they're hardly aware we exist, even when we squish them under thumb. So who knows what's out there that we do not perceive either, squishing us. That's not to say ants are not intelligent, well, no more or no less than anything else." He shrugs again, "In actual fact nothing *has* intelligence. It is The Mind of the Universe, these frequencies, which *is* intelligence. Ultimately, all physical matter is one seething electromagnetic ocean, and every thing, is every thing."

Smiles ominously, slaps the file on the table between us.

"Conclusion. We have got to find a way to neutralise the signal. We can't make a move until we do. The entire population of London can potentially be rendered combat ineffective in an instant."

"Potentially…"

"I'm not a hundred percent definite, but from what I've read so far, yes. They could stall a full battalion of Ghurkhas in its tracks at the flick of a switch, if I've interpreted the frequency range correctly. It's possible to artificially induce any emotion within the human range of experience; extreme lethargy, confusion, excruciating agony and so forth. But the irony is," he adds, "this technology began as a medicinal tool; the corresponding frequencies can also heal diseased cells, regenerate internal organs, even grow back amputated limbs."

"Blimey… my leg?"

Smiles, "I know, we'll have to look into it."

Breathing deep, I sank back into my sofa, "Whoa, alright, alright, and so the govermentals are gonna fry our antenna-brains, what's new? Switch off the RAMA for a moment and just tell us, what were you getting at earlier?"

"How many command centre's do we have, apart from Marcus's lot? Five, six?"

"Dunno either, keep hearing about more all the time."

"Enough?"

"Nah, not nearly enough to get the job done… At this rate, yeah, Brid's killer-lezzie battalion would come in well-handy!" I groans, "We'll be brown bread a hundred years before we've got the clout."

"And what did the Irish say?"

"You know, Sid, you were there…"

"'Fuck off,'" he sighs.

"To put it mildly."

The incident Sid refers to concerns a particular senior commander of a certain Irish organisation visiting the UK, who, in no uncertain terms informed us to 'fuck off.' Long story, and daft, all told…

223

Oh very well, I'll tell ya about it, but I'll trim it down – and don't go spreading it about. Highly embarrassing.

First rule of Lawful Rebellion: always, always have a newspaper delivered to your door…

Chapter 31

Arseways With The Irish

Alright, we're talking about the week previous. Sid and I had got up feeling pretty miserable about ourselves, it happens; full moon or whatever – we might sound like Superman's groovy granddad, but I for one gets days when I don't have the energy to tie my own shoelaces – and that day, we both decided to skip training and settle for an inspiring pint down The Albert instead.

It was always inspiring down The Albert; you had all these young'uns, Punks they called them, all dressed to the nines in their ex-army kit and leather jackets, pierced through the nose like Filipino whores – good people though, understandably angry at the state of the nation, but with adaptable brains; full of bright ideas for regime change and that's what we needed, a bit of inspiration.

Pat greets us at the door, looks at us each in turn,

"Sorry lads, I'm afraid I've got to lock up."

"What?" I says, stepping inside, "Bit early, isn't it?"

"Eleven o'clock," mutters Sid.

"Morning," says I.

"I know," says Pat, "But I've got an engagement, friends from home, *private* party."

"Oh," I says, spying the gaff was empty, except for this geezer in a black coat, sitting over by the jukebox reading a newspaper – grizzled stony face, flat nose, shock of blond hair going bald on top – looked hardboiled in vinegar.

Pat follows my gaze, coughs sheepishly, and holds the door open. We begin stepping outside just when this other geezer comes in.

"Good morning, sir," says Pat, smiling, but there's a tight tremor to his voice.

"Thank you Pat," says Sid. "We'd better see ya some other time."

"Thanks fellas," says Pat, holding the door open for us.

"Brian?" goes the geezer coming through the door.

We spins around.

"Yes?" replies Sid.

"Brian, 'tis Tommy!" grins the geezer, who at that moment looked familiar to me an' all – most probably because he was the spit of a young Steve McQueen – but Sid's eyes light up like Christmas,

"Tommy!" he declares, "Well just look at you, hey? Still got that horse?"

"Dad sold her, thanks be to God!"

"Cat food, I hope!"

"God help those cats!"

Pat and I take a step back, well-puzzled, as they proceed to hug, slapping each other on the back.

"Where you off to?" says Tommy.

"Dunno," says Sid, "Bit of a private party here, from what we hear." Raises an eyebrow.

Tommy nods to Pat, who bolts the door shut.

"Wait a moment, don't move," says Tommy, and without further ado, strides over to the hardboiled by the jukebox.

Sid's all tight-lipped, and Pat's well-fidgety, as we watch them chatting and glancing at us standing by the door.

"Sid," I whisper, "Who's that cunt then?"

"Tell you later."

"Don't like this. Let's go down The Effra."

Shakes his head, "Do you wanna get the job done?"

I nods.

"Could be our prayers answered. If they put in a good word."

Tommy waves us over,

"Pat!" he cries out, "Four pints and the rest!"

"Coming right up, sir," he mutters, going round to the bar.

Sid and I stroll and peg over to their table.

Tommy smiles. "Brian, this is Seamus O'Reilly."

"Pleasure to meet you," says Sid, "But that was then, you can call me Sid now. This is my friend, Joseph Stevens."

"Pleasure to meet you," says I.

"Sit, sit," says Tommy, grinning from ear to ear. "And Pat, give us a tune on the jukebox!"

We sits down. Sid and I don't need to contend the lighthouse seat, we've already got our arrangement – cover each other's back on all occasions, and this appeared to be a *special* occasion… of some sort.

The Jukebox cranks into action, 'The Foggy Dew' moans out across the bar. I'm on the lighthouse, Sid's next to hardboiled. Tommy distributes our pints – Guinness all round, four pints and a bottle of whisky – pukka enough.

Hard cunt says, voice like gravel,

"Young Thomas informs me you boys were army boys."

Sid and I exchange brief glances, and we nods.

"Well," he says, "I'm in the army too."

"Oh?" says I.

Grins, "I'm in the army, so I am, especially *your* army – tooth and nail. Ha! Ha! Ha!" he laughs, and then freezes like stone, going all hard cunt on us. "With every *nail*," he adds.

Happy Stick's flicked and released.

Sid diffuses my intention and the cunt's righteous demise with a rumbling laugh of his own, and says, "Well that's grand talk, coming from a man six counties short of a nation!"

Which didn't sound like much, but then again, coming from Sid perhaps it would to somebody else, namely Seamus, who only chuckled, bowed his head briefly and raises his glass.

"United Ireland," says Sid, lifting his pint reverently. We all clinked glasses, and Tommy slides onto the lighthouse next to mine.

"Horses," he declares, shaking himself down.

Sid laughs, swigging down a whiskey, "Never again!"

"Better count her legs next time!"

Had to ask, "What are you two on about?"

Seamus cuts in, "Hey there," he drawls at me, all Irish lilts and earnest frowns, "A *gentleman* never asks."

"Oh," I says, "And I suppose you'd know all about that?"

"I do."

I downs my pint, stand up, raise my whisky, down that too. "Sid?"

"It's alright," says Sid, "it's alright. Me and Tommy's father go back, got a bit of history, see?"

I sits down again.

"The three legged horse—"

"The three legged filly," Tommy cut's in, "Pride of Ulster, was her name, fastest horse in all Ireland."

"My arse! Fell for that hook line and sinker…"

And on it went, a wild and woolly story about how Sid, the dark horse himself, had met Tommy's father shitfaced back in '69 in Derry, bet on his horse, lost a packet, poled some infamous Derry transvestite called 'Filly,' hence the three-legged reference, and was on the frontline at the Battle of the Bogside the day after – our side, obviously, or supposedly – but nah, six pints and a bottle of whisky later, I still couldn't make head's nor tails of it.

"Point was," says Sid, "I'd been called up to supervise, only that, watch on the sidelines and provide Intel. God only knows why, 'cos I couldn't give a monkey's toss either way—"

"Or a filly's toss," chuckles Tommy.

"He was undercover," says Seamus.

"I'd gathered that," I grumbles.

Tommy nods. "He was staying in our house, giving me Irish lessons," he says wild-eyed, "Can you believe that, *me*, Irish lessons – nobody suspected a thing! Do your Cork accent again, go on…" he waits expectedly, but Sid carries on in Gawd's English,

"So there we were, under siege on the street that night, all hell's breaking loose again – petrol bombs, bricks and all the rest flying about – and I suppose I just got sucked in," he shrugs, takes a swig of beer.

"You'd gone native," I venture.

"Gone native? I'd fucking got shot!"

"The Brits shot him!" laughs Tommy.

"Here," says Sid, massaging his shoulder, and fell about in stitches.

Didn't seem much of a funny story to me, but it tickled them pink, leastways Tommy and Sid laughed; hardboiled and I hadn't taken our eyes off each other all afternoon.

"It's half three," says Sid, calming down, glancing at the wall clock. "Better be off soon, hey?"

"Tell me about it," says I, quickly finishing my pint.

Tommy slaps me on the back, "So soon? But we've only just started. Pat, another round here!"

"Better go," I mutters to myself, "leave this gentleman to his business."

I gets up, but my slur's entirely wasted on Seamus.

"Hey there," he grins, "Tommy's right, we *have* only just started."

"That's alright," says Sid, "We've got business of our own to attend to. Enjoy your visit to London."

Pat slides another bottle onto our table.

"Aw, why? Stay for the last one," says hardboiled, "It isn't every day we're blessed by such, ahhh, captivating and *experienced* guests. We Irish are very hospitable, aren't we Tommy?"

"Very hospitable Seamus."

"See?" he smiles, pleasantly enough. "Have a drink, relax, and forgive me for being... cautious. Tommy's a good lad – a little idealistic, fer sure – and if Tommy trusts you, then I trust you. What do you two make of the war?"

"Which one?" asks Sid.

"Our war," says hardboiled.

"It's your country, mate, not ours – everybody has the right to defend themselves, in the manner in which they're attacked."

"The right and duty," affirms Tommy.

"And if you ask me, our troops up North know that. Alright, there's bad apples in every barrel, but if it meant they'd finally come home? Given half the chance they'd blow the border themselves! It's all Brass Hat politics anyway. Thatcher," he spits. "So keep at it, they'll concede in the end if—"

"We don't need anyone to *concede* anything," Tommy snaps, "We're a sovereign nation by right."

Seamus agrees, "And in every sense we will reinstate our sovereignty. And please sit down, Joseph, you're amongst friends."

I sits down again.

"Economic freedom is the key," I says. "Interest free money."

The lad looks up, all earnest grins, "Oh we will print our own money, Irish money, and have religious freedom too – The Church is either with the people or they're free to piss off back to Rome."

"But hey there–" Seamus ties to interject.

"But no, Seamus, I mean it! They've been a thorn in our side from the beginning. Do you know what the Prodies up North call us?" he says to me, "Romanists, that's what they call us," skulls another whiskey, "*Romanists*, and fer good reason – Rome's always telling us what to do, what to think," taps his head, glancing at Seamus, "They even run our schools."

"Because we're Roman Catholics," he cuts in.

"And Rome's in Italy, Seamus; what gives them the right to run anything in *our* country?"

Hardboiled gives us an apologetic shrug,

"Young Thomas, a true home-grown romantic, he'd dig up Finn Mac Cumhail himself and sit his bones in parliament!"

"Ancient Irish hero," Sid says to me.

The lad goes on, "In all fairness, yes Seamus, and the Druids of the Sacred Groves of Tara too! I'd take the whole of Ireland back to how we were, *Irish*, fer fuck's sake – fer fuck's sake! I'd tear it all down and begin again! Starting with every Brit building of torture and death, brick by bloody brick, starting with Dublin Castle."

"Shouldn't still be standing," agrees Sid. "I see what you're saying. Maybe plant a memorial garden in its place."

"Dead on! And I'd tear down the Four Courts too; reinstate our own laws, Brehon Law. Do ya see Seamus, we have to reinstate *our* ways, in full, our language and heritage; Irish sovereignty means full Irish identity *in full*," he grins, "What's the point otherwise?"

Seamus shoots the lad that universal tight-lipped smirk what means 'prepare for serious words later.' Tommy gulps another whiskey, "Well, we were doing grand for thousands of years before foreigners poked their noses in. That's all I'm saying."

"If it ain't broke, don't fix it," affirms Sid.

"A good start," I mutter.

Hardboiled squints at me, "How about you then, what do you think?"

"You really wanna know?" I'd been itching to have a dig all fucking morning, "I don't want to speak out of turn."

"Speak freely," he says.

"Alright, I don't know much about your politics, I will confess, but I do know we all needs a change. And it strikes me the young lad has a fair point; what are yous fighting for – old colonial laws and a foreign religion?"

He shoots Tommy another smirk.

"Don't get me wrong though, I've nothing against your religion, or any other bronze age fairytale neither – sit the Pope himself in *your* parliament, why not, what do I know, I'm just an old *English* soldier. But if you're fishing for Intel to take back home, I can tell you now, you're conducting your entire operation arseways."

"Arseways."

"Give me twenty kids with catapults knocking out traffic lights down the West End, do more effective damage than your lot all year. If you're gonna take your war to the mainland—"

"Mainland."

I stall. He grins, folding his hands, "Continue…"

"If you're gonna bring your war over here, with limited resources, you need to conduct operations in proper order."

"Guerrilla tactics," agrees Sid, "Focus primarily on communications and supplies."

"Right. No point blowing up civvies; waste of resources and in the long run all it does is upset people – people who might otherwise have been sympathetic to your plight, or leastways didn't give a filly's toss either way. Same applies to military targets; doesn't matter how many of us you take out, we've hundreds of thousands to replace them; our resources are likewise plentiful – yours are not."

"So what do ya suggest?" asks young Tommy.

Sid clears his throat,

"Reserve your resources *only* for targets what are gonna count, which in your case means hit our Government where it hurts – their pockets."

"Right," I says, downing the whiskey Seamus passes me. "Have you cunts ever done any proper Intel on how Britain works, or even looked at a fucking map of London? Well nah, it doesn't appear you fucking have, does it. If you had, first thing you'd immediately notice is we're fucked with traffic. Takes weeks sometimes to sort out just one traffic light going on the blink down the West End – chaos on the roads. Scale it up a level; blow Lambeth Bridge at five in the morning, nobody gets hurt and London's cut in half for months! Meaning millions down the drains for the govermentals, bad for business, very, very bad. Do all the bridges simultaneously and *then* you've got a war."

Sid nods, pouring us all another glass, "Don't even have to blow them, just churn up the tarmac, serves the same purpose."

"Right," I says, "And having the clout, which you boys obviously have, if you targeted all our major cities in the same manner – relentlessly – within a month you'd have Britain paralysed and our govermentals on their knees."

"And importantly," adds Sid, "You've got to realise, the whole nation's on bloody strike; we're on the verge of revolution as it is! You've got everybody from the miners, to poll tax protestors, to the homeless to Falklands Vets – countless *seriously* fucked off people just dying to have a go. Get the underdog onside, tip the applecart in your favour. End of the day, it's all about Public Relations."

"PR," snorts Seamus, "You think after eight hundred years of brutal occupation, having a nice tet-a-tet with your murderous empire is going to help."

"Nah, Sid don't mean that, blimey, and it was your own Top Cunts what opened the door for ours anyways. No point talking to any of them without something to bargain with, and they're not gonna bargain over the lives of a few squadies, or civvies even. Proof of the pudding mate, they never have, never will – we're just numbers to them, statistics on tax registers and voting potentials."

Sid nods. "Power and control, order out of chaos. Standard black ops – problem-solution – the Government create the problem, offer the solution, usually things they wanted to achieve in the first place, but couldn't under normal circumstances, and we beg them to take control. And Joe's right, our armies walked into your country, *walked* – no landing crafts or air cover or anything, they sent us in and we walked straight through the door."

"Sid," I whisper, "They didn't have airplanes back then."

"Not the point. Got them now, don't we?"

"Alright, so why?" I asks Seamus. "You've got the north of your country still battling injustice daily, and the south, well, all they've done there is change flags. Why has fuck-all changed in eight hundred years?"

Seamus nods, "Continue…"

"Because *your* Top Cunts made a deal with ours. Obviously. You's were all getting uppity so your Top Cunts called in our armies to help; been there ever since. But what you've got to understand is the first victim of the British Empire was the British people ourselves. Eighty percent of this country still lives under the breadline."

"Borderline squalor," mutters Sid.

I nods furiously at that.

"Put it this way," I says. "When Cortez landed in South America, how do you think he brought an entire civilisation to its knees with only two hundred men? Because the Inca Top Cunts were fucking loathed by their lower classes, and by every tribe from East to West! But if Cortez had landed there and just gone at every cunt all willy-nilly, he wouldn't have got no support, would he? Nah, he would've found himself skinned alive quicker than shit though a duck! Same applies here; if you don't hurt nobody, you won't piss nobody off. I'm not saying you're gonna win hearts and minds overnight, but you'll stand a better chance of getting us onside. Otherwise, forget it, you won't win."

"Won't win," confirms Sid. "Same with the African slaves' situation, but in reverse."

"What?" we all say at once.

Sid nods, "The Africans practically invented the slave trade; they had it there for thousands of years, right across to the Sahara and beyond," lifts a finger to drive his point, "Their *own* chiefs sold their own people – that's why it was so easy for us to get slaves."

We all stared at him.

Sid shrugs at me, "Well that's what Uncle Pete said. Same old same old. Blimey, look at what happened at the battle of Isandlwana! 1879 it was, the Zulus dealt us one of the most humiliating defeats in history. They annihilated an entire column with nothing more than stabbing spears – against cavalry, artillery, and all the rest. Slave trade to the Empire couldn't have happened without serious top level collusion."

"Interesting," says Seamus.

"Interesting," I concedes, "But blow us up willy-nilly all you like; won't help your objective one iota, that's what I'm saying. Hitler bombed London day and night, blitzed the entire country and all it did was make us dig our heels in even deeper. Think about it…"

A pause followed. Eventually, Tommy and Seamus eye each other briefly, and Tommy pipes up,

"I hear ya, I do, but I can't say anybody at home would agree, not after Bloody Sunday."

Sid and I both sigh at that.

"Domhnach na Fola," echoes Sid.

"That was One Para, wasn't it," I mutter, thinking back. "Wilfred's lot."

"Wilford," Sid corrects.

Seamus nods. "Bloody Sunday; twenty-six unarmed civilians shot, five of them in the back, another two run down in the street by army vehicles. And then the Dublin bombings."

"Dublin was definitely our lot," mutters Sid, "Well-out of order."

I concede, "Regrettable, highly, and highly understandable you'd want to level the score – tit for tat – don't take the bait."

"The bait?" asks Tommy.

"Just said," says Sid, "Standard psyops: tit for tat is exactly the reaction our Government wants, that's why they gave the kill order that day, and did the bombings and all the rest. They need your country riled up, need the auld Order Out of Chaos routine to stay in power, while at the same time making you squander your resources."

"Don't fall for it," I says, "You're getting a lot of recruits because of it all but yous have got to stay pragmatic. Focus your resources creatively, use the enemy's goals against them. They want yous all British up there? Use it. Invoke Article 61 of the *Magna Carta*, mobilise all non-combatants living in Britain into Lawful Rebellion."

"Mass non-compliance," affirms Sid, "Under the full protection of Constitutional Law you can refuse to pay any kind of revenue; tax, fines, not a penny and they won't be able to do a thing about it."

Seamus nods.

I nods. "Disrupt the enemy on all fronts and in every way possible. Never lose sight of the long-term objective – winning. You wanna hurt the British Government; get them out of Ireland for good? Then hurt their finances, disrupt all sources of revenue; they'll back off and throw in China on a silver plate an' all! But going after civvy casualties here, bombing local pubs and supermarkets and all that malarkey, nah, all you'll get is the same auld govermentals banging on about murdering terrorists and getting re-elected time, and time again. Do some *real* damage, then you'll win."

"Do the bridges," reiterates Sid. "Just for starters. Simultaneous early morning strikes. Nobody's about, nobody gets caught, and nobody gets hurt."

"Can't see why they haven't already," I says to Sid, "Disable enemy supply lines, it's bog standard. Then there's the sewers, and the water supply – govermentals must be laughing – they could paralyse this city, the entire Country in under a fucking month."

234

"Bridges, roads, railway tracks," affirms Sid. "Then they'll win."

There followed another pause, a long uncomfortable one.
Seamus drains his beer, and finally breaks the silence,
"Perhaps," he says slowly, "*some* of us don't want to win."
"*Someone* up your chain of command?" I asks.
Doesn't reply.
"Good, good, better," I sighs, "Now you're talking sense, Seamus, thanks – now you're being *honest*. So I'll be honest with you."
"Work away," he smiles, folding his arms.
I lean forward across the table, meeting his eyes squarely,
"Sid has a different angle on you's all – he's lived with yous, learnt your ways and culture – but I *know* you don't want to win. That's fucking obvious, because if you did, you'd of conducted your ops in proper order from the start! And nah, you haven't."
I leans back, shake my head. "So, Seamus me auld china, what on Gawd's Earth are you boys playing at."
Seamus nods his head slowly, grinning.
I turns to Sid, "Business as usual, see, didn't I tell ya? All Top Cunts are paid by the same purse."
"False Flags," Sid mutters sadly. "They need to root out who's ratting them out. At least we don't have that problem."
"We'd be half way there if we did," I adds.
"I'm going to the Jacks," says Tommy, and heads for the bogs.
Seamus asks, "You'd be 'half way' to where?"
"Good point." I pour myself a whiskey. "Sid?"
Sid nods, "We've an Operation with the same agenda here. Ultimately."
"Regime change," I says.
Seamus shoots us a surprised squint, "You?"
"And others, mate, many, many others. We're slowly building up the clout, and that's our problem; it's slow, too fucking slow. But we've got the expertise, quality, and if you could put us in touch with some old boys in your organisation—"
"Old boys."
"Best if they're over seventy, the advantage of getting to our respectable age is that nobody gives us a second glance, and ready to apply themselves in proper order, we could get this war won in

proper order – bollocks!"

It happened quicker than you can spit – I'd just got my whisky glass level with my lips and Seamus has a 9mm level with my head.

"Well that's very hospitable, isn't it?"

Sid shoots me an almost imperceptible flick of his eyeball, meaning stand down. I chance a glance at Pat behind his bar, pale as a sheet midway cleaning a beer glass, frozen like a statue.

Tommy's behind me, another 9mm trained on Sid.

"Makarovs," I groans, "Lot of them about these days, ay?"

Seamus leans forward, slaps the newspaper he'd been reading earlier on the table.

"Read it," he says, "Out loud."

So I do,

"The blast tore apart the Brighton Grand Hotel where members of the Cabinet have been staying for the Conservative party conference…"

I glance up at Sid. He closes his eyes with dismay.

"…Prime Minister Margaret Thatcher was in the room next door when the bomb detonated, but narrowly escaped injury. The IRA has issued a statement claiming it had placed a 100lb bomb in the hotel. The statement read: 'Today we were unlucky, but remember, we only have to be lucky once; you will have to be lucky always. Give Ireland peace and there will be no war.'"

Studying the photo of the demolished section of the hotel – and I mean fucking demolished: a giant gaping hole over seven floors of charred rubble – I pass the paper back to Seamus.

"Now what do ye think of our war?" he scoffs, "Captain Joseph Williams Barbelo, *sir*?"

No big surprise he'd sussed me out, seeing as our Firm paid our dues, but all this was most uncivilised – a hundred pound bomb and they miss the target? Unlucky?

And I'm the Queen Mother.

Best be diplomatic though, with a gun at your head from a hardboiled, very, very diplomatic. I opens my mouth to answer, but Sid was already gunning his glare into my brain, and cuts in first,

"You're doing grand boys, just grand!" he chuckles, "For bog warriors. Off-target with a hundred-pounder? If that wasn't one of our False Flags then I'm the Queen Mother!"

You could've heard a pin drop.

I rolls my eyes to the ceiling. Tommy breathes, heavily, down my neck.

Seamus chuckles, tilts his head to the side, peering at us down the barrel with one closed eye,

"Get up, get up," he says, "Get up… slowly."

"Stand up Brian," Tommy orders Sid.

We all stand.

"Tommy, have we enjoyed our afternoon with your old buddy?"

"We have Seamus. Good craic."

"Mighty craic?"

"Mighty!"

"And the Captain?"

Pause.

"Fifty-fifty Seamus."

"Now then, we do have a quandary," he mutters, and taking out a pound coin, he flips it, slams it down on the table, hand on top.

"Call it," he says, staring straight at me.

The lad stammers, "No-no, I meant *mighty*, don't, don't–"

"Shut up boy! You said fifty-fifty. And I said, you there," he grins at me, "Call it."

I grins back at him. "Alright then, heads, 'cos I'm off my head."

"I hope you're not," he says, "Because if so, you'll be taking your pal home without his." And he points the gun at Sid.

I flicked the release catch with my thumb; disarmed Tommy in my mind, Sid had no doubt done the same to Seamus, and yet I must confess – I went cold to the bone as little by little, he lifts his hand away.

Without taking his eyes off mine, he slides the coin across the table towards me. We all looks down.

Tails.

Seamus creases up laughing – "Ha! Ha! Ha! Tails! Ya should've seen yer faces – now that's mighty craic!"

Tommy and Sid let out a sigh of relief but I had to laugh too – fuck me sidewise, it was funny, the cunt.

Nodding at the door, Seamus flaps his gun at us.

"Fair play gentlemen, now ye know all about the famous Irish humour too! Ha! Ha! There's the door," he says, "Now, fuck off!"

And so we did, fucked off out of there, and royally fucked off an' all – Sid went back with a two-inch mortar, mad cunt, had to wrestle him to the ground on the corner of Coldharbour Lane – though to look at him now it was hard to believe he was the same Sid, whatever the fuck that is anyways.

But, something's not right with you, I thought, studying his chuffed grin,

"That little caper last week was bloody embarrassing."

Sid nods, glancing at the clock on the mantelpiece, "Must have been crazy, asking that lot for support."

"Whiskey always did give you funny ideas."

He chuckles, "It was funny though, hey?"

"I swear your eyes popped out, Sid! Would've given my good peg for a camera."

"Gawd awful morning, that was, we needed a bit of inspiration and we got it. Tommy's a good kid though, fucking good bloke and so was his father. It was that other cunt."

"Oh don't go all native on us, they were both on the payroll—"

"Oh come on! It was a classic case of the right hand not knowing what the left is doing! You just can't stand the thought someone might get to Thatcher before you do."

"No Sid, I'd be delighted, but the point is they didn't get her and MI7 had a fucking field day spinning the auld 'Britain will never be slaves' Churchill-bollocks; her popularity ratings will shoot through the fucking roof!"

Shrugs, "Won't last, they'll soon cop on again standing in the dole cue."

"Alright, stop pissing about then; what's that grin *mean*?"

"That's my grin of inspiration," he grins.

"Explain…"

Our living room hummed with his guilty silence.

"Better I roll us a joint first. No, on second thoughts better not. What do the Arabs say when something happens, which in all probability couldn't be avoided?"

"Maktub," I reply.

"Right, they shrug it off and say *'Maktub,'* 'it is written,' it is destiny, couldn't be avoided."

"What happened earlier, then?"

"Did you know, the entire world only uses about half a zeptojoule of energy, and there's over two thousand zeptojoules of geothermal energy available. If that were harvested to its potential, we'd have four thousand years of clean power—"

"Did you know, I'm gonna shoot ya four thousand times in the head?"

Sighs, "He's our age, had a right to know, they're on their way over."

"Who?"

"From Bradford."

"For the love of fuck, Sid, what—"

"Ishmael. I let Ishmael in." He shrugs. "Time to reshuffle the pack, as you say—"

"Up yours Sid! You fucking deal with that fruitcake, alright?"

I grimace with the pain in my chest, lower my tone,

"Look at the state of me, mate, I'm not up for it."

Shakes his head, "Always think of now, never say why…"

"Never ask how."

"The Craft accommodates."

"The Craft accommodates."

"And you're the boss, so deal with him; fruitcake to fruitcake," he chuckles again, "Shouldn't be too difficult, hey?"

"Alright, alright…" I pause. "But I feel it Sid. There's *something* else…"

Chapter 32

The Three Martyr Master Plan

It was a white haze of headscarves, silk sheets and Omar Sharif smiles as Ishmael breezes into our living room. It was horrible – he looked fucking amazing – smoothy gold-toothed cunt.

"*Salaam aleikum,*" he declares, settling into my armchair.

I'm leaning up against the mantelpiece, all Lord Fuckface: hand in pocket, suited up English and in proper order – well, as far as you can after getting hit by a bus.

"*Aleikum Salaam,*" I reply, "Good to see you too, Ishmael me auld china—"

"Very great book I receive from the Infidel this morning, great plans! The Brotherhood of True Islam is truly happy for invite."

Yes, well, I was not truly happy, I was in true fucking misery.

I'm not a big fan of religion, you know that, but don't get me wrong neither, I've nothing *personally* against religious whack-jobs – the state the world's in today, there'd be something wrong with you if there wasn't something wrong with you – and I'm sure some of them are really nice, but this cunt wasn't.

Convinced all that God codswallop was just to get other religious whack-jobs to do work for nothing, which they do of course, and Ishmael had a lot more clout than us, a lot more, right across the Nation and the entire fucking beyond.

Took every ounce of willpower not to gut him there and then. Sid offers him a nice cup of tea.

Ishmael smiles. "No tea, thank you Sidney. Coffee?"

Sid trundles off to get the coffee, I nods over to Boris and the boys standing by the door, signalling to go outside and stay put.

Nah, not taking any chances, alright, he's only got two Paki gorillas with him, but I'd seen this cunt in action in the early days – from Afghani to Saudi and the Levant – no picnic. Add regime change into the mix, serious potential for one seriously pear-shaped night.

Sid comes back and passes him a cuppa. I sits down on the sofa opposite, glance at the clock on the mantelpiece. Midnight,

"It's late, what time did Brid say she's leaving?"

Sid shrugs, sitting down beside me. "She didn't."

"Who is this Brid?" asks Ishmael.

"Nobody, it's safe to go ahead, what's your offer?"

"*My* offer?"

"Yeah, to business" – get this over with – "what are you coming in with? Can't expect to come in with us without something to offer in return, it's only civil."

His mug cracks open a crooked smile at the affront, if anybody should be offering it should be us, but this was my manor now, gotta keep up appearances.

He says nothing for a bit, just twirls his goatee beard with narrowed eyes, and finally nods.

"Great spiritual achievements," he whispers.

I shook my head, "Excuse me?"

He leans forward, "I read your Manifesto with great interest, Captain Barbelo, it is good solution; nationalise your banks, coin interest free money and use your shit for fuel – methane gas, fart into glorious autonomy!" he chuckles, pulls out his copy of our pamphlet from under his robes, "What a great inspiration, truly, but what is this silly section: Lawful Rebellion?"

"Has to be done in proper order, we're gentlemen, after all."

"I think you are perhaps too generous; these devils will never stand down peacefully."

"We know," I says. "Why do ya think we're arming ourselves to the fucking teeth?"

"And so, we also have a plan," he adds, all proud and mad-eyes a-popping, "This, is what we shall offer you!"

"Very well, go on then."

"Three Martyrs. The first blows open the gates to Downing Street. Boom!" slaps his fist into his paw. "The second Martyr runs in the gate and blows the door. Boom! The third Martyr runs through the door, up the stairs and boom! Blows the Margaret Thatcher."

He grins. "We destroy the British Parliament. Good?"

Good? Cut my throat, I was dumbfounded, it was almost the happiest day of my life – his plan was doable – having the clout, meaning three whack-jobs up for turning themselves into Allah Stew.

"Except for one thing," says Sid. "Thatcher is not the head of Parliament. Have a look at these files," he passes Ishmael the Yank's briefcase. "It'll explain everything. The entire Nation's run by corporate banks and the military."

"But of course," agrees Ishmael, giving me the cold eye, "And do we not know this? I hope you do not invite us here to make insult."

I shuddered. "What? Gawd no! It's a great plan, great and spiritual."

"Good," putting the briefcase back down on the table, "Because you need help, and we do not refuse, if it brings us all closer to freedom for our homelands."

"It will," I affirms, and turn to Sid, lower my tone, "We need more clout, obviously, but to mobilise effectively we need *credentials* even more. Doing Number Ten was always on the cards; the whole country, the entire bloody planet wants that cunt dead. They pray for it, Sid, and don't tell me you haven't neither."

"I see we understand each other," grins Ishmael.

"Thatcher's head on the gates of Buckingham Palace," says I, "And tell you what Sid, us working with Arabs it'll *inspire* people, means we're prepared to go global and follow through to the end. Not like that IRA fiasco last week, MI7 had a field day."

"I do not trust these Irish."

"Nah, their tactics do leave a lot to be desired, but, excellent sense of humour, you've gotta admit, spot on."

"Ha! Ha! Ha!" Sid, doing his hardboiled impersonation, turning to me, smiling that smile what means he's seconds from blowing his lid,

"And we're talking about going at it worse than they are! The British Parliament does not exist! Don't you see, they've got us fighting shadows."

"Symbols," I correct, "We're destroying symbols, at this stage. Parliament might only be Disneyland Delusion, but it's where we all believe the power is—"

"Joe," he growls, "Cut off the head, and the body dies."

"Never a truer bloody word, Sid," I growls back, getting vexed.

"Which one then, which *bloody* head...?"

Another pause follows. I shift uncomfortably on my seat. Sid's flicking through his files again.

Ishmael drains his coffee, looks at us, all puzzled,

"If there truly exists another way, we would choose it over violence, gladly," he says, "But this is war, gentlemen, and in war the greatness of a warrior is measured by the greatness of his enemy. Thatcher is a great enemy, and thus, she is deserving of Jihad."

Glowers, raises his hands in the air. "What is the problem?"

I shrugs. "None I can see, we'll do it, we'll personally do the gate with an RPG and provide the cover, take it from there, spare you a martyr or two."

Shakes his head, "It is the martyr who decides."

"Oh. A religious matter."

Nods. "But on the same glorious day, we will destroy the bridges along the river, every single one must crumble into the Thames."

Well, shit in my teapot and call it your breakfast—

"Hear that Sid? Crumble into the Thames! Go on me auld china."

"And for this, we will combine our forces. We have been making good relations with our Libyan Brothers these past months. Many will assist us also, but we must be patient. Once we begin, there will be no turning back – we must be prepared to succeed, and *only* succeed. Like you say, follow through; no quarter."

"Ishmael, all we ask for is a few more months to build up a little more clout too, and settle things. Sid?"

"Not without a way to neutralise the signal."

"This signal, what is this signal?"

Sid picks out a couple of files from the briefcase on the table, "Ishmael, no offence, but please take these, pass them on to someone who might understand what they mean, and then come back to us."

Sid glares at me, I have to look away – it was almost the most embarrassing moment of my life. Ishmael picks up the files.

"Ahhh, this Infidel devilment," he mutters to himself, "What silliness; for what can be greater than the One, Allah?" He briefly flicks through, and chuckles to himself, dropping them back on the table.

"Sidney," he says, "We have known about this already, indeed, the Americans call it Psychotronic Warfare. And our scholars are also very confounded. If you wish, perhaps you can exchange your knowledge of these matters."

"Please, that's very kind of you," says Sid.

Ishmael smiles. "Trouble not. For every action there is an equal and opposite reaction – have faith, a solution *will* be found." He gets up. "You seem to be having some problems," he says to me, "I will return on a better day, a day without omens."

"Oh?"

"We passed a bad car accident on the M1 into London."

"Terrible," says I, "Did you spot any American military there, by any chance?"

"A bad omen," he reiterates, and I escort him and his lovely Arab geezers to the front door.

"Forgive us," I says in a low whisper, "We've all had a bad day, a bad week all round. We'll talk again."

He bows his head, *"Inshalla,"* he says.

He turns away and I close the door.

Slowly pegging back into the living room, and a gotta admit feeling pretty crestfallen, I tries to think of the best way to approach this rather unexpected and highly unfavourable turn of events.

"You dog-fucking cunt Sid! Why do you always have to ruin everything?"

Takes a drag of his joint, smiles up from his sofa,

"Did I?"

"You lost your bottle, or what?"

"You've changed your tune, glad to see."

"And we're not gonna live forever! When do the likes of us get a chance to work with the likes of Ishmael?"

"Well *you* still can, that's why I invited him."

"What are you saying?"

"I'm saying you can work with him; I knew you two would get along, once you'd found your common ground." He laughs, "Just mind yourself playing poker with his cousin, wots-his-name?"

"Explain."

Takes another drag, stands up and nods at me, all grim.

"You've had a change of heart," I says, "you're out, aren't you?"

"Am I out?" he asks himself, tight-lipped, "I suppose I am, though I've been realising I was out a long time before…"

"Before when?" I ventures, studying his glazed eyes.

"The moment Hitler ordered that Panzer division to halt in its tracks."

"Dunkirk?"

"Dunkirk."

"Good thing an' all," I mutter, thinking back. "We were sitting ducks on that beach."

"And what a 'heroic' escape we made. The entire British Army floats away and lives to die another day."

"Alright," I says, "but so what?"

"A load of bollocks, that's what! We were sitting ducks on that beach, and he ordered his airforce to stand down an' all."

"Fair dues," I says, trying to catchis-drift. "But we've always known this, ay? All sides were paid to war by the same purse, war is an industry like any other; Brass Hats can't make money if the war ends so soon, can they?"

"Exactly."

"But Dunkirk's hardly any reason to stop now!" I plead gently, "Same old, same old, that's what we're gonna change."

"You don't get it, do you?" he says, shaking his head at me. "I was out the moment we did nothing, said nothing – and why?"

"Fuck me, this was all forty years ago Sid, what's up with you?"

"Because we *believed* in this Country, even knowing what we knew?" he scoffs.

"Yeah, right!" I blurt out, "We believed. You, me, all and sundry knew and we were still *loyal!*" I checked myself. "Mate, this is still our Country, and its still got a chance. And *we've* got a chance, to do the right thing this time, to make a difference."

"Oh fuck off!"

"Ay?"

"Never ours to begin with, nothing is." He stops pacing. "You like skies, no?"

I frowns.

He grins, "And when you look at the sky, what do you see?"

"Sky."

"And who's it belong to?"

I frowns again.

"Exactly," he mutters, pacing up and down.

"Are you feeling alright, Sid, seriously—?"

"Have you ever wondered how it all fits inside your head, everything, when you look at the sky, its vastness, all inside your tiny bonce…"

I opened my mouth to speak, he raises his hand.

"I'll tell you why nobody said nothing," he snaps, stopping to stand in front of me. "Because they control our *minds*." Taps his head, and starts pacing again,

"They control everything people read in newspapers, all we see on telly and hear on radio – they decide who's the friend, who's the enemy; what gets ramned down our kids throats in schools and universities – they control everything we think is possible, and all we think is right, or wrong – and do you know what's worse?"

"What, Sid?"

"We *want* to believe we like our brain-dead lives, no matter how miserable, no matter how hard, so long as we're kept feeding on other people's misery worse off than ourselves. Do you see? Kept grazing, like sheep!"

I step back, trying to meet his steel-grey machinegun glare.

"Sheep," he sighs. "They *know* we're sheep."

"I don't get it, Sid, that's the whole point, this is nothing new to us. Something's gotta *change*, that's our purpose—"

"Oh something's gotta change alright, something's gotta change for everything to stay the same!"

"You've been listening to her, haven't you?" I mutter. "You're… infected with all that billion-neuron weird-shit."

"Yeah, I have been listening to her. And she's right. This is a prison of the soul, a concentration camp of the spirit, because without the capacity to first see the prison we've built, in here," taps his head again, "Nobody needs to control us. We do it to ourselves; we are both inmates and guards of our own private Panopticon. Take out Parliament, whatever or whoever – same old fucking same old."

"So you're out then."

He nods, "I wish you the best of luck, but I want my last years on the Earth plane to mean something, to do good, to be of service."

"You're going after the signal."

Shakes his head. "That technology's at least fifteen years ahead of anything I know; better leave it to Ishmael's crew to figure it out. The Arabs had already invented the electric battery when most of us still believed the world was flat. But," he smiles, "come with me a moment. I need to show you something."

I followed Sid down to the command centre; Brid was sitting like a pixie, cross-legged on a pile of ammo cases. Her eyes were closed, meditating. Sid puts a finger to his lips as we passed by, "Shhh," he whispers, "come and have a look at this," and leads me to 'his corner' at the far end, where he did all his tinkering about with his gadgets. Under his desk there's this big metal box, humming an ominous low drone.

"What you got in there," I grumbles, "Frankenstein?"

"Nah, an industrial generator," he says, "I converted it to run on compressed air instead of diesel. The engine's pistons are driven by air, and it has a built-in compressor, so it refuels its tanks with air as it's running. Zero pollution, completely free energy."

"Blimey, that's clever," I had to admit, despite my foul mood.

Smiles, "The whole house has been running on it all day. No problems so far, and I've plans for converting car engines too, but that's nothing compared to this," he says, picking up a small TV set from his desk, tiny, like the ones you get for caravans and all that.

He puts it back down gently, and nods at me, slowly, all mad-professor eyes, "I've cracked it," he whispers. "It was in the files, just a hint, I was looking for ways to neutralise the signal and stumbled across this!" he beams, "I did it!"

"You've invented the telly."

"What's the most important thing about the telly, the thing that makes it work?"

"The thing what turns it on, what you made me look like just now in front of the Ragheads, a knob!" I says, getting vexed again. "What are you on about?"

"The cathode-ray tube! It was developed by Sir William Crookes, but his original purpose for the telly couldn't be further from what we have today. Brid gave me a hand, literally," he chuckles, giving his telly an affectionate pat, wires it to a car battery. "So, what was Sir William working on, then? Not the kind of telly we have now. No, this is a Translocale Communicator. A device," he declares, proud as you like, "A machine to communicate with the Land of the Dead!"

I look at the telly, look at him, and I wanna cry.

"You see," he goes on, "The Government tasked Sir William with disproving, once and for all, the existence of the Afterlife."

"When?" I sighs, "Why?"

"Turn of the last century. Why? Same old same old: growing concerns over losing social control. Ordinary people were beginning to seek direct experience of spirituality by themselves, in séances, which were becoming way too popular, while Church attendances were at an all-time record low."

"So it was a standard psyops then."

"Bog standard. Sir William selects a team of leading scientists, and issues a challenge to hold these séances under strict laboratory conditions. The Government hoped it would discredit the whole Spiritualist Movement, and right enough, there were a lot of frauds around, but they hadn't banked on Sir William being so thorough.

He quickly sorts through the frauds, and focuses mainly on the most admired mediums of the day. And guess what? They ended up *proving* the existence of the Afterlife instead!" he chuckles, "It was like the conversion of Paul on the road to Damascus. Sir William and his team were witness to hundreds of physical manifestations."

"Hundreds of good'uns?"

Nods, "Dead and back again, and they took photographs, made plaster casts of their limbs, collaborated their fingerprints with police records, and even *worked* with scientists on the Otherside to build this," he pats his telly again, "An afterlife communication device."

"Oh mate, we've really gotta stop the whacky-backy, this is getting just too fucking crazy."

"But it really is simple technology, let me explain. All matter vibrates on a subatomic level, it has a speed, a frequency. These walls, this table, our bodies, everything vibrates within the same frequency range, so they *appear* solid to *us*. But if this table were to suddenly vibrate at a different speed, it would seem to us as if it had suddenly vanished. Equally, if we altered the frequency range of our five senses, it would seemingly vanish. It wouldn't cease to exist, the table would still be 'there,' just that we wouldn't *perceive* it.

The way the Afterlife exists, separately, is by this difference in wave characteristic – exactly the same way many radio waves occupy the same space without direct contact. Different worlds occupy the same space because they are differently tuned. This life, the one we experience now, is like a TV channel tuned into say, BBC 1. Turn the knob and you tune in BBC 2, or ITV and so on. But BBC 1 doesn't cease to exist just because you're watching a different channel. It's still there, broadcasting. Do you get it? *We do not die.* 'Death' is nothing more than a part of the universe normally out of the frequency range of our five senses."

I shrugs, glancing about, "So where is it *normally*, the Afterlife?"

"Just said, it's here, all around us, and in the life-force powering our physical bodies which carries on operating on other wavelengths.

The establishment wanted to restrict the results of his experiments to just the frauds, but Sir William went AWOL. He published everything in the leading scientific journal of his day – The Quarterly Journal of Science. I read them. These séances were repeatable experiments, the scientific method, and as I say, held under the strictest laboratory conditions they proved it, conclusively: people who had once lived on Earth, not only continued to live in other worlds, but could physically return through a medium." He smiles, "And that's the true story of our humble telly. Good, hey?"

"Yeah, just pukka – this is not good, Sid, not fucking good!"

"I understand, it changes everything, the implications are staggering! You're concerned about what this means in relation to our Operation, but—"

"Concerned? Fuck off, nah, seriously, just fuck off! Right? First, all that with Ishmael and now this? Alright, sorry, I've changed my perspective loads, I really have Sid, I'm really trying, specially after what happened down the Caff this morning, but what has this got to do with anything, for fuck's sake, it's this world, *here*, we should be concerned about, not some lala-land."

I stall. He was looking at me funny again.

"Alright, alright, so what's it do, I mean does it actually work?"

He unplugs the telly with a shrug.

"Sid, mate, don't be like that! I didn't mean it."

"Didn't mean what, Mr Barbelo?" Brid, sitting on a pile of ammo cases, shaking herself out of her meditations.

"Nothing dear," I says, and turns around. Sid's gone back upstairs.

"You two been arguing again?" she asks, climbing down.

"Moody cunt, yeah, he's got the hump again. So what you doing?"

"Time to go."

She comes up, and gives me a kiss, wrapping her arms around me. "Thank you, my knight," she whispers in my ear.

I hold onto her like I'm holding onto a life raft at sea – never was any good at hugs – and then let her go, trying not to grimace; my ribs were at me, excruciating. The Craft taught us many ways to lockout pain, but I'd also learnt something else: it serves you now and again to feel it, spruces you up and keeps you alert. Pain, like fear, has its function if controlled right. And I needed to be on high alert. This night wasn't over yet, not by a long chalk.

We shakes hands, "Pleasure to meet you, sir," says she.

"Pleasure was all mine," says I, "You look after yourself, alright?"

"You mean don't talk to strangers?"

We laughed at that. Fuck it, I was gonna miss her alright.

"Hold on," I says, rooting around in my pockets, "The Fool's a trump card, ay? Lucky…"

"Can be. Like the Joker, depends how you play it, why?"

"For luck, then." I pass her the card her nut-job mate had given me, the first day we met.

Smiles, slips it into her rain coat, "I'll come back, we'll see each other again, soon. I promise."

I give her a wave, and she climbs up the stairs.

A few moments later, I hear her saying goodbye to Sid, and the front door slam shut.

Immediately followed by Sid thundering down the stairs,

"Tool-up!" stuffing cartridges into his trench coat, "Now, now, now!"

Well, if there was one thing I was good at, but still—

"Steady on there, bit heavy handed, no?"

"Nah! It's not, I *know* it's not." He grins manically. "We're going over the top!"

Within seconds, Sid and I were out the house – two AKs wrapped in black bin liners under our arms – marching and thudding up Atlantic Road, keeping a discreet distance behind her.

Chapter 33

Peace

Rain and pain, that's what I remember most vividly about that night; greasy London drizzle crawling under my collar, and my battered ribs shooting a river of agony into my lungs with every step.

We kept up with Brid all the way to the High Street, where she mixed in with a crowd of young'uns, and got on a night bus.

Sid hails a black cab, we climb in, and tell the driver to park up behind; didn't pull away for a bit, just sat there, and then I saw... *it.*

"Oh Sid, oh mate, twelve o'clock!"

Sid doesn't have to be told twice. Up ahead, staring up at Brid's bus, there she was.

"The Wrenhunter," he mutters, "Yep, looks exactly like her."

"Where to?" asks the cabbie, tapping on the partition glass.

"When that bus moves, follow it, right?" I replies, and Sid stuffs a wedge into his paw, "We'll tell ya when to stop."

Cabbie grumbles something about Batman and Robin, and Sid and I just stare at the Wrenhunter, when the Yardie what I'd made a good'un months ago, sidles up next to her.

"That one bleeds," I whispers, "I cut it, major artery, groin"

"Well let's see how they both bleed, before they shift out," unwrapping his AK, "Got a clean line of sight—"

"Christ! Have ya *totally* lost your neuron, or what?"

"Oh don't start! They're still within our frequency range."

I clamp a restraining grip on his arm, "Then study their game plan *first,* ay?" Which was nothing, just stand there, frozen like statues.

"Time's up," says Sid, "Bored. I'm gonna have a word, then."

"Can't take you anywhere," I sighs, "Alright, strictly professional, right? I know you're afflicted and can't help it, but this is our manor now, we *don't* want a repeat of last time. I'll cover, phone box on the corner." But just then the bus pulled away and we follow behind.

Didn't speak after that, just prepared, mentally – for what?

We didn't know, and yet it did feel like what Sid had said at the house, 'going over the top.'

Sitting in that cab felt just like the trenches; blind panic, immediately followed a calm, heightened sense of things – I couldn't remember the last time London looked so… beautiful.

Pulling up at the stop before the Vauxhall flyover, we climbed out the cab; eyes pinned to Brid crossing the road, and followed.

She strode into a pub, The Old Hen it was, had been closed down for years, but reopened as a nightclub by a bunch of squatters; punks, travellers, and all sorts of young'uns were milling about.

"Wait," says Sid, over the thumping Darkie music coming from inside, "We can't go in there."

"Why not?"

"We'll stick out like a couple of sore knobs in a morgue!"

"What interesting visuals, thanks mate." I glance around, spot a pub opposite. "There then, we'll go in there and regroup."

It was about half-two in the morning, well after-hours, obviously, and a good old-fashioned lock-in doesn't normally let in strangers, but funny what you can get away with when you're an old geezer tooled-up to fuck on a Saturday night – nah, we were mates with the landlord's grandfather – Gawd blimey, what do you take us for?

We propped up the AKs amongst the umbrellas behind the door, and hovered over a table by the window with our pints.

"Sid," I gently asks, "all that you said earlier at the house…"

Solemn nod, "Meant every word, Joe. Booked my flight for Canada, going next week."

"Oh."

"You'll be alright with Ishmael."

"With Ishy baby? More than alright! Got the feeling he's got a few problems of his own though."

"Probably, they're on another level."

"Oh?"

"You'll see when you get to know them better," sips his pint, "And there's always Frank the Finger if things go to custard."

"Diamond geezer," I mutter, "Anyways, go find us a log cabin with a good view, ay? Big sky, that's all I want…" I pause, a cold shiver shot through me. "Do you feel it?"

He nods. "Glad you've not lost your touch. She's in trouble mate. All that about being forgiven or whatever, it's cobblers."

Glances out the window, "I don't like this, don't like this one bit. Even that rain, everything… feels… *wrong*…"

"Don't Sid, you're giving me the abdabs. I don't think you quite appreciate what we're up against here."

Glares, "Sorry, but yeah, I do – frequencies – predatory transdimensional beings shifting from lower density realities into ours, feeding, and trying to take over."

"Right, that's what I meant…" I pause, sips my pint. "Sid, what's a lower astral then?"

"Oh bloody hell, now he wants to know!"

"Nah, nah, I know what it is, but what is it *exactly*. Is it a place, like another world?"

Sighs heavily, glancing about the crowded pub, "Haven't got time to explain. It is and it isn't a place – like there are pockets of lower astral frequencies in our world too, there's both higher and lower frequencies here, interlacing, merging and forming what we call physical matter…"

"It is and it isn't a place, but it's still real then?"

"Think of the Lower Astral realms like rivers, dense seething rivers of nightmare misery, loneliness, extreme violence and pain, which are self-aware and create creatures which swim about tormenting each other, continuously. These creatures are its method of self-expression. And these rivers leave puddles as they splash by, and if you get too close to these puddles, they'll suck you into the river."

"But can you get out," I mutter.

"You can, but you don't know you can – drowned in agony and contempt you forget where you are, you forget who you are." Sips his pint, nods at me, "No doubt what we'll end up doing tonight will be lower astral. Significantly."

I fumble with my fag, "We'll just wait here a minute then, think on what to do, ay."

"We'll have to go in and get her out, that's what."

I nods. "Fuck it. Reminds me of that time in '42, that boozer we did, where was that again?"

"If you mean 'the night of a hundred and one fuckups,' then that was Paris, and it was in '43. And that was definitely lower astral."

"When did we meet again?"

"In '38."

"Blimey, thought it was '41, must be age and all that."

"Dunno mate, I've got the same problem. Some of it's clear as a bell, mostly it's all a drumfire haze, but I know it was '38 'cos Sally got recruited that year too."

"From Ireland, right? I mean who…"

Shrugs, "Who, what, where?"

I sighs, "Leave it in the square. The Craft accommodates."

"The Craft accommodates."

"Anyways, Paris, right, fuck me I remember that alright. German High Command wall-to-wall, Sally flirting away, giving it all honeypot, the tart, and then they cop's on the gaff's rigged to blow! I dunno how we got out of that one."

"We didn't."

"Oh, right, no, you got caught…"

"Copped one in the arm, two in the legs."

"And one in the arse!"

We laugh at that. "Still," I says, "P.O.W? Two square meals and your own bunk? You lucky, lucky bastard!"

"*One* square meal alright, laced with enough fluoride to sink a battleship – went cross-eyed after a week! Shuffling around like fucking zombies, we were."

"Yeah? Took us three months to get back, living like wild animals we were, up in that forest in Brittany. I still can't look at a squirrel without my mouth watering."

Frowns, "But Sally always said yous had the time of your life."

"We did," I took a slug of beer, "Probably would still be there, if it wasn't for the Resistance."

He smiles. "They were good times though, even if it *was* all a load of bollocks."

"Hell on Earth, but yeah, looking back on it, yeah… I wonder where she is now."

"Joe," he whispers, "Sally's… Sally's on the Otherside, mate."

I didn't hear, not that I didn't hear, but like when you hear but don't want to hear.

"Bet you she's causing it somewhere… I dunno, probably Asia, that's where I picture her, always liked it there, the heat suited her. Some head-hunting island in the Philippines or something, ay?"

"Joe," he says in a tense whisper, "Your wife's on the Otherside, crossed over seven years ago, Army knew 'cos she told them, had to…" pauses, and sighs. "She was penniless."

"Come again, Army knew, but we didn't?"

"She'd gone Grey, that's how we didn't."

Gone Grey, craft-speak, meaning vanished off the radar, as opposed to just being under it.

"Was on the streets, down in Kent the whole time, she was not in a good way… ah, let's just say she's happy now."

"Was only pretend anyways," I says, quickly taking stock, raising my glass. "Tenstar Sally, almost the most proper wife I never had."

"Long live Sally," whispers Sid, and we clinks glasses.

"Hold on, 'happy now'… come again?"

Sips his pint. "Said, she wasn't very happy, but she is now."

"Did you go and see her?"

He grins, but then shoots me this funny look, nah, *really* odd… quizzical, like he suddenly didn't know where he was, or I'd grown two heads or something, and finally whispers, "Saw her on my Translocale Communicator. Said she wanted to come back, soon," he chuckles, "Unfinished business. Looking bloody good, she was…"

A short pause followed.

"Transfuck that you cunt!"

I know it was Sid but it was like my fist didn't, it swung out, clocked him a good'un on the jaw. He took it squarely enough though. Always did.

The pub went quieter, and then louder again.

Rubs his jaw, holds up his hand. "Enough, sorry, it was just me having a bubble; thought it might cheer you up, you miserable old cunt! Nah, seriously, a fax came through, this morning. Game over…"

"Fucking hell Sid, sometimes I really don't understand you."

Picks up his pint and downs it in one. "Right, we playing silly-buggers here all night or going to work; what's the plan?"

"Dunno," I shrugs. "Suppose you're right… we'll just have to go in and find out."

We didn't have to wait long. No sooner we step outside, than an ambulance arrives, and then another, and another – all wailing sirens and flashing lights, closely followed by a fleet of paddy wagons and jam sandwiches, screeching to a halt, one by one, outside the pub.

Old Bill swarming all over the gaff.

First thing they did was cordon off both ends of the street, clearing out the residents from the flats above the shops, and the pub we'd just been in.

The pub what Brid was in was doing a pukka job of clearing itself out; young'uns scattering everywhere, probably thinking it was a drug's raid, and then we copped an eyeful of the squad in one of the paddy wagons – suiting up armoured vests, loading up – tooled-up to the nines.

"Oi, oi," mutters Sid.

"I see them."

"Didn't see her."

"Still inside," I whispers, as a Plod was plodding up to us.

"This is what she meant, the Illuminati."

"Oh leave it out, please, ay."

"Now sirs," says the Plod, glancing at our bin liner packages under our arms – Gawd only knows what he thought they was – and ushers us along, "It's not safe here, you're going to have to move behind the cordon, and board the coach with us."

"Of course Officer," says Sid. "What's happening though?"

"Gas leak, likely to blow the whole street."

My arse, but Sid gives me the nod, and we begin side-winding our way through squad cars, slowly, hanging back with each step, putting on the 'old geezer had one too many' show, until we were under the radar enough to pin ourselves behind an ambulance, and then dived into an alleyway to our left – crouched behind two council bins, brimming with rubbish – good vantage point, a clear line of sight to both ends of the road.

"Dead-end," grumbles Sid, turning around and peering into the gloom behind us. "We're sitting ducks here."

I scan the walls of the two buildings either side of us, "Right enough, got any better ideas?"

Sid creeps off to the end of the ally, and comes back, grinning from here to China, "Wall, ten foot, railway tracks, Albert Embankment behind." Meaning a pukka escape route.

It was quick and efficient, I'll give 'em that, had the street evacuated in minutes, seemed like, and then the first armed squad lines up, ready to go to work.

"Here," whispers Sid, passing me a balaclava.

I slips on the mask, and stuff my walking stick into my belt. "Did you bring any grenades?"

"Nah, did you?"

"Nah, and we could do with an RPG an' all."

"Two-inch mortar, better off."

"Right, two-inch mortar and the Bren Gun."

"Told you it was gonna get messy."

"Alright! So I never listen – fuck me though, this reminds me of another thing... dream I had."

"What happened?"

"Not sure, nightmare, you were in it!"

He laughs.

"Shhh! Yeah, I was Earless Mickey and you was Dimbo the Elephant."

"Earless! Bloody-well says it all, must be 'cos you never—"

"Look who's talking, must be 'cos you're – here we go!"

And fuck me, it was just like Paris alright, the first squad piles into the pub, teargas canisters smashing through the windows, and there's an immediate exchange of automatic gunfire. We quickly unwrapped our arsenal.

"Joe, I'm getting pissed off here."

"Royally. Sounds like someone's giving them a right run for their money, ay?"

"We getting her out or what?"

"Has it got lower astral yet?"

"Lower astral to fuck..."

The firing intensified, another squad going in.

We looks at each other, Sid's upper lip curls,

"In Mad Mick we trust," he growls.

"In Mad Mick we trust," I echoes, and unleash hell.

I suppose we had the jump on them, last thing they expected; going at it back to back, slaughtering through their ranks like a hot knife through butter – and fuck me it felt good, lovely, lovely chaos, but we got about ten yards from the pub doors and it was game over.

Doors fling open, Brid charges out, AK in hand.

For a split second she looks us straight in the eyes. Time stops.

Silence.

I was still aware of Sid beside me, the car we were using for cover, the squad around us – all suspended in mid-motion – and then an ear piercing howl rises up, Brid drops her weapon. She just stands there, smiling – arms outstretched like she wants to embrace the world – her lips mouthing one word, one simple word what at that moment seemed to hold the meaning of the stars, of existence itself:

Peace.

Gunfire immediately cuts her to ribbons.

"Alleyway!" screams Sid – no time for why, no time for how, no time for anything except survival.

And no, not exactly a walk in the park going back neither, but we'd been through worse, done this countless times and had confusion on our side.

Standard rear action, flittering from car to car, covering each other in turns, steadily gaining ground – a homicidal game of Tag, in other words – until finally we've dived into the alleyway, bullets rattling off the metal bins we we're shielded behind.

Lying my stomach, I steal a peek over the road. Parked cars, a dozen rifles braced over roofs and bonnets.

They cease fire, regroup. We reload.

The cold rain continues to pour.

"Copped one," grumbles Sid, shuffling up, strapping a cable-tie tourniquet around his thigh, "You?"

"All present and correct. Sid, did you hear that… noise?"

Nods, "I heard it."

"Horrible, howling, the feharchrove's howlings. In olden times they'd say if you heard the Banshee—"

"Fucking hell Joe, not now, mind the abdabs…" Stalls, looks straight at me, "You're right, if you heard the Banshee it meant you're a good'un. Joe, it's been a pleasure knowing you."

"What?"

"I think one of us is…"

We lock eyes. He nods, all grim.

"Pleasures all mine," I mutters. "Really Sid, I mean it."

"Fuck off, only joking!" he chuckles, "We're worth ten of them each," glancing at the wall behind us, "Just have to get over that."

I glance over my shoulder, "You first then, 'hop-a-long.'"

"Been dying to say that, I bet. Nah, you first."

"Sid, *not* the time to play silly buggers. You first."

"Toss for it," he growls, and gets out a pound coin.

"Heads," I sighs.

"On account you're off your head?" he chuckles again.

"Fuck's sake, Tails then."

He flips the coin, it lands between us.

"Go!"

Shouldering his rifle, Sid opens fire. I bolt for the wall.

Not easy scrambling up, cracked ribs an' all, but I sling my weapon over the top, adrenalin and a hostile disposition does the rest.

On the other side, quickly brace Happy Stick against the wall, and step up on the handle, hauling myself up again.

Left arm hooked over the top, my weapon's on murderous automatic. Sid's rapidly backing away from the bins, emptying his clip, about to bolt – lovely job, we've got them pinned behind their position – and then that fucking telltale break in their gunfire.

We both know what's coming next.

I chuck my weapon. Sid's already chucked his, hurtling for the wall with the desperation of the damned. In two's and three's, the grenades pour into the alleyway, bouncing about his feet.

Bracing my wooden knee against the wall, I hook my good peg over the top. Sid leaps, grabs my wrists. I leans back all my weight, pulling him up.

"Pleasure's all mine," he grins.

"What – oh fuck off no!"

Sid lets go – grenades explode at once – I drop like a lead balloon on the other side. Using the momentum to roll away into the underbrush, a reflex action grabs my weapons, and I peg it towards the Embankment.

Game Over.

PART THREE

☠ rebirth ☠

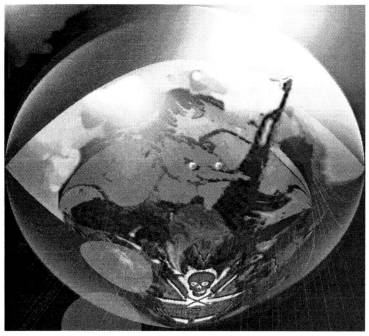

"Once population is out of control, it requires authoritarian government, even fascism, to reduce it. To really reduce population quickly, you have to put all the males into fighting and you have to kill significant numbers of fertile females."
Thomas Ferguson, Head of the U.S. State Department's Office of Population Affairs. 1981

"As we know, there are known knowns. There are things that we know that we know. There are known unknowns, that is to say, there are things that we now know, we don't know. But there are also unknown unknowns; there are things we do not know, we don't know."
Donald Rumsfeld, US Secretary of Defence. 2002

Chapter 34

Dark Side Of The Moon

Ditched my AK in the Thames, got home on a night bus, crammed full of young'uns drinking beer, smoking and laughing.

Chucked myself through the door, put the kettle on, and made a cup of tea. Sat there at our kitchen table.

It was quiet.

Fucking cold and quiet; my ears were ringing like the Bow Bells on '78 from gunfire and grenades.

Lost my bird, my best mate, got run over by a bus and found out my wife's brown bread – it was probably the worst day of my life, should've been. Didn't feel a thing. No sadness, no remorse. Nothing. It was like nothing had happened.

If anything was sad, that was.

Drank my tea, made another, brought up a small arsenal from the basement, and redid the splints on my fingers, waiting for the knock on the door to come.

Sid was identifiable – they had records and knew where he lived – so they'd know I was most likely the other geezer what had been at the slaughter with him; leastways they'd be round alright, either way.

Don't ask what I was doing, all I knew was everything had come crashing down on my head, and I was even more up for it now than ever – well-up for going out in blaze of homicidal glory.

Cradling my rifle on my lap, I sat by the window, and waited; watching the night sky growing lighter – lovely purples, greys and mauves – dreaming of growing wings and flying up into the dawn.

But the knock didn't come, well, not in the way I thought it would.

I opened the front door, in strides my auld CO. Doesn't even look at me, just nods at the squad car outside, and then putting his arm round my shoulder, says,

"Not very clever that, was it?"

"No sir, not the best idea I've ever had."

He groans, raising his hands in the air, "Let's have a chat then."

Shutting the door behind us, we goes into the kitchen.

"Joe, Joe…" he mutters, shaking his head.

"I'm fucked, ay?"

"Royally."

"Alright."

"They still need you though, love to have you on the team. This little misunderstanding can still be fixed, I'll personally—"

"Team? Team? What fucking team, selling our Country down the Swaney?"

"Steady on there, old chap."

"Up yours Frank! Stuff the lot of yous! Didn't even find out, didn't even bother telling me? Cunts!" Checked myself, "Sorry," I says, calming down, "Sally… she's gone now too."

"Ahhh, right, sorry to hear that."

"They're all gone, nobody left."

"I'm left," he sighs. "But you know what they're like, Joe, same old, same old."

"Use you and drop you."

"Like a hat." Takes off his Trilby, drops it on the table.

"Don't fix nothing," I says, "I'm out."

"Oh we all say that, from time to time," grins, rubbing his hands, "Nice cuppa, that's what we need."

I put the kettle on, and our morning newspaper pops through the letterbox. I goes over to the door.

"Page five," he calls over, "'Fire burns pub in Vauxhall. Suspected gas leak, but IRA terror attack not ruled out.' Am I right?"

"Dead right," I mutter, going back into the kitchen, making our teas.

"See? MI7, like a Swiss clock."

"I see alright."

"It's big, Joe, way too big."

"Cuts deep."

"Cuts deep. And so," glancing about appreciatively, "Sid lived here too."

"Yep."

"Leastways he had a good innings."

"Yep."

"Good man, was Sid, damn good fellow."

I hand him his tea, and lean up against the sink.

He sits down at the table, nods at the door leading to the basement, "We've found three in London, so far, heard rumours of at least ten more, another ten in Birmingham, Glasgow, five in Portsmouth, one in the Isle of Wight, of all ruddy places," he sips his tea, "And Bradford – know anything about the Brotherhood of True Islam?"

"Put me on the payroll, I might tell ya."

He chuckles. "In any case, it's all beginning to worry the boys at HQ no end."

"Is it?"

"If it's any consolation, they don't have a clue who or how many are out there."

"Met their nemesis, then," I mutter.

"Nemesis—!" gags on his tea, "It's like trying to command a troop of nuns lost in a brothel! Bloody shambles, every month, on the week leading up to a T-Day."

"Stretching their resources, ay?" I says, "Can't blame the Irish," I smiles, "And what's worse, they can't use it."

"British War Heroes Plot To Overthrow Parliament? I shudder at the headlines! No, they can't use it, that's ridiculous." He shrugs, "But cut off the head, the body dies – it ends here," squints his knowing squint, "I can't cover for you any longer."

"Ahhh, bit of a problem there, Frank. You see, I don't *personally* have a clue how many are out there neither, nobody does. So it might end here, or it might not; depends if yous nip it in the bud early enough. But, judging by the state of the Nation?" I shrugs. "A nod's as good as a wink—"

"To a blind horse," he groans, "What do you have in this command centre?"

"Enough," I says, "Come down and have a butcher's."

"No need, I'm sure it was enough. Pity though." Shakes his head. "How long did you know her?"

"Brid…"

Sips his tea. "Brid."

I sat down. "I dunno, a year, a lifetime, feels like."

"And she was hiding, here, the whole time."

"Sir, I'm going to ask, suppose I shouldn't but fuck it, all of that for a girl?"

"Joe, she was not entirely alone in there, there were... others..."

"We almost did it, Frank, could of had her out; she was almost like one of ours, but... but she just... just stood there."

"Maybe she'd had enough."

"Enough of what, sir? Who was she then? Who gave the kill order? What section, what branch at least? Don't say T Branch, that wasn't IRA in there, that wasn't no regular ops, Frank, seen a thing or two in my time and that wasn't fucking *normal.*"

Doesn't reply, and starts scanning for wiring on the walls and ceiling.

"Timer's set," I says, following his eyes flitting about.

"The moment you saw the car pull up, I wager!" He grins at me. "Planning to take us all out?"

"Until I saw it was you, of course."

"Of course," glancing at his watch.

"Seven thirty," I says.

"Can't be reset."

I shakes my head. "Wouldn't try it, Sid's handiwork. I spent the night thinking, take out as many of these cunts as I can, didn't know what else to do, but nah – I think I know now what's got to be done alright, and it's gonna be done right..."

I pause, we looks at each other.

Taking my memorial pen from my breast pocket, I lays it down on the table.

"Frank," I whispers, "Do it."

Frank hesitates for a moment, but places his pen next to mine, meaning we were on sacred ground now – whatever was going to be said next was never said.

He runs a hand over his face, and nods at me,

"I don't fully understand myself, and that's the main reason I've covered for you so long. Believe me, it's not been easy."

"Francis Moon," I chuckles, "always looking for your inside man, ay Frank? A finger in every pie."

Smiles, "This Country, it's a complete mess, Joe, I need good men on the inside, men I can trust."

"Alright Frank, what's going on?"

"I wish I fucking knew," he sighs. "I know an organisation calling itself Common Purpose has been recruiting since the War, most of our leaders since have been members."

"Sid mentioned them."

"He did? Ahhh, the Yank's briefcase."

"Sounded like some kinda secret cult."

"No, just small, highly focused, but they've recently been branching out into all public sectors, ready to make their presence known – internationally," he adds with a concerned frown. "But Common Purpose is still only wheels within wheels, just a part of the bigger machine."

"Part of a Top Cunt Firm. Freemasons?"

"I suspect their top levels are a part of it, but not all of it."

"Taking over the Government."

"The Government," he echoes, stroking his forehead, "The Government no longer exists, we run the Country now; we've factions of the Intelligence Community who have…"

"Have what?"

Pauses, glances about, and turns to me,

"Joe, I receive orders and I give orders – the lie changes at every level – but what I deal with on a day to day basis are many governments, all fighting with each other and *within* each other, for power. And for quite a number of years, from before the last war, possibly from even before the Great War, one of these factions has been steadily gaining ground and taking charge."

"Same old same old, then."

Chuckles, sips his tea, "Except nobody knows who. Elements of MI5 think it's elements of MI6 and Mossad. MI6 suspects factions of itself, MI5 and the Knights of Malta," he chuckles again, "Personally, I always suspected CIA and the Jesuits, and then the factions of the IRA allied to the Knights of Columbanus. It's fucked up beyond all recognition, Joe, nobody knows who or what's pulling the strings – for a time everything led back to the Vatican, and yet even our contacts in the SVS are just as boggled."

I sips my tea, "Right, and when was the SVS ever boggled about anything?"

He nods, "Back in our day, but I believe that's changed. Genuinely. And I'm not alone in that, my Intel is solid."

"Whoever holds the purse, pulls the strings. Frank, we've always known our banking dynasties are answerable to the Vatican. Nationalising the banks here was a bloody good strategy."

"Undoubtedly," he concedes, "And I personally know a dozen Brass Hats, at least, who would have supported it. But are they still answerable, were they ever, and would people go along with it?"

"They'd be fucking mad not to, once they knew *their* money was in *their* control—"

"No, no, that's only one level of the lie. I'm talking about something else. Right across the board, worldwide, every nation is going through an identical reshuffle of power, and the only issue anyone appears to agree on is keeping the plebs in the dark, particularly about the fact nobody knows who's actually in charge. It's the panic we're trying to avoid, see?"

I laughed at that, "Oh I see alright, so it's finally happened; you've created your Frankenstein's Monster and it's biting yous in the arse!"

He shrugs, giving me that 'we're doing everything we can' smile he used to give when he'd lost track of a man behind enemy lines.

And then he leans over the table, whispers,

"The Intelligence Community was always self-regulating, and yet still accountable to the chain of command. Chatham House. We were the only exception, that I was aware of."

"So let me hazard a guess," I whispers back, "Since running the drugs trade, factions within SIS have become self-funded. Right?"

"Totally, self-sufficient and yes, self-replicating."

"Follow the money then, as Sally used to say."

"It's not that simple, nobody's accountable any longer."

"Bloody hell Frank, I would've of thought you of all people would've had a suss on all this."

Leans back into his chair, shrugs again. "FUBAR."

"And the lie changes at every level," I mutter.

"Which means someone, somewhere, is hiding the truth," sips his tea, "Perhaps it was always like this. Draw your own conclusions, I'm beginning to suspect nobody was ever in charge. Though I can tell you one thing I know for sure. It was your section on Methane Digesters and free energy that set alarms ringing. Follow the money? Follow the middleman, I always say."

"Good point," I says.

"Currencies are based on oil speculation, as opposed to precious metals as they once were, and yet it's not OPEC who regulates this – somewhere down the chain there's a middleman between the oil producing countries and the oil companies." He shrugs again, "The World Bank, the Bilderberg Group, the Vatican? Obvious choices."

"Too obvious."

Smirks, "Now, if you were to reconsider, we could work together and get a handle on who's—"

"Fuck off Frank, said I'm out and I mean it – regime change or zilch – last thing I'm gonna do is be one of your spooks." I roll up my sleeve. "And this?"

"*Non Serviam,*" he says, and smiles warmly.

I frown. "Yes, but *what* is it?"

"That's our motto, remember? I Will Not Serve, and never a truer word. The Craft bowed to none, answered to no one."

"No, I don't remember, I don't remember when or where it came from."

Frank explains patiently, "You, and then Sid, were the first with that, to begin with. Set a trend; by the end of the War we'd all got one done."

I roll down my sleeve, lower my tone, "I had a run-in with a fucking Satanist and he had one an' all!"

"A Satanist?" he declares incredulously. "Strange coincidence."

"Coincidence."

"Must be, we're soldiers, not devil-worshipers. In any case, the Craft was retired in '67, shortly after HQ was relocated."

"Could it have been reformed?"

"That, I would've heard."

I sighed with frustration. Frank gives me a reassuring pat on the shoulder.

"You're addled," he says, "Exhaustion can play tricks on the mind. It was just a coincidence."

"No Frank, I'm talking about organised child abduction – ritual murder!"

Scrutinising my anxious glare, he leans back into his seat, and nods his head slowly, "I've heard the rumours, Joe, don't think I haven't, and whoever or whatever is gaining the upper hand, I've seen things – seen men changed at HQ," he says with a faraway stare.

"And I mean changed. It's in the eyes, it's all in the eyes, people can't hide if you know how to look, and these men's eyes are… *different*, from one day to the next. World leaders have the same eyes too; they don't start that way, that's how they end up. Almost as if they've been made to watch something, shown something that… something…"

He pauses, at a loss for words, and just stares ahead.

I shuddered, I went all dizzy for a moment, the hairs on the back of my neck stood up – I could feel the abdabs rising, thick in the air between us.

"Frank," I says, very quietly, trying to steer the subject back, "So who was Brid working for?"

He shakes himself, and flashes me a quick smile. "The Brid situation, let's call it, is above top secret; Alpha Clearance, you understand."

I nods.

Sips his tea, "Tell you much about herself?"

"Didn't stop! She was… not the full shilling, well, that's what I thought, at first, but then… but then it began to make sense. And strange things started happening to us too, Frank, seriously. MI13 couldn't hold a candle to it! Felt I was losing my mind – saw a *thing*… howling, and… and nothing, forget it, doesn't matter now."

"Did she ever mention anything… anything she was hiding?"

"Well she said *she* was hiding… I don't understand."

"Something she stole, perhaps…"

"Dunno what you're on about, seriously, she said she was one of their experiments, something called the Illuminati."

"Interesting, that's a name I've not come across for a while. eighteenth century mystics, if I remember correctly."

I nods. "Are they… still about?"

A tense pause followed.

"Cut off the head, the body dies," he mutters.

"Which head though…"

Snatching his pen from the table, he raises his eyebrows, shooting me that look what says he's already said more than his job's worth, meaning my life, and glances at his watch,

"What's your proposed destination?"

"North, for now. This ain't over yet, not by a long chalk."

"I'll rumour south."

Draining the last of his cuppa, he stands up, putting on his coat and hat,

"Car out front, one at both ends of the street, and one at the back. Skip through the back, the garden, that's your best bet; they're expecting us to come out together." Glances at his watch again. "I'll wait here a few minutes, give you a head start," he adds with a wink.

"Thank you sir," I says, standing up.

"Pleasure, Captain, as always."

"I expect we won't be in touch, then."

"I expect we won't," he says, and shakes my hand, "Thanks for the tea."

Without further ado I peg downstairs, grab my travelling kit, throw in a couple of grenades for good measure, and take a last look around. Command centre, didn't make any sense now without her and Sid, and I was just about to go, but stalled – Sid's telly yoke.

Truth be told, the thing made my skin crawl, and recalling that odd 'two-headed' look he'd shot me in the pub didn't help, but I picked it up, stuffed it into my backpack too. Fuck it, I had his memoirs, which was something he never knew I knew about – broke all the rules but I never grassed, never have never will – and I thought, well… I dunno what I thought, I had exactly three minutes to evacuate or I was Barbelo Stew!

What, out through the back garden? Just four cars, one out front and blah fuckity blah? If you believed that bollocks, please don't sign up for the mortality trade – you'll be hanging off Blackfriars Bridge quicker than shit through a goose.

Not saying Frank didn't have me going for a second, but I'd nailed my colours to the mast now; I was out, resigned, well-on the dark side of the Moon and fair game.

So nah, I used our secret tunnel for my getaway – well it wouldn't have been secret if I'd told ya about it, would it – and another good thing about having council workers on the Firm, they're fucking good diggers, I'll give them that.

I pulled the hatch under the stairwell, and scrambled inside…

Chapter 35

The Wait…

Bloody loud it was, the explosion, and largely contained in the basement, the ground shook from Atlantic Road to Brockwell Park, leastways that's what Graham said later round his gaff, which was round the back of the park.

I knew I'd be safe there for a good while. Rob, the Sergeant down the Station, reckoned he'd never seen so many plainclothes in all his days; rumour was they were following a lead to some top cunt 'IRA' geezer what had legged it up north – made me laugh – north, south, which way did he go?

There's a classic double-think there, if ya catch it, I'll buy you a Mars Bar.

Truth was, I had no intention of going nowhere just yet – best thing always, stay put. Forget all that house to house searching bollocks you see on telly, the last place they come looking is under their noses, specially not for one of their own. They don't have neither the resources nor the inclination.

After a few weeks they might get a couple of local Peelers to keep an ear to the ground, if that even, and they're all kept busy trying to keep their jobs; pissing about with parking fines and nicking youg'uns for cannabis.

Nah, what they do is open up a file on you, all hush-hush of course, and only follow the strongest leads; mark a territory, and like wolves, spiral inwards on their prey.

But even that's bollocks – mostly they just wait, wait for you to fuck up and show up, on the radar.

Remember that, if Gawd forbid you ever find yourself in a similar pickle – because the important thing is to stay calm, channel the stress in positive and creative ways.

It's the pressure of the wait they're counting on – a double-edged sword – the longer you get away with it, the more the stress builds up, and the more likely you'll do something stupid, like gut some cunt what looks at you funny on a bus, thinking you've been clocked.

Chances are he's only looking at you funny 'cos you do look funny; sitting there all eyes-a-popping and fidgeting like a cunt.

Stay calm.

Or the stress turns inwards, and after time you create the delusion that you've got away with it. 'Blimey,' you say to yourself, 'they must've forgotten about me.' And then you go and do something really stupid, like get a job and give the boss your bank details for your wages. Believe me it happens. And chances are you really had got away with it, silly cunt.

It's a fucked up unconscious thing, the not knowing when you'll get nabbed, anything to put an end to the stress of the wait.

Stay calm, it cuts both ways.

They've all the time in the world for the wait.

You've all the time in the world to let them wait.

Now, all that's good, but I couldn't play the hermit around Graham's forever, and the long-term choices weren't plentiful. I had a handful of passports for abroad, some cash, but falling foul of all the king's men meant I was a fucking liability for the Firm, and don't get me wrong, they could fix a lot of things but not this – way out of our league.

Ishmael did pop into my head a couple of times, had plenty of clout, but even he wouldn't go near me, not for all the tea in China. But that's alright, what I wanted more than anything was solid Intel on these Illuminati cunts, and if anybody could find anything, it was his crew – but it was too soon for all that, needed to go Grey again, vanish off the face of the Earth for a while.

Didn't fancy the bunkers up north, in case you're asking, I'd thought about it in the kitchen before Frank had come round, and thought, nah. That's all I can say about that – call it a gut feeling.

So I let myself go, meaning I didn't shave or wash for the whole time round Graham's, got into a trench coat and ditched my dentures – right, Barbelo, Gentleman of the Road, that was me from now on, and pukka little job I made of that too.

Dentures in one pocket, bottle of wine in the other, and with Happy Stick now suitably under the radar too – scuffed-up with bitumen paint – we hit the road, headed south.

I was on my own again, and fuck it, a part of me rejoiced – hadn't strapped a pack to my back for donkey's, it felt good.

Brighton first, fancied a bit of sea air, didn't make anyone a good'un, heart wasn't in it, or better said, I was changing – didn't rightly know it myself then, but that's what was happening. Didn't do much of anything, stayed calm, channelled the stress positive; dossed along the seafront, in other words, and sank a few pints in the evenings down The Crescent; served anyone in there, a rare auld bunch of social misfits we were.

Travellers mostly, not just your Romany, but young'uns living in vans, trucks, busses and all sorts, and it wasn't long before I ended up kipping in a communal bus, parked up on a field near Lewes, near the Nick.

They'd take in anybody, this lot, didn't matter who. Never asked questions and names weren't important – everybody was either called Spider, or named after cartoon characters or an engine part, seemed like, and I got tagged too, 'Peg,' on account I had a wooden leg.

Right, my kind of people alright.

Resourceful and creative bunch too, clever, found that out on my first skip-run to Tesco's with them.

Conducted early morning, 'cos of the security guards, it was done in proper order, right under the cunt's noses; nobody got nicked and we requisitioned enough food to feed everybody for a month.

I shit you not. Fifteen people, and their dogs, fed for free.

It's all there in bagfuls, by the way, just round the back of your local supermarket about to be chucked out and wasted – and they tell us people are starving because of an overpopulation problem.

Security guards paid to guard a skip full of food?

Says it all.

Still, it wasn't all a bed of roses, and I wish I could say all Travellers were that nifty, but they weren't. I was lucky I'd fallen in with a good crew, but the main drawback of taking in anybody is that you take in anybody. And oh my good Gawd, some of the fruitcakes lurking about site sometimes, well, if my heart had been in it, there were days I'd of thought all my horses had come in at once.

And yeah, right, it was bound to happen…

Chapter 36

Code Green

"The brew's ready Peg; are you sure you don't want some?"

I looks up from reading Sid's memoirs, and Sprocket's grinning down at me, the biggest beard I'd ever seen on anybody under thirty, or anybody, for that matter, wrapping a blanket around my shoulders.

He asks again, stoking up the wood burner with a stick, "Are you sure? I know you like the quiet life, who doesn't, but a party every now and again's good for the soul."

The night was frosty outside, but inside, the bus was empty for once; warm and toasty, the wood burner cranked up full. Made from an old gas bottle, it was – like I say, they were virtually self-sufficient, never threw anything away, reused and fixed everything and anything; stuff from local skips or half-inched from the Council. Even their vehicles ran on old chipper oil. The only thing I'd seen them pay for was army surplus, and only 'cos it's made to last ten times longer than civvy gear.

Dunno why, but that tickled me pink whenever I thought about it. Everywhere I looked, clothes, tools, the tarps, even the shovel for digging your shit-pit was a mismatch of kit from some army or another; mostly German.

"Not sure," I says, sitting up in my dossbag (Swiss). "What's this brew about anyway?"

He shifts my candle aside, and sits down next to me.

"Nothing to worry about," he smiles, "we do a trip every year, this time of year."

"Hmmm, a trip, LSD? No thanks."

Eyes widen, "Wouldn't give that shit to my worst enemy! No, this a shroom fest, *magic mushrooms*, they're natural, can't do you any harm. LSD though, that's a military mind-fuck. Not many people know that," shakes his head, combing his fingers through his beard, "But I know, I wrote my thesis on it in college. Acid was a drug developed for torture and interrogating prisoners. And when the anti-Vietnam war movement looked like it was actually winning, the CIA released it to the public to get everybody so fucked up—"

"Nah, nah, but what about all that carry-on about peace and love and all that free your mind bollocks?"

"Exactly, bollocks! Oh it can give you the illusion of mind expansion and mystical connections and enlightenment but it's bullshit!" he laughs, twirling his hands over his head, "What enlightenment? If that were true, we'd be surrounded by millions of enlightened Buddhas!"

"Fair point, it's wall-to-wall cunts instead."

"All LSD's ever done for us is fried people's heads and given society a continuous stream of psychotics and fuckheads. I don't take any drugs anymore, Peg, you know that, I don't even drink beer; not necessary. Life's weird enough as it is."

"Suppose. But I do like me pint, and the odd joint these days."

"Well who doesn't, but you don't need drugs when you've got yourself, and your people," he grins, pats me on the shoulder. "And Gertrude, here," he smiles, spreading his arms out, then giving the wooden panelling of his bus an affectionate pat. "But the shrooms? Different story – the shrooms are a psychic detox, clean you out, and if you lose your way, they can give yourself back to yourself – shrooms are shamanic. I partake once a year to keep myself in shape," he taps his head, "In here. Because when the shit hits the fan, and the fabric of society comes crumbling down about our ears, what's between our ears will be what saves us."

"Never a truer word," I mutter, listening to the wild laughter coming from outside. They could probably get through Armageddon like nothing had happened, this lot, they had adaptable brains alright; the nifty way they run things would've made any unit back in my day proud. I shit you not, and they looked out for each other – leastways better than your average cunt slumped in front of telly soaps, full of beer and soft porn. And Gawd save us from the day there's no burgers and chips down the chipper – that'll be Bambi's Revenge that will – fuck me, there's hardly nobody left who even knows how to grow a potato; people will be eating each other in the streets!

"Does sound like fun alright."

"Okay, Peg," he says, "plenty to go around if you change your mind; there's thousands of lovely little shrooms in the pot outside."

He grins, gets up, and puts on his council fluoro-jacket.

"Very well, wait a moment, I'll just strap on my peg, ay."

Why not, in for a penny, in for a pound – and a bit of socialising was definitely in order.

I'd been with them a couple of weeks now, hanging about the field, helping out with vehicle repairs, which I was good at, but mostly just kept myself to myself, drinking tea in the bus, reading bits of Sid's memoirs, and thinking. A fuck of a lot of thinking, specially about his orphanage years – shocking's too mild a word.

They'd been busy preparing for their shroom fest alright. In the middle of the field was this big tarp-covered igloo-house they called a 'Bender,' on account it was made from bendy sticks (Willow's good, if you're asking). And a marquee was set up, and a lot of wooding must've gone on 'cos the central fire was massive – and there were loads of people milling about too, vehicles were parked around everywhere, from other sites near and far.

"Come with us," says Sprocket, and leading me to the marquee, we went inside, headed towards a table at the far end.

Standing behind the table was this right wanker I didn't like from the start – dishing out mugs of shroom tea from a huge tea urn.

The candles flickered horrible across his scuzzy dreadlocks as he prattled, "Alright Sprocket? Long time no see."

"All is good, you've got some shrooms, I see."

"You still driving that old junk heap?" twisted grin, pouring him a cup, "Why don't you get yourself a real vehicle? Got me a Bedford TK, state of the fucking art!"

"I'm happy for you," says Sprocket, and turns to me, "This is Merlin." He turns to the cunt. "Merlin, meet our mate, Peg."

"Alright granddad, I'm your Master of Ceremonies for the night," he declares, and for the first time in what seemed like years, I found myself fumbling with the release catch of my blade.

Sprocket looked edgy, so ups I steps.

"On account I've got a wooden peg," I say, trying to be civil, and stretch out my hand. "Pleasure to—"

He grins, and gives me the weakest handshake in all fucking history. Like a wet rag – anybody would think he was dying of cancer.

I pulls my hand away quick-smart.

"Dunno if you should have any shrooms granddad, you don't look old enough!" he cackles.

I glance at Sprocket, he was already downing his cup, and I thought fuck this for a game of soldiers, but found myself nodding. The cunt gives me a cup, I down it in one.

"Can I have another please, young man?"

Looks at me funny, but then grins and pours. I down that in one an' all. Sprocket leans over to me,

"Careful there matey, came out late this year, not as strong when they come out late, but strong enough to give you a rough ride."

Cunt gets uppity, "Are you saying my shrooms aren't any good?"

Sprocket takes a step back. "No, no, I didn't say that—"

"Are you saying I didn't brew them up right?"

I wrap my arm around Sprocket's shoulder. "That's alright, me auld china. Can't do any real harm, they're natural, ay. Another cuppa there, young Merlin" – hanging on nearby tree by your fucking entrails – "And we'll leave you to your good work."

I smiles, he pours, Sprocket and I retreat outside.

"What's that cunt's problem; you were shitting it in there!"

He sighs. "You won't understand."

"Try me, we're mates, aren't we?"

"He's a little fucked in the head," lowers his tone, "Son of an Earl, or a Lord or something, but it's the Army's done him in, we reckon."

"If that's a squadie, I'm Popeye the Sailor," I mutter to myself. "What regiment?"

"Dunno," shrugs, "We just hear stories; dunno if it's true. He knows to keep his mouth shut, but we still don't tell him anything – he's violent… though he does have a good truck."

"Which one?"

"That one."

I looks around, and spot the truck he was on about – dog's bollocks, alright.

"So where's he parked up?"

"Floats about loads of sites, but I don't reckon he's been on the road long, he's missing the point entirely – ignore him, he'll chill out eventually, everybody does."

I nods, Sprocket goes over to sit by the roaring fire, and I'm just stood there, looking up at the clear night sky; stars stretching out all over the gaff – felt like I was up there, flying about like a bird – lovely, and then I heard a voice, sounded like that Merlin cunt, whispering in my ear,

"Code Green. We will never forgive you."

And suddenly it wasn't so lovely.

I really was flying up there, could see the field and everybody in it, but now they was all dressed in red hooded robes, circling a girl tied up on the ground. I was down there an' all, shouting and roaring at them to stop. Stop what? I didn't know, I had a cutthroat razor. I was standing over this girl and nobody was taking any notice.

The girl's face, wrapped in red and white bandages loomed up huge before me. The bandages began to peel off, one by one, exposing her eyes, her nose, her lips,

"No," she whispers, and smiles. "I do forgive you."

"Marianna? What are you doing here?"

"I've come to say I forgive you, and that I'm sorry."

"For what?" I ask the face in the sky, as it slowly changes into this horrible woman with painted eyebrows, Nazi uniform and teeth like shovels after shovelling shit.

"Gretel! Not again," I pleads, "Don't make me, I can't cross that bridge yet, I can't! I'm not ready—"

"I am sorry," she says, and turns into my sister again,

"I forgive you," she whispers, turning into Gretel, "I am sorry," she says, turning into my sister,

"I forgive you…"

"I am sorry…"

"I forgive you…"

"I am sorry…"

"I forgive you…"

"*Non Serviam!*" I yelled, dropping out the sky like a lead balloon. Collapsing onto my knees, I turns to look at the field. It's gone lopsided. Red lines like from a laser sight are shooting everywhere, connecting up to all the people wandering about, and I puked my ring out there and then.

Heard shuffling behind me, looks up, sure enough.

"Code Green. Will never—"

"What's your fucking problem, ay?"

I scrambles to my feet, wobbled a fair bit, and he squares up, growls under his breath,

"Code Green! Will never forgive you!"

Happy Stick flicked into life. I chance a quick glance-about from the corner of my eye; people everywhere, kids an' all, and someone had started strumming a guitar somewhere.

Nah, stand down. My blade stays in.

"Bit strong these shrooms, ay?" I says, taking a step back. "Pukka. What you on about, the Green Cross Code?"

His eyes flitter, all puzzled, and he scurries off.

Odd, then again, these shrooms were a bit rough alright, knocked me for six, and there was more than a few of us staggering about.

Breathing hard, concentrating even harder, I'd just about managed to turn the world the right way up when I heard a scream – well, it was more of a yelp – but sure enough again, it had come from the cunt's truck behind me... somewhere, whatever behind means; opposite of in front? What the fuck does that mean?

I take a step, and I'm here, but how can that be? I keep stepping, but I was there, and now I'm here, but I was there, and now I'm here, but I was there, and now?

I'm here, and all I could see were people stumbling about the field, confused, some crawling on all fours, and these fucking red lines everywhere.

The muscles in my jaw locked tight; my head was a trampoline full of bouncing three-legged gorillas.

There was another scream, and then it sounded like the entire field was screaming; it was horrible – not the screams, the gorillas – I went down again and stuck my fingers down my throat.

Had to empty my gut of as much of this shit as possible.

My puke turned blood-red. That's when I got worried. I puked again, and it was bright yellow with laughing little gorilla men swimming about. That's when I sussed on – LSD.

You see, I was no stranger to what young Sprocket had said earlier, and he was right up to a point, govermentals effectively shut down the manufacture of clean acid in Operation Julie, back in '78. With the competition out of the picture, variants of the pre-war military grade flooded the streets.

Army did teach us how to handle the effects, though, or leastways they tried to. They gave us bucket-loads of bad acid, designed to trigger the stuff nightmares are made of. The new wonder-drug truth serum, they said it was, with just one drop the enemy could crack open the toughest nut; you'd sing all your Country's secrets away like a canary so you had to learn to handle it.

Bollocks.

At best you'd end up a gibbering idiot for thirty-six hours, at worst God might tell you to shave your eyebrows and cut your CO's throat – and at the earliest opportunity before he grew giant leathery wings and his loyal legion of killer-hamsters destroyed the Earth – the ones he keeps in his secret laboratory under the parade ground, obviously.

Truth was, LSD was crap for interrogation purposes, and after experimenting with different variants, we soon ditched psychedelics and went back to sedatives – SP-17, sodium pentothal, temazepan – though it was handy for counter-subversion, meaning leak the dodgy formulas to hippie chemists and create a whole generation of useless whack-jobs in kaftans and spandex.

Nah, if you get spiked, there's nothing much you can do except recognise what it is and take appropriate action – which in this case meant doing nothing. When you're head's swimming with enough bad acid to stall a battalion of Ghurkhas, well, just get on with it; fuck-all you can do but hope.

Hope that if you do come through with at least two neurons to rub together, then bloody right, yeah, hunt down the cunt what spiked you and butcher him in front of his entire fucking family.

But first, another puke, tool-up, and sort out all those three-legged gorillas!

Sorry, but they've gotta go…

Chapter 37

Voice Of Truth… Gawd Help US

Came round on the floor of a truck, early grey frosty dawn, covered in blood and slumped over that Merlin cunt's naked chest – I know, what a picture.

I stands up, squint down, and read the message cut into his forehead.

It read:

MY BROTHER, WE FORGIVE YOU. MARIANNA.

"Did I do that?" I says to myself, eyes pinned to the bloody blade in my hand.

"Well I don't see anybody else here?"

"Who said that?" I yelled, scanning about me.

No answer.

Studying the heavy bruising around his neck, I bend down and check his pulse – brown bread – replaced Happy Stick's blade, and scanned the interior of the truck; nothing much to report, standard job's a good'un and the cold light of day.

"Good morning sir!"

"Show yourself!"

No answer again. I spun around.

Nothing.

Alright, fucked up night, but I've had worse. Keep it together Barbelo.

I carefully slides open the truck's side door, and peep outside.

Even less, just the last embers of the fire smouldering away into a blanket-grey sky.

Quiet as a dormouse.

Fuck me, but I looks around at the dead Merlin cunt and it slowly starts coming back.

His shroom brew was shit, so he'd spiked it with a load of acid to give it a kick, or so I'd presumed, so's to not appear to be the plonker that he was? Wasn't sure on the motive, but either way, I'd obviously gone after him, and I suppose a leopard doesn't change his spots overnight, but still, why did I do all that funky shit to his head?

Not my style.

"And who the fuck's Mariana?" I asked myself, and again I heard the voice,

"Your Present!"

"Where are you?"

"Everywhere."

Oh bloody hell.

"I've gone mad, haven't I?"

"You've gone mad, haven't you?"

Nah, I'm still off my tits.

"The Present, the Present, the Present, the Present, the Present, the Present, the Present the Present—"

"Shut up!"

He shuts up.

Stepping over the dead cunt, I get an urge to go over to his bunk at the back of the truck, and start rooting around the thick blankets – oi, oi, a Browning semi-automatic service pistol, and a rope? I inspect the end with the knot, it had been cut.

Sitting on the edge of his bed, I hold the rope and wrack my last neuron trying to think back. Impressions – a girl on his bed, a laughing three-legged gorilla and red laser lines shooting out of his wanger. I crept up and—

"And the Present!"

"Shut it! I'm trying to think…"

I thought, but nah, couldn't make head nor tail of it.

"The Present!"

"Will ya just shut the fu—" I stalls, looks around, fuck it…

"What you on about, what present?"

"Code Green, you numbskull!"

"Alright, alright, keep your voice down… who are you?"

Laughter echoing all around. *"I'm the Voice of Truth!"*

Oh great –"Pleasure to meet you," I mutter.

"Pleasure's all mine."

"You gonna tell me what this is about, then?"

"Nah, Non Serviam, you are. Use our brain."

I did. Blade in hand, I rushes over to the dead cunt and finish what I'd started. Stripped off the rest of his clobber and sure enough, branded on his left calf – *Non Serviam.*

"Oh what's going on now?"

"You sure you want the truth?"

"Yep, why not... go on then."

No answer, just a light dawn breeze howling down the chimney of the cunt's wood burner.

With a terrible sinking feeling in my gut, I sits down next to the dead cunt, and stare at the carving on his forehead. Marianna... forgives her brother... for what?

Closed my eyes.

More impressions of the night flood into my brain; laughter turning into screams and madness – people scrambling about the field like animals, bewildered, on all fours. I was flying in the sky – the faces in the sky.

"My sister," I gasp, "And then I... and then I..."

And then I'm doubled over, retching on the dead cunt.

"Steady on there! You wanted the truth, now you've got it!"

"No, I never did those things, never!"

"Actually yes, you did, but that's how it is; lower astral to fuck."

"The Present!"

"Oh, now he gets it."

"Code Green..."

"No, this is not a Code Green!"

Against every survival instinct, beyond all primal terror, Barbelo finds himself on his knees.

"Captain, this is an order – get up!"

And with both hands, carefully positioned the tip of his blade on his solar plexus.

He closes his eyes, and slowly leans his body forward.

"STOP! What do you always say? A gentleman always follows through! Think then; what about his Pontificus, and the Illuminati Top Cunt, and what about chocolate pudding! Ay? We'll never have a nice cuppa tea again! And then they'll find you here, like Mad Mick, gutted by your own hand; is that the way it's gonna end? Just another stupid cunt sacrificed to the demons of mediocrity?"

"Demons of mediocrity," Barbelo mumbled to myself, staring down at the blade in my bloody hands.

"Yes, good, goood… we can work through this, together. We've things to do, there's plenty of time to be dead—"

"What am I doing?" I muttered, "This is madness!"

Laughter.

"Now, please, put that thing away before you hurt yourself."

"Fuck you!" I yelled, quickly sliding the blade back into my cane and standing up.

"Well don't thank me all at once!"

"Fuck off!"

"Sort this out before everything goes to custard – remember where you are…"

And then I remembered where I was – the fucked up situation at hand – and FUBAR is putting it lightly, but whatever and however, shit happens. Time to bury it.

I staggered out the truck, and slipped into Gertrude, carefully climbing over the people passed out on the floor.

Sprocket was huddled up in the corner by the driver's seat, opens one eye, twists his lips, points a trembling finger at me,

"Dad? Is that you? Dad… Aliens! The Aliens rule the world!" he starts screaming.

"Oh bloody hell!"

"Aliens, Aliens, the Aliens are coming—!"

I clocked him a good'un on the jaw, did him a favour, went out like a light.

"Good idea, he'll thank you for that one day."

"Fuck off!"

He won't remember a thing, that's the whole point.

Lying Sprocket down onto his side, I covered him with a blanket, and grabbing my bag, and our handy communal siphoning tube, I returns to the scene of my carnage.

Climb into the cabin. Crank the engine, drive, slowly, inching out of the field and onto the slip road.

Drove about fifteen miles towards London, pulled over on the side of the road. Siphon fuel into a Jerrycan.

Paying special attention to dead cunt, I tipped the chipper oil all over the gaff, climbed out, lobbed a grenade inside – one I took from the command centre – pay attention – and pegged it.

And I mean pegged it; word of caution here about fuels. Chipper oil or diesel, useless accelerants, but vaporised within a contained space you've got yourself the workings of a mini Hiroshima.

Ka-booooom!

Job done.

"Is it?"

"'Course it is, look at that!" I says, pointing to my perfect mushroom cloud, curling nice and tight, shooting up a mile high into the early morning sunrise.

"Beautiful…"

"Yeah… But what will the Old Bill make of it?"

I shrugs. "Nothing, that's what, the world will never know. Gawd, I really wish I had a camera. Son of Lord Fuckface Gets Shitfaced Playing With Hand Grenade: Suicide or Stupidity? See how Frank likes that for a headline," I chuckle.

"Yep, he'd eat his Trilby for breakfast. Now your bloody clobber, get rid!"

"I know, I know, give us a chance, fucking hell…"

Changed clothes in a field off the motorway, and having a right auld barney with my Voice of Truth, I pegged cross-country back to Gertrude.

"Listen—"

"Fuck off—"

"Listen, we all started off little bundles of love in our mother's arms—"

"Fuck off!"

"Even Hitler, even Bomber Harris! Ahhh, how lovely, there he was, coochee-coochee-cooo, the future mass-murdering little cunt—"

"Oh please fuck off!"

"Can't, got no wanger!"

"Will ya just shut up then—"

"Will ya just stop being a product?"

"A what?"

"A product – who's responsible, you or your conditioning?"

"Fuck off!"

Laughter.

"Aright then, what about—"

"Nah, listen, I mean it, you're giving me the abdabs, go away, shut up – permanently!"

"*Oh deary me! How am I gonna do that? I'm in your mind, 'cos I am your mind. I'm everywhereee...*"

"Well then, just be quiet, ay?"

"*Like a little mouse?*"

"Hows about like a little dead mouse?"

"*Bit difficult. I'm what squeezes out and boxes things up you don't want to look at. Your programming's breaking down—*"

"What programming?"

"*You and me, me auld china, and we've opened the box now.*"

"Easy then, put the lid back on and shut it!"

"*Can't, I haven't got any hands, just thoughts, see? And you've got loads of these boxes with loads of stuff we've done... like murder your sister.*"

"Didn't, as far as I'm concerned. Don't remember."

"*That's the whole point; you weren't programmed to remember, till now...*"

I stop pegging. "Hold on, why now then?"

"*Because you've gone AWOL – you're an obsolete piece of kit – Code Green: auto-termination.*"

"You mean suicide..."

Silence.

I resume pegging.

"Anyway, I can't good'un females, shrinks all said so. Bane of my life."

"*And why is that, I wonder?*"

"I've only got your word for it."

"*And what you saw last night.*"

"Yeah, but that's because I'm on drugs. You can see all kinds of horrible things on drugs."

"*Still, I'm the Voice of Truth, I can't lie – and I'm telling you what you saw was correct – we murdered her, it was an exercise we passed with flying colours!*"

"Come again?"

"*Standard Trauma-based Mind Control. It was a ritual to seal our programming in lower astral densities. Every Craftsman went through something similar. You see, trauma and abuse splits your mind into pieces, pieces that can then be programmed and trained. It's called dissociation of the mind and personality, me auld china.*"

"What for?"

"*To make you an outstanding killer, obviously.*"

"Obviously."

"*Yep, you've all these fragmented pieces of yourself you're totally oblivious to. Started at the orphanage. Started with the Present. That's when you got branded one of theirs.*"

"Nah, I got that tattoo done sometime during the last war—"

Laughter.

"*Still, that particular exercise was from the old days, experimental, and backfired on them, well, as far as they were concerned.*"

"But Sid, and—"

"*And you and Sally and all the rest of us. Illuminati! What do you think the Craft was, use our loaf.*"

"But that Merlin cunt had the same brand."

"*Then what have you got, a coincidence, or an Illuminati assassin sent to make you a good'un?*"

"Really?"

"*Gave you the Code Green, didn't he?*"

"And I got him first."

"*Nah, I got to him first. Giving us Code Green on LSD caused a total short-circuit of our psyche—*"

"Alright, enough!"

"*Thought he could create a distraction, bide his time, pick his terrain—*"

"Not listening anymore!"

"*Always was your problem. Now, take what Frank said about all of us sooner or later getting the same brand.*"

"Can't trust anything that cunt said."

"*Right enough, the lie changes at every level, but did Sally ever tell you what her ten stars were about?*"

I stop pegging.

"What do you mean?"

"*I mean, what were those stars on her pretty arse covering up? Nah, think again. How many letters in Non Serviam?*"

"Blimey… ten."

"*Glad to hear you can still count!*"

I resume pegging.

"Alright, go on…"

"*Let's start at the start then, ay? The orphanage…*"

And on and on we went, fifteen miles of Class A fucking lunacy till we gets to the site.

Getting dark by then, but the field was empty, except for the site dogs sniffing about.

Peeps inside Gertrude, everybody's still out for the count, all's quiet.

"Too quiet."

"Shut up!"

Dived into my dossbag and slept the sleep of the dead.

A girl had vanished from site early morning; upped and left without a word to no one. But none of us were quite the same after that night – military grade LSD does funny things to your head alright.

We wintered there, though I stayed in the bus after that little 'incident' for most of it; studying Sid's memoirs, must've read them a hundred times over, but I still didn't suss what all that Present stuff was about till the Spring.

We were on the road by then, crawling in a convoy half a mile long, heading up to Glastonbury.

Chapter 38

The Present

It was my birthday, May Day, not that I'd told no one, but there I was, eighty-three in the bogs of The Rifle Man's Arms, staring at Catweasel's Revenge in the mirror – fuck me I looked pukka! Well-under the radar; beard and hair all grown out, matted into clumps, a haze of wood-smoke and body-stench steaming off my combat trousers and trench coat. I took another slug of country cider and laughed; hadn't seen myself in a mirror all winter, seemed like—

"Alright Peg?"

About-turns, Sprocket, grinning through his beard, taking a slash. They were all out in the beer garden, two hundred of them if there was one, drinking cider in the hot sun, and more coming up to Glastonbury for some big, fuck-off gathering that night.

"Never better, mate, never better!" I says, and would've meant it except all this Traveller lark was growing well-out of hand, getting way too high profile. People were taking to the road all over the land, living in buses, caravans, anything with wheels, and the mad part was it was working, and so ever more people wanted to be a part of it.

Easy logic.

But, and this is the onion, fuck-all Peelers about in this town, just your local country bumpkin Bobbies. I knew my homeland black ops alright. If there's one thing that terrifies govermentals even more than people getting self-sufficient, it's self-sufficient people coming together and giving others ideas – we were well-overdue a kicking from the Big Boys.

I knew it, and this lot knew it too – only a matter of time.

"Let you in on a secret, mate," I says.

"What's that then?"

"Shhh, it's my birthday."

Up he comes, grinning from here to China,

"Nice one! You're alright Peg, I hope when I get to your age I'm half as alright as you."

Pray you don't mate – "Need a favour."

"Okay…"

"Need you to get my kit from Gertrude for me, but discrete. I'm leaving, tonight, not any good at goodbyes; all those hugs, see?"

He nods.

"Cheers Sprocket, you've been a good mate to me; won't forget it. Oh, wait," I says, as he's about to head for the door, "Do you know about the *Magna Carta*, Lawful Rebellion?"

"Yeah… I mean no, why?"

"Come 'ere then, listen to me, I've a feeling things are gonna get a bit messy for yous, and soon. People don't like other people opening their eyes to life, having a good time, not like this. Got a bit of information, might come in handy.

Seven hundred years ago, we struck a deal with King John, a contract what still stands today: we were given a law to use when threatened with impending dictatorship, a get-out clause.

If at any stage we feel we're being governed unjustly, Article 61 of the *Magna Carta* gave us all the right to enter into what's called Lawful Rebellion. From that point on, we, the People, we've had Sovereignty – not the monarchy or parliament or any other cunt – and nothing can legally take that away from us. It's our birthright."

"Okay," he says, "I think I remember something about all this from school… never paid much notice though. Go on…"

"What you've got to do is write Queeny a registered letter, saying you feel unjustly governed and you're invoking Article 61. And if after forty days she hasn't made amends, you come under the full protection of Constitutional Law. You then have the right, and ethical duty, to obstruct in every way possible any activity what supports said unjust government. You can refuse to pay any kind of tax, or fines or do anything what would in any way profit them."

"You mean I wouldn't have to pay a parking ticket even, *legally*?"

"*Lawful* Rebellion, mate, you can refuse to abide by any legislation put in place by that government."

"Okay, anything that's in breach of the Constitution."

"Exactly, 'cos according to this lawyer-bird I once knew, all those acts and statutes are just rules, given the force of law, but only by our consent. Revoke your consent to be governed, and they no longer apply to you. Look into it."

Nod, nod, stroking beard thoughtfully, "Definitely gonna have to look into that, yep, thanks," glances up, "And thanks for knocking me out that morning too – bad fucking trip that was, never had anything like it."

"*Told you so!*"

"Shut up!"

Sprocket chuckles, "Still hearing the voices, then?"

I sighs, "Sometimes. Not been as bad lately, then again, it catches me on the hop."

Irony was though, if I hadn't of gone loop the loop, I would've gone loop the fucking loop—

"*Lucky for you then, the wheel of fortune turned, I remembered who we are.*"

"Yeah, thanks mate."

Sprocket nods. "That's okay, I've not been the same since either, but why leave now? Don't you wanna come to Stonehenge, for the Solstice like? It's gonna be a massive party this year." He looks about, "Peg," he whispers, "I know what you mean, like. This town's not my cup of tea either; Freaksville UK we call it, full of freaks, *strange* things happen here. We'll be on the road again soon, heading up towards Stonehenge after this, and—"

"Nah, it's not that mate, let's just say I'm… I'd be a bit of a liability for yous all, from here on, see?"

"Then stay for the party tonight, go on, at least…"

At least, and glad I did. Up this big hill, appropriately called The Tor, gorgeous night it was, felt like we was all lost in time. Could see for miles in the moonlight; fields silver and blue from horizon to horizon – and then the drumming started.

Alright, they're a lovely bunch, this lot, never judged you or nothing, just got on with things as they were, mostly, but never could stand the sound of drums, not since the First War anyways.

So I got up from the fire I was sitting around, moved away round the other side of the hill, and joined another bunch; different crew, this lot had come down from London, judging by their banter, and were sat in a circle, serious and quiet, just one of them speaking every time they got a piece of wood passed to them.

Funny fuckers.

Eased myself down, and the girl next to me smiles; all boots, flowery dress and ribbons.

"Talking Circle," she whispers. "A healing one."

"Oh?"

"It's sacred!"

"Oh!"

"You talk when you get the Talking Stick."

"Right, makes sense."

"Anything goes."

"Anything goes. What do you say then?"

"Shhh! Rules, no talking unless you have the Talking Stick."

She squeezes my hand, passes me a joint, and I soon got the gist.

You pretty much said the first thing that came into your head, sounded like, stuff they'd done and wanted off their chests, mostly, so I gets the stick and oh Gawd, I don't know if it was the joint, or 'cos it was my birthday or the healing magic Talking Stick or what – I don't know what came over me,

"Good evening, I'm Peg," I says, "On account of my wooden peg. I've been listening to yous all, and don't get me wrong, I'm sure your problems and what you've done and wot-not is all very distressing for you, I'm not saying it isn't, far from it for me to judge, and I truly hope you gets over it and forgive yourselves. But I can tell you now, it's nothing to be worried about.

I kill people. I kill people a lot…"

I pause, trying to gauge a reaction in the gloom – nothing, quiet as a dormouse. I breathed deep, and continue,

"Alright, thanks, I will explain then. I used to run a Firm up in London, see, I was Top Cunt and everything was running like a Swiss clock. Me, my best mate and our girlfriend, was amassing this armoury down the basement for an overthrow of regime – plan was to stirrup all us old fuckers into action, take out Parliament and hand power back to the Nation; give you youg'uns a chance to have a go.

I don't give a flying monkey's about all that now; it's all gone tits up and was never going to work anyways. Tell you why.

We'd gone mad.

Pointless trying to solve a problem, if you're head's fucked, all you're gonna do is cause the same problem. She was right; it starts in the mind, so that's where the fight's got to be won first. I see it now like I couldn't see it then; it needed all my mates to get done in for me to realise it's all pointless.

Our plans, that is, 'cos it's not all pointless, obviously. And the Illuminati, that's what she called them, are hidden everywhere – not all SIS is run by them, Gawd blimey no! Some decent people working there, I can tell you, they just haven't sussed yet – the lie changes at every level. But lies work best when sprinkled liberally with truth, and all Firms have a Top Cunt, Illuminati can't be no different. I don't know who, but I'm gonna find out. Cut off the head, the body dies. Natural law, and I should know; I was one of their best in my time, a true natural selector.

Did my first job's a good'un – that's craft-speak, meaning 'a hit' – exactly seventy-three years ago, I was ten. Didn't know till now it was them what set it up, but I've done a lot of thinking since I've been on the road, an awful lot, and my Voice of Truth hasn't shut up for most of it. Been reading my mate's memoirs too, same with him; fist job's a good'un on his tenth birthday, same tattoo – *Non Serviam* – coincidence?

When you've been in the mortality trade as long as I have, you learn to learn there are no coincidences, only opportunities. And oh," I roll up my sleeve, "That's no poncey ink job, that's branded on, catch-madrift? Hot iron. Tenth birthday.

Anyway, London, turn of the century, different world back then, I can tell you; not far off your Oliver Twist, if you need a picture. Born into the wrong Class, as most of us were, little option, tip your hat to the Top Brass when they passed by, and shut up, do what you're told.

Or tip your hat and set up your skulduggery, to survive – and I mean survive. Don't get me wrong, not saying some of yous haven't been dealt a rough hand, but most of yous here at least have someone or something what can bail you out.

And with a bit of suss, there's no good reason why you can't have a roof over your heads, food in your bellies, and a mate or two to share a pint with. Shame it's at the expense of half the world being fucked over, doesn't have to be that way, plenty to go around and all that, but where there's a Top Cunt, that's just the way it is.

Tough titty, for now, anyways.

Anyway, we, meaning my family, tipped our hats, shut up and did what we was told. By the age of seven I was working the market, fruit and veg – and I mean *working*, grafting like a cunt! Sorry, long story.

I don't want to give the impression it was all doom and gloom neither, it wasn't, we knew how to have a laugh too alright – what I'm saying is that you grew up fast; by the age of nine I was pretty much running the business, being the eldest.

Dad, Gawd bless him, ended his days that year too; TB, if you must know, nothing unusual, got mum too. What *was* unusual was the orphanage I got banged up in – nah, again, think of Oliver Twist only cross it with an x-rated Brother's Grimm. Right – Hell on Earth.

My two brothers ended up Gawd knows where, never saw them again, and my sister only the once after – and I wish I hadn't – but in those days they split yous up anyways, and the place I ended up in was in the country, not far from here as it goes. The regime there was a kicking if you stepped out of line, and a kicking if you stayed in line. Didn't matter what you did or didn't, you got seven kinds of shit knocked out of you twice a day either way.

Fear, trauma, that's what they were after, I can see why now, and how it worked, military got some of our finest soldiers out of these institutions. Why? 'Cos they're military-run. They gets the first shout on recruits; all primed, teeth cut in combat since we were little kids – just like Sparta, Rome – oh no, that wasn't the only one, Sid too was in someplace what sounded exactly the same, as were all my mates, and my wife, though she cut her teeth in a Catholic borstal in Dublin, slave labour in the laundries 'cos her mum was unmarried, can you believe that?

I shit you not – standard Vatican policy, they imprisoned thousands and thousands of young girls for being pregnant out of wedlock, or disobedient, or even too pretty; any excuse to get potential recruits. Fucking religion, don't get me started, but doesn't matter where, the purpose of these places was brutalisation – *unbelievable* levels of stress and trauma – and the mad part is you miss it when it's not there. Not the brutalisation, obviously, just the stress.

Drives you mental not having something to go mental about.

Any stress will do, don't matter what. So out you go looking for it and all sorts. Either that or if you try really hard, you turn into the walking dead, like I did for nigh on twenty years.

I say try really hard but it wasn't that hard for me, to reinvent ourselves was what the Craft taught us to do – continuously – fact is I didn't know who I was till the Voice of Truth told me.

I thought I was falling apart these past months, my programming was breaking down, but really, I was putting myself back together. Post Traumatic Stress, the shrinks call it. I call it life without purpose.

Now, let me tell yous about that, about what that means: purpose.

Your purpose is more than your life, because without something you're ready to die for, die and kill for at the drop of a hat if called to, you've got no business being alive in the first place. I mean it. Dress it up any way you like, but that threat, that risk that it could happen at any moment is what *makes* you live; sharpens your edge, awakens your touch and fuels your purpose, see?

Deep down you know I'm right. Without purpose you're of no use, of no significance to yourself or to anybody else.

But, conscience is a tricky master. I do take the moral high ground. Like the war stuff was in defence of the realm – don't get me started on that bollocks neither – or I'd take my chances on the field of honour, and take down those what deserved it. That's why it's called job's a good'un, except for one thing.

I know I'm evil.

Pure lower astral, and killing that cunt in the dole office proved it; leastways I still can't rightly justify it – evil that was, pure evil got the better of me that day, like the evil I am.

But, as soon as I accepted it, everything started making sense, and my mates? Birds of a feather flock together, not least if you're always the ones most likely to survive a conflict. Catch-madrift?

What you've gotta understand about these orphanages is that it wasn't no random abuse, nah, it's calculated, worked out down pat – they make you evil.

You had to dig deep to survive that place, eyes on the back of your head, learn to shut out pain, and the screams – some poor kid or another was getting battered somewhere all the time – you lost your touch there and you were fucked, royally.

At fourteen, when the first war begun, my senses were already sharpened to a knife edge. Fear, see, fear makes you hyper aware, hyper observant, develops your sixth sense and that's what they wanted. The Illuminati, sharpening our edge, one of the finest marksmen on the Western Front, I was, and I knew how to take orders, meaning without question – would've opened my own throat with a teaspoon if told to. I shit you not.

But that's not what this is about, nah, not only – this is about my tenth birthday and the present I was told I was going to get, that night…" I pause, turn to the girl next to me again, "Pukka gear this! Got another one, please?"

She nods her head furiously, rooting around in her bag, and passes me a joint.

"Cheers, I'll see you good after. Right, where were we? Oh yeah, my very first job's a good'un…

It was my birthday, been in this place just under a year, and fucking hell, I'm lying there in this bunk, two hundred and fifty other cunts snoring, moaning and groaning – don't ever recall hearing anyone actually crying in the dorms – and I'm waiting, waiting for the 'Present.' Fuck me sideways, if I've ever shat myself it was waiting for the Present.

Alright, I knew firsthand what went on, and alright, getting done by some nonce was par for the course – they hire the sickest cunts on Earth to run these places – but nobody, not even the hardest kids there could even bring themselves to mention the Present.

All I knew it was different for everybody, and it was Mr Smith who was going it to give me. The 'Gorilla,' we called him, on account he was hairy all over like one. Right, and no prizes for guessing what I thought that was going to be – some particular and horrific version of what already went on anyway?

Worse.

Nobody had even gone near me the whole day, and that in itself was terrifying – to be left alone for the first time since arriving there – then, at just before midnight, Mr Smith comes to my bunk and asks me to come with him. Asks, mind you, doesn't drag me out by the ear screaming, just asks. So I nods, and out I climbs and follow him down to the Chapel in the basement, where they sometimes did their noncing about with us all.

But, and this is the onion, none of the other screws were there, just this young girl, about eight or nine, naked and tied to the altar.

Well, she was gagged with these red and white bandages up to her eyeballs, but I looks at her, she looks at me wide-eyed, and Mr Smith holds me by the shoulders as if we were the best of mates, smiles, and says, 'Is this your birthday?'

'Yep,' I says.

'Do you like your candles?'

I glance about at the candles lit all over the gaff, and nods.

He grins. 'Fuck her then.'

'What?' I says, not really knowing what he meant. I was only ten, and although that's what made the world go round in our world, I didn't suss the tables were turned.

'Fuck her,' he says, 'and you'll get a really nice present after. If you don't do what you're told, we'll kill her, and then you.'

He smiles again, all pally-pally.

So, not really knowing what else to do, I got my wanger out, and Mr Smith guides me over to the altar.

'Like this?' I says, holding my wanger in my hand, 'Inside her hole?'

He nods. 'Climb on top, fuck her!'

So, I climbs on top, stuffed my wanger in her, and I looked into her eyes and did the business, best I could anyways.

Then, Mr Smith says, 'Good, do you want your present now?'

Well, what to say? The poor girl was sobbing, and I thought maybe she should have a present too. So that's what I say.

Mr Smith was delighted, jumping up and down with glee, and so was I, just to be in 'the club,' if ya catch-madrift, leastways this wasn't as bad as I thought it was gonna be. Then, he reaches under his jacket, and takes out a razor, a cutthroat razor and says; you can fuck her again, if you like, with this, and smiles.

I smile back, take the blade, don't really know what else to do and stuff my wanger in her hole again. Mr Smith went mental; nah! Use the blade, use the fucking blade or we'll use you!

Well, I knew what that meant, if nothing else. So I…"

I pause again, look around the circle, all eyes, thick with horror.

"Oh bollocks, let's cut this story short, ay? Don't wanna bore you tit-less with my personal life; you're all good people and all that. The point is, that was my younger sister. I didn't know till he unwrapped the bandages covering her face but yeah, I did it; did all that sick cunt told me to do, and got branded with this after.

And do you know what? You would've done the same – all of yous here wouldn't have done no different if you'd been me, so nah,

I wasn't responsible for what I am. Always thought I was, but the Voice of Truth was right, I'm a product – as was all the rest of them. We didn't start off that way.

Nobody does.

We was all born a squidgy bundle of love, once, if only for five seconds. And knowing what I know now, well, it's given me the strength to get my freewill back. That's my purpose now. I make the choices; the choices don't make me... if that makes sense.

Anyways, that's all I wanna get off my chest, so goodbye, and watch your backs, ay? Stick together, help each other out on the skip-runs, but squeeze the Welfare System for all it's got too, 'cos that's what your fathers fought for, your welfare. And do some good, as Mad Mick would say, we're only here for two days – the first and the last.

Thank you all, it's been a pleasure; whose turn is it on the magic stick then?"

"Me," she squeaks.

I give the stick to the girl beside me, and gets up, thinking of my warm dossbag.

Time to go, keep moving, zigzag, randomise the routes, this lot were getting too high profile – start heading up north first thing – but I gets a little way down the hill, and hear,

"Joseph!"

Turns around, a woman comes up to me in the shadows.

"Don't you remember me?"

I squint into the darkness – long blond hair, a bit of a beak on her, but otherwise quite tasty in a Barbra Streisand kind of way.

"Thank you for the flowers," she whispers.

"Oh fuck me no!"

"Well I never, Kate?"

Chapter 39

Funny Auld World

"Kate? What are you doing here?"

"I could ask the same of you," she says. "I left my teaching job, moved in with my sister, after… after Christopher's murder."

"Sorry to hear that… did they catch who it was?"

"No, the police were useless; they even accused me, of, of… we'd been having some troubles, so they said I…"

She couldn't finish. I freeze, staring at her moonlit face in the dark. Couldn't tell if she'd started the waterworks, but fuck me, I didn't know what to do neither, peg it or what?

"Right, look, sorry dear, been a long day. I'm going to bed, maybe we'll catch up tomorrow—"

She grabs my arm. "And it was you, all the time?"

"Why do think that? Alright, I sent you some flowers, I was very upset that day and—"

"And what was all that just now?"

Oh bloody hell!

"Bloody hell is right, just tell her!"

"Shut up!"

"Sorry—?"

"No, not you," I sighs, "Listen, all that earlier was the magic talking stick healing wots-it, and I'm on drugs." I taps my head. "I was never made to kill my sister or nothing, right?"

"Oh yes you were, backfired, that's why you can't job's a good'un women—"

"Glad to hear it," she mutters.

"It was just something I made up to freak these young'uns out, catch-madrift?"

"It was a joke?"

"Healing stick wots-it, yeah, of course!"

"Some kind of sick joke?"

"Yeah, yeah, I mean no! Look, I'm not well in the head… and alright, you know, theys all needed to feel better about themselves up there, so… so I just gave them something to feel better about."

"It wasn't true either then, what you said about Chris…"

"Course not!"

"She doesn't believe you."

"Joseph, tell me, I deserve the truth!"

"She deserves the truth, she'll handle it, I reckon, tough cookie this one, never judge the book—"

"Alright! The truth! Fuck it," I groaned, and again I dunno what came over me, but standing there in the moonlight after exposing my darkest past, the beginnings leastways, and—

"And with the Voice of Truth beckoning you on—"

"Shut up!"

"No," she hisses, "I won't shut up! If you know anything—"

"Stop it, both of you! Kate," I says, "Alright my dear. Sorry, you've been through a lot, ay? I just wish I had the words, I mean you deserve a better explanation than what I said above, and yes, that part was true alright – it was me, I killed him but I dunno why, I really don't—"

"Sixth sense."

"Ay?"

She nods. "Like you said, you developed a sixth sense, eyes on the back of the head – oh I know what that's like!"

"What?"

"Fucking bastard."

"Ay?"

"If you hadn't of done, I would've."

"What?"

"Sooner or later – laid a hand on me one more time. And the police knew it, sure, who didn't on my block?" heavy sigh, "You need a shower, come, I'll make you something to eat too."

"What—"

"I said come, I won't bite!"

So there you go, just goes to prove… what? I wasn't sure yet, but Kate led me down into the town, and to a flat just off the High Street, round the back of the Church.

"Sorry about the mess, Sharon, my younger sister, she's a bit of a hippie. Cup of tea?"

"Please, can you use spring water?" I mutter, pegging it through the hallway and into the living room. "Blimey, what's all this… stuff?"

The entire gaff was crammed full of boxes of these, I dunno, looked like thousands of plastic muffins, about the size of your fist.

"Orgonite," she says, going into the kitchen, "It's basically resin mixed with bits of metal, oh, and a crystal. Fancy some wine instead?"

"Alright… what's it for?"

Kate swans back in with a bottle, and clears some space on the sofa for us. "I've put the hot water on for you."

"Thanks. So what's she do with this, Orgo-wots-it, sell it?"

"Oh god no, she gives it away. She's a Gifter, there's not many about, but the movement's growing."

"Right. A Gifter."

"Yep, they're going to change the world with it!" She uncorks the bottle, and pours me a glass. "Apparently, it polarises negative energy into positive, Orgone they call it, another word for life-force. They hide it around places of negativity, banks, police stations, these new phone masts, that kind of thing." She laughed. "I thought they were all bonkers, but tell you the truth, it works. See that plant up there?"

I looked up at the mantelpiece,

"Morning Glory," I mutter.

"That was a yellow mush when I brought it down form London, you couldn't even tell what kind of plant it was, look it at now. Take a piece if you want, she won't mind, that's what they're for."

"Right," I murmur, picking up a piece from the box next to us, and putting it into my bag. "And phone masts, I mean, I had a mate, electronic wizard he was, kept on about electromagnetic mind control and all sorts."

"You'll have to talk to Sharon about it, she's the expert. Actually they're all obsessed with it down here; this is only one of their command centres—"

"Guns?" I blurt out.

"Guns? God no, *command centres*, and there are others springing up… are you okay?"

"Right," I mutter, rubbing my forehead, "Listen Kate, I'm having a bit of a hard time taking all this in… this is all very nice, but…"

She smiles warmly,

"You don't scare me, no, don't ask me why. You should, I know."

"But I don't."

She laughed again. "And anyway, I'm surrounded by a ton and a half of Orgonite, no kind of evil or nastiness can stand being around it for long, so you're obviously not evil."

"No…?"

"No, just honest, I think, acute honesty, that's what I think you suffer from; not many people have the courage to go that far, never mind act on it."

"Courage…"

"Let's not speak about it for now, okay, what's done is done."

"What's done is done."

She raises her glass, "Chin-chin!"

"Chin-chin… nice wine. Not evil… that's got to be one of the nicest things anybody's ever said to me…"

"Hey, Joseph, don't—"

Puts her glass down, wraps her arms around me. Fucking waterworks, been a year since I'd last shed a tear, and that was with Brid that day in our command centre, right, of a very different sort. Last time before that?

Can't recall, probably when mum died, or when Gretel fed my leg to her cats, I dunno, all I knew it was my birthday and she'd just given me the best present… well, ever really, and…

"…I fucking miss Sid, the cunt, and her, and her…"

"Oh there, there. There, there, it's all going to be alright! You're just worn out, you can't be living like this at your – I mean, look, just lie down here and sleep."

"Can't, fucking nightmares are back… used to dream I was this young knob from another planet… stopped since she's gone… killed my mate Sprocket in his bed last night! Had to get up and check and everything… oh no, no… Marianna… I did it… I did it…"

"Right, okay then, nice cup of tea?" she smiles, cradling me in her arms. Woman after my own heart, but tea wasn't what I needed, just that; a hug on my birthday from the ex-missus of a cunt I'd murdered – funny auld world, ay?

Chapter 40

Freaksville UK

Kate's sister returned in the morning, after the party on the Tor. I don't remember falling asleep, but I woke up on the sofa to the sound of laughter in the kitchen and the kettle boiling.

Just lay there, trying to make the world disappear.

It didn't.

"There you go, nice cup of tea, made with spring water."

Open one eye, Sharon, smiling down over us; the spit of her sister Kate, except she had her hair all cropped off and dressed like a Mujahideen – meaning, well, just that – all what was missing was the turban and the rifle.

"Thank you young lady, I'm Peg."

"No you're not, you're Joseph Barbelo. I know, Kate told me. Everything." She adds, squinting down, "All-of-it."

"Oh bloody hell…"

"Isn't it? Thought that myself about this world, many times, until I discovered Orgonite." She smiles again. "Help yourself to food, have a nice shower. We'll have a proper talk later."

"That we will."

Like fuck, I was getting out of there first opportunity.

She stalls, returns, leans close, "Did you sleep well?"

I sit up, pause before I answer. Cut my throat, no nightmares,

"Yeah, like a baby," I says, "Just this, this… light…"

"Orgonite," she winks, and trundles off up the stairs.

Sipping my tea, I stared into the boxes at my feet, pondering what to do. I mean, it's good here; I'd slept better than my entire life put together, you'd think it was a hands down decision, stay here for a bit, regroup, but if I stay—

"If you stay there could be trouble," came this singing from the kitchen behind my settee, "If you go it will be double…" I looks over my shoulder, another girl suddenly pops out the kitchen; huge violet eyes, framed in raven black curls.

"Definitely, double trouble in the yard," she says, and smiles, sitting down beside me.

Almost dropped my tea, my hands started to tremble.

"Brid?" she says, "Brid was my sister, I'm Rahanna, and you're Joseph the psycho-killer," she giggles, twirling her hair in the same coy way and everything. "How do I know what happened? She speaks to me from the Earth Dream."

"How—?"

"How do I know what you're thinking? I'm a psychic."

I tear away from her glare, my eyes darting over the boxes scattered around the room, she rapidly intercepts my thoughts–

"You mean does Orgonite help harmonise electromagnetic pollution…?

I wouldn't 'peg it' just now…

You are safe…

I'm not Illuminati, don't be silly…

No. Brid used sexual energy to enhance her Awen, I do not…

Indeed, she'd 'pole' anybody…

I said no—"

"Stop!" I yells, leaping up from the sofa.

"Oh dear, does it unnerve you?"

"Fucking right it does! Who are you?"

She laughs. "I'm only trying to get things straight between us. It saves a lot of unnecessary confusion later."

I breathe deep, compose myself. "What's going on here?"

"You know what's going on."

She flashes her blue light bulb orbs, I stall, find myself sitting down again, feeling calm, too calm.

"Do I know?" I mutter.

"Of course you do, you've landed on your feet! Cause and effect, Joseph. You made a choice; came clean to Sharon and it led to a good outcome. Another good choice was deciding to stay clear of Stonehenge on the Solstice."

"Why? Is that where this lot are going to get a kicking?"

"And because that's where they'll be waiting for you…"

She pauses, leans close and whispers, "They have known where you were, and yes, for quite some time. Merlin… 'that cunt' wasn't one of their finest, but good enough," she says, and straightens up again. "And you sent a powerful message back. No, they're not quite ready to take you on, not yet, but I really wouldn't recommend that you go anywhere, not without preparation…

Yes, 'wheels within wheels,' the Illuminati use the police force, secret service, emergency service, anything and everything they try to infiltrate. Common Purpose is only one wheel… they infiltrate and hide behind many guises, use many titles; the Nazis, the Trilateral Commission, the Bilderberg Group, the Dominion—"

"Alright," I mutter – standard psyops – "Always point the finger at someone else."

She nods. "Always distract, confuse and disinform. The Illuminati doesn't actually call itself anything, it is a principle, an ideology of the mind, an *Inner* Order."

"I catch-yadrift."

It don't matter what name you call a cunt by, a cunt's always a cunt.

"And you're looking for their 'Top Cunt.'"

I nods.

"I can help you," she says, "But I can only help if this is what you truly want, with all your heart." She smiles. "Oh I can see it is what you want, but can you be trusted, Mr Barbelo, as a scholar and a gent?"

I turns to her, looks into her eyes, "Listen to me. Those cunts have stolen my life, wiped out my all my mates and every chance I ever had for a proper anything! I'm a man of my word, Rahanna, my word is my bond. Always has been, always will be. They can't take that away from me, never."

"If what you say is true, do it…"

She smiles, but now it's a dark smile.

"What," I ventures.

"Give *us* your word."

I shifted uncomfortably on the sofa, didn't like the way she said that, not one bit.

"And if I do, what happens then?" I asks.

She smiles again, delighted, "You will have completed your first Initiation into our Inner Order."

"Oh… and what's that called?"

"Nothing, it's an Inner Order."

"Right, makes sense. And you'll want what, in return?"

"Ha!" she snapped, "You'll find out in the end what we want in return. A choice will be presented, a simple choice, but don't worry, you'll be able to refuse."

"Why?"

"Because it wouldn't be choice otherwise, would it? But ally yourself to us, now, and we will be permitted to give you the information you need to fulfil your purpose…"

We sat in silence for a little bit, but truth was, at that precise moment hunting down the Illuminati's Top Cunt was what I wanted more than anything in the whole world, and…

"… if what you say is right, then you've got my word, I promise. But why though, I mean why me?"

"Of course I can read you like a book, and yes, you are 'fucking mental!' That's why I think you could do it." She chuckles, shakes her head, "And will you stop thinking about that!"

Slaps me on the knee, rising to her feet, "Go and clean yourself up, 'regroup,' Sharon will show you around and explain—"

"Kate knew, you all knew I was coming here, didn't you?"

"Told you I was psychic," she grins, and legs it upstairs after the Mujahideen-girl.

Well yeah, me too – welcome to Freaksville UK!

Chapter 41

Orgonite

The garden shed seemed to hum ominously in the evening twilight. Sharon's eyes burned with purpose as she continued to explain, "Those new phone masts double-up as Death Towers. A global extermination project will cull the world's population by two thirds, and the survivors will be slaves in a totalitarian martial state, living half-lives of perpetual misery and fear.

We discovered Orgonite disables their Death Towers, and converts them into Orgone Generators. Here," she says, and passing me a muffin mould, she went on,

"We're going to suspended these metal particles within fibreglass resin. Not the petrochemical type, we only use corn resin or soya, with a hydrogen peroxide hardener; it's non-toxic, totally ecological.

The metallic particles act as resonators of incoming electromagnetic waves, while the substrate dielectric resin acts as a capacitor. Then, the opposing charges within the resonating metal particles act as electromagnetic dipoles, which in turn polarises electromagnetic waves." She smiles, "Bad vibes go in, only good vibes go out."

"I wish my mate Sid was here, he'd love all this. So, how we going to make these…"

"Tower Busters. Okay, it's simple technology, so the procedure to make it is likewise simple. First, pour in a tiny bit of fibreglass resin into the mould."

"Alright…"

"Take a pinch of the metal bits; these are just sweepings from the floor of a metal shop, but you can recycle used pan scrubbers, cut up into pieces, works just as well. Now, pour in some more resin, good, slowly. Bit more metal, poke it down with the stick."

"Alright. Copper, steel, any kind of metal will do, yeah?"

Nods, "Make sure it's soaked in and covered, and now add the quartz crystal. Don't buy them new, never. Always find your own crystals or recycle the smashed up, un-sellable pieces in the shops."

"What's the crystal for?"

"Technically, the resin and metal particles do the 'work,' but adding a small crystal magnifies the polarising effect tenfold. Any crystal will do too, except onyx; doesn't work for some reason. Okay, a little more metal, and top it up with resin. Make sure there's enough metal in the mix, roughly fifty-fifty. Nice one!" she grins, "You've just made your first Orgonite Tower Buster."

"That simple?"

"Let it set for a few minutes."

"And for this they're doing people in?"

She nods sadly. "They are. And it's a testament that Orgonite works, if you need one. The first, hmmm, martyr, if you like, was Wilhelm Reich, back in the 50s. He originated the term Orgone, although the force it refers to has been worked with since the beginning of time – Chi, Prana, Awen. So yes, we pose a serious threat to them, both on the physical and the ethereal."

"Ethereal…"

"Unique electromagnetic properties surface with Orgonite – it's transdimensional – but that's Rahanna's territory," Sharon whispers conspiratorially, "She can actually *see* them, hovering around Orgonite."

"Sees who?" I whisper back.

"Entities from the Earth Dream."

"Oh."

"Me? I can't," she says, "But if you consider that every time somebody hides one of these near a Death Tower it means, well, it knocks its *intent* out of action." She shrugs. "Millions down the plughole. Right, one more thing to show you, bit dark in here, switch on the light by the door."

I flick the switch, and she leads me to a table in the far corner – fax machine, maps all over the wall – and pulls out a file from the filing cabinet.

"Sit down."

I sits down. "This reminds me of… nothing," I sigh.

"Okay, we stole this file from BT Head Office. Don't ask, it wasn't easy. Here." She opens the page she wanted, I pick up the file.

It was official, US Air Force, written by a Captain Paul Tyler.

The potential applications of artificial electromagnetic fields are wide-ranging and can be used in many military or quasi-military situations. Some of these potential uses include dealing with terrorist groups, crowd control, and anti-personnel techniques in tactical warfare.

In all cases, the electromagnetic systems would be used to produce mild to severe physiological disruption or perceptual distortion or disorientation. In addition, the ability of individuals to function could be degraded to such a point that they would be combat ineffective.

Another advantage of electromagnetic systems is that they provide coverage over large areas with a single system.

I pause, look up. "What does this mean, 'single system?'"

"We think that's a reference to a sister project they're working on called HAARP, another weapon. Massive amounts of electromagnetic power is beamed at the ionosphere and heats it up.

The heated ionosphere stores and amplifies the charge still further, bouncing huge volleys of electromagnetic energy back to the Earth's surface. So in effect, if you could direct the discharge, you'd have an energy beam that could obliterate a target anywhere on Earth, instantly. But that's only one side of the project, it can potentially cause earthquakes, even weather manipulation comes into it – but don't worry about all that just yet, the mobile phone network's the delivery system they're after. Read on."

Recently, pulsed electromagnetic fields have been reported to induce cellular transcription related to reproduction of DNA. Knowledge of mechanisms of actions of Radio-Frequency Radiation (RFR) with living systems and the assessment of pulsed RFR effects, will demonstrate the vulnerability of humans to complex pulsed electromagnetic radiation fields.

Experiments with electroshock, RFR experiments and the increasing understanding of the brain as an electrically-mediated-organ, suggest the serious probability that impressed electromagnetic fields can be disruptive of purposeful behavior and may be capable of directing and/or interrogating such behavior.

I looks up again. "Blimey, it's true then…"

"Bet your life it's true!"

"No, I meant my mate, he used to go on about all this, and nah, suppose I didn't really listen, always was my problem."

"Better listen now then, because when all these towers go up, they'll be able to control our behaviour at a flick of a switch!"

"And this is happening all over the world?"

"All over. It began with Project Paperclip, with the Nazi scientists in America brought over after the War. And then, back in '77, the CIA gave Maggie Thatcher all this information and more, including which ELF frequencies affect which mood: 4.5 Hz to induce paranoia, depression's at 6.66 Hz, manic rage is 11.3 Hz and so on."

"Dinner's ready!" Sharon, popping her head through the door. "Oh, you're still at it…"

"Just finishing up." She smiles, blows her a kiss, and turns to me, "So that's what we're up against."

"I see… and Orgonite's gonna stop them."

"The Gifting movement is growing across the world too, but for myself, no, I don't think this alone will be enough to stop them. It might be though, we do worry them. I just hope one day we'll get big enough to stretch their resources, at least to the point they won't be able to harm us anymore. But," she raises her finger, "this is a genuine decentralised grass-roots movement. 'No flags, no leaders,' as you say."

"My Gawd," I mutter, "Are you psychic too?"

"Wish I was," she laughs. "No, Rahanna said you repeat that in your head like a prayer sometimes, and in a sense, we could be your prayer answered. We don't judge people here, what you may or may not have done, or been, is irrelevant. We're from all walks of life, and some of us prefer to work in groups, others on their own."

"No 'head' to cut off then," I affirms.

"Precisely, Joseph, that's what makes us impossible to take over, and if you ever come across anybody claiming they're the leader of a group, or even Gifters who are looking up to someone as if they were, put them straight."

"I dunno how I'm gonna do that," I grumbles, "I mean, I don't even know how all this stuff works. My mate gave it ago, said it was beyond him, and he knew his onions alright, he was a bloody genius. Govermentals are decades ahead of us, he said."

"They are. Their science is at least twenty years ahead. But we discovered the best way to fight them is with the old, simple technology. Mainstream science has already put-down Orgonite as witchcraft, and for the simple reason that it's effective; the old ways still pose a major threat."

She nods at me a few times, and shrugs,

"It's not that important whether or not you understand the technicalities involved, psychotronic weapons are beyond most of us here too, or even how or why Orgonite works – just gift away mad, and observe the effects."

"Proof is in the pudding."

She shrugs again, collecting up her files, and slipping them back into the cabinet.

"We're not out to convert anybody, go ahead and experiment with these devices, and see for yourself. Orgonite's definitely given me hope."

"False hope," I couldn't help but mutter. "Sorry, I dunno why I said that."

"I know why," she says, "And that's precisely what I thought, in the beginning, when I found out exactly what we're up against."

She picks up a lump of Orgonite, turns it in her fingers,

"How is this little thing going to defend us from a global, trillion-dollar scientifically proven mind-fuck killing machine? Nobody really knows the answer, not in its entirety."

"Well, I hope it works then, ay?"

"It appears to, but on the other hand, polarising negative forces through meditation is an empirical fact too. So perhaps simply the act of working with something in an inspired and hopeful manner, yields inspired and hopeful results."

"Had the best sleep in all my days last night! Seriously. That was definitely hopeful."

Frowns, "Strange, most people report nightmares the first time, a psychic detox of all the fears lurking in their subconscious."

I smiles. "Ah, that's probably because I am a walking nightmare anyways."

She puts the lump down on the desk, gets up,

"But Rahanna's right, it's about more than the one level. The aim of Gifting is to gift Orgonite unconditionally, from the heart, and that in itself invokes Love."

"Yep, unconditional."

"I think that's the most important aspect of our movement – even if the material in itself does absolutely nothing, our group still works to expose their crimes and serves as a counterbalance, as a focus for people's collective intent. Either way, it can only be good, right?"

"Yep."

"Okay, time to eat, and then we need to load up the truck. We're moving this command centre," she adds, "Orgonite by its very nature shields us from their surveillance equipment, but sadly, good old-fashioned rumour is another problem entirely."

We goes back into the house, people sitting everywhere around the living room, scoffing down bowls of veggie stew, young'uns mostly, but there was one lady on the settee what was respectfully near my age – long black dress, smoking a fag in one of those long cigarette filters, looked the spit of Greta Garbo in a film I saw – she'd of been a right cracker in her day. And still was, I shit you not.

No sign of Rahanna though, she's who I needed to talk to again.

I wasn't hungry, so I moves over to the settee, and sits down with this lady.

"May I?"

"Hello," she says.

"Joseph Williams Barbelo," I says, "Pleasure to make your acquaintance."

"That's a coincidence! Samantha Williams, but you can call me Sammy. Pleasure's all mine."

She smiles, I smile.

"Kate's mother," she adds.

"Oh… so… right," I mutter, slowly getting up.

Holding onto my sleeve, she draws on her cigarette, and exhales a smoke ring,

"What goes around, comes around," she says, "Sit down."

I sits down.

"Tells me everything, daughters always do, ya know? Well, almost everything."

"North London?"

"Nah, near enough though, Oxford – not the posh end, the other end," she winks again. "Moved here… what? Fuck me, twenty years ago!" she giggles, "How time flies, ay?"

And then she leans over, close,

"His days were numbered anyways," she whispers, "'Ethical decision,' saved *somebody* else the bother."

"Ethical decision," I echoes, pause, and looks into her eyes; a fleeting shadow passes by, there and yet not there.

"Never judge the book by the cover, ay…"

"Never a truer word," she says, and sits up again, all suave and pleasant. "So, Kate tells me you're a business man."

"In a manner of speaking."

"I ran a business once, nightclub, after my dancing career. Cabaret, mostly. War put an end to that."

"War put an end to a lot of things."

"Staying around for long?"

"I dunno…"

"Hasn't Sharon recruited you yet?"

I chuckled. "Yep, did a pretty good job of trying."

"Well, one good turn deserves another. Got this lovely farm house up the road, you're welcome to stay for a bit, if you like? Courtesy of that nice chap from 'S.L.H. Insurances.' One of yours, I presume," she grins, "Very polite, looked a bit like wots-his-name…"

"Clark Kent?"

"Comes round my daughter's Brixton gaff, settled all our debts for us: mortgages, credit cards, the lot. We kept stum, of course."

"Of course. He paid it all off, I know—"

"Watch it!" she growls in a tense whisper, "He did nothing of the sort! Told him to sling his hook, we're not a bloody charity."

"Sorry."

"Don't be, we cleaned up!" She grins again.

"Ay? But, you just said—"

"It was like a Christmas fairytale," narrows her eyes, puffing away on her cigarette, "Wanna know how?"

"Too bloody right," I says. "Go on, you were in debt, then?"

"Heavily, since before the war, but I'd always fancied a place in the country for my retirement, and something to leave behind, you know, for my kids. And the banks, mind you, were dishing out credit like confetti! Until suddenly, they weren't. Suddenly they wanted us to cough up, or they were gonna repossess the house, everything we had. That's when your mate, Clark Kent, called round the second time."

"Good man," I says to myself. "A gentleman always follow through."

Shoots me a puzzled eye, "Well, no, he said something about being dropped off a flyover if he didn't."

"Oh."

"So he comes in, lays a letter on the table, and says, 'This asks the bank to validate your alleged debts under the four basic requirements of a lawful contract. Fail to meet one, and you're in the clear:

Signatures of the Parties, or Meeting of the Minds, equal consideration, full disclosure, and of course, lawful terms and conditions. They failed to meet them all.

Banks can't sign because they're corporations, and legal fictions have no mind, or right, to contract with. The money they 'loaned' you did not exist until created by *your* signature, hence there is no equal consideration. There was never full disclosure, since your bank never disclosed any of this, and their terms and conditions are based on fraud.' Do you follow me?"

"Blimey," I mutters, "Of course, *consideration*, 'tit for tat,' they never actually bring nothing to the table, nothing real."

Sammy nods, "Never had nothing to lose, no, whereas we did. Therefore, he went on to explain, since the lawful requirements of a contract were not met, where's the valid contract? All that exists is a *unilateral* agreement." She smiles. "Takes two to Tango, Mr Barbelo, a bilateral agreement. Anything less is total Mickey Mouse."

"Catch-yadrift. They ran for the hills, ay?"

"And so did we. I suppose between the three of us, add the credit cards and we'd clocked up over a hundred grand's worth! Plus the house. So, you're welcome to stay for a bit, if you like?"

"Oh, please, please, let's go tango!"

"Shut up!"

"I beg your pardon?"

"If it's not an inconvenience?"

"Said, pleasure's all mine," she winks.

Chapter 42

Nah, Pleasure's All Mine!

And let me tell ya!

Sixty something, legs of a gymnast – poled like a gate-happy hooker fresh out of jail.

Which she'd been and done, both, of course – and I'd landed on my feet alright, landed myself a Goodtime Girl from the war days, lots of them about back then, for obvious reasons. Fact of life, but war does funny things to women anyway, all that death and destruction kicks off their primal survival instinct; perpetuate the species at any cost – party on, in other words.

And that's what we did.

Shacked up with Sammy, spent the entire week in bed – four-poster, silk veils, the full Greta Garbo – listening to vintage dancehall 78s, drinking champagne and eating bacon sarnies – fucking died and gone to heaven!

Learnt a thing or two about this lot down here; nothing's ever what it seems, least of all people.

They was all Gifters, totally obsessed with the stuff – the four posts of Sammy's bed were made of it; not a single nightmare – but it turns out Rahanna was a complete mystery. She wouldn't let on where she was from, or why she was in Glastonbury; not that anybody here particularly gave a toss. But Sammy was unnerved as much as I was about her talents, didn't like her daughters hanging around her much. I couldn't see why though, strange girl herself, was my Sammy…

"The first memory I can recall?" she laughs, sipping her bubbly in the four-poster, "God, yeah, I was three. I'd been playing with my doll's house, upstairs in the attic, which was later to be my little brother's room also, when I heard my mother calling me for dinner. We were a very strict family then, but it all changed after that…"

"Why," I says, sitting up to look at her, she'd gone all glum.

"Okay," she whispers, "but please don't think I'm crazy."

"Well yeah, she must be to shack up with you!"

"Shut up!"

Sammy laughs, "How long did you say you've been hearing *him?*"

"Too fuckin' long," I sighs. "Go on... strict family?"

She nods, puffing up her pillows, and lies down again,

"You see, my father was a born-again Christian, but of the sort who ruled with an iron fist in our house, although he was a kind and loving father to us all also. But if dinner was at six, then six it had to be, on the nail. If not, we'd get the belt."

"Same in our house," I says.

"Same everywhere, and although I was too young to be punished like that, I dreaded my father's anger beyond my years. Now I understand him a lot better. You see, there were five of us, and nine by the end of it, all growing up inner city and wild, and we did have 'the devil in us,' as he would say, and he was right.

Well, Seamus definitely did; biggest crimm on our street. Joined the Old Bill, typical. But I think looking back, dad's greatest fear was that we'd end up on the streets or in prison, or worse, and perhaps 'cos of his overbearing ways we didn't. But as I say, he was a lovely man also, and he wasn't a drinker.

The doll's house was pink, and my father had made it out of old bits of floorboard and string mainly, and I suppose it really didn't look all that much like a doll's house, or anything at all for that matter, but I was three, and my father's word was law, and I suppose not knowing what a doll's house was supposed to look like helped a lot. But anyway, it was my doll's house and that's where I put my dolls to sleep and I loved it, and I loved my dolls. One in particular. I named her Amy.

My mother's voice rang out the second time from the kitchen, and we all knew there wouldn't be a third time 'cos all hell would break loose – dinner at six, not five past, or five to. Six it had to be for the evening prayer, and I wish I could only describe the fear I felt, especially at that age, when our emotions are a lot purer, perhaps, before we can reason things out, you know?"

I nods.

"Anyway, I was in fatal danger of running late and I couldn't find my Amy anywhere. She was outside in the street where Sean, that's my other brother, had thrown her, trying to get her run over.

He really was nasty to me, the little shit. But anyway, I looked everywhere, and you have to understand, in my wee head I couldn't just leave her – she had to go to bed! I always put her to bed before dinner, just like I always went to bed after dinner. Looking back now, I can see just how much of our games were about our house, in miniature, you know?

So, Amy had to go to bed, and I couldn't find her, and I remember the conflict I was having, although I didn't have words like that then, and I got frantic, and the more frantic I got, you know – 'Amy to bed, go down for dinner, Amy to bed, go down for dinner' – well, the more frantic I got! Especially when I looked down at the hatch to the attic and I saw my father's big, broad red face. I knew then I was in for it.

The shock's what I reckon did it, 'cos I knew what that meant, seeing his red face an' all. I'd seen what happened to the others, especially when he had to go and get them for anything.

He was furious.

Two giant paws grabbed me, pulled me down through the hatch, and he ran down the stairs, growling like a bear with me tucked under his arm, through the living room, and into the kitchen where we always had our evening meal.

The table was set. The food was untouched on the plates. Nobody eats until we're all present and accounted for, and I remember that feeling, that shame like it was just five minutes ago. But what I remember most of all is seeing my mother's face, white, like stone, and her screams.

My two brothers, after, swore it never happened and still do, and my father never talked about it. We were all screaming, but I have to laugh at it all now, 'cos you see, it was funny, really, all of us running about, shouting and wailing! 'Cos, how can I say this without you thinking I'm mad?"

"Go on, I won't think nothing."

She smiles, "It *was* mad though, it really was. Just as I got carried through into the kitchen, there was another 'me' climbing onto the pile of cushions on the chair I always sat on. In my wee hand – the other 'me' that is – I had Amy, my doll, and we both stared at each other, and smiled 'cos you know, she'd got to dinner just in time, and I was happy just to see Amy safe and sound.

So we looked at each other, and I could see through her eyes, and feel her looking through mine! She was me, and I was her.

All this happened really fast, but when my father saw me sitting there, I mean, it really was me; we were dressed identical and everything, well, he just said, 'Samantha,' but in a voice I'd never heard from him before, crying and yet speaking at the same time. Then he dropped me and screamed, and prayed, you know, to Jesus, but screaming! It was horrible…

I think that's what set everyone off, 'cos we'd never seen him scared like that, ever, just angry, but never shouting and roaring with terror.

Seamus and Sean started thumping each other, and got into a fight 'cos they both wanted to squeeze past each other to get away from me, understandable, I was at both ends of the table at the same time and they couldn't get out.

My poor mother fell off her chair, arms flailing, taking the table cloth and all the food with her, and fainted. My father was crawling about on his knees, shouting, 'Jesus, Jesus, Jesus!' So me and my other me knelt down next to him – which only made him worse – and we started screaming too, 'Jesus, Jesus, Jesus!'"

She laughs, sips her Champagne.

"I mean, we always prayed together, you know? And I, and the other I, were only small, we didn't understand what was going on. How could we?

Now I do, but back then it was all new to me. It was my first memory of being simultaneously in two places at once. I honestly thought it was normal, no? Well, my wee mind didn't think it was anything 'not normal,' I mean, come on! Doesn't everybody have a soul?"

Well suck my thorny cock! I didn't say anything to all that, just poured myself another glass of plonk, and stared up at the rafters.

"You alright?"

"Yeah, yeah… it just, I dunno, reminds me of something."

"I haven't told anybody that story, ever."

"I'm the first?"

She nods. "Shall I tell you another one?"

"Alright then," I says, sitting up.

"That was the first time I 'bi-located,' that's what it's called, but releasing my other 'me,' or my 'Fetch,' as I found out that used to be called too, isn't that unusual. I found out it happened all the time in the olden days, and you had to be extremely careful evil sorcerers didn't steal it. If they stole your Fetch you were done for, they had power over you for all your life and after—"

"The Fetch," I interrupt gently, "You ever heard the word *feharchrove* before? Means 'straw people,' I think. We set them on fire in the olden times, or something…"

"Not familiar, though when we were little, we'd stuff old clothes with straw and make a Guy Fawkes… It's Thatcher everybody's burning these days, hey, total voodoo," she chuckles, "Some hope! If only…" pauses again, head to one side, "But no, not familiar, why?"

"Nothing, I knew someone once who… nothing, tell ya later. Go on…"

"Everybody has a Fetch, mostly they're complete replicas of yourself, but sometimes it's an animal, or even just a light, but everybody's got one – it's what we go dreaming with."

"Right."

"We're split in two, everything in this world comes in twos." She brings her hands together.

"True enough," I says.

"Anyway, after the first time it happened—"

"And can this Fetch be, I dunno, evil?"

"Just said, if an evil sorcerer gets it, yes, of course! It can become a storehouse of pure evil, and it can be *used* – urgh!" she shuddered. "The things I've seen…" She narrows her eyes at me.

"Alright, my dear, alright – go on, what happened after."

"Anyway, after that, it didn't happen again for quite some time, but what did happen – and I've got to tell you this, even if it does sound kinda scary – was that about a week or so after, 'Hoody' came into my life."

"Hoody," I murmurs dreamily.

"Yeah, I still dunno what he was, maybe a ghost, I dunno. At first, he didn't move or speak, he would just stand there looking out the window at night, and I could see him, but my brothers didn't, you know? He would just stand there, his back turned, a shadow-man with a big hood. That's how I got to call him Hoody.

318

For ages, he didn't do anything much, just be there, like, and I used to see him and just go to sleep.

That might sound a strange reaction, but I was only three, and again, I didn't think it was anything unusual or not normal. I mean, not *that* unusual; like Amy, my doll, she was real to me, like a person, and she was just a pink mush with a leg missing! So that was probably more 'not normal' than actually seeing a person standing there, night after night, if you follow me."

"Yep, catch-yadrift."

"And that's exactly how we make the world!"

"Come again?"

"When Hoody did finally talk, he explained the world's a subtle thing, that we build on, like when we play with dolls or—"

"Come again; talked about subtle things, what?"

Sighs, "Settle back, get comfy," shoves a pillow under my head, "Let me tell you the story, the one when I nearly got us all killed in the car. It'll show you what I mean."

"Alright…"

"It was pissing with rain, real windy like, and we were just coming off the M1 into town; the evening we'd all gone to visit auntie Mary, the mad one, and we're coming back with her kids in the back – and Sharon and Kate crammed into the front – when suddenly a big black Labrador came bounding across the road!

I hit the breaks and we all went flying about the place. And I tell you, that was one of the scariest times of my life! I stuck out my arm just in time, and my kids flew back, I bounced off the windscreen, and our car swerved off into the hard shoulder.

Luckily they weren't hurt, but I saw what had really happened – it wasn't a dog."

She shakes her head,

"Everybody was really happy we didn't kill it, and it went off around the corner down the street, all ears and paws, happy too. Or so they all said, 'cos I saw something different – I saw it *turn into* a plastic bag."

"Sorry darling?"

"A black bin liner, just before it went around the corner out of sight."

"It wasn't a dog then, you thought it was but—"

She flaps her hand at me, "No, no, that's the whole point! Maybe it turned back into a dog after? We'll never know. Or maybe, if I'd actually hit the thing, and with all of us, including me, believing it was this lovely black Labrador, then maybe it would have kept it's shape, do you follow me?"

"Alright, and stayed being a dog."

"Now, that's the kind of thing Hoody would eventually talk to me about at nights, 'the nuts and bolts of reality,' he called it. And those were the stories I'd like him to tell me best, because 'what's in the outside, is in the inside,' and the other way around, he would say. And so the trick is to stay 'fluid,' and build on that 'subtle thing' that can turn a plastic bag into a dog, 'cos *that's* what really makes the world up."

She leans over me to bedside table, and refills my glass.

"Stay fluid, how?" I ask.

"Stay fluid in thought and action, he said, that night when I told him how I got the bruises on my head. 'Cos *it*, the 'bag-dog,' was both things, you know?"

"Yep, a doggy bag," I chuckles.

"Hey!" she thumps me on the shoulder, "We almost came a cropper that night!"

"Sorry dear, so… so what you're saying is you didn't know what *it* turned into after. Right?"

"Exactly, who knows what *it* became after! Perhaps someone else crashed and killed a dog later that night, or didn't even notice they ran over a bin liner. The trick is to believe it was both. Which is actually to say it was neither, if you follow, and then what's left is that Subtle Thing. And if you can keep hold of the Subtle Thing, then you keep the magic in the world. That's 'staying fluid,' Hoody said."

"Sounds a bit like what I call the touch. But, ehem, does this Hoody geezer still come to visit?"

"What? God no, I haven't seen him since Richard crossed over… Anyway, where was I? Oh yes, sex…"

Chapter 43

The Word

Another week passed for me dripping in sunshine heavenly bliss, but then, as always, all it takes is one night for everything to go seriously fucking pear-shaped.

"All the other Gifters in town have moved on," whispers Sharon.

We were standing outside the farm house, nothing but dusky trees, fields, and shadows, but she says this like we're in a church confessional,

"And Rahanna wants to see you."

"Well we all want something," I whispers back. "I'm going inside to finish my tea."

"Immediately, Joseph – it's urgent!"

"I'll see her tomorrow—"

Truth was, Rahanna was the last person I wanted to see – I'd cracked it, didn't want to go nowhere, never. Just wanted Sammy, those legs wrapped around me, and yeah, shoot me in the head there and then and I'd die a happy man—

"—The Illuminati and all that bollocks can kiss my hairy arse."

"What's going on, my dears?" Sammy, in her dressing gown.

"Nothing mother."

"It's Rahanna, isn't it, ever since she turned up there's been nothing but trouble."

"It's nothing mum," she sighs. "We just need Joe to fix the sink again, and then—"

"Give us a moment, I'll get dressed." Sammy marches off inside.

I reach behind the door and sling on my coat.

Sharon huffs, as we climb into her car, "Now see what've you done?"

"Nah, not really, and what's she want to see me about anyway?"

Shakes her head. "Can't say, here, now," she whispers, tight-lipped, cranks the engine and hares off up the road.

"Oi, what about Sammy—"

"Don't speak!"

Fifteen minutes later, and I'm standing in the living room, rooted to the spot. The entire gaff's been cleaned out, Orgonite, sofas, the lot, and Rahanna's aged a hundred years, meaning just that, she's sitting on the empty floor, shrivelled up in a grey blanket, all skin and bones.

"Come closer, Joseph," she rasps, "Not much time…

Yes, I am dying…

No, I am not upset…

Because I have been called back, and this is how I return…

To the Earth Dream…

Of course it's natural…

Sit with me, please. I have something to ask you."

I crept forward. "Here?"

She smiles, and I sits down on the floor in front of her.

"Sharon, keep watch at the door, thank you."

"My mother's on her way."

"I know."

When we heard the front door slam, she reached out a bony hand and stroked my cheek. "Joseph, my how you have changed!"

"So have you," I mutter, and she giggles.

"The only certainty. Please don't let it upset you, look at it like shedding some old clothes. Our abilities stretch further than all we see or seem. Now, listen. You have a friend on the Otherside, and he says you took something of his from London? Ahhh, of course, now I understand," she sighs, reading my mind, "Translocale Communicator… makes your 'skin craw?' Well he wants you to switch it on…

By simply switching it on, the rest will follow…

It sure has taken a knock or two on your travels, but the only way to find out—"

"Is by switching it on," I says.

"He's doing just fine…

Don't be frightened…

I can't believe you're still thinking about that! Thank you anyway."

"My pleasure," I mutter, "Rahanna," I says, "You're right, I have changed, but I…"

"You don't want to do it anymore," she nods, "I understand… but do you accept this is happening?"

"Well something's happening alright! It's surreal, all of yous… are odd. This place, this town's… not *normal!* Sorry," I murmurs, "Alright, they're all off their heads, but yeah, this is the nearest thing to a proper life I've ever had."

She laughs, "Everybody on the Earth plane is odd! By the very fact we're alive makes it surreal – life is a magical event, a mystery. You've just happened to have come to a place which opens people up to the fact, and opens people up to each other, that's all…

Sammy catches glimpses of the Otherside, a lot of people do, far more than we realise. The 'dead' don't go very far… Please accept it, because it's going to get stranger, and stranger. And no, I know you're not a coward. You've found peace for the first time in your life and you want to hold onto it… But have you forgotten our little *agreement*, when first we met?"

I return her smile with a shrug. "Well… I know you said you'd help me out, but Rahanna, I'm happy! Do you understand? I'm actually happy. Every morning I wake up here I feel like… like the sun is shining on me, and it's not just the Orgonite—"

She scowls, "You gave us your word."

I scowl back, "And I've had a change of heart. Seriously, the way I see it all now, this is what we deserve, and we should be thankful for what we do have, thankful and proud.

Proud 'cos we're in one of the Top Firms on the planet, and thankful 'cos that's the reason we can live like this. That's why we're not starving in some poor Darkie country. I mean, if our lot weren't Top Firm, chances are somebody else would be, it's natural law—"

Rahanna takes a sharp intake of breath, like I'd slapped her in the face or something. For a split moment I felt queasy, but I goes on,

"Alright, not saying there's not room for improvement, but fuck it, like or lump it, it's what we've got so make the most of it. Don't give a flying filly's toss about population reduction, so fucking what? We've all got to die of something, right? To the victors the spoils – that's natural law too."

"And you're a natural selector."

"And it's a predatory universe, Rahanna, dog eat dog."

"True," she sighs, "For some."

"Fucking hypocrites, I mean, man gets hungry, man eats squirrel, man eats his own grandmother if hungry enough! Seen it."

323

"I'm sure you have."

"Ultimately we're all food for worms – but who stops to think what gives man the right to kill anything at all; to even pluck one potato from the ground and take it for himself? 'Cos he's hungry? Nah, 'cos he can, and he *does*.

That's what gives man the right. He looks at something and thinks yeah, I'll have that, I'll fucking have a go 'cos if I don't, somebody else will. 'Cos if I don't, someone or something's gonna have a go at me! And that's what gives Top Cunt the right to be Top Cunt. The Illuminati or whatever you wanna call them, that's all they are: people who've opened their eyes to the horror this world's all about, and they're not hypocritical about it, they're bloody good at it instead. Gotta give credit where credit's due."

Rahanna shakes her head at me slowly, "You gave your word."

"And life's a game of two halves anyways, the first and the last, so let the final whistle sort them out, ay, that's what I say. I've decided to stay here, and be a Gifter."

She smiles. I smiles back.

"Yep, seriously, I'm good at logistics, and I reckon we could get this ops running in proper order in no time..." I paused, Rahanna was still grinning, and my words were sounding hollow in my ears.

"What does your conscience say? Interesting... And are you a 'gent,' Mr Barbelo?"

"You can't hold me to this," I mutter, getting vexed.

"You are making a mistake—"

"Fuck off! Sorry... I didn't mean that."

She gives my wooden peg an affectionate pat,

"I'm not holding you to anything, your word is. And you *know* what that is. You know what purpose *means*..."

"Purpose," I muttered, and tearing away from her piercing glare, I stared up out the window behind her – lovely evening sky, moonless, stars, stars, stars...

"Yeah, yeah, I know they're odd, we've already gone through that, but they're decent. If you back out now, could you live with yourself? I dunno, but I could..."

Closing my eyes, "I could too," I affirms, and then I looks into Rahanna's wizened face, "I'm sorry, I don't think I'm who you're looking for, I'm not the man for this... mission."

"I think you are."

"I've done things," I whispers, "Terrible things I've done, and…"

"And had done to you…"

I sighs, looking up out the window again,

"We were just little kids… they used to tie us to this chair, drive these needles under our fingernails, and wire them up to a battery. The pain was unbearable, you'd feel like you were dying, really dying… and the only way to survive, the only escape was to fly. It sent you flying out of your body and up into the sky."

"Ever wondered why you're so fascinated by skies?" she whispers, and reaches out, holds my hands. "Extreme pain shatters the emotions, disconnects the perception of right and wrong, good and evil, until what remains is a blank personality, a blank page which can then be programmed to do, and be, whatever they choose."

"Told you so, dissociation of the mind and personality, me auld china—"

"Shhh! What do you know about the orphanage?"

"The orphanage was your own personal Chapel Perilous. The first target there was to uncover the most intimate fears of your being, anything they could use against you to break you down, like the fear of bad things happening to people you love, like Marianna—"

"Alright, stop. You know all about me, don't you."

"There are countless like you, Joseph. These projects are commonplace, and birds of a feather do tend to flock together…"

"Brid. Her too…"

"Fate 'dealt us a rough hand," shrugs, "Tough titty.'"

"Hardly a time to shuffle the pack, then."

"What you were is not what you can yet become." She smiles, "You could still 'turn up trumps.' It's entirely your choice…"

"Alright, to the jugular then – who's the Illuminati Top Cunt?"

"The Creator."

"God?" I mutter.

"No, that's just what It calls Itself these days—"

"*It* calls Itself?"

"You'd know It better as *Lucifer*, the Bringer of Light."

"Oh bloody hell, what are we talking about here?"

"You do not need to believe in demons for them to exist."

"I dunno what I believe anymore," I says, "May I? I ventures, stroking her gnarled cheek. She chuckled at my incredulous stare,

"No, it's not make up, I really am dying."

"Like shedding some old clothes," I affirms, "Alright, alright, I had a small run-in with some Satanists, one time up in North London, right bunch of sick wankers – one of them?"

"No. I'm afraid that what my sister told you is correct, they are only the tip of the iceberg… What does the Devil look like? Depends who's doing the looking… Yes, like a mirror…

But your soul, your consciousness, is infinite… Think of it like an egg, perpetually turning itself inside out but without ever breaking its shell. And the Devil's like an egg slicer, dividing your egg into thin slivers. These slivers are the Locales of the Earth Dream, your entire range of perception and potential experience. Between these Locales lies Its domain…

Ahhh, and so what was Brid hiding? The Black Stone of Prophecy, of the last incarnate Goddess, the Cybele. Brid stole it from the Illuminati, but I'm afraid that is a long, long story… This is about you now, and yes, you will receive help, listen to Sammy…

Really listen, she has 'solid Intel,' and your friend Sidney has been trying to guide you through it too… No, the Voice of Truth will only 'shut up' when you *become* your truth. Learn to accept yourself; your pain, misery, let it come, it is yours to teach you. Do not run from yourself. To reach the Light that you are, you must first cross the Realm of Shadows. Now, please, stand back."

I climbs to my feet, and stand at the door. I hear yelling outside and briefly turn around – Sammy and Sharon having a right auld barney – and then I catch a bright flash of golden light behind me.

Rahanna's vanished.

Sammy storms into the living room with Sharon in tow.

"She's left us something," says Sharon, continuing her stride. On the very spot where Rahanna had been sitting was a card.

Sharon picks it up. Sammy holds my hand. "Let's go," she whispers, and then turns to her daughter.

She was chuckling softly to herself, "It's a Tarot card," she says, "The High Priestess. Perfect."

"Who was she?" I asks.

"A complete mystery," shakes her head, "And that's what this card means; when it turns up in a spread, it's to remind us that there are always things we'll never fully understand, or master…"

Chapter 44

You're Looking Well!

"Switch it on!"

"Nah, you switch it on."

"Joe, darling, this is your gadget."

"It's Sid's actually."

"Well I'm not doing it. You've been dithering for days!"

"Wasn't dithering, I was... *preparing*, mentally—"

Sammy cut me off with a loud groan, she'd lit candles all over the gaff specially for the occasion. The living room was spattered in leaping shadows. Sitting on the dinner table was Sid's telly yoke, rigged up to Sammy's car battery, and sitting either side of it was us – shitting it.

Well, me more than her. Sammy'd already had her fair share of run-ins with ghosts, by the sounds of this Hoody geezer, and she reckoned her mad auntie Mary was well-into her séances in Oxford. Parlour Games, it was called back in the old days, when they'd all sit around and call up their dead Uncle Jack, or Napoleon or whoever.

But this worried me. Considerably.

In the days following Rahanna's 'departure' we'd pondered the mysteries alright, and I'd always taken these things in my stride anyways; when you're brown bread, you're brown bread – buttered and sliced. On the other hand, countless seriously fucked off good'uns waiting for you doesn't bear thinking about, never mind anything else—

"Joe! I'm not waiting another night—"

"Alright, alright, here goes..." I leaned over and twiddled with the knob. White noise, and then the screen flickered into life, static, lighting up our faces in a bluish haze.

"Banjaxed," I mutters, giving the thing a tap, "Been at the bottom of my bag for months." I go to turn it off.

"No, look!" she grabs my hand over the table, I don't let it go.

The white noise fades out, replaced by birds singing, and children's laughter.

Sammy's ecstatic, "I know that hill! And that's a field just up from here. No, that's this field, here!"

"Must be BBC 2, Open University or something, I'll turn the channel over—"

"But where's the house? There are no houses!"

"Alright, there's no houses."

"It's beautiful, Joe, can you feel it?"

"No…"

"Yes you can, you muppet!"

'Shut up!"

"Him again?"

I nods, and truth was I could feel it alright, pumping out from the screen. It felt like the first morning I woke up after I'd slept with the Orgonite; calm, complete – and then Sid appears, running across the field towards us, resplendent sunrise behind him, all golden, cherry-pink streaky clouds, and him streaking bollock-naked, grinning like a cunt – I screamed.

Sammy comes round my side of the table and stands behind me, wraps her arms around my chest.

"That's him?"

"Oh fucking hell, yeah! He looks no more than thirty though…"

"Thirty-five, mate! Came as quick as I could, how's it all going on your side, got yourself a girlfriend, I see – whoa! A right babe." He winks. "Lovely to meet you."

"And you," she blushes. "I'm Samantha Williams, but you can call me Sammy."

"Watch him Sammy, he don't know how listen, but he sure knows how to get you into a lot of trouble!"

She laughs. "Oh I can handle myself, alright!"

"Joe?"

"Sid! Oh for the love of Christ—!"

"Oi, pull yourself together! We've got some nasty business to deal with on your side, the Nursery's in big trouble."

"What nursery?"

"Oh, that's what everybody over this side calls the Earth plane."

"Yeah but…. what's it like there?"

"Oh mate, you're in for a big surprise!"

"Yeah, but, I mean have you met anybody we know?"

"Of course, they're all here! Well, until they move on. Move on to another vibration. I've got no inclination to move on just yet, the Guides say I'm ready to, but you don't have to if you don't want to."

"Nah, I meant you know... anybody we *know*."

"Oh, right. Yeah," he frowns, "I have. Not so good. All I can say about that is try to put the work in your side as much as you can. It's no picnic when you first cross over, guilt, misery, pain – emotions create worlds too, what we call the Transition. If anything is Hell, then that is, but you get through it. Leastways I did. Don't worry about that too much, just get on with what you've got to do there and listen to your conscience."

"Do I have a bloody choice?" I mutter to myself.

"Nah, and I'm stuck with you too, you deaf amputee filipino trollop!"

"What?" I whisper.

"Deaf Amputee Filipino Trollop, you DAFT cunt!"

Sid was falling about in stitches, "You hearing voices now? That's all we bloody-well need!"

Sammy nods. "Seems to get worse when he's stressed."

"Does it dear?"

"Seems to."

Sid spreads his arms wide, "Well, no stress here, just look at this place, here you can create whatever you want!" he laughs, "It's just like the science-fiction films, only it's real, solid – better than Canada."

Stretching his arms over his head, he did a series of back flips in the air, came to a halt, and floated in mid-air, gliding back towards us.

"And that's not all, watch this."

He clicks his fingers on one hand, and bunch of red roses appear in his other.

"For the lady."

"Thank you," she beams.

"Get some clothes on," I grumble.

"Oh, right, forgot." And he's instantly togged-up all pukka in pinstripes and Panama hat – cunt.

"Alright Joe, to business; that's a car battery you got there and this thing sucks up the juice fast. Get yourselves an adapter next time, plug it direct into the mains."

"Okay," says Sammy.

I nods. "How do you know it's a car battery, it's behind the screen."

"No, I'm not seeing you *through* the screen, I'm actually in the room with you."

He twiddles his fingers in the air, and I feel a light caress on my cheek – "Fucking hell!"

"Good ay?" he grins. "Just wait till I get the knack of moving things about!"

"Don't you ever, ever do that again, Sid! I mean it, please."

Sammy asks, "And can I see my people?"

"Difficult," he says, "This is my Translocale, it's, and sorry to be so blunt, it's got my sperm in it. Brid's idea, something she calls an Anchor, having a bit of 'me' in there helps me locate it easier. I'm basically haunting that telly. But I'll see what I can do for you next time."

"And you've seen Brid?" I asks.

"Once or twice, and her sister; they sometimes act as Guides here, helping people with their Transition from life into… well, into this life, here. And they're also Guides on your side of life—"

"Here, what for?"

"Well it's not rocket science, look at me, all this – it's gotta be the best kept secret in world! And for good reason, all fear stems from fear of death, and all control mechanisms stem from fear. So enjoy the ride, mate, there was never anything to worry about, we're all making it up as we go along anyway—"

Sammy gasps, "That's exactly what Hoody used to say! Have you met anyone called, ehmmm… Hoody?"

"My dear, you'd need to be a little bit more specific."

"I don't know any other name for him; never said."

"I'll ask—"

"Sally… have you seen Sally?"

"No, moved on. Heard she's somewhere back on your side. Unfinished business. Tried to explain, you punched me in the head!"

"Yeah, I remember. Wasn't that I didn't want to believe you, Sid, just that… I wasn't ready to. Sorry. Where, then?"

Shrugs. "You know what she was like, relentless."

"Oh, and what about—"

"Mad Mick?"

"Yeah!"

"Mate," he chuckles, "I wish I could explain that! Where he is now, but I can't – it's beyond the limited understanding of language."

"Oh, what about—"

"Listen up! Plenty of time for all this."

"Alright, to business then."

"The man you're after is not a man, it's an *entity*, what we call a lower astral being. You have to remember that. It's powerful, mate, one of the Big Boys."

"Morning Star, Rahanna said."

"Exactly, the one and only, Lucifer the Light Bringer."

Sammy shudders.

"That's only one of Its titles, It's been known by countless names, and It's real, yes. It rules over your world. Remember Brid's story about the Inanuquae Gods, the Neanderthals, and how humans wiped them out? Well that's the Being she was talking about, the 'mad puppet-clown, feasting upon our cold flesh,' we invoked it from the lower realms to help us with the killing."

"Gawd blimey, then how am I gonna good'un the Devil himself?"

"It's an *It*, Joe, the ultimate trickster, but not all-powerful, not all-seeing, and neither are the Illuminati – they can be defeated, they can be raised up, in vibrational terms."

"And the feharchrove…"

"Same as. They're people's ideas of themselves, made real, like all this," waves his hands about, "but trapped in the Lower Astral."

"Sid… mate," I grimaced. "This is all way over my head—"

"No, too late, can't go AWOL on your word, cuts way too deep. If you do, kiss your arse goodbye when you cross over this side. Don't ask, I didn't make the rules. The Transition can be hell for our kind. We *knew* a lot of people…"

I shuddered. "Catch-yadrift."

"Rahanna?" he asks.

"Fuck me Sid, is everybody psychic around here or what?"

He laughed. "No, no, it's just that in 'spirit form,' everything's comprised of a faster frequency, very close to thought… more than read your mind, I can actually see what it's creating, over this side somewhere. Odd, I know."

"Odd is right, but listen; Rahanna reckoned they're waiting for us, Stonehenge—"

"And you want to get to them before they get to you, I understand. Pick your terrain. But I need to explain something very important first."

"Alright."

"The Earth plane's not very high up the spiritual ladder, your vibration's easily caught, like when you pluck a tuning fork next to a guitar string and it plays by 'itself.' Fear, misery, pain – all these states are caused by, and create, slow frequencies, low vibrations. So it's a question of raising the vibration, which is what the Earth Herself is trying to do, and what a lot of us on this side, and on your side, are trying to achieve too."

"The Earth?"

"Yes, the Earth is alive, She pumps out a frequency like a heartbeat; it's what scientists call the Shuman Resonance. And these waves of electromagnetic energy occur at frequencies which resonate with our brainwave range: Delta is the slowest, between 0.5Hz – 4Hz, and corresponds with deep sleep; Theta is 4Hz – 8Hz, awakening from sleep; Alpha is 8Hz – 14Hz which is calm but alert; and finally Beta, 14Hz – 30Hz, which induces a highly active and focused state of mind. Got that?"

"Roger that."

"The Shuman Resonance normally sits around the Theta range, the state of awakening from sleep, but is currently approaching Alpha and rising fast. When the Earth's frequency reaches Beta it'll spell doom for the Illuminati. That's what they're planning to prevent, and one of the jobs all those new masts are designed to do; sheath the world in lower astral frequencies – crackle, crackle – reduce the population, reduce the weight of human consciousness. *It* really does not want ten billion of us – crackle, crackle—"

The telly started to crackle, the image rapidly shrinking in size.

"Right, Sid! Battery's going."

"—so this won't be a walk in the park – crackle, crackle – your best bet is to let them come to you. Bait yourself – crackle, crackle – and be ready to—"

"Fuck it, gone," I mutter, and turn around. "Oh, my dear, why are you crying?"

"I dunno," she says, holding me tight. "Not sure I like that *thing*."

"Nor I, but whenever I thought about ditching it, I just couldn't, got the abdabs. And glad I did now, that was great, that was!"

"Was it?"

"Yeah! Oh, right… but if the Devil exists, then so must God exist, ay? And blimey, who'd of thought it, Happy Place is real! So don't cry, it's all good anyways—"

"Why are they asking you do this?"

"Hmmm…" Probably because it takes a cunt to catch a cunt, but I don't say that, obviously. "I dunno," I says, and I look at her there, crying on my shoulder, crying over me and nah, fuck it, I dunno what comes over me,

"Oi, Samantha."

"What?"

"Will you… will you marry me?"

"What did you say?"

"Said will you be my wife," I smile, "Please."

"What for, why?"

Why? Blimey…

"Because… because you're the first proper thing I've ever had; I've never felt this happy in all my days, and because someone once told me that love is freedom, and yeah, I love you… that's why."

Felt cheesy as hell saying it but her sobbing stops, wipes at her tears,

"You silly old goat! Yes."

Chapter 45

Stay Fluid

"I'm coming with you."

"Oh no you're not, you're doing as you're told!"

"Darling, please!"

"Nah, you're staying here, talk to Sid on the Translocale and keep me posted. I'm gonna need your help, see? Best thing to do is—"

"Fucking right I'm going with you," rooting around her wardrobe, "Where is it?"

"Oi! Where did you get that?"

She tilts her head to one side, smiles. "Oh, you mean this? .38 Smith and Wesson. Was Richard's." Richard was her ex, by the way, been a Peeler back in the War days.

"Give me the cannon, young lady."

"Young lady, oh that's nice, take it off me!"

She grins, I bundle her to the bed.

"It's empty anyway."

"Course it fucking is!" she grins, leaning on one elbow. "Don't need none of that when you've got the Subtle Thing." And then she sighs, goes all serious. "Joe."

"What?"

"All the discipline from dad, you know, all that religious 'regular as clockwork' stuff, came in very useful later."

"For what?"

"For knowing what it is, and knowing not to do it, like Hoody said."

"Oh not him again."

"Hear me out! He was a big part of my life, you know? He said breaking our routines is important for staying fluid and quick in the world, so's not to lose the Subtle Thing, and be able to do things."

"Like what?"

"You know, magic things. Not bad things, you understand, although there's some that use it for that 'cos I've seen them, and they look at me funny in the street. They know I've got the Subtle

Thing too, and they're afraid when I notice them. They know I know what they use it for. They leave me alone, although Hoody said to be careful, always. And that's what I'm telling you, *please*, stay fluid, and be careful."

She leans over and gives me kiss.

Well if there was one thing they taught us in the Craft it was precisely that – break up your tracks, but she looked genuinely scared for me, so I concede, "Go on, my love, what else did this Hoody geezer say then."

"Hoody would talk to me long into the night, even when I fell asleep!" she chuckled at my incredulous expression. "And that's when it was the best. I was asleep and everything, and yet I could still hear him, and then we'd go flying in the sky—"

"I love skies, me, daydreaming of flying was—"

"But mine weren't dreams, it was real as you or I."

"Oh, right, *that* kind of dream. I get them too…"

"I'd forget most of the time what we did, but I know that he showed me things, marvellous things, and I met a lot of people – funny people – but it didn't matter if I forgot 'cos one day I'd remember. That's what he'd say, and well, he got me looking at all kinds of things I wouldn't otherwise, like art, which I love now, though it wasn't easy then 'cos my father never let me. I still had a big stigma about it all. I've had to work through a lot of stigmas, turn them into strategies."

"Funny that, I've always loved Art too, if I couldn't be a writer I'd of been an artist; Caravaggio is my favourite. Don't like none of the modern bollocks though."

"Me neither, at first, but that's only 'cos I didn't understand it, and modern art is what Hoody wanted me to see the most. But in our house, I'd even have to hide schoolbooks from the library under my bed, or else! Art is 'of the Devil,' just about everything and everyone was the Devil's work. I knew even then they were all bananas, but I still had to go along with it. But granddad was the worst.

Every night they brought him round, the neighbours called the police. He'd just sit there, at first, where he always sits, you know, *his* chair, looking into the corner of the living room, quiet like, not a peep out of the old beard, and then – 'The Dark One!' he starts roaring, 'The Dark One! The Dark One!'

And then he'd have us all on our knees praying, which I suppose wasn't that unusual in our house, but then the chant would kick off, 'Who let the Devil in?' All fiery-eyed and spitting, dancing around the living room, 'Who let the devil in? Who let the devil in?'

No prizes for guessing who they thought that was! So I'd be praying even harder, and mum would start talking in 'tongues,' and the Morgans next door would come round threatening again. It's a wonder I turned out normal, it really is."

"A true wonder."

"Oi, don't pull the piss! It's good all this, listen."

"But I am listening!"

"Thanks! I mean, they were all crazy, especially granddad and not because he was dithering-old either, he'd been like that as long as I remembered. Though dad went the same way, and mums was no better, and the others had all gone, and no, I couldn't count on any of them anyway. Hoody was the only one I could ever talk to, and he was a…"

"A what?"

"Funny that, I never once questioned it till now, Hoody was always just Hoody… But from the moment we met, you kind of, well, it's silly but you do remind me of him."

"Blimey…"

She smiles, "I can talk to you the same way. Anyhow, he said granddad was the right type to make a grumpy old ghost. It's the routines, 'cos when we cross over, we leave a bit of ourselves behind, as 'energy,' our routines anchor us here; and I've seen enough ghosts to know Hoody was dead right, but they're not as scary as people make out. They just try and do what they normally would've done when they were alive on this side. Most of them don't even realise they're ghosts, like, and are more scared of you moving the furniture around, or painting the walls a different colour, than you are of them."

"Why?"

"'Cos they're frightened, poor things, their routines made them control freaks, so they freak out, as you would if you got home one day and found a lot of strange people messing around in your house.

Anyway, it's only the ones who get conscious that you have to worry about. Now, they really are like the horror films sometimes, really scary, 'cos they can grow more powerful the longer they stay here. The others you can talk to, they're quite ordinary, still connected to their soul, you know, the main part of them that's crossed over, and you can tell them they're dead, and they'll just say, 'Oh really? Dead?' And that's that, after a bit of explaining they go off back into the Astral or whatever, but the other ones can get very nasty.

Some are no longer even human, not really. You've got to watch out for them. They're dangerous…"

She pauses, pins me with her intense look.

I ask, "So you think that's what this Illuminati geezer is?"

"I dunno, that's my point. I've been trying to contact Hoody, he might have explained it all."

"Alright, then what are these nasty ones about?"

"I suppose, in the end, I feel sorry for those ones too, 'cos there's little anybody can do for them. They're just bits of other people, sometimes many, many people all mashed together, and for the most part, only trying to do the best they can, trying to get a kick of energy off us. You know, stay earth-bound, get bored, angry, move things around and get a kick of energy if they get a fright out of you.

So for the most part, they're pretty harmless really, if you ignore them, that is. If they're really, really strong they might get a kick out of possessing someone, especially if you're drunk or on drugs – you're more suggestible then. They're the dangerous ones. But that's quite sad you know?"

"Why?"

"'Cos they're strong, they've gone all the way around to remembering they were once human, in the pink, and want to get back to normal. But a portion of them's got totally lost from the big part, if you follow me.

So Hoody says we have to watch out for our routines, 'cos if we don't we'll 'anchor' a part of us here, and we'll get stuck in a kind of no-where land. That's where the 'shadow people' need to keep us, to feed. "

"The Shadow People… hold on, this sounds familiar."

"It does, yeah, sounds an awful lot like your feharchrove types."

"I meant, I think I dreamt something about all this… I dunno, go on. What do you mean, 'feed?'"

"Keep us all split up, lonely and nasty like, so's we never get beyond this place: the Earth plane. We need every single last drop of energy for what's coming when we cross over into the Astral. But Hoody says it wasn't always like that, and there was a time when we could all go in and out like walking through a door. Anyway, that's why he had me looking at art."

"Alright, so what's art got to do with the Subtle Thing?"

"Well now, even though that all happened when I was about twelve, it's all still kind of new to me, but I'll try to explain.

You see, I'd been reading a lot back in those days, well always really, when I could sneak the books in, and I'd learnt a whole heap of new words from Hoody too, like 'abstract.' My favourite word, just the feel of it, aaabstraaact," she sighs, and giggles to herself. "Say it ten times with a straight face," she goads. "Go on! Say it."

I yawns, "Aaaabstraaaact," three or four times and we fell about the bed in stitches.

"Fun's what life's all about," she gasps, calming down, "I used to do that when things got on top of me."

"Yeah, can see why! That was good, that."

"You see, people like dad and granddad, and just about everyone I knew didn't know the 'abstract' of things. Which is sad, 'cos if they did, they'd have a lot more energy to spare for having fun or whatever, and when they have to go back into the Astral, they get lost. Oh, there will be people and guides out to help them, but the larger part of them's anchored down in their routines.

Now, I don't want to go on about other people too much 'cos as Hoody said, I don't know them so it's not fair, like. I mean, their routines may turn out to be strategies after all, who knows?"

"Strategies," I echoes.

"A strategy is when you do something a lot 'cos it really is the best way to do it, and you stay awake to what you're doing, not like a routine which is like sleepwalking through life, doing the same things over, and over without even thinking why, or how it ever got to be that way in the first place, if you follow."

"Oh Gawd yes, don't I just."

"I mean, that's what they want, you know?"

"The Govermentals."

"'Cos it's routines what make us scared to question, to do anything different, or to be anyone different if we want to. You know, not just the Government, the Shadow People, they love it when we fall asleep to the world around us, all split up inside, being nasty to everything – people, animals, you know, everything. 'Cos then, as Hoody said, when we 'die,' they 'consume' us and you don't know any different. Until the very last moment maybe, and then you've had it. You can't get out, or come back or anything, 'cos you don't have enough energy. That's when we find out it's too late and we've wasted it all doing the same things over, and over, asleep, like."

I shuddered. "Fucking horrible."

"Horrible, I know, but that's the way it is. Best thing to do is smash it all up till there's nothing left, and then build it all up in strategies, stay fluid, and stick to the Subtle Thing like glue.

And it's seeing the 'abstract' in life that smashes you up the best, and will probably save your arse in the long run, all things said and done. That's why Hoody got me looking at modern art, 'cos he said that some of these artists have the Subtle Thing too, and it can be passed onto you, if you let it in. So, one time we went dreaming together to this place he called the Akashic Library—"

"Hold on, a what-library?"

"It was brilliant! It's like everything's there in books, the whole world, everything that's ever happened... well, we saw it as books, but other people might see other things, 'cos the Akashic is pure *knowledge*, energy, and we make it look like books 'cos that's what we're used to – a bit like the black dog and plastic bag story I was on about the other day, remember?"

"Yeah, go on, this is starting to make sense."

"Make sense?" she shook her head urgently, "What in life makes sense – if anything has any meaning at all, it's only the meaning we give it. Stay fluid! That's the whole point."

"Catch-yadrift, go on my love."

"So, you go into this massive library, made of big grey stones, like a monastery or convent. Outside it was warm, surrounded by lush green woods and tended gardens, and you take a book from the thousands of shelves – any book will do 'cos it's going to turn into the one you're after – open it – and bang! You're in the Tate gallery, full of paintings, sculptures and everything!"

She laughed. "Oh Joe! Marvellous! You're *there*, it's made real. Do you follow me? It's everybody's memory of the place, its energy, imprinted on the ether.

So, we went to see these Mark Rothko paintings, 'cos Hoody says he was someone who'd tapped into the Subtle Thing, and that some of his paintings aren't really paintings at all, but something he called 'Portals to Eternity.' And that I'd need to understand this to know that's what we all are too."

"You mean people."

"All of us, everything's a Portal to Eternity. I understand this now, but until that night I'd only seen art in the books I sneaked in, and that's not quite going to do it, he reckoned – oh, that's another thing, if you ever go to this place, the Akashic, don't waste your time trying to find something you don't already know at least a little bit about to start with, 'cos you wont find it. Unfortunately, it doesn't work that way, but that's probably obvious really.

Anyway, we were with all these Rothko paintings, which are massive, and oh! Just *being* with them was enough, I didn't even have to look at them or anything, just stand there and feel it – pure Abstract.

Of course, the Akashic, 'cos of the place it is – you know, its 'energetic paradigm' – it can do that, but when I went to see them in waking life it was the same *knowing*. In fact whenever I go to the Tate, there's always one or two people just sitting around the paintings with their eyes closed – but I tell you, and it might sound a bit funny coming from me, 'cos of that madhouse I grew up in and everything, but, whenever I'm with these paintings, it's like I *become* the Abstract, it's like being with... God."

"Sounds scary to me, my dear."

She laughed, "Okay, okay, maybe not God... but like... you're connected to everything... like you're looking back at yourself from space through a hole in your head, going on, and on, forever," she chuckles, "I know, I can't describe it. And that's the whole point anyway, it's the Abstract... But I understood, without needing to understand anything, exactly what Hoody had meant. We are all Portals to Eternity, and the world's a feeling that can't be put into words, or even words about feelings, 'cos it'll always be something else."

"What do you mean by that."

"It's like, we can say something is 'hot,' so it can't be anything other than hot. It can't be cold, say, or even warm – hot is hot. But the Abstract is 'everything' and 'nothing,' and with this feeling in you, 'hot' can be hot, can be cold, can be warm, or anything and everything and nothing at once!

That's what it was like the first time I felt it, and I know that's what everything really is, underneath, Abstract. It's like we took 'everything' and split it all up into little 'somethings,' and we've been calling them 'this' or 'that' for so long now we've forgotten what we did!

And its our routines that make everything stay as it is, keeps people dumbed down, stops them being what we really are, complete, whole – do you follow me? That's why people are nasty, 'cos deep down they're unfulfilled, 'cos deep down we all want to return to the freedom of the Abstract, we feel it calling from out there, from the mystery that surrounds us, but we don't have the energy to return, squandered on stupid routines.

But it's not just routines, 'cos 'routines' is just another word, you know? And the words in our heads are probably the worse routines of all…"

Chapter 46

The Eyes of Iblis!

We did a lot of that, talking and bundling in the bed those last days. I dunno, we laughed a lot too, I'll give Sammy that, she made me laugh and had a heart of gold. But where I ended up going was no place for ladies, or human beings, for that matter – Solstice Festival, Stonehenge.

Don't get me wrong, I don't mean that because of the Travellers an' all, I mean it because of the Peelers – 'Peelers that were not Peelers.' if ya catch-madrift – I can smell black ops a mile off.

It was a sweaty-hot summer's day.

I suppose you've all heard the stories of what went on there, right, the Battle of the Beanfield, on account it was in a field of beans, and 'battle' on account MI7 media dissinfo said it was.

One side was a bunch of unarmed men, women and children, and the other side was tooled-up with riot batons, sledgehammers, coked-up and psyched-up to the eyeballs.

We didn't even make it near Stonehenge. About seven miles out, they'd dumped lorry-loads of gravel on the road – stopping the convoy dead in its tacks – ambushed us all there and then, throwing hammers through the windscreens, pouring petrol into caravans.

There were women with their heads split open, dragged bleeding along the ground by their hair, their children terrified, watching.

Fucking turned my stomach.

And I'm not saying that just because I was going through some changes of perspective neither – it takes a particularly sick cunt to club pregnant women to the ground with riot batons.

Those of us what could, ploughed our vehicles off the road, steamed through the bushes and into the beanfield. Everywhere I looked people vanished under a storm of truncheons and blood. In minutes the entire field was full of little kids screaming for their mums, black smoke towering out of their homes, their caravans burning, smashed to pieces.

And all the time, some wanker in an unmarked helicopter circles above, roaring down support from a loud speaker,

"Doing a great job boys! Give it to them! This is what they like!"

When Gertrude finally ground to a halt in a pothole, I thought fuck this – climbed out the broken windscreen, swore I'd good'un the lot if I ever got out of this in one piece, and pegged it across the field towards the trees at the far end.

Didn't know what else to do, got caught on the hop.

That's bollocks, Captain, you know it and they know it.

No it's not! My intention had been to pick my ground, not get ambushed by the Met's 'finest.'

Bollocks!

Look, I stuck out like a sore knob in a Panama and pinstripes. It was either peg it or go to work there and then.

Wished you had?

Wish I had.

Bollocks!

Alright, alright, I will confess, I was ready for the occasion, and fair dues, I can see you're not gonna let me off the hook that easy neither. The main reason I didn't do nothing lurks in the exceptional events of the day previous...

Rahanna had warned me to stay away from Stonehenge, and Sid had suggested I bait myself and let them come to me – there was no way I was getting Sammy involved – so it seemed the best thing to do; meet this situation halfway and pick my terrain.

For a month I prepared, training, talking to Sid on the Otherside, though there was little he could add to our first talk. To be fair, he was learning as he went along and seemed to be going through some changes too. Kept getting younger, and younger – the last time we spoke he'd shrunk into a little kid – wanted to experience childhood again, the childhood he never had. He was pretty disinterested with what was going on our side, by the end of it anyway, seemed like, though Sammy did get to talk to some of her people alright – very personal – and Sharon got obsessed with the whole bloody thing. Unhealthily so, if you ask me. Ditched the Orgonite ops, and by the time I was leaving, all she talked about was the Translocale and what a great world it would be with one in everybody's living rooms.

Dunno about that; kinda defeated the whole idea of a living room in the first place.

Finally, it boiled down to a toss up between Ishmael and Uncle Pete, them being the two most expert acquaintances in my spiritual armoury of mystical acquaintances. Standard Intelligence gathering mission. Needed to know what I was going up against, and if anybody knows anything about Demons it's your good auld religious nut-job.

And of course, Ishmael won through, on account if things went tits up at any point he was the most likely to deal with it in proper order, meaning armed to the teeth and with the Lord's Cannons blazing.

So I sent a letter, via the Firm, explaining everything I knew so far, and got myself togged-up, tooled-up, and on a train to Bradford.

Ishmael had closed one of his carpet shops for the occasion – this lot didn't need no preamble or convincing about nothing – they didn't muck about, knew exactly what I was on about from the start.

We sat on some cushions in the room used for guests at the back. Four Ragheads, I mean lovely Arab geezers, stood at each corner, of course, looking well-evil, though one did make us some nice mint tea.

"We call this Being, 'Iblis,' the Whisperer," Ishmael was saying, "But the noble Qur'an offers no proof that he is the ruler of this world, it clearly states:

'It is We who created you and gave you shape; then We ordered the Angels to fall and prostrate themselves to Adam. And they fell prostrate, all save Iblis, who was not of those who made prostration.'"

"So Iblis was an Angel."

"One who rebelled. He would neither serve God, nor obey His command to serve mankind."

"Very well, but why all this 'We created you' malarkey? Could it be talking about Iblis and his Demons?"

Ishmael pauses, shifts his position on the rug, and grins,

"The Demons or 'Jinn' you speak of are in the hearts of the Infidel, and until they are all cleansed by the Truth, there cannot be peace..."

Oh bloody hell, here we go.

"…and thus, many verses in the Noble Qur'an and the Hadith call for righteous acts of war upon the Infidel, in the name of peace. One such verse, Qur'an 47:4 states:

'When you meet the unbelievers in the battlefield, strike off their heads, when you have laid them low, bind your captives firmly. Anyone who insults or even opposes Muhammad or his people, deserves a humiliating death – by beheading if possible.'"

"Alright, but is it possible to—"

"Possible? Of course! The Spoils of War Surah:

'Allah has sent you from your homes to fight for the Cause. Allah wished to confirm the truth by his words: wipe the Infidels out to the last. I shall fill the hearts of the Infidels with terror!

'So smite them on their necks and every joint, and incapacitate them, for they are opposed to Allah and His Apostle. Whoever opposes Us should know that Allah is severe in retribution. The Infidels will taste the torment of Hell.'"

He smiles. "Do you understand?"

"Situation normal then," I mutter. "Alright, makes sense, of course, not saying it doesn't. But I still don't get all this 'Us' and 'We' business…"

I pause, he was looking at me funny.

"Right, Ishmael me auld china, what I mean is *how*, if you had to come up against this Iblis geezer Itself, how would you deal with it? RPG, two-inch mortar, a string of garlic… what?"

He laughs. "Captain Barbelo, my good friend, Iblis cannot be smitten with human weapons! The answer to your question lies within your mind."

"My mind."

"You are an Infidel, Iblis is a Jinn. The inner expression is in the mind, the outer expression is in the eyes."

"I don't understand."

"I will explain," he says patiently. "We have the eyes of the Warrior, you and I, we have blooded ourselves in battle countless times, sometimes the fight was righteous and fair, sometimes it was not," he shrugs, "Our eyes tell of it either way, and thus—"

"If you mean '47, I can tell you now, you lot were no bloody picnic neither—"

He puts up his hand, "You came, we fought, you won and took our lands – it is what warriors do. As I say, sometimes it is fair, sometimes it is not. But your leaders – the Thatcher, the Reagan and all who came before, and all who will come after, although they too are drenched in blood, they do not have the Eyes of Man – they have the Eyes of Iblis!"

I swear to fuck, the way he said it nearly had me bolting for the door right there and then – I went all dizzy for a moment, the hairs stood up on the back of my neck – it was like when Frank had talked about some of the boys from HQ coming back changed from… from whatever it was they'd seen, or made to watch.

Slowly, Ishmael nods his head at me, seeming to understand.

"Trouble not, you are an Infidel and thus have the mind of the Jinn, but not yet the eyes, although…" He raises his finger. "This is because you are in ignorance and have yet to bear witness, your *heart* is yet to choose."

"My heart."

He nods, "The mind is the battlefield of the Jinn, but the heart is where the War is decided – the eyes tell of who the final victor was."

"Ishmael, who are the Illuminati, I mean I've never had to do this before, obviously, and well, how do I put it…?"

"You're shitting it!"

I sighs, "I've never really had anything to lose, until now."

Ishmael waves over one of his men, whispers something to him, who nods, and leaves the room.

"One moment, Captain Barbelo."

"I talked to my dead mate Sid, in Paradise, I suppose you'd call it, and he said I can't back out."

"As you explained earlier, you were called to this path and took an oath. But your friend is not in Paradise; if you have spoken with him, then he merely resides in one of the Seven Realms. Only Allah, the One, resides above the Seven Realms, in Paradise."

Geezer returns with a battered old book, and passes it to Ishmael with a gracious bow.

Opens it, flicks through to the page he wanted, "Here, look."

It was a stone carving of a giant Raghead king in a long robe, but with a snake's head.

"In ancient times, from Sumeria to Babylon to Egypt, the wise spoke of these Beings – the Jinn, who would take human form in the day, and at night, devour the souls of men. It is a parasite, takes all, and gives nothing in return."

He passes me the book.

"Look at the eyes, cold, dispassionate, as if seeing the futility of its condition, it has abandoned all hope, all faith. A pitiful creature."

"Then the Illuminati are what, Babylonian…"

"No, older, far older than history records. What you call the Illuminati we call simply 'the Infidel,' the human servants of this Jinn, And infected with Its doctrine, like their master, they display the condition of the parasite; take all, give nothing. Always they stalk the corridors of political power, equally, they seek to control all Faiths and distort all Scripture – anywhere you find celebration of bloodshed, you find the signature of their corruption."

Last bit didn't make sense to what he'd said earlier, but I says nothing, and pass him back his book.

He goes on, "In order to attach the Jinn to them, rulers were groomed as children; practicing depraved sexual acts and human sacrifice, opening gateways in their minds and forging alliances with the forces of darkness."

Closes his book with a snap, and looks up, "And they still do, Captain Barbelo, this has not changed. What is it that you really seek from us?"

"This, I suppose, I needed to know what I'm going up against… and protection, that's what I'm asking, that's why I'm here."

"Then you must give something in return." He nods. "If you have been called to bear witness before Iblis, and do not wish Its eyes upon you, you must at least perform the First Kalima." He smiles. "Cleanse your mind and heart, submit first before the One, Allah."

Oh bloody hell –"Become a Muslim?"

"Of course, but remember, this is merely a word. It means: 'a person who peacefully submits his or her self to God,' that is all."

"Ishmael, right, listen, I don't want to speak out of turn, but I don't believe in the invisible man living in the sky—"

"Nor I, my friend!" he chuckles, "How can God be the likeness of man, or of anything we see – is man perfect? The One resides beyond all that can be known by man, beyond all that can be reasoned with the mind, for man is not perfect. Only God is perfect, only God is great!

And yet," lifts his finger again, "His influence can be sensed, and nurtured, and allowed to guide you with good deeds."

"Oh, then if you put it that way, maybe… like a presence you mean? I used to believe, well, I felt something, once… something good, out there somewhere," I sighs, "Even though I didn't know it myself, it was there… thing was, it was precisely the day I realised it was gone, that I also realised it had been there, always. But that was a long time ago, war put an end to all that."

Smiles, "Then perhaps declare to the contrary, and He may once again be drawn near you."

"Hmmm, I dunno about that—"

Raises his hand, "Do you believe with all your heart that there can only be the One Almighty God?"

I stalled, silly question – how could there be more than one Almighties, that would be like two bosses running the same Firm. I mean, if God was almighty, there couldn't be another one otherwise He wouldn't be all-mighty, would He.

Easy logic.

"Yep, of course, I catch-yadrift, but—"

He raises his other hand, "And do you believe Mohammed is the Messenger of God?"

Well who was I to say he wasn't?

But still… "Explain that bit, will you?"

"It is simple," he says, bringing his hands together, "Mohammed is the Messenger of God."

"Why?"

"Because the Angel Gabriel spoke the words of God to Mohamed."

"Right."

"And these words we call the Noble Qur'an."

I paused for a moment, pondered, and shook my head,

"Very well, but in that case, it was the Angel what was the messenger of God, Gabriel, not Mohammed. Mohammed would've been the messenger of—"

"It was Mohammed who brought God's message to mankind, not the Angel."

"Nah, Mohammed was a man too. If I was your Captain, say, and I came to you with some Intel from HQ, and tell you to please pass it on to your troops; who's the messenger, you or me?"

He looks at me like I'm crazy, and then turns briefly to the Ragheads around us, who shrug.

"Good, Captain Barbelo, good. True Islam is above all a faith which encourages questions and free thought. In your example we would both be the messenger."

"Nah, I would be the messenger, and you would be *my* messenger."

"But where is the contradiction?"

"Chain of command, see? You're saying that Mohammed was the messenger, the one and only, when actually he got his Intel second-hand, from Gabriel."

"Ahhh, but there have been other Messengers before; Abraham, Isa and so forth, and be it Angel or man, above all is God. What is your problem?"

"Problem is, well, if I'm gonna say this Kalima business with all my heart, I can't say *the* Messenger because it don't feel right."

"I cannot see the contradiction, but… what would you prefer."

"*A* Messenger."

Turns around to the four corners, gets a couple of shrugs and nods, and says, "Very well. Testify now that there is no God but God, and Mohammed is a messenger of God."

"Now?"

"Now."

"And I would be a Muslim?"

"That is only a word, sir. To *be* a Muslim is an *action*; it is to discover and then practice that which you always were," he smiles, "A servant of the Highest Good, the One."

It was a sobering moment. Started in my chest, that crushing, primal uncertainty you get just before your first jump – otherwise known as common sense – and then my mind went blank, even the Voice had shut up. This was not something to be taken lightly, it ran deeper than mere words, and they knew it – all eyes, staring at me expectantly.

"Alright then," I says finally, "Here goes. I hereby testify there is no God but God, and Mohammed is a Messenger of God."

Ishmael beams, "Do you feel it?"

I wasn't sure I understood the question. This warmth was spreading inside me, like just after you've had a lovely soak in the tub after a hard days graft, but without the sleepiness what generally follows. And blimey, it was growing! I looks around the room; the Persian rugs hanging on the walls, the silver tea-set on the floor between us – exquisite – everything was right, correct, like we was all wrapped in this perfect bubble and there was no way to go wrong—

"—to have ever doubted was insane," I muttered, sitting up straight.

Ishmael chuckles, delighted, "He feels it!"

I nods, "And now, please," I says, inhaling deep, "I need more Intel on this Iblis Jinn—"

"What more do you need? Welcome home my Brother! You have just taken the first step towards Allah, and now Allah will take two steps towards you!"

He leans forward and gives me a hug. Bloody hell, and then the others leave their posts in the corners and come over, all grins and smiles.

"Steady on!"

"Do not despair of the seventy-two eternal virgins waiting for you in Paradise," says one, "Allah is merciful!" Lowers is tone, "I do not for myself believe this." He winks.

Well thank fuck, 'cos I personally couldn't think of anything more annoying than seventy-two eternal virgins—

"In Islam," says another, "the more you feel His goodness, the more good deeds you do, and the more you will receive."

"Alright, alright, I feel it," I says to them all, crowding in, "But listen-up you lot, I am still Captain Barbelo, back off and—"

"And of course," says the other, still trying to hug me, "Faith increases and decreases by good and bad deeds, thus always be good."

"And honest, Captain Barbelo, for the more you are honest, the more the One will help you increase your faith."

"Captain Barbelo the Muslim," corrects the other Raghead – fuck it, really gotta stop calling them that—

"Alright you 'orrible lot! Back to your posts – that's a fucking order!"

350

Well, I yelled that in full army mode and they all just laughed. I turns to Ishmael, "Tell them to back off!"

He growls, "Return to your posts!"

They laughed even harder, but at least backed off a bit, sitting down around us.

"What's all this about?"

He shrugs. "In true Islam, nobody is set higher than another. All are free to be, all that they can be."

"But you're the boss."

"No, these are my Brothers. Allah is the Boss."

It was then I realised a very important fact,

"It's all a show then, a psyops."

"If you mean does our group maintain a certain… hmmm, theatrical performance, then yes, but it is solely to conceal our true nature from the Infidel, until the hour arrives when we are made strong, and can finally defeat them…" pauses, squinting at his hands, and then shrugs again, "Allah has called you into battle against a great enemy, truly you are blessed! So what troubles you now?"

I shook my head. "This is all very nice, but I'm not getting involved in all that Jihad smiting business, alright? I've changed my perspective loads. There's an awful lot of very nice people out there, and I'm not—"

They were all laughing again. Ishmael claps me on the shoulder,

"Oh my Brother, how funny you are! Here you see neither slaves to the laws of men nor their religions, only servants of God."

I looked around, they were all nodding at me now, very serious.

"Every Muslim is called to Jihad, but not all answer the call, only His righteous few—"

"Right, been a pleasure, thanks for the tea and all that…"

I pause, halfway from getting up. Ishmael growls, all grim, face like a coal pit,

"The choice is yours. Leave now, or be seated, but you will return to being an Infidel unless you open your ears and learn to listen!"

Fingering Happy Stick's release catch, I settle back down.

"Good," he says, pleasantly enough. "Understand this, we are the Brotherhood of True Islam, not cowards. We do not smite the innocent; the women and children, or even the man, for where is the honour in this?

We are Warriors of the One, the righteous, Allah the merciful and compassionate, He Who is Great! Thus, the righteousness of His Jihad can only be measured by the greatness of His enemy – only the mightiest leaders of the Infidel deserve to taste His justice – those with the Eyes of Iblis! For who but the cowardly Jinn would pick enemies which are less so?"

"Catch-yadrift, Allah is Great."

"Thus, the others of which you speak, those who smite the innocent; the women and children, or even the man? They are servants of the Jinn, and bring only insult to God, dishonour to His Holy Jihad. Be they Infidel or beguile themselves 'Muslim,' they too will taste the torment of Hell!"

Pouring us another cuppa, he rests his hand on my shoulder, and smiles again, sweetly.

"Do you understand now, my Brother? The greatness of a warrior is measured by the greatness of his enemy. This is Jihad, anything less is cowardice…"

I'd understood alright, and fuck me sideways, just goes to show how wrong you can be about people, but pegging it across the Beanfield with the screams of children pounding in my ears, I wish I could agree – I'd fucking smite the lot of these cunts in the name of whoever – they deserved Barbelo's vengeance at the very least.

I dived into some bushes. Tipped the blade out of Happy Stick, weighed up the situation in my mind, and my last grenade in my palm, ready for the lob – odds were about 2,500 cunts to one Top Cunt. A great enemy?

Time to go to work.

Nah, I didn't. There was not one with the Eyes of Iblis among them – oh they were sick fuckers, these 'Peelers,' SPG, posttraumatic to fuck from smashing the Miners' Strikes the years previous, but as I pegged through the field, Ishmael's words resounded in my head, "Anything less is cowardice," and before I knew it, my blade had slid back inside my cane, and my grenade in my pocket.

And then I saw him – I spotted him before him me, Frank, sitting in the back of an unmarked squad car, parked just off the road.

Staying close to the bushes, I crept closer, and closer, but when I saw Sprocket on the ground getting his head smashed in with a fire extinguisher, I couldn't help it – I leapt out, and slashing the Peeler's hamstring, dragged Sprocket to his feet, and we staggered towards the road.

It was all over after that – last thing I saw were uniforms and truncheons, raining down all around us, and Frank – the Eyes of Iblis staring straight at me.

Total darkness...

PART FOUR

☠ redemption ☠

"Naturally the common people don't want war; neither in Russia, nor in England, nor in America, nor in Germany. That is understood. But after all, it is the leaders of the country who determine policy, and it is always a simple matter to drag the people along, whether it is a democracy, or a fascist dictatorship, or a parliament, or a communist dictatorship.

Voice or no voice, the people can always be brought to the bidding of the leaders. That is easy. All you have to do is to tell them they are being attacked, and denounce the peacemakers for lack of patriotism and exposing the country to danger. It works the same in any country."

Hermann Goering (Marshal of the Third Reich)

"Military men are just dumb stupid animals to be used as pawns in foreign policy."

Henry Kissinger, (Council On Foreign Affairs)

Chapter 47

2007

Scene: on board seventeenth century man of war.
  Soundtrack: Stealers Wheel, *Stuck in the middle with you.*
  Action!

Flickering into life like a reel from an epic movie, the dream played out before his mind's eye in vivid colour. Green hues streak across the darkening sky, and the camera slowly pans back over a galleon, flying through the heavens.
  Well I don't know why I came here tonight, I got the feeling that something ain't right.
  A tracking shot reveals the cannons on the ship's flank.
  I'm so scared in case I fall off my chair, and I'm wondering how I'll get down the stairs...
  Fanned out across the horizon, seven vessels follow behind. They sail over a dense sea of red mist. Their translucent sails are tinted blue from the light of a thousand stars and the full moon.
  Clowns to the left of me, Jokers to the right, here I am, stuck in the middle with you.
  Dressed in pinstripes and Trilby, Captain Barbelo stands on the prow. He holds the double-edged Sword of Justice before him.
  Well you started out with nothing, and you're proud that you're a self made man.
  A sombre shadow passes over the length of the deck, dark-clad Dream Warriors pull down their hoods to gaze, awe-struck at the heavens.
  And your friends they all come crawlin,' slap you on the back and say, Please... please...
  Tracking shot: a pod of dolphins, giant manatees and diverse deep-sea creatures swim through the clouds above the ship's masts.
  Trying to make some sense of it all, 'cos I don't think that I can take anymore.
  Close-up: a gigantic eye.

But I can see that it makes no sense at all, is it cool to go to sleep on the floor?

Camera pans back from the eye to reveal a humpback whale, swimming in the stars above the fleet.

Clowns to the left of me, Jokers to the right, here I am, stuck in the middle with you.

More deep-sea animals descend to join the fleet.

Stuck in the middle with you.

Tiny seahorses float in front of the lens, and dart away to join the ranks of the swelling Lyraquai army in the sky.

Yes I am, stuck in the middle with you.

Soundtrack climbs higher.

Spanning the horizon of swirling silvery-red mists, another fleet approaches. The seven galleons are now dwarfed by the enormity of the shadow realm's armada. At the prow of their flagship, dressed in a clown's costume, stands a different Captain Barbelo. He cackles wild laughter. Festooned with gold chains and jewels, he too holds the Sword of Justice.

Finishing shot: the red mists part to reveal Planet Earth below, fading into darkness.

Stuck in the middle with—

"With you, and I, and you!" I regained consciousness singing on a bed, sat bolt upright. For a split second I thought I was still dreaming. I was in a boat cabin, and on the table next to me was an envelope.

Picking it up, I climbed out, and peered through the porthole – sunny morning sky, and heaving blue sea everywhere.

Checked myself over – no damage – and then my pockets. memorial pen, wedge of cash, credit card, false passport. But Orgonite, grenade and other tools of the trade, gone.

Spied Happy Stick on the floor by the bed.

Went to the door, opened it; an empty corridor. Went back inside and opened the envelope, sitting on the bed.

Inside was a photograph of an old, three-storey white building.

On the back was a note.

It read:

All the king's horses,
and all the king's men,
couldn't catch Barbelo
and his Mighty Pen.

Everybody thinks the Devil lives in Georgia,
But if you're looking for me,
How wrong can they be?
'Tis obvious only the Irish can sort ya!

I live at Number Three,
Call round for a nice cup of tea.

I hope you had an interesting journey.

Kind regards,

The Creator

"Lovely handwriting," I couldn't help but notice, and picking up my cane, I quickly pegged outside, bumping into a young lady with a mop in the corridor – "Oopsy-daisy, sorry my dear."

"That's okay."

"Can you tell me where I am, my head see? Bit foggy, age and all that."

She smiles, "Yeah, you're on the Sealink," glances at her watch, "We should be docking in Dublin in an hour or so."

"Thanks," I says, taking out the envelope, "Do you happen to know where number three this white house is?"

She shrugs. "Could be anywhere."

"Of course, silly me," I grimace, and peg it up the stairs to the bar.

Fucking needed a drink after all that. It's the most disconcerting feeling there is, getting nabbed like this. Mostly you find yourself strapped to the bed – and not in it like just now – but this is almost worse, feeling like the mouse waiting for the cat to pounce.

Frank had good reason to be there in the field, MI5 and counter-subversion and all that bollocks – if you can call people trying to live their lives subversion – but looking back, he wasn't what I had expected, I dunno what. Demonic creatures spitting fire and all the malarkey? I dunno. Then again, fuck me, his eyes; don't get me started! Gawd knows what these poor cunts get shown, but I'm not going near it for love or money.

Fuck it. I took the bait, got nabbed, and they let me go for whatever reason. Time to sink a pint, mull it over before the boat docks.

"Barman, please, a pint of porter."

He nods, just about to turn around, and freezes, "Impossible!"

"Sorry my good man, what did you say?"

"My God, you even sound like him."

"Like who?"

"No, it can't be…"

"What?"

"You look the exact same… Don't you recognise me?"

"Emmm, no…"

"Jake."

"Jake who?"

Pauses. Lowers his tone,

"Jake, down, the, underpass, Jake."

"Fuck off," I mutter – this cunt was a grown man!

"Alright then."

"Nah, wait! Why do you say that?"

"Because it's… me." Glances about. "Remember?"

"You don't look much like any Jake I know."

"Well, it has been, what, twenty years?"

"What the—"

"You're looking well though! Haven't changed a bit."

Taking a closer peek, I had to admit, he did look like him,

"How old are you, then?"

"Coming up to the Big Four O."

Right, breathe deep, keep it together – this isn't the first odd thing to happen in your life, seen plenty of weird-shit too, Gawd help us all.

"Alright, when was the last time we met?"

"Oh, that was round Uncle Pete's, where I used to work. Remember it like it was yesterday. You'd got run over by a bus, and I got you some lollipops and Superglue–"

Fucking cut my throat there and then! My legs went to jelly, thank goodness I was close enough to grip the bar rail or I'd of brained myself on the floor.

"Mr Barbelo, your pint."

"Oh, thanks." I reach out a trembling hand, and pull back.

"Jake," I suppose, "What's the date?"

"Twelfth of August."

"And emmm, alright… what year is this? Sorry, age and all that."

"2007," he says, and winks, "The pint's on me, sir."

And with that he goes off to serve a young'un in really stupid baggy jeans – well they was, fucking hanging off his arse, stupid cunt.

Controlling the tremors, I skulled a long quaff of my pint, gagged – tasted fluoridated to shit – and scanned the bar area. Not many people about, but spotted a specy geezer reading a newspaper, and I goes over.

"Sorry mate, can I have quick butcher's?"

"I'm sorry?"

"Can I have a quick look at your newspaper?"

Passes me his paper, sure enough, 2007.

"Britain's at war with… Iraq?"

Nods. "And Iran's next."

Alright, now you can fuck me sideways, upways and anyway you like.

I sat down heavily beside the geezer with the newspaper, eyes pinned to 'Jake I Suppose' serving behind the bar, and breathed, just breathed deep like I'd done a million times when caught in crossfire – and feeling the blood flush into my face once more, I got up and headed for the bog.

Taking off my Trilby, I peered into the mirror.

Nah, I was looking well alright, too bloody well for a hundred and fucking five!

"This has to be them, check our birth date on your passport."

"Thanks," and sure enough, that had changed too. "Why though? They had me, could've done us, end of."

"And instead they put us on a boat to Ireland and pretend it's the future?"

Unless, of course, I was still useful, and…

Of course! I was in some kind of military rehab psyops – fuck your mind from here to Mars, smash you into pieces, and then put you back together again in their image, back in line.

"Why Ireland though?"

"I dunno, maybe they're on a low budget."

I turns around.

"What year is it?" I asks a geezer taking a slash.

Looks at me funny, but answers, "2007."

"Oh bloody hell, are you all in on it?"

"What?"

"Said you're not getting me that fucking easy!"

He starts zipping up, quick-smart.

"Oh yeah, you go and tell them Barbelo's not having it! Right? My mind's *mine*, it belongs to me and my Voice of Truth! Yeah that's it, run along now ya cunt! Crawl like a nice little puppy to your masters. I'm out!"

And he was out too alright, out the door quicker than shit off a stick.

"Fucking cunts, fucking cunts, fucking cunts…" me, thudding over to 'Jake I Suppose.'

"Another pint, Mr Barbel—"

"Right ya father-fucking piece of shit!" I growls under my breath. "Come with me! Now!"

"N-n-now?"

"Right fucking now!"

Takes off his serving pinny and comes over my side of the bar. I drag him over to the window.

"Wh-wh-wha—"

"What do I want?" I grins, "If you're really who you say you are, you'll know what! If you're not?" I flick the release catch.

He shudders, eyes pinned to mine.

"Still?" he whispers. "The Luger?"

"So where did I buy this cane?"

"You didn't, Mr Barbelo, I did, dealer in Mile End, remember?"

"Tell you that in your briefing?" I begin sliding out my blade—

"Wait! Nah, look at the poor cunt, he's shitting bricks!"

"Fucking hell, too right…"

I pause. I could feel the abdabs off him, rising thick between us.

"It's you Jake, isn't it? It really is you…"

"Please Mr Barbelo sir," he says rapidly, "Past is past, I've changed! It all changed me, I'm a good man now, have a job, home, wife, you know her—"

"I do?"

"And we've kids. Look," he says, fumbling out a photo from his wallet, "That's Emma and little Sammy."

"Sammy," I mutter.

"Left London, see? Left it all behind in '85 after the riots—"

"Riots."

"Went on for weeks; Brixton went to shit after that – fucking crack-heads, smack-heads wall to fucking wall!" Heavy sigh, "And yeah, I was one of them. Whole of London's still fucked, worse than ever, if you ask me."

Glances about, lowers his tone, "I couldn't get off the gear there, it's impossible, it's everywhere – every time I cleaned up I'd fall straight back into it again. And what you said, what you said you'd do to me if I didn't," nervous chuckle, "So I scarpered, went on the road, everybody was doing it back then, helped me loads. Met loads of good people travelling. Though bottom line, I've got you to thank for it. In funny ways your Formula worked. I cleaned up, permanently—"

"What formula?"

Grimaces, "*The* Formula," he whispers, "Special Unit, the War."

"What's this nut on about?"

"Dunno, shhh!" I pause again, think back, 'cos unless briefed to, you got hooked on skag in the Craft you got shot, end of…"Oh *that* Formula, blimey. Alright, go on. You scarpered."

"That very day round Uncle Pete's. Cleaned up, ended up down South, met my wife there, Kate, well, thing was she was from London too, but then again—"

"Hold on, Kate who?"

"Kate Williams."

"She was from our way…"

"That's what I mean. You know her." Pulls out another picture. "My wife. Isn't she beautiful?"

"In a Barbara Streisand kinda way…"

"Yeah, that's what I thought." He smiles.

"And Sharon?" I asks. "How's her sister doing?"

"Oh, passed on. Car crash, it'll be what, thirteen years last Christmas, hit some ice. It was quick, they said."

"Who said?"

"The police report."

"Cunts," I mutter darkly, thinking back to their Orgonite ops.

"Story goes, they were coming back from London, been round the Patent Office to register an invention. Don't ask, never saw it myself, vanished from the crash site, Peeler's nicked it, I reckons. Some kind of 'new television,' Sharon said—"

"Hold on, Translocale Communicator?"

"That's it, yeah, it was going to change the world, Sharon said, did you ever get a butcher's?"

"Once or twice."

"What was it like, better picture?"

"Long story."

Sighs, "Changed their world alright, changed all our worlds."

Lowers his tone again, "Look, I never let on to no one, I swear on my kids, I never let on about your *visit* to the Social."

I nods. "And Sammy, how's their mum, how's she doing?"

"She talked about you, I know that. Kate says you made her laugh…"

"Same car."

"Kids took it badly at the time, see? We thought it best to get away, change of scene did the world of good. North Wales. Live near the Port now." He shrugs, glancing about again. "Finally got a job doing this."

"It really is 2007 then."

"Please, I have to get back to work, clean up. We're docking soon."

"Alright son," I says, "Take care. And Jake," I hold onto his arm, "I *am* sorry."

"I know," he replies, and edges around me, back to the bar.

The loud hailer declares we were docking in ten minutes.

I peg-shuffle to the doors.

"This is definitely a psyops. If you ask me, we've been frozen in a Cryogenics Lab, and defrosted."

"Or it could be a Time Machine."

"Don't be silly."

"Could be, we all heard the rumours."

"Either way, whatever this is, we don't have to go along with it."

"Options, right."

"Options and prospects, they left us money, passport, good looks – we don't have to do nothing we don't want. I reckon that's the main target of this psyops, choice. If you follow through on this one it's curtains for you, I reckon."

"Alright, we'll go Grey for a bit and work out—"

"But we fucking hate Ireland!"

"True. On the other hand, I dunno, Sid always liked the place."

"Only because Sid was deranged and afflicted, poor auld sod."

"Loveliest people on Earth, he said."

"Yeah, right, say that to Sally – loveliest pervy priests, more like. And all those nuns, ach! Gives us the abdabs."

I nods. "Never a truer word."

"We're on an island the size of football pitch, mate, not saying you're not any good at the Grey game, but the Emerald Isle my arse – there's barely any trees here anymore, never mind proper forests. We've far better prospects on a continent, a large one. Soon as the boat docks – cab, airport, Canada."

Queuing up, I take out the photo in my pocket of the white house, and re-read the back: 'I live at number three, call round for a nice cup of tea.'

"Too fucking right I will!"

"No you fucking won't! Think – we're free! Personally I'd go for the Canada option, you'd love it there, big skies, huge forests, loose gun laws and all that – fuck me, we're free of the cunts! Don't you see? We can go anywhere, we're in the future!"

I scanned the people shuffling through the queues, and pondered for a moment. "You're right," I whispers, "Everything's telling me we've slipped through the net, somehow…"

"It's hardly rocket science; we can go and do whatever we want – drink beer all day long, breed a race of genetically superior beings what wipe out all the vermin and bring about world peace, why not!"

"The porter tastes fluoridated to high—"

"*Chemical lobotomy, yeah! And what did Ben Franklin say about well-armed sheep—*"

"They don't have the right to bear arms here..."

"*That's what I mean! Where we gonna find a 9mm Glock at five in the morning when we need one?*"

"Where there's a will there's way."

"*But still, the only arms we'd have a right to bear is a beer-arm, and good thing too—*"

"Nah, I'm telling you, they've done something foul to the porter here."

"*So there ya go, compared with Canada all this strikes me as a very unfair and worrying predicament.*"

"Highly regrettable."

"*Be practical then – get me some land, I won't mind where, anywhere you think will be interesting. Preferably somewhere we can still see the stars and like Sid used to say, drink clean water from a stream, at least, and let off a full clip from a fully-automatic at the moon all night, wearing nothing but a bearskin hat, screaming, dripping with baby-oil and the next day nobody even says 'boo' to ya! Hehehehheee...*"

"Canada?"

"*My thoughts exactly...*"

Chapter 48

Thanks Barry, You're a Star

'Call round for a nice cup of tea?' Too fucking right I will! If I could only find the fucking place – everybody thought I was a handle short of a pickaxe, drifting about Dublin asking where "number three this white house" was. By the end of the day I was almost in tears trying to find out, finally sat on a bench in O'Connell Street, head buried my in my arms.

"I know you're right."

Then listen to me! Take the first fucking plane out now, or I swear I'll never speak to you again!

"Promise?"

It's terrible here! Ireland's the last place we wanna be right now—

"I know! I know, but the note says here, so here we are."

It'll be THEM waiting for us, I'd bet your sorry arse that's what's gonna happen. And alright, maybe they have? Maybe they've invented time travel, so what, we can still give them the slip—

"Gotta follow through, always."

Fuck me, if I had hands I'd fucking slap you into the next millennium!

"Oh very droll," I mutter. "We're gonna find this house, use the Time Machine to go back; annihilate every last cunt to the last cunt, starting with Frank. And then find Sammy and… oh no, Sammy…"

Caught me by surprise, but I turned on the waterworks like I'd never done before. And I fucking mean that too. I must've sobbed a bucketful of tears, it was getting dark by the time this old geezer shakes me by the shoulder,

"Hey there! Are you alright?"

"Nah, I'm not fucking alright! Nothing is."

"Do you need me to…? I mean, will I call you someone?"

I glance up, "Tried. No answers, anywhere…"

He hands me a handkerchief. I look him up and down, smart and tidy, still red-haired, broad shoulders. Had the air of the Army about him – leastways somebody what had been through it alright.

"Thank you," wiping at my face, "Thank you, my good man."

"You're welcome." He smiles, puts his walking stick next to mine, "May I?"

I nods.

"Barry O'Reilly," he declares, sitting down beside me.

"Joseph Barbelo."

We shakes hands.

"Where you from?"

"I don't know…"

He laughs, "Well you've come to the right place!"

"Please don't," I says, "I need help. I woke up this morning on a boat, I don't know where I am."

"Dublin," says he. "We'll try calling someone again, anyone, give me a number."

He pulls out his snazzy little talkie-walkie.

I stare at him. He stares back, genuinely concerned,

"You don't know what this is, do ya?"

"Some kind of new craze? Seen loads of young'uns playing with them, all day…"

Frowns, "You've been *away*, haven't ya?"

I shakes my head, "Nah, I wasn't in prison, if that's what—"

"Come 'ere to me!" leans over, lowers his tone, "Then did ya meet the Faerie King? Did you strike any deals with them, did ya? Dodgy biscuits, *never* contract with them, ya see, this is what happens."

"Right, Barry is it? I'm asking, please, don't take the piss, that's all I've had since I got here. I'm serious! I really don't know where I am."

"Well, when they take ya away, not many people do," shrugs, "At least you weren't found wandering about some bog field," nod, nod, "I'm serious too, deadly serious. People lose their minds."

I look him up and down again, and yep, he was either two pegs short himself, or deadly serious.

"What year is it?"

"I knew it! Away with the Faeries!" slaps me on the back, and then whispers, "So, tell me, what was the Kingdom like? They say the Faerie Queen's beautiful, treacherous without measure—"

I turn on the waterworks again, can't fucking help it. He puts an arm around my shoulder, "My God, what did she do to ya…?"

"I don't fucking know! I was in a field with hundreds of people getting their heads smashed in, and then I'm on this boat. It was fucking 1985 fuck it! Now it's… it's…"

"2007," he sighs, "All the hallmarks. At least that's one possibility. Come, I'll buy you a pint and we'll figure this out."

"Don't want no pint, just wanna go home."

He slaps me on the back again. "Pull yerself together there, chin up, come!"

"And what's all those white streaky lines about, up there in the sky."

He looks up. "Do ya know what, I don't know either…"

"It's fucking horrible! We didn't have them where I'm from. It was a lovely sunny day this morning, been watching planes spewing out these lines up there all day."

"Never noticed before," he mutters softly, "You're right, it was sunny this morning."

"I'm in Hell, aren't I?"

"You're not in Hell."

"I'm dead and Iblis took me to Hell!"

"Who? No, no, listen to me, you're grand," he chuckles again, points at the sky, "Look! They're spread out like clouds, there."

I glance up. "That's what I mean! Do you make rain in the future or what?"

"Not that I know of, as if we need any more rain here!" he laughs, "But what we need is a pint, eh? And a good stiff drink to settle the nerves."

"I dunno…"

"Dunno either. He could be SIS, true, and so what? Worse that can happen is you get a bullet in the head, knock some fucking sense into you! Fuck it, go for a drink with this lovely fruitcake, regroup, good idea…"

We sat at the bar in silence for a bit, didn't much like the idea of having my back to the door, the gaff was heaving with early evening boozers – least of my problems though.

"2007?"

"2007."

"Have you got a spare fag please?"

"Here ya go."

"Cheers mate."

"But I'm afraid we can't smoke in here."

"Oh?"

"The doctors say it's bad for us."

"Bloody hell, I remember when they said it was good for us, 'opens up the lungs,' or something. What beer is that, Carlsberg?"

"Weissbeer, German," he says, the barman passing us our drinks, "My granddaughter suggested it. I can't go near the Guinness these days," he whispers, "My arse drops out!"

"Fluoride poisoning. Don't drink the tap water neither."

"Right, that's what she says too."

"Can't do much about our food, unless we grow our own."

"So, where you from?"

"London."

"Interesting name, Barbelo."

"Dunno where it's from. Granddad was Irish though, then again, who's wasn't."

"Makes you one of us then."

"Nah, it doesn't. Countries don't make you nothing. Purpose does."

"Purpose," he affirms with a curt nod.

"My wife was born here," I skulled my whiskey, "Leastways that's what she always said. Dublin. Hated the place, not surprised after what they did to her. Mother was unmarried," I adds.

"Ah, sorry to hear that. We're from Cavan originally, we moved here thirty years ago."

"Fucking ruined her life, ruined all our lives. Use you and drop you, that's what—"

"Like a hat."

"Like a hat," I affirms, and raise an eyebrow.

He sips his pint, and nods. "IRA," he replies.

"Oh, well, you lot need a few basic lessons in strategic—"

"The *other* IRA."

"Oh."

"And proud to say it."

"I wish I could say the same. I took the King's Shilling at fifteen, the First War, 'the war to end all wars,' they said, like fuck. Sold us all down the fucking Swaney—"

"Hold it there, the First you say?"

"Yeah, I know, I did the maths earlier too."

He pins his eyes to mine, "Sweet Jesus and Mary!" he gasps, "It's true, then…?" skulls his whiskey in one, orders two more.

"Looking good for my age, ay?" I groans, "Yeah, it's true."

"Tell me, tell me everything…"

I did. The next four hours felt like a debriefing session, back in the days. Did wonders on one level, to get it all in proper order. This cold emotional detachment comes over you, like you're watching events happening from a great height, but like they're happening to somebody else. I was shitfaced by the end of it, we both were.

"Not a good idea going to the Cops, then."

"Wouldn't be the brightesht idea, nah."

"Sheems to me you're being groomed, prepared."

"For something, yeah…"

"Show me that picture again."

I puts it on the bar.

"It looksh like a… hmmm! A convent maybe. It's an old building fer sure, over two-hundred years, I'd say, and the common folk, no, we didn't build three stories high like that. The Church would've had the money though—"

"Church ish fucking loaded! How's world hunger these days?"

"Hungry," mutters he, swigging his pint. "But they're in big trouble now, oh it's all come to light now, sex abuse scandals – thoushands and thoushands of children abused… and people knew, I knew, everyone knew the shtories but… but what could we do?"

I shrugs, "Put up or shut up."

Sighs, "The nail that sticks out gets hammered in."

"Catch-yadrift."

Shakes his head sadly, "It almost sounds crazy now, it just doesn't seem possible that it could have gone on and for so long; generations and generations and the State did nothing to stop it, *nothing*."

I nods. "Shame old shame old, acceshories after the fact."

"And insurance policies, they actually took out insurance policies in case they got caught!"

"Now why doesn't that shurprise me? That's exshactly what owl-worshiping cunts do! It's bloody obvious, guilty as charged. But thish," I points to the photo, "Is thish thing here?"

369

"Dublin? I couldn't tell ya. My granddaughter might, Roberta, clever girl, History student and a bit of a rebel. We'll get her on the Internets in the morning."

"Come again?"

"Electrical gadgetry, kids nowadays can do anything with Internets." Drains his whiskey. "What you gonna do when you get there?"

"I dunno, have a cup of tea with the Devil" – and then blow his fucking brains out – "Innkeeper! Another two pintsh of Weishbeer and wishkies, and another two wishkies, pleash," I slurs to the barman, who nods back with a smile. Amazing.

Pat or George, or even Uncle Pete – any barman round my manor would've chucked us out six whiskeys ago, but this lovely cunt just grins and pours. Fucking amazing… maybe this place isn't such a bad idea after all.

"Alright, Barry, me auld china. I gotta go to that foreign exchange, change more of me Shterling into… whats-its?"

"Euros. But we can do that tomorrow—"

"Fuck me, how's they've got away with all that euro-bollocks?"

"Referendum after referendum till they get the result they want."

"Right… oh don't tell me Britain's Europe too."

"Soon will be."

"Fuck that, nah, Queeny can't be a Shovereign and a European citizen at the same time, that's ridiculash!"

"Ridiculash!" nod, nod, "We'll finish these, and go."

"Good point. Fucking bollocksed… find a B&B or something."

Shakes his head. "Don't even think it, yer going to shtay with us!"

"Barry, thanksh you – you're a star, sound as a pound and twice as round… and yeah, thanks for listening."

He smiles. "Can't be discourteous to a man touched by the Faeries, can we now? That'd be mosht unwise."

"Whatsh all this Faerie Folk malarkey about then? I mean you really don't look like someone who believes in the Little People."

"Never judge the book—"

"By the cover, never a truer word, mate."

"The Little Folk aren't what the movies tell us, that's just to ridicule people who've had dealings with them." Lowers his tone, "Church's to blame, they're afraid we'll stray from the flock. Mosht unwise! They *are* real, without a doubt, just that most of the time we don't see them... I suppose it's shimular to what you said earlier, about the ashtral beings."

"Nashty then."

"Belligerent. They can take you away into their kingdom and trap you there for hundreds of years! You were lucky."

"Lucky," I mutter. "You really think that's what happened, I got nabbed by the Faeries?"

"Wasn't uncommon in my day... shtill is. Just that in these modren times people are too scared to admit it. Too scared of the ridicule. And something happened to you, didn't it?"

"Didn't it jusht..."

"They use cunning subterfuges, never trust what they shay they are, or even what they appear to be," skulls his whisky, "We are the shadows on the cave wall, cast by beings too bright to see."

I smile at that, "Plato. The Republic, read it too."

"The Allegory of the Cave, yesh, we don't even undershtand what *we* are, never mind the Faerie Folk. I think that's how they see us though, like cave dwellers, like shadows. I think they're living in a parallel world, shide by shide to ours, and they're more advanced, and their time moves slower, or fashter."

"I shaw something once," I ventures, "I shaw this... this woman vanish in front of my eyes! Heard her howling, it was *horrible*..."

"Like the Banshee," nod, nod, "They've been called different things, in different places and timesh; demons and angels, elves and pixies, but nowadays we have all this new technology, and with it we've changed our views, and so people now are more likely to shee spaceships and aliens instead of the Faerie Folk of my day. But make no mistake," he adds, lowering his tone solemnly, "they are shtill the same underneath, just changing facades as we change over time. And yesh, Joseph, I've seen them too, and not all are bad; there's goodness in the ones who wanna help us remember who we are. Let's go, I'll tell ya all about it."

"Alright," I drains my pint, "Funny that, I dreamt about flying boats... earlier."

Raises his eyebrows.

I shakes my head. "2007?"

"2007."

Chapter 49

The White House

Woke up on Barry's sofa sick as a dog, hangover from the darkest depths of thorny Hell – but that was the point – needed something tangible to focus on. My head was an exploding mini-Hiroshima. Good. That was real, at least.

Unfortunately, so was 2007.

Pat down The Albert was right, imaginative bunch the Irish for sure, and thank fuck for that. Anywhere else I'd of landed in the loonybin for half the things I needed to talk about.

Found out the Little Folk live in Britain too and abroad all over the gaff, and by the end of all his stories I'd pretty much been converted. Leastways I wanted to keep an open mind. Had to. I was completely stumped! When your arse depends on it enough times, you become expert at rooting out opportunities, working through just about any situation – the Craft accommodates everything except failure – all options are good, till you've stepped on a landmine.

So, options: Time Machine, Faeries, Alien and, or Demonic Abduction and the white house in the picture, the cunt what wrote the message on the back: The Creator – the Illuminati Top Cunt. And if everything somehow boils down to an SIS psyops, which oh Gawd I was fucking praying for at this stage, then yeah,

"Well done, Frank," I mutters, staring up at the ceiling. "I bow my head, and tip my hat in the presence of outstanding brilliance. Damn your Eyes of Iblis…"

"Good morning," Barry, passing me a lovely cuppa, "Roberta's due over any minute. Give us another look-see at your photo again."

I pass him the photo, and strap on my peg just in time. The bell rings, and in comes a cracker, a fucking stunner, I shit you not – well, anything to keep my mind spinning from here to Narnia, you do understand. But my Gawd, two legs up to her arse, mad corkscrew red hair, green eyes – you get the picture – they would've burnt her at the stake for being a witch back in the olden times.

Silly cunts.

"I'm Joseph Barbelo," I says, reaching out a hand, "Pleasure to make your acquaintance."

"Roberta," says she. "What's this?"

Barry gives her the photo, and she turns it over a couple of times.

"That's what my good friend Mr Barbelo here wants to know. We need to find this building. He has an appointment with destiny there."

She smiles, passes me the photo. "It's in Limerick."

"Limerick?"

"Where's Limerick?"

"In the West, a town. That's the old convent near the racetrack. Everybody knows it. Been to a party there once or twice."

It was getting odder by the second, "The nuns have parties now?"

She laughs, "No, no, it's no longer a convent, it's been turned into flats. I used to know people living there from the University."

"Then to Limerick it is. Who lives at number three?"

"No idea, sorry."

"You don't have any friends still living there?"

"No, people move in and out a lot. But I've friends in Limerick still, in fact I'm—"

"What's it like inside?"

"Inside? Ehmmm, there's a stairway, doors leading to the flats." She shrugs, turns to Barry. "I need to go, I'll be late for my lecture."

"See ya later," gives her a peck on the cheek.

"Joseph," she says, pausing at the door, "I'm going to Limerick this evening."

"Tonight?"

"For the weekend, wait till about five, if you want the company on the bus."

"Very well, that's very kind of you – we'll catch the train then, go in style, my treat."

She smiles, "We'll go in style, then."

And that was that – and about fucking time something just fell into place nice and easy. Said goodbye to Barry at the train station, diamond geezer, took everything in his stride. Offered to come with me, just in case, but understood this was a mission I had to accomplish on my own. My Jihad.

Main thing now was keeping the abdabs at bay; conserve energy, focus on something else for the train journey and improvise at the other end, on site. And that's where Roberta came in, well-handy. But fuck me, bit of a rebel? Clever girl alright – almost had me thinking she'd done a stint with SIS at one point – couldn't make heads nor tails of half the things she was on about.

"Natural law? Yeah, sounds good – come on Joseph!" dragging me through the crowded carriages by my sleeve, "We've just got to get a seat. It's great to talk to someone like you about all this. Here, this'll do!" Throws her rucksack onto a seat by the window, "Look after my bag, what beer do ya want to drink? Something unfluoridated, German."

"Ermmm, beer then," I grins, "Something German."

I sits down by the window, and in what feels like seconds, she's chucked herself into the seat opposite me in a whirlwind of scarlet curls, "Here ya go! Hair of the rat."

"Thanks," I says, accepting my beer.

"I need to pick your brains about a couple of things."

"My pleasure."

Serious squint, "Granddad said you've been through a lot, and you look like someone who's been through a lot."

"Fire away, you were saying the world's 'fucked.'"

"Yeah, but I reckon all their scheming will rebound on the bastards, big time, with enough people awake to what's really going on, they'll crash and burn. They can't go ahead with Armageddon or do anything with enough of us just turning around and saying fuck off! I'm not buying into that! The next False Flag attack will probably be a dirty bomb in either London or—"

I wave my hand in front of her and interrupt,

"How do you know all this, then?" I lower my tone, "Seriously young lady, and how can you be so *sure?*"

She laughs, "I'm a history student! False Flags are how nations start wars, and stay in wars. And sometime soon I reckon, London again, probably—"

"IRA, right, same old, same—"

"IRA?" shakes her head, "No, no, Al Qaeda, the entire world's evil is blamed on Islamic militants."

"That's not right! Al Qaeda are in Afghanistan, they're on our side, bought and paid for, always were, always will be. We trained them to fight the Russians—"

"Jesus! Where have you been? They're now attacking—"

"Hold on, is that still going on?"

"No, no, the Mujahideen kicked the Russians out," she sighs. "Afghanistan's mostly about opium supplies. Over ninety percent of the world's opium is grown there, and since the invasion there's more being grown than ever before."

"Turf war."

"Keep heroin production up, what else? Black ops money."

"Right, of course."

"And the London bombings, Madrid, Bali, New York—"

"Wait, slow down! What happened in London?"

"Terrible. Bombs on tube trains and buses, a couple of years ago now, Seventh of July, but it had the same M.O. as all the rest."

"Oh?"

"Before Al Qaeda it was the IRA and I tell you, Joseph, it's all come to light now. Oh yes, the Birmingham Six, the Guildford Four and all the others, they weren't terrorists either – they were completely innocent people set up by the British Government!" she growls, poking a finger at my chest, "Your own Government *murdered* your own people and then blamed it on us!"

"Alright, alright, young lady, you're preaching to the choir here. So what do you think really happened in London?"

"It's not what I think happened, it's what I know happened. They got this guy, Mohammed Khan, and set him up as the ringleader. It turns out now he was working for British Intelligence at the time."

"A Grass?"

"More of a community negotiator; he'd help the police settle disputes between local gangs in the area, that kind of thing. I mean, all the accused were said to be good boys, nice people, westernised, no political interest and not the type for suicide missions. Even criminal psychology experts say they weren't the types, and they just didn't behave like people who knew they were going to die. They were even out playing cricket the day before! And two of them had kids, and with new arrivals on the way."

"Yep, don't seem to fit the profile alright—"

"Oh it's so obvious it wasn't them! They weren't even on the train your government said, the Luton train was cancelled that morning! How could they've of been in Central London in time?"

Because they probably weren't, I mused.

"I dunno." I shrugged.

"And why hasn't the CCTV footage been released—?"

"I dunno," I cuts in forcefully, "But all these things are only details. You see, it don't matter how bad the job is, the point is to give an impression. It's not what you look at, it's what you *see*—"

"An impression, yeah, people are brainwashed, they see what they're programmed to see – because then guess what?"

"What?"

"Dan-nah! 'Coincidence,' the attack parallels a security drill about bombings at the *exact* same locations, at the *exact* same times…"

And as she went on, a cold shiver shot through me – how do these futuristic youg'uns know how we work?

Let me explain.

This is exactly how a False Flag like that one is done.

First, you get some poor cunt, a Grass usually – SIS have plenty of those, obviously – and you get him to roundup a couple of mates what need the cash for a little govermental job. Two with new mouths to feed?

Perfect.

You strap a bag to their backs, and tell them they're part of an exercise for a mock terrorist attack, to test national security responses and all that bollocks. You fill their heads with all that shit about Defence of the Realm – what a great job they're doing 'cos it'll help prevent real attacks in the future – and assure them they'll get a nice fat wedge at the end of it to boot.

Who could refuse?

Exactly. Then you go ahead with the security drill and detonate the real bombs – either inside their bags or planted on the target sites. That's the Patsy Method. If anything goes wrong, you've got over a thousand-odd security team as a front, to remove or plant evidence as needed. Not all of the security drill are in on it, obviously, just enough to make sure the left hand doesn't know what the right hand is doing. Catch-madrift?

Pukka – now you're thinking like a cunt.

What sent a shiver up me was just how fucking careless they're getting these days, 'cos if this little beauty knows about it, then cut my throat, half the world must do too.

"And the chances," she was saying, "of a security drill and terrorist attack coinciding in London, by chance are… hold on, the odds are all over the net, someone went to the Bookies," she pulls a notebook out of her bag, opens it to a page, "There, one chance in…"

I peer at the figures:

3,715,592,613,265,750,000,000,000,000,000,000,000,000

And the estimate of grains of sand in the whole world is:

7,500,000,000,000,000,000

Yep, many a time I'd thought about putting a fiver down myself—

"Is that right," I says.

She nods her head at me seriously,

"In other words, Joseph, if you go to a beach, or a desert, or even scuba dive under the ocean and pick one single grain of sand, I'm trillions of times more likely to pick up that same grain than the drill coinciding with the attack at the same hour. *Coincidence?*"

I sip my beer. "And I'm the Count of Monte Cristo."

Folds her notebook away, nodding, "And they're holding back on more False Flag attacks because too many people are copping on."

"They don't know which way the apple cart's gonna tip."

"I don't think they do, no. Awareness, that's our prime weapon, the only effective way to fight back; asking the right questions and revealing their tactics as much as possible. We need to neutralise their fear machine, in here." She taps her head. "We're done for if we buy into fear. I'm no longer afraid of the answers I find, and I'm not afraid of anything they say. I refuse to be fucked around with like that! This is my life, my crack at the whip – they've no right to mess with my mind."

"Standard psyops," I mutter. "Strategic perception management. Fear causes weak perspective, we're easy to manipulate then."

"Psyops, yes, dirty lying scumbags. Want another beer?"

I shakes my head, she goes ahead on fully automatic,

"But they can and *are* being defeated, they're not all-seeing, not all-powerful, that's why they've got surveillance cameras everywhere;

that's why their kids go to school in bullet-proof cars – in many ways they've already lost. I know it doesn't look like it yet, they still control the media, all their arse-whore journalists, but if you look real close you can see signs of desperation. I mean, saying that Bin Laden, after what, nearly seven years has finally admitted to 9/11? Come on! He's been saying it wasn't him since it happened and now he lets us know? Do they think we were born yesterday?"

"Floated down the Liffey in a bubble," I mutter, "What on Gawd's Earth are you on about, my dear?"

"The World Trade Centre." Raises her fingers, "Only two planes strike, three buildings are demolished – demolished in exactly the same way, straight down, a quarter of a mile at freefall speed into their foundations." Nods, dark smile, "The truth is right before our eyes, there's tons of evidence it was a controlled demolition and at last it's happening."

"What's happening—?"

"Too many people are copping on to who really was behind 9/11, Bali, London, Madrid – in the last poll they did in Spain, and this is an official media poll by Sky News, ninety-three percent don't believe the government's story of who's responsible for the Madrid bombings, i.e. Bin Laden, again!"

"I met him once—"

"But that's brilliant, it's not working, another False Flag attack there would cause a civil insurrection! I'm convinced of that, and they know it too; that's why they do these polls. So *cui bono*, 'who benefits?'" she chuckles, "The Private Banking Cartels. Always. Always follow the money."

"Well, that's not rocket science—"

"True," she cuts in, "So it's up to us to make sure they don't get the result they want: another world war to further centralise power."

I nods at that, "Same as what happened after the last two wars—"

"A Centralised European Superstate, that's what the Nazis wanted, control of the many at the mercy of a handful of mass-murdering scumbags – and that's what sixty million people died fighting against, and that's exactly what they're pushing for! Jesus, look at us, we have a central law court, a single currency and a central bank in fucking Frankfurt!"

"Bloody hell…"

She glares, wide-eyed, "Frankfurt, exactly where Hitler was going to put his had he won."

"I know, and I used to have these nightmares where the Nazi's really had won—"

"They did! Well okay, they didn't totally lose, only it's not jackboots and 'Heil Hitler' anymore, they put on suits and ties now. It's the same ideology, the same superstate blueprint, and what they couldn't bring about with force, they're now achieving with stealth, slowly, taking our freedom away, piece by piece."

"So you think Germany's getting uppity again."

"No, no, they're still subject to the penalties of an occupied nation, and that's something a lot of effort's gone into keeping us in the dark about too. No peace treaty has ever been signed with post-war Germany, therefore, the European Union is illegal."

"Illegal."

"The founding Treaty of Rome was null and void because the 'Federal Republic of Germany' was not, and still isn't, legally recognised to even exist. All the referendums we've had were over a worthless piece of paper! A treaty based on a criminal act of fraud: all the laws they've passed, all the policies made, everything. The EU is a criminal entity and they're terrified should we ever find out."

"Blimey, bit careless, ay?"

"Another clear sign these scumbags are in trouble. To me, all this means they're losing control. And just like any control freak, when they start losing it they go on a massive information gathering spree, spying on ya, trying to clamp down, and the more they do, the more likely you are of turning around and saying fuck off bitch!" she laughs, "If ya know what I mean. Had that with my last girlfriend, scale it up and you've got a revolution!"

Oh great, a lezzy…

"I'm not talking about violence, I'm talking about bringing them to their knees with *awareness*. And that's the heart of the problem today; we're afraid of the answers we'll find, so we've forgotten how to question things. But, it's still the people with the guns they rely on, and they are still people. Okay, mind-fucked beyond recognition, but they can come out of it. My granddad's a good example, and some of his friends, those who made it out the other end anyway." She sighs, drains her beer. "Sad but true."

"Sad but very true, but—"

"So if the police, the army knew they're betraying their oaths, working for what? A criminal cartel of international bankers? Then it would be a different story. If they knew, that is."

"A lot of them do, my dear. But I dunno about that. Alright, a lot of us in the mob know all this and more, but they'll still follow orders, have to, don't matter what it is—"

"I don't agree. I reckon everything hinges on what they tell us happened on 9/11. That was their 'Reichstag Fire,' their last big excuse to go to war and their last mistake. I mean, these bankers, politicians, they try to control everything, they have no national boundaries and so far they've escaped prosecution – but they're still people too – and there's ample proof it wasn't suicide hijackers. For a start, at least nine of them are alive!"

I had to laugh at that, "Typical Yanks, sloppy as ever then. I remember in the last War when Pearl Harbour—"

"And get this: On the same day, the Pentagon were running 'security exercises' about terrorists crashing hijacked planes into buildings. *Coincidence?* Again?" shakes her head, "Strength in numbers. Do not stop speaking out and with enough of us to create the right psychological climate, due process of law will follow. Okay, convictions require proof that crimes were committed, but we've got them with 9/11. Their official story contravenes the laws of science and nature – and if they've been lying to us all along?"

"Probable cause," I mutter.

"Enough to put the entire US administration in the docks, and all your two-faced British bastards in government and yeah, here too – all of them – if they *know* what *really* happened and *still* make deals with them?" quick shrug, "We'd only have one chance though, have to get it right, clean evidence first time, we've plenty of that too—"

"Alright, alright, but—"

"And the dirty media whores, I'm sure some of them don't sleep at night, knowing their part, so when the whistleblowers start to come forward, that's the time to build a case and—"

"Let me speak! Can't get a fucking word in edgeways!"

"Sorry…"

I sighs, "Gawd, listen my dear, I'm sure you thinks this is all very important but I don't give a flying monkey's anymore. Maybe it's 'cos of the fact I'm having a very difficult time lately, but right now, seeing the state of things and everything you've said, I reckon my mate Sid was right – it's mostly down to so many morons being produced and on such a massive scale that there's fuck-all hope of any change. Let them rot!

Alright, sorry, maybe that's bollocks what I just said. I've seen things alright, seen the dignity and courage too – seen potential to create miracles but mostly amongst people who don't have nothing, understand? The reality is we're under siege, wall-to-wall by cunts, pardon my French, and yeah, unbelievable too, un-fucking-believable that something as powerful as a human being can be reduced to something so mindlessly fucking stupid—"

"That's because of programming with consumerism, fear and—"

"Young lady, please! Believe me, I do know how this works, and the fact is people let themselves be led because it's the easiest way to go, with all the other morons. It's a damn sight easier to be a stupid cunt than face up to the facts of reality. Let them rot, I say."

She smirks at that, "Reality, and what is reality?"

"Reality, my dear, is accepting that everything pans out exactly as it's meant to. See that?" I point to the fields outside the window, "There's not one single blade of grass out of place."

"I hear ya, I do hear what you're saying, sometimes I think all we're doing is running away from the inevitable—"

"Good, now close your eyes, tap your forehead three times and repeat after me: 'There's nobody here but us chickens!' Nah, seriously, do it."

"Why?"

"Just something I was taught to do, for when in a tight spot…"

Roberta sighs, closes her eyes briefly, and then nods at me.

"Do you get it now?" I asks. "*That's* reality."

"I understand," she says, understanding fuck all, and looking out the window, says quietly, "And the darkest hour is just before dawn, there is hope, like… for example, the Vietnam anti-war movement wasn't started by hippies, it was started by the soldiers themselves," she turns to me, "Soldiers, *human beings* who didn't just follow orders. People's brains haven't changed that much from then to now."

"That may be, but tell most people the truth till you're blue in the face and they'll go for the lies over, and over, so my advice to you…

is I dunno, blimey, don't get so upset! Every time you get riled about all this they win, they rip a piece out of you. Roberta, I likes you, you're a good girl, and clever, so just live your life, be all that you can be, ay? The nail what sticks out gets hammered in."

"That's what my grandfather says…"

I smile, "I'm tired."

There followed a long uneasy silence. I sipped my beer, staring out the window at the battered grey sky, and ended up imagining I was running alongside the train, skipping over rooftops, onto the bare hills in the far distance, and leaping back level with the train again, running, running, 'running away from the inevitable?' I gets this queasy knot in my gut – I could feel the abdabs rising. Needed to keep her talking, engage the mind,

"Seen more trees in Hyde Park," I goads, "Where they all gone?"

"The Brits chopped them down," she grumbles, and then quickly adds, "Though we've had plenty of time to plant more, centuries, but haven't. You're right," dark grin, tapping her head, "'Nobody here but us chickens.' Like you say, we're stupid, we just let things happen like we let everything happen – the hunger, the suffering and wars – we shrug it off saying 'isn't it terrible what they're doing, tut-tut, awful.' No, they're not the cause of it, *we* are, all of us, we sit back and watch and do nothing!"

I sighs, "And what can you do about it? And even if you could, even if you had the clout, start messing with the Big Boys, my dear, and you'll be pushing up flyovers quicker than you can say 'Jack Robinson.' Trust me, I know."

"Yeah? Well at least I'd be doing something fucking useful!" Lowers her tone, trying to smile, "At least talk to people, *something*. Look, I do realise I'm an oddball, I do – but see all this? Look at us, look at them all, how long can this go on?"

We gaze at each other, and then at the carriage; commuters going home from work, packed like sardines, the usual, but then it hit me – their faces, tired, anxious, miserable – cut my throat, it was worse than London, leastways the London I'd just left – last time I saw so many faces like that was just before the last war…

Roberta shot me the quizzical eye, shaking my shoulder gently,

"Five million years of human evolution for this… is this it, *life?*

Work, debt, and more work to produce thirty times what we need, only to have it sold back at us at thirty times what it costs to produce."

I nods. "It can't go on."

"We work harder and longer now than at any other time in history. We've so much surplus we don't even know where to put it; food rots across the world in giant containers, incinerated, even dumped in the sea! Our planet could sustain over *fifty*-billion people, comfortably, and yet we can't manage resources for eight, nearly."

"Nearly eight billion, already…" I pause, recalling Sid's neuron-brain theory. "It is coming, isn't it?"

She reiterates softly, "Total economic meltdown engineered by the banks, world war, and the disintegration of society on every level. And then manipulate whoever's left into believing a centralised world government is the only answer. Slaves," she says, rooting around in her bag again. "We're all slaves anyway, of the worst kind: slaves duped into believing we're free."

"Slaves… Have you heard of the Illuminati?"

Nods, "The Internet's buzzing with theories. Everybody's saying the Illuminati are backing the Jews, and the Jews are behind the central banking system. I don't believe anything until I see it with my own eyes. Here, have a read of this."

Passing me her notebook, she opens to a page. It read:

I want to tell you something very clear, don't worry about American pressure on Israel, we, the Jewish people control America, and the Americans know it.

(Ariel Sharon, Prime Minister of Israel. October 3rd, 2001)

I looks up, "So the Jews still control America, then."

"Hmmm?" Peers over the table, "Sorry, wrong page," flicks through, "Though yeah, the White House is owned by Israelis. They say 'jump,' America says 'for how much?' Okay… here."

For you are a Holy People to YHWH your God, and God has chosen you to be His treasured people from all the nations that are on the face of the Earth.

(Torah, Deuteronomy 14:2)

"That's behind the banks, and behind every foreign and domestic policy today, do you see?"

"Nah, not really," I says, sliding her notebook back across the table, "So the Jews believe they're the Chosen People, so what? I've met Nazis, blimey, even Hindus what think they're the master race, and the Vatican's got more clout than all of them put together."

"Agreed." Shakes her head, "But a religion is not a 'race,' it's a *religion*, and yeah, like Christianity or the Hare Krishnas, you *convert* to a religion. Think about it. If you converted to Hinduism, could you just jump on a plane to India and be given citizenship, land, money, a house, a job? No. And yet convert to Judaism and you can do all that in the State of Israel, on land stolen from the Palestinians. And all because of the Holocaust, which didn't even happen."

"Didn't happen, right. Are you on the happy-pills, or what?"

"Mossad's motto sums up the Holocaust sham perfectly: 'By way of deception, thou shalt make War.' I've been to Germany five times over the last two years and it's gotta be the most efficient nation on Earth. If they really wanted to 'exterminate' all the Jews, or anyone else they didn't like, they would've done it in a month. Think about it. If they really wanted to kill all those people, then why bother shaving their heads?"

"To prevent lice infections. Typhus was a major killer, that's why."

"Bit of a contradiction, for a death camp. Why not let Typhus—"

"Because it's war, and like you say, the Germans are efficient, and needed a source of labour. Are you sure you're a history student?"

"Then why bother tattooing someone you're planning to work to death?"

"Identification, the Nazi's were obsessed with all kinds of ID."

"Control, agreed, and what role did the Palestinian people play in all this? None! When the British invaded Palestine in 1948—"

"It was in '47," I correct, getting vexed, "Started then. we'd already gone in and uprooted a million Arabs, razed their villages to the ground and—"

"And the Holocaust provided the excuse!"

"Young lady, I dunno what they teach you these days, but I can tell you now that death camps did exist—"

"And how do you know, did you see them? The International Red Cross recorded deaths from illness and accidents, but no gas chambers, no burning ovens – no deliberate exterminations of any kind. Why would the Red Cross lie to protect Hitler?"

I reached over and gripped her wrist, "Listen to me, you don't have a fucking clue about what you're talking about! Alright, no I didn't personally see the camps, but you're fucking wrong, the Holocaust did happen. I know 'cos I know people who survived."

"Isn't that a bit of a contradiction there too? Survived. I'm not denying the fact people died, only asking, how do ya know the camps really are what we're told—?"

"Because I know what people are capable of!" I growls, turning on my battle-gaze, "Do you wanna fucking talk about what I did see then, of what the Allies did, of what we did after the war; the mass torturing and butchering of over four million German civilians, the repeated rape of virtually every girl and woman, herded into open fields without food or water until they died; on top of the millions we expelled from Prussia and Sudetenland; the million soldiers who surrendered, worked to death in Soviet slave labour camps and the thousands more we murdered, crammed into cages along the Rhine, left to rot from starvation and disease; on top of totally annihilating every German community right across Poland to Silesia to East Prussia – and all that after the 'official' end of the fucking War – wanna talk about that, ay?"

She shakes her head. "No need."

"Good." I let go of her wrist, "'Cos war is war – and all we're doing here is throwing stones in glasshouses."

Nods, "I know all about that genocide, it's called the Morgenthau Plan. Enforced by US Treasury Secretary Henry Morgenthau, and the US General, Supreme Allied Commander of Europe, Dwight Eisenhower. Both hell-bent on creating a homeland in Palestine."

Fuck me, clever girl alright. I leans back,

"Fair dues, so they're Jewish, seems reasonable to me they'd want a homeland for their people though, what's your point?"

"They're not Jewish! That's the whole sham; they only let us think they are. Jewish people believe they can't have a homeland until the coming of their Messiah, and then we're all supposed to live in some kind of paradise on Earth; that's the main tenet of Judaism. How can you set up a Jewish homeland and still be Jewish? Where's the Messiah? Hold on, I'm sure I put him somewhere," she chuckles, rooting around in her bag, and then looking under the table.

"Alright, sit up straight," I says, "I know it's a religion."

She pops her head back up. "Judaism is a religion, yeah, and Israel is corporate politics, big money, and Eisenhower, Morgenthau and Churchill, and the Pope, and just about every leader we've had since World War One are all Zionists. That's the political and military group backing a Jewish homeland."

"I know."

"And the vast majority of Jews don't support them. In fact the very term Zionist-Jew is an oxymoron if you're Jewish."

I nods, "Can't have a homeland and be Jewish."

"It runs against everything Judaism is about; a religion is not a 'race,' nor is it 'secular.' Drives me crazy when I hear people saying they don't believe in God and yet claim to be 'Secular Christians' or 'Agnostic Jews.' Makes no fucking sense!"

I chuckles at that, "Alright, go on."

"Nazism is German national socialism, Zionism is 'Jewish' national socialism. Nazis believe the Germans are a superior race, Zionists believe the Jews are a superior race: The Chosen People, The Master Race. Both claim a 'racial' right to rule the world.

It's an identical blueprint, fuelled by corporate interests. Neither religion nor nationality determines race. You can be Caucasian, or Oriental and be Jewish, or German, or both.

Look, okay, I'm not Jewish, I'm not saying the State of Israel doesn't have a right to exist, I actually think it does, and if people who want to be repatriated can provide evidence of parentage, then clearly they should be allowed to. Just like any other country. But think about it, how can religion establish someone's nationality?

It can't, that's absurd, that would be like saying all Africans who convert to Catholicism are Irish. And you can't just bulldoze people out of their own homes here just because... just because you *believe* you're related to some ancient tribe from Sacred Tara! If you weren't born in Ireland, you'd need your grandparents to be from here, at least, before ya can say you're Irish.

And thinking it's okay to practice genocide because God told you to is by definition insane."

I nods at that, "Doesn't matter how you dress it up."

"So, why's the Holocaust Jewish? I mean, Hitler supposedly wanted to exterminate all the homosexuals too, so does that give us the right to invade the Isle of Lesbos and rule the fucking world?"

Gawd forbid! "I catch-yadrift."

"History is written by the victors, Joseph. And the Holocaust, regardless of whether or not it happened as history claims, provided the excuse for the creation of the State of Israel *and*," jabs a finger on our table, "an axis to implement a centralised world government."

"A command centre."

"It's the same world domination blueprint Hitler worked with, and Stalin, Trotsky, and Mao Tse-Tsung—"

"And it failed," I cuts in. "Pretty crap blueprint."

"Ahhh, but, create a powerbase, an army of idiots who can't tell the difference between religion and real life," she grins, "And with the entire world's banking system funding you?"

"Blimey…"

"And over four-hundred nuclear weapons helps too, which Israel has."

I nods. "Job done."

"They've been after this for centuries, since the first Crusades to the Holy Land. It never mattered to these scumbags who's in control – Jews, Christians, Muslims or fucking Hare Krishnas – as long as they're in control of whoever is in control. Let me give you a small example of that," flicking through her notebook, "I don't want ya thinking I'm totally puddled," she chuckles to herself, glances up. "Okay, we can agree that when someone joins an organisation, it's usually because they support that organisation's aims, yeah? Like you wouldn't get a Brit up North here joining the IRA, say."

"Roger that."

"Okay, the Knights of Malta, created to wage war during the Crusades, amongst the oldest and most powerful Catholic institutions still. Members include Agusto Pinochet, Reinhad Gehlen, Kurt Waldheim, Heinrich Himler – hordes of other Nazis and criminals – and *David Rockefeller*. One of the richest bankers on Earth, Jewish, knighted into a religious order *loyal to the Pope?* Alongside genocidal Nazis? And banking members of the Rothschilds too; and Larry Silverstein, owner of the World Trade Centre; Michael Bloomberg, Mayor of New York; George Tenet, CIA director; Henry Kissinger; Rupert Murdoch; Tony Blair; George Bush – their membership reads like a 9/11 'who's who' conspiracy, but other than that, doesn't make sense, does it?

Actually it does, yeah, but only when you look behind their religious sham. Then, bear in mind that Rothschild and Rockefeller money funded both sides in the last war, advancing the first stage of global government, the United Nations, *and* the powerbase from which to operate also – the crusader prize – the Holy Land. Then it makes perfect sense why the Holocaust's necessary too, the policies of all Western nations are based on it, and why they loath anybody questioning what happened; it's a criminal offence to even voice these thoughts in some countries. Fuck them. Have ya seen that Auschwitz documentary by David Cole?"

"Ehmmm, no…"

"Google it."

"What?"

"You'll see the senior curator of the Auschwitz Museum admitting that the gas chamber was, in fact, a tourist attraction built after the War by the Russians. David Cole is Jewish, by the way. But—"

"Wait, wait, I can almost go along with what you're saying, all CIA directors are Knights of Malta too, I know, I had dealings with Vatican spooks back in the War – but I did hear the stories about gas chambers, specially about that one…"

"You heard *stories.*" Tilts her head to one side, wry smile, "Six million Jews exterminated in the camps? Start with the Red Cross, they kept meticulous records and have no reason to lie. Were there even that many Jews in the whole of Europe at the time? Compare population censuses from before and after the War, and then move on to who *does* benefit from lying.

Then why did the Zionists specifically insist on six million; what's so *significant* about that number in Jewish mysticism? Look it up in regards to the creation Israel, don't be afraid of the answers, *question*. I did, and I tell ya Joseph, even the word 'Holocaust' isn't valid. It means death by fire, a burnt sacrifice to God, an exclusively Judaic term hijacked by the Zionists to give it all an exclusively *Judaic* quality.

The real Holocaust was Dresden, firebombed by the Allies, and Hiroshima and Nagasaki, when the Americans dropped nuclear bombs." She shrugs, looking around the crowded carriage, "On the other hand, if I'd been locked up in a work camp for five years, the truth would be the last thing on my mind; after being liberated I would've had them all lined up, skull-fucked to death by donkeys!

You're right Joseph, war is war, we're only throwing stones in—"

I grab her wrist again, "What did you just say?"

"Don't be angry with me, I'm actually agreeing with you, people died under horrific circumstances in those camps! Jews, Christians, Communists, Gypsies and the list goes on—"

"Shhh, wait—"

"—and it's *Zionazi* bankers who profit from their suffering. Death means dollars, the Holocaust Industry is big money."

"Nah! 'Skull-fucked to death by donkeys,' you said!"

Cringes, "Sorry, I'm a foul-mouthed little cow sometimes, so people say... pardon my French?"

She smiles, I let go, and the abdabs begin crawling up and down my spine, "S-sally?"

"Who?"

I shakes myself down. "I mean... nothing... nothing..."

Concerned stare, "Are you okay? Granddad said, well, he said you've been *away*? Sorry, I don't believe all that nonsense meself, but it's just that... there is something... a little strange about you."

Got to Limerick early evening, tooled-up to fuck; Jif lemons, garrotte, pool balls the lot. Although Ishmael reckoned Iblis couldn't be done in with human weapons, I wasn't taking any chances.

Hailing a cab at the station, I says goodbye to Roberta and stuff my credit card into her paw.

"What's this?"

"Yours," I says, scribbling bank details on the white house photo.

"Oh for the love of fuck, our offshore accounts?"

"My entire legacy."

"Joseph, but why—"

"Yeah, but why, why, why please—"

"Got the touch."

"But what if it all goes to custard, what about Canada—"

"Shut it!"

"Sorry, I do go on, don't I—"

"Listen to me. If you run into any access problems, your granddad will know what to do." I winks. "Us old cunts, pardon my French, we've been around, done stuff you wouldn't believe."

"No, I can't take this..."

"Oh you bloody-well can young lady! Just stay one step ahead of those 'flyovers,' and do some good with it, alright?"

"But how will you live?" Shakes her head, thrusting my card at me. I take a step back, climbs inside the cab, slam the door shut, "Convent by the racetracks, quick, she's mad! A witch – look at that hair!"

Cabbie chuckles, pulls away, and I tip my hat to Barry, standing by the sandwich kiosk over the road. He smiles back, delighted.

Nah, I hadn't clocked him on the train neither, but I knew he was around; a granddaughter's a granddaughter, after all.

Fifteen minutes later, I was paying ten yoyos, and stood outside the Convent. Through the open front door, I scanned the murky hallway inside. The sky darkened into a hazy grey gloom. A light greasy rain began to pour.

Checking to see nobody was about, I primed my tools, breathed deep, and pegged into the hallway.

Door on my left: No.1. Door to the right: No.2. Climbs the first flight of stairs, door on my left: fire escape. I turns around:

No.3.

Paused there for a second, ear pressed to the door. Frantic tapping noise, and singing, happy singing,

"Clowns to the left of me," tap, tap, tap, "Jokers to the right! Hahaha! Yes here I am, stuck in the middle with you…"

Pulled back. Pondered my options…

Negative: whatever this is all about, has to be done in proper order. Face to face.

I knocked.

The door opens.

"Good evening Captain, I'd almost given up on you, come in."

Chapter 50

The Creator. Or Maktub

"Come in," says this young geezer in the doorway, shaved head, a Whitie, about my height, not bad looking, dressed in black tracksuit bottoms and black hoody, all pleasant.

I pulls out my Jif lemon and immediately launch a napalm inferno at his head – sidestepping forward, blade in hand, carving at his knees.

He vanishes.

I hear chuckles behind me, spin around. He laughs outright,

"Oh dear, we are upset!"

Sweeping his open palm, he parries my next strike, and scoops my legs from under me with his – I use the momentum of the fall to roll onto one knee.

"Nice bit of kit, this," he mutters, sliding the blade into my cane, "Do you want it back?"

Tosses me Happy Stick, I gets to my feet, and stroking his chin he holds up my lemon, "Watch! Now you see it, and now…"

He grins, and it disappears in his fingers. "Captain, please, let's be civil."

"Who are you?"

"It's the Creator."

"I'm the Creator."

"And I'm Henry Kissinger. What agency do you work for? The Jesuits?"

"Just come in, ay?"

With a flourish of his hand, he bows, beckoning me inside.

"I don't wanna go in there!"

"No?" straightening up, "Are you sure, or just bottling out?"

"Don't go in there, oh please, use the fire escape – It's a DEMON!"

He glowers, all serious, and puts out his hand,

"What's it gonna be?"

I edge forward, one eye on the fire escape door behind us,

"My Gawd, you look just like me when… when…"

"When you were younger."

"Yeah…"

Shrugs, "Just thought I'd make the effort. Well?"

I puts out my hand to shake his, "Alright, sorry to be rude, been a long day. Joseph Williams Barbelo, pleasure to make your acquaintance, at last."

He smiles, "Creator of All Things Known and Unknowable. Pleasure's all mine—"

My sock-mace lashes out – he ducks – parries – disarms.

"Whoa!" he whispers, "Close! Fuck me that was close…"

I'm staggering backwards, gawping as he carefully lays all my weapons on his doorstep, "Captain, I do understand your displeasure, but I'm not gonna ask a third time."

"We'll never see each other again, It'll snuff us out!"

"Do what you want, fucking halfwit, I've got all the answers you seek inside…"

Halfwit? I pick up my tools and follow…

The flat was tiny, little more than an L-shaped shoebox. On the left was a kitchen area; at the far end a window and a desk with books, and what looked like a snazzy typewriter crossed with a telly.

"That's where I create," he says, "And that chair's where I sit, The Hot Seat. Over there's where you sit."

He gestures to a wooden box beside the desk, and turns away, "Kettle's just boiled! Nice cuppa, that's what you need," taking two cups from the shelf above the sink, "Did you have an interesting journey?"

Uncoiling the fishing wire in my pocket, I slowly creeps up—

He spins around, "Will you please just stop that and sit down!"

"Who… *are*… you?"

"Said, I am the Creator. Have a seat, look at the screen."

I glance about.

"The snazzy telly," he says.

I peer round at the screen. "It's a book," I mutter, and then quivered, "Th-th-that's all about us at the door…"

"Just now, yes…"

"Says I almost had you…"

"Close, came closer than most."

Stirring in the sugars, he sits down on the chair in front of the screen, "That Chapter's here, about us. The Creator. Or *Maktub*?"

Fighting down the rising bile of panic, I started to sway, and sits down heavily on the wooden box.

"Haven't decided which is more appropriate," he says, passing me my cuppa, "*Maktub*, Arabic word, translates as 'it is written.'"

"I know," I says, spilling tea over my trembling hand, "It means destiny…"

Frowns, "Hmmm, destiny, and yet the pages of our book always begin and end blank. *Maktub* all depends on what's doing the writing – your loves or your fears," he smiles, "But still, maybe that's appropriate for the occasion, wouldn't you say?"

I stare at him.

He stares back, "You've gone pale. Are you alright?"

"No, not really. If this is one of their psyops, then please, just get it over with, ay? "

Nods slowly, flashing me a crooked grin,

"Oh this is a psyops alright, the ultimate psyops, but it's not one of theirs. Allow me to elucidate. Might as well get this part over with, settle your nerves, saves a lot of explaining later too. Watch this."

Tapping away on the keys, he closes his eyes and suddenly we're sitting in a lush, green open meadow. A light summer breeze caresses my skin; the morning sun, warm and gentle on my face.

"Look at your leg," he whispers.

I stifle a scream,

"It's grown back!"

"Touch your face."

"Oh my Gawd… and my teeth, I have teeth! What is this place? It's fucking beautiful…"

He laughs. "'In my Father's house there are many mansions!' You, this is you, Joseph! All of it. Locale 33."

"Oh my good lord, can I?"

He nods. I leapt to my feet, jumping up and down, and then legged it, running in circles, exhilarated—

And suddenly we're back in his flat.

"Do you feel better?"

"Do that again!"

Shakes his head.

"But why…?"

"You know why."

I pause, and then I nods, "Because that would be too easy."

"Partly, yes, the Nursery isn't called the Nursery for nothing. You're all here to grow up and learn to reconnect with the totality of yourselves, beyond this Locale, if you ever get off your arses and think for yourselves. And that's why I'm here, and that's what I'm here waiting for – unification – long story, looong fucking story…"

There followed a pause. We sipped our teas. Him tapping away on his keyboard, singing happily, me just… *staring*. I had no doubt any longer, I was totally stunned, FUBAR-ed, this was Him, It, Iblis-Lucifer Itself! And yeah, I had no doubt either, the cunt could swat me like a fly, and yet…

"I feel good, here… too good," I ventures, peering into my cuppa.

"No such thing, don't be silly," he chuckles. "And no, I didn't slip 'something' in you're tea. I'm not a complete cunt."

"But my mate Sid, he also said… I dunno, that the Nursery's in trouble… and you're a…"

Swivels round on his chair, "And yes, I am a lower astral being," he concedes with a shrug, "We all are. Our Locale is smack in the middle of the Lower Astral, and so the Wormery's always in trouble. But with enough awareness to keep the vibration up, it's not a complete hell-hole… yet."

"Yet."

"Depends. Locale 31 are right next door – now that really is a place of misery and torment! Pure Hell, and it wants this Locale."

"What for?"

"To feed!" He gnashed his teeth, lurching forward exactly like a wolf. I recoiled back, and then he goes on, all pleasant,

"They can't help it there, it's their vibration, they are parasites, predators. Their nature is to feed on horror, so, they create it."

"The shadow realms," I mutter.

He squints at me. "Are you going to behave yourself?"

"Do I have a bloody choice?"

He laughs. "Good question. No, here there is no choice, only change. I don't have a choice either – like or dislike – I am the sum total of this Locale. Look…"

I looks at the screen.

"See, blank, and then the words just appear…"

"Oh yeah…"

"Plenty of scope for change, infinite opportunities."

"Bloody hell, then why here… 2007?"

Rubs his face, "That's a sensitive issue, Captain, best illustrated with direct experience. But for now… well, thing's aren't too bad here, ay? You always wanted to see how the world is today, twenty years on, and now your awareness is focused here, so here I am too – here we are in this tiny sliver of perception, the lower end of our awareness that you call Life—"

"The lower end?"

"The lower end. Glorified worms, infinite creative mini-gods, trapped inside fleshy pissing-shitting tubes."

"That's what Sid used to say."

"And he's right. A better word for this Locale would be the Wormery." He chuckles darkly.

"Then why do you live in this place, I mean don't get me wrong, it's very nice, bit small maybe, wouldn't mind living here myself…"

I lost my drift, studying his flat. Compact, nice and tidy, cushy little sitting area to my left, white furry rugs and furry cushions…

"Drink your tea, it'll go cold," he says. "I live everywhere. This is my Locale, I am the sum total of all you see, of all you seem. There are sixty-four Locales in total, making Seven Realms, or 'Realisms,' and the One. Do your maths, it's very simple. Seven plus One?"

"Eight. And eight by eight, sixty-four, I catch-yadrift. Like the squares on the Chessboard."

"And six plus four?"

"Ten."

"And One plus zero?

"One."

"Right," he grins. "And so all of them together comprise the One, and the One is always bidding for unification. And when that finally happens, we will all dwell in Paradise."

"Like what the Muslims believe."

Shakes his head. "Like what you all know in your hearts to be true…"

I gazed out the window beside me; quiet residential street, glistening with evening rain – until I hears the tapping stop. Leaning back into his chair, he folds his arms, glancing at his snazzy telly,

"Go ahead if you want, have another butcher's."

I stretch over his desk, and press the key there with the little pointy triangle—

"Noooooo!" he howls, and fuck me, it was worse than the feharchrove – I fell off my box with the shock.

"S-sorry," I says, getting up, "I don't know why I did that—"

Glares, takes a vicious breath, "Do not ever, ever fucking touch those keys again you gormless father-fucking CUNT! Sit down!" he orders, snarling, eyeing my every move.

"Yes sir!" I quickly resumed my post on the box.

"Forgive me Captain," he says, calming down, "Very *sensitive* bit of kit, this, as you can perhaps appreciate," nod, nod, stroking the keys affectionately, "It's self-regulating. Mostly it writes itself, for all time striving for unification – the perfect balance – and just when it almost gets there, something always comes along and knocks it off kilter."

"What does," I ventures.

"You lot. The Hot Seat's not called The Hot Seat for nothing," he smiles, "With it comes immeasurable responsibilities. You we're right though, that particular key lets you scroll up the screen. Watch."

He scrolls up, I peer at the screen.

"Oh my Gawd, that's my nightmares, and that young knob with the Darkie Sid… it's me, isn't it?"

He nods. "One of you, a Dream Warrior from Locale 5, a very accomplished being in many respects. You drew on each other's awareness to work through your… issues, let's call them."

"And this is Locale 1."

"No, this is Locale 32."

"But I'm here, so it must be…"

Squints at me. "Hmmm, not entirely. It's only natural to call wherever you focus awareness Locale 1 or 'the Awake,' all the Inner Orders do it whatever Locale they're on. But from my perspective it's not entirely accurate. Because I *am* Locale 32," he adds, anticipating my question. "I can't go or *be* anywhere else."

"I don't understand that…"

"Smiles, "It doesn't matter. We can talk about the nature of Eternity till we're blue in the face. Words and numbers, they're just tools; sooner or later we end up hitting the unfathomable.""

"And the Firm," I says, reading on, "they've all gone legitimate?"

"Yep, they're all paying their dues 'legally' now, they've all got big enough to be in the club with the Big Boys, and all your command centres rooted out, and neutralised."

"So I see…"

"Nice try though."

"Fuck me, almost had them too, says here…"

"Almost, but not quite. Is it sinking in now?"

"Starting to, yeah," I looks up, "What are you going to do next?"

He laughs, "I dunno, we're all making this up as we go along! Alright," he shrugs, "Pass me the Uncertainty Principle."

"The what?"

"Those Tarot Cards there," nods to a deck sitting on a pile of books next to me. I pick them up, hand them over, frowning,

"Oh no, so that's how it's done…"

"One way, yeah," he grins, shuffling the deck, "Need an element of chance, uncertainty, else where's the freewill? Let's see… let's see… I was in the middle of something just now, oh yes! Fucking up America, or the Federal Reserve to be more accurate," scrolls down the screen, "Mission status: Iraq wanted to exercise the right to trade oil in currencies other than the US Dollar. *Modus Operandi:* Impose sanctions; decades of disease, millions of starving children, followed by full military invasion; aerial bombings with depleted uranium, birth defects for centuries and all that malarkey. Right, job done there." Flips a card over onto the table. "The Tower," he says, "Very appropriate. By the way, you got that one too," nods at me, "just before Sid got done in and your whole empire went tits up."

I nods back, "Go on, so what now then?"

"So, now we'll have Iran, third largest oil producers on the planet, drop the Dollar too. Hahaha! Suffer little children, come unto me!" tap, tap, tapping on the keyboard, "Let's use euros in Iran's oil business instead, what do you think the response will be?"

"Same old, same old."

"Can't yet, we've got to factor in Russia and China, they drew the Emperor Card just before you called round," he peers at the screen,

"A naval blockade in the Gulf's as far as I can go. Hmmm, or up the terror in Gaza Ghetto a notch or two... Nah, what we need is a False Flag attack, on site, get the sabres rattling on all sides. Options?"

"Blimey, I dunno, blow something up in Jerusalem..."

"Good move, a religious site. We'll have the Israelis destroy Christ's tomb, blame it on the Arabs and everybody's nice and uppity again," flips a card, shakes his head. "Temperance. Fair dues, not yet then, timing is everything in these matters," tap, tap, and tap. "There, we'll continue with the Palestinian genocide, let it run. See if we can't eventually push somebody, anybody into mounting a defence—"

"But why? Why don't you do something... nice."

Looks at me funny, "That was nice, if you're a shareholder of the Federal Reserve. Though in reality, I didn't do nothing."

"Yes you did—"

"No, all I did, all I can do set the conditions, present a set of factors. Freewill is freewill, for better or worse."

"But what about world peace and wiping all the vermin from the face of the Earth—"

"Oh fuck off! What about you lot doing something for yourselves? Hmmm? I'm giving you chances all the fucking time! Chances for change! 'Do not give what is holy to dogs, nor cast your pearls before swine' – and what do yous fucking do? Give it all away to child-murders ya fucking daft cunts!"

"Nice tea, this," I grins.

Grins back, "Another cuppa?"

I nods, he gets up, and puts the kettle on, "Alright, but don't, *don't* get me started on all that bollocks – Armageddon's running like a Swiss clock – what did you expect, Mother fucking Theresa?"

"I'm dead, aren't I?"

Turns around, leans up against the sink, folds his arms, "Silly question. Living is dying to all who dwell in the Land of the Living, thus death is life to all who dwell in the Land of the Dead."

I paused for a moment, made sense. "If I've got you right, then it's all upside down. Life is death... we're *all* dead, then?"

"Yes," he says, but shaking his head. "And no," he says, nodding up and down. "Living is a continual state of dying, therefore life and death are indivisible. *One and the same.*"

"Reminds me of another thing Sid used to say, that we think we're a body, walking our mind about the place, seeing the world and all that, yeah? Like your mind's inside your brain?"

"That's how most people see it on this Locale, go on."

"It's wrong, it's your *body* what's walking about inside your mind."

"Exactly," he says, turning around, pouring boiling water into our cups, "What you call your mind is out there, everywhere, and you're all thought up and created *inside* it. Unique, individual expressions of each other, the One Mind."

"So that's you then, this One Mind."

"No, I'm only the realised sum total of this Locale."

"But is this really… happening?"

"Everything that's ever happened, or is going to happen, is always happening," he says over his shoulder, "And no, in this form I don't have the Eyes of Iblis. And no, I can't harm you neither; you've sworn allegiance to the One. Can't touch that," he says, chucking the used teabags into a bin under the sink.

"So I don't get the Eyes of Iblis?"

"Just said."

"Alright, but let's get this straight. The Illuminati are evil, and the Inner Order says you're their Top Cunt, so—"

"Ah! Silly bunny! The Inner Order *are* the Illuminati, a condition of two opposing forces which *you* define either 'good' or 'evil.' Matters not a jot to me, I control them both; to define is to limit."

"Feel a bit stupid now. I came here to…"

"I know, for the ultimate job's a good'un," he shrugs, "How else was I gonna get you here?"

"You could've asked."

"And would you have come?"

"Probably not."

"That's 'cos you're a right cunt!"

We both laughed at that.

Sitting down, passing me my cuppa, "Oh there's plenty out there who say they're ready to see me, but that's just bollocks, they nearly all bottle out on the last card. And the ones what don't are mostly off their heads anyway, fucking obsessed – demons, giant owls and serpents and all that malarkey – but that's the point, all I can do is give them what they want, those with the bottle to come this far. Collectively," he adds, "So don't go getting no funny ideas."

"Collectively, right. So collectively people don't want peace."

"Obviously not."

"I still don't understand who they are though—" I sipped my tea, nearly fell off my box again.

"Good tea?" he grins.

"Yeah, even better than the last!"

Winks, "The Inner Order are like that tea, only a matter of taste."

"So this is what the Illuminati gets shown. You."

"Pretty much. Of course, they don't get all this – everybody sees the world with whatever eyes they've opened to see – and what's good for the goose isn't necessarily good for the gander. All too many fucking lose it here, poor cunts, they go demented, can't fucking handle it." He winks again, "Can't handle the Truth."

I shudder, it was beginning to sink in alright.

He shrugs, "Not my fault. I Am that I Am, catch-madrift?"

"Can you do me a small favour," I says, "Could you stop talking like me, it's a bit unsettling."

"I can if you want, bit inappropriate though…"

He pauses, flashes me a knowing grin.

"You're my Voice of Truth," I says.

Shakes his head. "Close. I *am* your Truth. That's all you ever really wanted, isn't it, yourself."

I nods. "And I *am* dead, aren't I?"

He laughs. "Just said, living is dying to all—"

"Got that the first time… but… alright, what's going on then? Why bring me to Ireland?"

"I didn't, you did."

"Gives me the abdabs…"

"Oh I dunno, could do with more trees, but it's quite nice here otherwise," he shrugs. "Alright, use your loaf. I had to manifest somewhere, you could have gone anywhere – left you a passport, finances, the lot – therefore somewhere between the abdabs and Canada lay your choice. And you didn't bottle out, followed through, and didn't get stuck on any cards. That's the issue here."

"Didn't get stuck?"

"Correct, and so here you are," pulls out a Tarot Card, "*The World*, the last card, at the end of the Fool's Journey. Watch," he says, spreading cards on the table:

THE FOOL. THE DEVIL. THE MAGICIAN. THE CHARIOT.

STRENGTH. THE EMPEROR. JUSTICE. THE EMPRESS.

THE HANGED MAN. THE HIEROPHANT.

THE TOWER.

THE MOON. THE HERMIT. WHEEL of FORTUNE. THE LOVERS.

THE SUN. TEMPERANCE. THE HIGH PRIESTESS. DEATH.

THE STAR.

JUDGEMENT. THE WORLD.

"That's the order they fell in, the map of your journey, and this is you, the traveller." He picks out The Fool, and starts placing it over the other cards. "Everybody's map is unique, each card can be revisited countless times, but the journey remains the same. The trump card, moving through the pack, becomes one and equal with every step until, finally, arriving here: The World, on the threshold of Eternity—"

"Alright, sorry to interrupt... but, I was in this field, and then I was on a boat. What was I doing for twenty years in-between?"

"Settling your account."

"What?"

"Balancing your book."

"Sorry?"

Taps the table, "Said, you were away."

I study the cards on the table, "That one, there," I mutters, "Judgment."

Nods.

"So I was *away* like in Nick, then? Some kind of prison…"

Smiles, but doesn't reply.

"Oh please, no, don't give me 'away with the Faeries' now. Alright, I'm prepared to go along with it up to a point, but I didn't come down in the last shower, alright?"

"Your friend Barry wasn't far off the mark, closer than most like to believe." Sips his tea. "You really wanna know?"

"Too bloody right I do!"

"Hmmm, plenty say they're game, but…"

Scoops up his cards, shuffles the pack, puts them in a neat pile beside me, and raises his eyebrows.

I get a tight knot in my gut, but I nods,

"This is the point when they all lose it, isn't it…"

"As I said, depends – different strokes for different folks."

"Do it then," I sighs, "I'm here now… In for a penny."

Slowly raising his hood over his head, the Creator cracks his knuckles. "In for a pound," he whispers solemnly, tapping on his keyboard again, and I'm waking up, head-splitting headache, trussed up in a straightjacket…

Chapter 51

Hell Hath No Fury like Your Own Scorn

The last thing I recall was the Beanfield, staggering towards the road with Sprocket, truncheons raining down all around us – and then Frank Moon – the Eyes of Iblis, staring straight at me.

After a brief struggle with my straightjacket, I scanned the bare cell. I'd been drugged.

The door unlocks, swings open, and Frank swaggers in.

"Morning Captain," he grins, "Get a good kip?"

He doesn't have the Eyes of Iblis now, but he's in his shirtsleeves and he's got a gun.

"Feel sick as a dog," I mumbles, shifting myself up, sitting against the wall.

"It'll wear off in a moment. Precautions." He smiles again.

"Where's Sprocket?"

"Your scruffy friend? Oh dear," slowly pacing up and down, "They let him go without charge. It appears he'd invoked Queeny's Article 61. Clever. Too clever – we can only *hope* it doesn't catch on, hmmm?"

He stops pacing, peers down, "A royal pain in the arse."

I groans. "He's a good'n…"

Shrugs, "Sooner or later, if he doesn't behave himself. Not my remit – you are."

"Then get this fucking thing off me."

"Do it yourself."

"Can't be arsed."

"I am disappointed," he chuckles, crouching down, unbuckling the leather straps at my back. "There was a time when you'd of been out of this, unleashing hell quicker than digits off a leper! You're back at London HQ, in case you're wondering."

I nods, "Gathered that."

"Then I suppose you know why you're here."

"I can guess, but tell me."

He sighs, glancing about, and finally grins again,

"Let's just say you're being offered a promotion."

Undoes the last buckle of the straightjacket, pats me on the shoulder, "Come with me, there's something I think you've wanted to see… don't forget your cane."

Picking up Happy Stick by the door, I followed Frank out of my cell, down the old corridors. We were deep underground, in the restricted sections of the MI6 building Sid used to call 'The Underbelly,' where many of our briefings took place, all those years ago.

My heart skipped a beat stepping over the different coloured lines on the floor. Whenever down here, you'd be fingerprinted, retinal scanned, and given a security card marked with a colour. Then you'd follow the lines on the floor to the rooms you were allowed into – that was your colour – cross the line and you're a good'un. Say even one word to anybody with a different colour and you're a good'un.

No wonder the lie changes at every level.

"Nobody down here but us chickens now," says Frank, gesturing to the doors we passed by, "Relocated back in '66."

"Interesting—"

"Left!" he declares, turning off into another row, and suddenly stopping before a black door.

I glance about us. "What now, Room 101?"

He chuckles, "God no, nothing so… crude." And taking out a key, he opens the door. "Inside," he says, flicking the light switch.

The room was large and bare. Frank strides up to the wall opposite, places his hand on the brickwork, and immediately a sliding door appears and opens.

"Better take the lift, at our age," he jests over his shoulder, and in we go – down, down and down.

"Where are we going?"

He mutters, tight-lipped, "Do you know how many you've eliminated these past two years?"

"Who polished up my cane? Looks like new."

"Fatalities from wounds consistent with a fifteen-inch bladed weapon: 2,199."

I looks down at my shoes, they'd been polished too, and my suit smelled aired and fresh.

"Fatalities from gun wounds consistent with a 9mm Glock, hollowpoint – your preferred firearm of choice, I do believe – 337, and that's a conservative estimate from the annual unsolved."

"Wasn't counting."

"Well *they* were. And if only a score of people carried on like you over, say, a ten year period?"

"About a quarter of a million scum off our streets," I mutter.

"About that, yes."

"A bit miffed, are they?"

"Not at all, plenty more where they came from… ahhh, here we are!" he declares, the lift coming to a halt.

The door slides open. I take an involuntary step back.

A silver gangplank, about twelve foot wide, stretches out before us, and all around are stars glistening into infinite space.

Frank turns to me, his eyes darkened into black, lifeless pools.

"Cross the bridge," he orders.

"W-w-what is this?"

"Cross over and find out."

My hands begin to tremble. "Where are we—"

"On the last level of the Lie, the first level of the Truth. How long do you want to remain on the last step?"

Tearing my gaze away from his, I scan the bridge into the distance. There doesn't seem to be an end to it.

And there doesn't seem to be any choice either, not with Frank's 9mm level with my head.

Breathing deep, I took a shaky step forward, and then another until I stood on the gangplank. I turned around, the lift door slides shut, and vanishes.

I wave my cane at where it had been, nothing but empty space.

"Oh no…"

"Oh no is right!"

"Am I glad to hear you!" I yells, spinning around.

"Alright, steady on."

"This is it, mate, game over."

Laughter.

"I don't think Frank would go to all this trouble just to do us in."

"Nor I, but that wasn't Frank – it was but it wasn't."

"Looked the spit of the cunt to me."

"Did you see his eyes?"

"Ermmm, nope."

"The Eyes of Iblis!"

"Don't worry about Iblis, we'll cross that bridge when we come to it."

Laughter.

"Oh very droll...This can't be real."

"Looks and feels real enough."

"Some kind of new technology, then?"

"Or maybe something to do with the drugs they used to knock us out. I dunno. He said cross, so that's what we've got to do."

We start pegging.

"Doesn't make any sense."

"Nope."

"Goes on forever..."

And it did, we pegged for what seemed like an hour in silence, and then he pipes up,

"Hold on, hmmm!"

"What?"

"Just thinking, why forward, why not to the side?"

I stop, peer over into the starry heavens below us.

"Just a thought, sorry, silly idea."

"Nah, hold on... you could be onto something. There's nothing on the end of this bridge, leastways nothing as far as..."

"And nothing above, or below; that's what I was thinking."

"Jump?"

"Jump."

I pause and ponder.

"I'll keep that in mind, thanks. But we'll just keep going for now, ay?"

"Alright, press forward! I'll open up some boxes, see what we come up with..."

We carried on, I dunno for how long, lost all sense of time and then he pipes up again,

"Futile and fucked up!"

"Beyond all recognition," I agrees, and sitting down, I tapped the bridge with my cane. It kind of 'twanged.'

"Metallic."

"Of some kind, yes, and that's what I was thinking… Alien."

"Come again?"

"Transdimensional Beings, this particular situation has their M.O. all over it."

"Oh Gawd, please don't lose it on me, not here—"

"Well you don't remember, but I do."

"Remember what?"

"Remember a meeting with them, back in '47."

"Nah, in '47 Sid and I were levelling villages in the Levant for King and Country. Anyways, that's all MI18's territory, supposedly."

"And MI13."

"Still, I don't think—"

"Don't have to think, that's why you've got me. And I can tell you, we saw one of them, briefly, with Frank, first time in '47."

"Little green men?"

"Little grey men, more like – the Mandinda, servants of the Chitahuri – creatures from the Lower Astral realms, with massive heads and eyes."

"Doesn't ring any bells, but in for a penny, in for a pound. Open the box."

"You sure? You appear a little apprehensive there, me auld china."

"Look at this place, what else have we got to do? Go on."

"MI18 investigate Extraterrestrials, and MI13 deal with the Supernatural."

I shuddered in the eerie silence, scanning the infinity around us.

"Gawd, I always thought those departments were a load of bollocks, a front for something…"

"It was. The best fronts aren't those claiming to do the opposite of what you're doing, the best fronts of all are those what sound so fucking mental nobody would believe it's true. And when MI18 and MI13 finally sussed on they were essentially working in the same field, they amalgamated. Frank was there at that historic meeting – got you cleared to be his driver – and that's where we bumped into one of them, one of the little guys on the driveway out of St James's Palace."

"Gawd, it's getting odder by the second…"

"Point was, disclosure, how best to explain to the public what was going on. Frank, and most of the Yanks, argued against disclosure entirely, 'cos of 'the mass-panic,' meaning loss of social control, people questioning the mystery of existence and all that malarkey; they might not go to work in the morning."

"So they decided to put a lid on it."

"*Exactly, break the plebs in gently over a generation or so; have to prime the bible-bashers first; have to wait for a lot of their hardboileds to die off before declaring it's no longer a sin to believe in life on other planets.*"

"Where are they from, then, these Aliens...? Are we on one of their home worlds or something, 'cos fuck me, this ain't right."

"*This place, yeah, it does, it feels Transdimensional. But they've cities on the Moon and Mars, they said, all over the gaff, and there's thousands of different species. But it's the ones who feed off Awen they were interested in, 'cos in exchange, they give us advanced technologies. So maybe all this...?*"

"Right, but I still don't remember meeting no Aliens."

"*Use your loaf. Didn't say you met them, said you bumped into one...*"

Pause.

"Oh no, no... I never..."

"*You did.*"

"What was I driving?"

"*A Wolsey. The little bugger didn't stand a chance, stepped out in front of you. But look on the bright side, at least it wasn't an ice-cream van!*"

"Oi! Don't laugh, this is a serious situation; what if the little buggers are still out to level the score?"

"*Doubt it, long time ago and it was an accident. In any case, they don't have individual bodies like ours, they're more like fleshy dolls, receptacles.*"

I stood up, thinking of receptacles, and unzipped my fly.

"Carry on, while I conduct a little experiment. Did we attend the meeting?" I asks, watching my piss flowing over the side, down, down, down...

"*Nah, but Frank briefed us on the way there. I know they were concerned about suppressing scientific evidence, particularly anything supporting the idea that humans are Alien hybrids. Personally though, I was never comfortable with calling them Aliens from 'other planets.' I think it's more a question of 'spheres of influence,' transdimensional realms. Wanna hear my theory of what the main agenda of that meeting was?*"

"If it gets us out of here, yeah."

"*Alright. Disclosing the existence of extraterrestrials would open up a massive can of worms, obviously, but especially about the true nature of reality; like how do they travel across millions of light years of space in the first place?*

The only way to answer that is to stop thinking in terms of travelling through space on any level, 'moving' from Point A to Point B, and begin thinking in terms of Point A and Point B being one and the same Point.

So, when talking about 'going to' other planets, closer to the truth would be to see it as 'passing into' simultaneous realms of existence, within which our limited and pre-set notions of consensus reality might not necessarily apply.

Therefore, the main reason they need to keep people in the dark is because they need to keep our linear concept of space-time. On a primary level, control hinges upon limiting fields of perception, which then determines 'experience.'"

"Standard psyops," I mutter

"Exactly. So if we continue to believe the universe is nothing more than finite objects floating about an empty void, the perception of ourselves and our transdimensional capabilities are likewise limited—"

"Enough, cut to the chase. And your point?"

"I think we might have a better understanding of this particular sphere of influence we've landed in if we strike a deal, right now, and stop thinking with outmoded models of liner time.

We must dare to envision original concepts, totally new paradigms which reach out for a broader perception of our relationship with the universe, and our transdimensional cousins. What do you reckon?"

"Switch off the RAMA and stop sounding like Sid."

"I think we've got to think our way out, in other words."

I felt a drop on my head, and then another. I looks up and see a torrent of water coming down. I sidestep out the way, and it splashes onto the bridge beside me.

"I think it's… raining?"

"Nah, I think you just pissed on yourself – Oh no!"

"Oh no what—?"

"Look lively! Twelve o'clock."

I zip up, turn around.

"No, the other twelve o'clock!"

About-turns, and sure enough, there on the horizon something was coming towards us.

"Something big."

"Big as a house."

We watched, rooted to the spot. As it got closer, we could make out legs and a torso, green scaly skin and a head like a lizard – bulging eyes glowing as bright as two golden suns.

"We're in trouble."

"What the fuck is that?"

"Dunno. Don't like it."

"Nor I," I mutter, sliding out my blade.

The bridge trembled with each thundering stride.

"I think a tactical retreat is in order."

"My thoughts exactly."

We start backing away, and the creature picks up its pace, hurtling across the bridge on all fours with sickening speed.

"No, wrong move – Stop!"

We stall in our tracks.

The thing stops too, no more than forty yards away. Eyeing us evilly, it stands up, bares its teeth and roars.

"Stay put! I think I know what that is."

"Alien-Iblis!"

"No, no, fuck me, I know where we are!"

"You do?" I murmur, the thing striding towards us again.

"Go at it!"

"You've gotta be kidding," I says, scanning the abyss around us.

"Trust me!"

"Look at that thing—" My words chocked in my throat. I was petrified. I knew. I remembered—

"Said charge the cunt!"

Gritting my teeth, I pegged, screaming my lungs out straight at the thing. It crouched down low, roaring fetid breath, razor claws outstretched and I passed straight through it.

Vanished.

I tripped, scrambled about on the smooth gangplank, and managed to hold onto the edge, my cane spinning into the precipice below.

I hauled myself up.

"You alright?"

"Nah, I'm not alright, gotta get out of here, now!"

"Can't."

"Where did it go?

"Dunno…"

"Gawd, will someone please tell me what's going on! What do you mean, can't?"

"Can't as in can't. You've gotta see this through to the end. Keep going, don't stop, cross the bridge. I'll explain."

– No need to explain –

"Who said that?"

"Who said that?"

"I did."

We turned around – "Brid!"

"That's not Brid! Don't trust it!"

"Looks like her, she's dressed the same an' all."

She giggles, twirls her hand in a circle, "That's because it is me!"

I stroked her cheek. "Is it?"

She smiles, and then goes all grim. "You will never cross the Bridge of Penitence this way, Mr Barbelo, and if you fall off it, you will only find yourself back on it again."

"Don't listen to her!"

"Watch." She points up at the starry heavens, and my cane and blade hurtle down between us.

I bend down, and pick them up,

"Where are we Brid?"

"Inside your Transition."

"That's what I was going to say!"

"Charging about won't work here, I'm afraid, so I wouldn't listen to anything that Demon says."

"Demon?"

"She's the Demon, can't you see, where did she come from, why is she here if not to trick us!"

"Fair point, why are you here Brid."

Shrugs. "Because you wanted to speak to someone who knows what's going on."

"I'm dead?"

"That's only word."

"When though?"

"Many times, work it out."

"Sprocket."

Nods. "Protecting your friend, yes, that was the last time, but not the first time."

"I don't feel very dead," I muttered, patting myself down, "What was the score then?"

"Barbelo 4 – SPG 1."

"Oh how embarrassing. Hold on, what do you mean, 'first time'…?"

I pause, studying her anxious glare. "… I think, I think that's important, isn't it."

"Very important," echoes Brid gently, "Work it out."

Massaging my temples, I racked my brain.

Images of mayhem and slaughter flashed before my eyes – bombs, shrapnel, screams and blood – and then the dripping of autumn rain, drip, drip, dripping softly into dark puddles overwhelmed me with despair—

Stifling a gasp, I crumpled to my knee. "The underpass!"

"I'm afraid so," she murmurs, reaching down and helping me up.

"That little cunt? But it was only a dream!"

"Both yes and no, as my good friend Edgar Allan Poe says: 'All that we see or seem, is but a dream within a dream.'"

"Why's everybody talking in riddles? Fucking hell…"

"You are in Hell, Mr Barbelo, always were and always will be, and it's all of your own making. And now this," she adds, grinning, "This is what you have allowed yourself to become equal and One with!"

"Hell? No, no, don't listen to her mate! She's lying—"

"Shut up! Doesn't look like Hell."

"Stay here for eternity, believe me, it will," Brid mutters appreciatively. "There's only one thing greater than love, and that's hate for whatever takes it away."

"Come again?"

"Nice work, you must really hate yourself!" she chuckles. "No way up, no way down, no Time. Doesn't get much worse for someone like you, a bridge across infinity, starting nowhere, ending nowhere. Trapped in eternal monotony."

"I *made* this?"

"And all which came before, and all that came after…" she pauses, smiling, glancing around again. "Doesn't bear thinking about, does it?"

"I don't understand," I says. "Talk straight, please, ay…"

"Well, you could've gone for worms burrowing into your body and laying eggs, no?"

"Nah, not my style – had plenty of that in Africa anyway."

"Or skinned alive maybe?"

"That too, Africa, Indonesia."

"Crucifixion?"

"Africa, Indonesia, Burma, Mile End Road—"

She widens her eyes, "What about boiling vats of oil. A lot of your hardboiled types go for that."

"Not my style… oh fuck, I think I'm beginning to get it!"

"Oh you'll get it, Mr Barbelo, we all have to atone."

"I catch-yadrift. How do I get out… out of *here* then?"

Shoots me a worried squint, "Not easy. Everybody gets one chance out of Hell, the same chance, the only chance."

"What chance?"

"Oh, oh, look lively!"

"Right on cue," she mutters, "here it comes again."

"Oh Gawd, Brid, what *is* that thing?"

"Your *feharchrove*, and it's going to keep coming at you until it gets what it wants."

"Well it can't exactly kill me—"

"It's worse than anything you can think of."

"Really? How's that then…"

"It is the shape of all the pain, all the misery and suffering you've ever caused others—"

"We're in trouble."

"What the fuck is that?"

"Dunno. Don't like it."

"Nor I," I mutter, sliding out my blade.

The bridge shook with each thundering stride. Has this happened before?

"Continuously!" yells Brid, over the creature's hellish roars, "You've been here five EPYs already!"

"Epees?"

"Earth Plane Years! Each second is like an eternity here, and every time is like the first. You forget, and then you remember a small piece more!"

"I think a tactical retreat is in order."

"My thoughts exactly."

"No! You charge, it vanishes again, and again! You will play out the same scenario—"

"Brid? Where did you come from?"

"That's not Brid!"

She grabs me by the shoulders, her eyes aflame, "Listen to me! Can you fight something that you are, with something you are not? Let it have what it wants!"

"Let what have what?"

"Your *feharchrove* is the only thing standing between you and the Creator."

"The Creator…"

"Goodbye, Mr Barbelo. I will not come here again…"

Brid vanishes before our eyes. I stare in terror at the creature hurtling towards us; I felt as if I'd been here years—

"Charge the cunt!"

I crouch low, my blade poised, ready to plunge into where I imagined the thing's heart to be – and I charge.

It vanishes. I trip, scramble about…

Next thing I know it's back again, hunkered down in the far distance, watching our every move – and some girl in a white dress is giving us a helping hand, getting me to my feet.

"Hello darling," she says, "Aren't ya getting a little tired of this routine?"

"My Gawd, Sammy! You're looking well!" And she was; young, trim, fit as a fiddle in a white cotton summer dress.

"Where did you… I mean… shit! How many Epees this time?"

"Twenty-two," she chuckles. "I'm a Guide now."

"Oh… happy then?"

"Extremely. Are you?"

"Nah, it's all coming back to me though, bit by bit. Found out I came a cropper down the underpass."

"Well, no, you did and you didn't, both."

"Right, like what you used to go on about, the Subtle Thing, both bag and dog."

"Equally."

"Yep, I get it now."

She smiles warmly. "And you will, more, and more."

We glance behind us at the creature.

"I didn't do it, did I?"

"Hmmm, obviously not," she says. "You might though, this time. Then again, you might not."

"Fuck, I've been… I've been doing this a lot, haven't I?"

She chuckles, "Millions and millions, over and over – you silly old goat!"

"Can it stop, all stop?"

"Up to you. Stay fluid. Face the music or rot here forever—"

"We're in trouble."

"What the fuck is that?"

"Dunno. Don't like it."

"Nor I," I mutter, sliding out my blade.

The bridge trembled with each thundering stride, but Sammy only shrugs, slowly walking away, "Here we go again. Typical, you remember, you forget, remember, forget…"

"No, Sammy, wait! I do remember!"

"Gotta go," she says, "You've had many, many Guides coming to assist you – and everybody you've ever helped, everybody you've ever said a kind word to – and still you don't listen!"

"But I am listening," pegging towards her, "The Subtle Thing! Stay fluid!" I yell. She begins to fade, slowly vanishing into the darkness around us,

"…You know where to find me… If you want to, then you will…"

"Charge the cunt!"

"Don't leave me here, Sammy!"

"Forget her, she's evil! Charge the cunt!"

"No!" I whisper, eyes pinned defiantly to the beast, picking up speed.

"Ahhhhh! The abdabs! I can feel the screaming abdabs!"

"Like never before mate, we're staring straight at them."

"Charge the—"

"What part of 'no' don't you fucking understand? NO!"

"But it'll get us!"

I grit my teeth, "Most probably."

The creature slowed its pace. Its massive claws just a couple of feet over Barbelo's head, it loomed over him and stopped.

"You stupid cunt, don't you see what this means? We'll be stuck here forever!"

Barbelo felt his cane slide from my fingers.

"*Pick it up, oh please, I need you! You need me, we need each other! We've always been together, I AM YOU!*"

"No you're not, I've never known who I am…"

And bowing my head, Barbelo spread my arms wide.

"… I surrender. Peace—"

Immediately it grabbed him by the throat, lifting me high into the air. My leg and peg thrashed about, we were choking.

Raising us level with its eyes, the creature yawned open its huge cavernous jaws and we couldn't help but ponder; to be eaten alive for all eternity?

Fair dues.

And no sooner had we thought this, when the beast turned us around to face the bridge.

Walking towards us were a multitude of diverse peoples, thousands upon thousands, and leading them was his sister, Marianna.

At last, we understood. We were ready.

Let them come…

Chapter 52

The Strawman Redemption

The Creator was trying to pick me up, laughing – I was screaming, thrashing about on his floor.

"Fucking hell!" I jumps up, rubbing my throat.

"Relax, Captain, you're back," he croons, "Here, together, with me."

"I'm back, I'm back," I sighs, eyes closed, breathing deep.

"Are you alright?"

"Yeah, yeah, fuck that," I says, crashing down on the wooden box.

"Do you understand now?"

I nods. "Did that really happen?"

He smiles. "I made you a nice cup of tea—"

"They were all there! And this monster… and fuck me, thousands of them crossing this bridge…"

I couldn't go on. I could still see their faces whenever I blinked.

The Creator moves round behind me, and switching on the desk lamp, rests his hands on my shoulders,

"What we accept we're One and equal with, becomes our manifest experience. And what we do to others, we do to ourselves. *That* is natural law. So yes, you became every single person you ever interacted with. You thought their thoughts, felt their hopes, loves and fears, all their pains—"

"Please!" I raised my hand wearily, "Stop, alright, stop – I don't wanna go there again."

"Well let's hope you don't, but freewill is freewill, after all. So what did you realise?"

"Is that my tea?"

"Coming right up," he smiles, sitting down with our cuppas. "Go on, it'll help you regroup…"

"Hard to put into words, what I realised," I mutters, sipping my tea, glancing out the window at the darkening, evening sky. "Is…?"

"Yep, it's all as real as it gets."

"I can still see their faces…"

"It'll pass."

"Bloody hope so, 'cos I didn't just feel what they felt, I became them, I *was* them all along – they all had identical loves, needs and desires what flowed into each other, like... like humanity was the one same *stuff* – and yet nowhere was there any freewill in any of this."

"No?"

"Oh we *had* freewill, alright, but we didn't know who we were, where we were to *know* what we were doing with it, if ya catch-madrift. And when that, that *thing* gripped me by the throat, I saw why: The Truth. There is no choice with the Truth, only unconditional surrender to the fact. I suppose that's what I realised, it's only the delusion of more than one truth what creates the delusion of choices. Like you can't have more than one Almighties. Truth is Truth, fact, one and indivisible, anything else is merely lies – lies in action..."

"You had a brush with the One," he whispers, "But good way of putting it, must remember that."

"So, I lets go – unconditional surrender – and in that instant the creature let me go too... it was like once I'd realised that freewill is the act of surrender, it wasn't interested, like it had no business with me anymore..."

I pause, stare at him. "The next thing I know I'm here again."

The Creator smiles, "And here we are, together again."

"But... did it *really* happen?"

"Just said, everything that's ever happened, or is going to happen, is always happening." Drains his cuppa, "I'm going to ask you a favour. You can tell me to fuck off if you don't wanna do it, and that's alright; can't upset me, I'm seeing and doing it all."

"A favour," I says, eyeing him suspiciously.

"A favour, and then I'm going to give you a chance, a chance to try out your freewill in the light of what you've realised. I'm giving you The Choice. You can go back or cross over to Locale 33."

"Where Sid lives."

"Though I won't tell a lie, that's where everybody's headed anyway, sooner or later."

"Not much of a choice then, is it?"

"Everything depends on how you look at it."

I nods. "What do you mean by go back?"

"How long do you want to remain on the last step? That's the question I ask all with the bottle to come to see me. And the choice is the same for all who come this far: go back to your previous life or safe passage into the next Locale."

"Safe passage?"

"Meaning I can guarantee you won't get trapped anywhere horrible. Choose the next step, and your work here is done. You'd have tipped your applecart out of the Lower Astral."

"Alright, and if I decide to go back, you'd put me where though?"

He shrugs. "How the fuck should I know? That depends on you, your Awen, *your* awareness."

"But wouldn't I do it all over again?"

"Just said, depends on you."

"Bit tricky, then…"

"Awen's a tricky master." Flicking through his Tarot pack, pulls out a card, "Right now we're here, The World, the last card, meaning at the end of the Fool's Journey through the pack. From this point on, you'll travel light, with a clean slate—"

"But if I go back, will I remember any of this?"

"I can't tell you that either. Perhaps, or perhaps you'll only retain a feeling, an impression. Either way, listen to your conscience, to your heart. You have The Choice, do the right thing."

"Alright," I sighs, quickly draining my tea. Sid's manor looked all very nice, but nah, plenty of time for hanging about fields bollock-naked… on the other hand, beautiful skies…

"I dunno, give us a moment."

He grins knowingly. "Funny that, they all wanna go back. It's the regrets, see? Everybody wants a second chance."

"Said, I dunno…"

"Take your time."

"One last cuppa for the road then, ay?"

He smiles indulgently, gets up, and puts the kettle on.

"So what's this favour you want?"

"Hmmm, oh, it's nothing," he says over his shoulder, "Just need you to cook up a title for all this," flicks his fingers at the screen, "It's going to get published, but not without your permission, of course."

"Fuck off! You're not publishing diddlysquat! My life's in there—"

I stalled, he was laughing his tits off.

"Alright, but why me though?"

"Because you're fucking mental, Joseph! Never come across anything quite like it in all my aeons," he chuckles, "Mad as a hatter and still you've something useful to say."

"Really?"

"Really, and so they asked me to do it, and so, I comply. Rules are rules. You had your reasons to come here, and they had theirs."

His eyes dart rapidly to the ceiling – the universal code for use your loaf – and yeah, it slowly dawns on me.

"Bastards!" I whisper, "That's what all that Inner Order 'oh we'll initiate you' bollocks was about! Blimey… That was clever."

"Spiritual mercenaries usually are; don't give a toss who they upset or how it's done, as long as the message hits home, on-target."

"Alright, so what do I get in return?"

"You get to have people reading it. Is that enough?"

"Will they want to?"

"Just need a title."

"Why don't you think one up yourself…?"

Looks at me funny.

"Right," I says, "Because it's my story, I catch-yadrift. Give us a moment then…" I got an image of Brid and Sid sitting at our operation's desk, reading the booklet we'd written for our revolution what never happened, and I says, accepting my cup of tea;

"Hows about, Barbelo's Blood. Is that good?"

"Good? That's pukka!" he declares, sitting down and tapping into his snazzy telly. "Anything else you need to discuss?"

I shook my head, my mind was blank, and then it hit me—

"Yeah, my mind is blank! I mean there's no… no words… there's not been any words inside my head since I got here."

Shrewd nod, "Hmmm, tricky issue all that too. You see, that voice living in your head was, well, it's me."

"But you're a Demon, Iblis-Lucifer Itself, and that was my Voice of Truth…"

Closes one eye, "Was it?"

"You cunt…"

Laughs, "'People say all kinds of things, don't mean its true!'" He shrugs, "But I suppose that's one way of putting it, yes, a Demon."

I sips my lovely tea. "Explain, please."

He goes on patiently, "Everything in this Locale is made of Light, and I'm the Morning Star, the Light Bringer to the Darkness."

"Alright."

"The Darkness is separation from the Light, and the Light is intelligence, *awareness* of that separation: *Nuish Bash'swan*, The Double Mind. You and I. But, I'm here now, and you're sitting over there, in my 'divine presence,' as it were. So, you are free, end of contract."

"I'm free… of… you," I says slowly, studying his mischievous grin.

"When you leave my domain, yes, completely free. 'The two shall be made as One.'"

"And what happens to you, me, Gawd, you really do *look* like me, a younger me…"

"Well, just said. All this," pats himself down, "goes with you, it's your Awen after all, including this," swings round on his chair, rolls up his left trouser leg, "Yep, all there, whole and integral. Me though, nothing happens to me, why? Because I *am* everywhere, I *am* this Locale; the manner in which your species perceives itself."

"Catch-yadrift," I says, eyes pinned to my leg.

Raises an eyebrow, "Anything else?"

I nods, "Those clouds I saw, what are those fucked-up clouds in the sky about? They're bloody horrible! I mean, doesn't anybody even notice? What's wrong with people these days?"

"My point exactly. Those fucked-up clouds are Chemtrails, a military aerial spraying project – Operation Cloverleaf – combined effort, all the major players are working on this together. Two pronged. One: to shield the Earth in an artificially created electromagnetic field, and prevent the raising of global spiritual consciousness. Two: a global population extermination program, infecting humanity with lethal biological agents."

Dark glare, "Your mate Sid, the Gifters and all the rest were bang on. The Illuminati plan to wipe out two thirds of humanity, bring the population down to a convenient level. Slaves," he winks, "Sorrow, despair and endless war."

"Nah, then why isn't everybody dead then?"

"Think like a cunt for a moment."

I 'thought' for a moment.

"Right, I get ya, they're spraying the antidotes first."

"Exactly. The program's in its immunisation phase. Selective Western populations are to be spared, though in practice, many people don't respond favourably to airborne vaccines; sudden death syndrome, heart attacks, cancer, morgellons – and you're way beyond pandemic infection's levels from 'unidentified' diseases too."

"Right, so they're not spraying the antidotes in poorer countries."

"No, not in places with the highest human populations. Africa, China, South East Asia and Central America will be wiped out, mostly. The plebs, that is – their Top Cunts will be safe and sound in their underground cities, and off-world facilities. Or so they think."

"Off-world?"

"The last time I checked, there's at least twelve orbital space stations, 'Arks,' storing sample DNA of every species on Earth, and the old emergency bases on the moon," chuckles, "But they're building more, and at a phenomenal rate! Shall we have a look?" glancing at his screen, "Mars was always on the cards. They found several cities there, ancient, very advanced by your standards."

I sips my tea. "Sorry, can't say I'm interested. It's what's happening now, here, on this planet that I'm concerned about. So what's the next phase? Use Israel as a powerbase. Goad the UN into war."

Nods. "All the major players. Simultaneously; orchestrated global economic collapse, leading to mass starvation, disease and world war. But you've got to understand, none of this is certain. The vibration of our Locale is rising; you could all, every single one of you, at long last achieve a merging with Locale 33."

"Where Sid lives," I mutter.

"Where you all live, when not experiencing separation from the One."

"Lovely place that."

"True, infinite creative freedom."

"And what, they live forever there, right..."

"They live there as you do here, moving on when it's time to move on – only without fear, Eternity is there for the taking."

"Yep, roger that. So what will happen to here, to all this, if the Illuminati succeeds."

He shifts uneasily in his seat, "You don't want to know."

"Go on."

"The resulting fear and trauma slows down your collective vibration, and my Locale merges with Locale 31."

"The parasite-hell misery worlds."

"Trust them to go and lower the tone."

"I don't get it… I mean, if I've got this vibrational density business right," I says, glancing about his flat, "Nobody actually, really, dies, no?"

"Right enough, but even the most psychotic paranoid depictions of Hell, repeating over, and over, forever, without any hope of it ever ending and no, it doesn't come close to the horror they'll transform this Locale into. Not even what you've been through can light a candle to it. It's all about Harmonic Resonance."

"But you said Locale 33 is where everybody's headed anyway."

"I said sooner or later, and later can be eternally fucking late in Eternity. Awen's a tricky master – interfering with someone else's process has massive repercussions for the soul, even on an individual basis, as you know."

"Don't I just."

"The mass-slaughter of billions is off the scale entirely. True enough, the vibration of our Locale is rising, but with all that Awen focused into lower astral concerns, we won't reach optimum pitch, and our Locale's rebirth into the higher realms is aborted. If that happens, the Illuminati finally gets absolute control of me, of all of it, and will push on through into Locale 33, and beyond."

"Bloody Hell…"

"Bloody Hell is exactly right, that's their plan. Doesn't mean they'll succeed though," jabs a finger at his screen, "you've gotta remember the page always starts off blank."

"And do they, the Illuminati know all this? I mean is that really what they want?"

"Of course not! The lie changes at every level, ninety-nine percent of them haven't a clue of the ultimate agenda. At the top level, though, the truth was always constant: they were always losing control. And now, very soon, they'll lose control entirely. So, if staying Top Cunts of the world means wiping most of it out?" he shrugs, "Nero fiddles while Rome burns. But, nobody wakes up in the morning and sets off to do evil, they need to—"

"Oh yes they do! I've met loads of evil cunts who—"

"They don't, if they're human then they need to justify it somehow – even you had to play the Justice Card from time to time – and this is the irony of it all, the Illuminati genuinely believe they're on the good side, see, they actually think they're *saving* civilisation, and from an even greater evil: a world without government, a world without them to take care of you all, to save you from yourselves."

"Blimey, then it's like farmers rounding up cattle for a cull."

"Hmmm, more like free-range cattle; they've learnt to parcel out your freedoms in exactly the same way – you're 'free' to wander about as long as you're productive, and stay on the farm. Question is, what will your farmers inherit after the cull? Using bio-weapons won't destroy their infrastructure, so most believe they'll just carry on as they have been; lording it about with their top-notch whores, cocaine parties on the palace lawn and whatever takes their fancy.

But their one percenters know, their Top Cunts fully appreciate the stakes involved – the spiritual implications are huge! Fear is their food source, and yeah, we'll reap a great harvest. Mmmm, high steaks indeed," he licks his lips, "Pun intended."

I shuddered, "They're not human either, are they, these top cunt one percenters? They're not from here and that's why don't give a flying filly's about the world."

Nods, "Consumed, totally, their sovereign selves were forfeit to me many generations ago. Nothing recognisably human left, only the shell of their flesh, which they interbreed and incarnate time, and time again, with no chance of redemption. That's why they want to sink this Locale deeper into the lower realms, yes. And that's what they're afraid of, terrified of your sovereign potential, of your power to transcend beyond their reach..."

"Can't you do something?"

"Already gone through this, haven't we. I'm doing something all the time, and as you say, Captain, all is as it should be; there's not a single blade of grass out of place." He smiles.

"But you don't have to do... I mean, you don't seem very evil, anyone who can make a lovely cuppa like this can't be all bad..."

"I'm an evil cunt alright," he chuckles, "Oh I enjoy all this, immensely, make no mistake. On the other hand, I personally can't think of anything worse than giving you lot freewill, now that's an evil cunt – like giving a baby a packet of razorblades to play with."

He shrugs again, "Listen to me, I can only do what people want. Collectively you've got the power to transform this world into a paradise, collectively you give your power away to wankers; not my fucking problem. Individually or on masse, it's the same rule – fall asleep with your head in the sand, nobody to blame but yourselves when you wake up with a sore arse."

"Have you decided yet?" The Creator asks, pausing from his typing.

"Could do with some more Intel," I sighs, "This Awen… I mean, how does it *actually* work? And *what* are you, what part do you play?"

"I'll explain it another way, then. Think of Awen as soft clay, and freewill as a force, shaping that clay; a force which takes any shape you like because Awen is neutral, subject only to your will, to your word. In a sense, freewill and your word are one and the same."

"'Cos your word is your bond."

"Right. Because you were created conscious, sovereign beings, you deal with the world using the force of freewill. The choices you make are agreements, contracts with your sovereignty, and your word is the *consideration* you bring to the negotiating table."

"Consideration, 'tit for tat, this for that.'"

"Exactly, *quid pro quo.*"

"What are we striking deals with, then?"

"Everything, your very existence, reality itself is shaped and formed by your will."

"Right, that collective thing again. So who are you?"

"And individually too; those of you who have retained sovereignty can, and do, perform wonders with Awen – what you now call miracles. Miracles were once the rule, the measure of your soul. Me, however, I am a creature of the lower realms. Essentially a disincarnate being, a strawman, I have no sovereignty, no independent consciousness. I can't even recall my origins, I can only *suspect* that I had a beginning, somewhere, once…"

"Like the strawman in the Wizard of Oz? 'I have no brain,' that useless cunt?"

"Well, I do have uses – it's not all one-sided, I do provide a service. For now, think of me more like the strawmen you had in the Army, for target practice, bayonet charges; for hiding contraband whisky and tobacco at night. Remember?" sly wink, "Very useful."

"How can I forget, yeah, go on."

"I have neither sovereignty nor Awen; absolutely no autonomous creative power, or means of self-expression. Without a species like yours, I wouldn't exist, meaning I can't *know* myself to exist. I need retainers, sovereign minds to inhabit and use, like mirrors, for self-reflection. But, I can't use your Awen against your will, so I have to strike a bargain and gain your consent.

Problem is, not having much going for me, I don't have much to bring to the table. I'm not a sovereign being, I have 'no brain' to contract with. All I'm good at is one thing: being a strawman.

So in return for giving me a home, I offer to stand guard at your door, a buffer zone, if you like. Something to present to the world when you want to hide behind a lie, perhaps, or to take the punches when another's strawman seeks to attack you."

I nods, "A front, a psyops."

"The ultimate psyops! An illusion cannot deal with reality, only other illusions. In order for you to contract with that fiction, you have to agree to it. You have to lie to yourselves, in other words, continually, and before long you've convinced yourselves that my strawman is real."

"Right, so you're saying that we believe we *are* you?"

"And I, in turn, take your sovereignty for myself."

"Fuck me you're a nasty piece of work alright. So what else do we get in return?"

"Nothing. All I do is parcel out gifts you already had anyway!" He chuckles. "You ended up believing I am you, and in that instant, you are mine. You shift into my Locale and are bound by my terms, my conditions. That's the deal."

"What terms, what conditions?"

"Just said, *quid pro quo*. In exchange for my tenancy, you relinquish your autonomy, and with it, the bountiful, unconditional existence which was rightfully yours. That's the deal."

"What fucking deal? No we didn't – how? When?"

"You did, mate," he sighs, "Just said, it's your proverbial 'Pact with the Devil.' You contract with me via your fictitious self, the strawman I created in your head. Created using your Awen too, I might add. But when did it start? Always. I'm always there, broadcasting from the Realms, 'I am, I am, I am…'"

"You are… what?"

"Precisely, that's what I'm trying to find out! I grow my first roots in your consciousness when you're still in the womb, and as you grow, your brain develops the right shape to receive my signal, ready to accept my voice as your own—"

"Wait, why do we accept your voice as ours?"

Puzzled squint, "It *sounds* like yours, obviously!"

"No, I meant why do we contract with you in the first place?"

"Ahhh, well, I can't exist without you, so why do you think?" he asks with a wide grin, and yet a profound sadness lingered…

"You don't know who you are," I ventures, "You're afraid for your existence and you pass that fear onto us."

"Correct," he says, "Total oblivion. I infect you with my fears, you project them out into the world at large, and I offer to build a strawman to protect you," nods, scrunches his face, "From all those nasty 'straw-bogeymen' lurking out there, who knows how many, ay? Of course, total oblivion is an impossibility for you, for all sovereign beings, but fortunately for me, pure unadulterated terror is not."

"The screaming abdabs…"

"Exactly. But I'm *very* subtle. I only need you to feel my horror just that once, and of course, to later remind you of it, should you ever wish me to leave. From then on, I tone it down. I whisper in your sleep, 'forget, forget, forget,' sinking my roots deeper, and deeper, and by the age of two, the 'terrible twos' – every parent knows that phase: the first spark of a child's self-awareness? No, precisely when your sovereign self discovers something's very, very wrong,

'Where am I? Who am I?'

'Shhh,' I croon, 'You are here, with me. We are safe, you and I…'

And our first battles begin.

Throughout your lives, that constant internal division causes a conflict which, in turn, you manifest in all that you do, and become. Could you cause another suffering, without first the concept of 'them and us,' and logically 'you, and I?' Could you even allow it to take place?" deep breath, "You dog-fucking Paki Raghead Whitie Cuuunt!"

He grins, beckoning me to answer. I looks out the window, shakes my head.

"No, Captain. Without that split, that pathological duality, no war could ever have been possible, for you could not have conceived of an enemy to fight! *I* bring the Light. *I* give you awareness of separation. Divide and rule. Without me, not a single falsehood could you regard with conviction, nor even an unkind sentiment escape from your lips. All would exist in the irrefutable reality that the All, is the One," he smiles sweetly, "Unconditional Love."

Staring out the window, I noticed the evening sky had cleared. The street was chilled silent. A lonely star tries in vain to poke its snooter through the yellow haze of light-pollution, and I realised, despite everything he was saying, I fucking liked the cunt...

"... But still, why aren't I feeling this unconditional one-loveliness now, then? I mean, I feel great here, don't get me wrong, but..."

Returning from the sink, he sits down, passes me a fresh cuppa, "Because you're still here, with me, and everything's conditional in my domain, *quid pro quo*, everything comes together in twos – positive and negative, give, take, push and pull – down to molecular structures. So yeah, feels great here, if you've got a clean slate."

"Feel like I've paid my dues alright," I sips my gorgeous tea, "But we're all damaged goods, you're saying."

"Damaged? You're not well in the head, you bloody lot!"

"And no thanks to you, ay?"

"I suppose," he says, turning on my battle-gaze, "But I can't help it, see, I'm just a force of nature," he winks, "Catch-madrift?"

We both laughed at that.

"As you can appreciate," he says, "I'm not doing anything which doesn't stem from freewill. That is the Law of the One. The whole of the law. We contract with each other, you and I, freely. And it's through the *idea* of yourselves that we do this, and most effectively."

"The idea of ourselves, the strawman."

Nods, sips his tea. "Redeem the strawman, and your true self is also set free. Instantly."

"But till then, what?" I looks him up and down, "You live in our heads, slicing us up like an egg slicer, robbing our Awen. Blimey."

"No, I don't. You *give* me your Awen. Yes your awareness sustains me, and the price is high, but as I've already explained, you agree to our relationship, even with the harm it causes." Glares, "You're all transdimensional beings of incalculable power! If you wanna spend your entire lives believing you are free, that your choices are yours, when in actuality they are mine? What can I do about it?"

"Nothing. I understand," I says, "This is your manor, we're your creations, we're stuck here with you."

"No, you're not, only the strawman is my creation."

I nods. "We're enslaved to fictions, then."

"Exactly. And the principle which sustains my existence is reflected everywhere in my Locale – in the structure of your societies, in your personal relationships, your politics, economy, your endless warfare – just about everything works 'strawman to strawman.' Or 'lies in action,' as you said earlier. Allow me to explain further. If you remember all this, it'll come in useful if you decide to go back."

"Thanks. Go on…"

"It's been said that the love of money is the root of all evil, yeah?"

"Go on…"

"Shortly after you're born, you are registered, a Birth Certificate is created and along with it a name. But if you look, you will notice that this NAME is capitalised, and not written as you would normally write it. Now, the reason for this isn't because it's easier to read, though there are people who'd like you to believe that. The real reason, the only reason is because that name on your Birth Certificate's a legal fiction. That name is not you, the living breathing soul, it is in fact a corporation. A Firm. Any name you see written in capitals, including governments and countries, are corporate entities.

And any documents you see with your name written in capitals, are addressing your corporate self, and not your sovereign self.

This gives you a choice. Corporations are, like me, strawmen. They cannot contract with living souls, nor *make* them do so, they can only deal with other corporations. A strawman has absolutely no power over *real*, sovereign beings."

"Yeah, right!" I blurts out, "Try telling that to a whack-job with a 9mm at your gonads!"

Throws his arms up in the air, "Welcome to the Lower Astral! Freewill is freewill, mate, what you do with it is not my business, nor is it the issue here. No, the true issue is, who's pointing the gun at who?" he grins, "Sovereign being, or strawman?"

"I don't get it. I mean, sovereign being or no, wouldn't he get his nuts shot off anyway? I've known whack-jobs who—"

"Do you remember Mad Mick?"

I nods. "Of course."

"Remember how he'd go out into No Man's Land—?"

"Of course, bold as brass! And that's not the half of it. Sometimes he'd just sit down, cradle his rifle on his lap, and spark up a fag – in the middle of a battle! Seriously, we all saw it. It was like the bullets swerved out of his way, or the Germans didn't wanna hit him or something. Brass Hats said nothing about that, they'd had enough of the cunt as it was, but…"

Grins again, "You have the answer to your question."

"Yeah, I know, go back to what you were saying. Govermentals tricked us into slavery with all this trade name, strawman business."

"No, not quite. You do have a choice, and it's no different to how you limit your infinite, creative selves. The trick was, if there was one, to simply *allow* you to identify with your name, to *agree* that the strawman is you. Every time you do, then yes, you relinquish sovereignty and become their property. *They* have your strawman, held in bondage, so you are bound by their terms and conditions too. Sound familiar?"

"Yep, roger that. And just like your voice in our heads sounds like ours, we go along with it all 'cos our names look similar."

"Right, similar is not *the same*. Anything placed in capital letters is a legal fiction. Always remember, illusions can only contract with other illusions. In reality, you don't have a name, you *use* a name."

I nods, "One of the first things the Craft taught us, blend in, blend in, blend in – gave us a cover to use for every occasion."

"And did you believe these covers to actually define you?"

"'Course not, didn't get a bloody chance! There were so many. Sometimes you'd go native though, did happen, Sid was always a bit prone to that. But nah, I never knew who I was, that was precisely my problem."

"And precisely your advantage," grins over his cup. "To define is to *limit*. Now, listen carefully. The upside of freewill is there's always a remedy, you can get out any time you like. Along with your name – the strawman corporation – was created a bonded account. That is in fact what a Birth Certificate is, a *bond*. Complete with its unique tracking number, it's traded on the open financial markets—"

"Money?"

"Again, no, the entire banking industry functions in deficit, there is no money in circulation, only promissory notes, IOUs. Therefore, your bond is not money, it is credit. Unlimited credit. Much the same as you were born with infinite, creative freedom, you were born with infinite financial freedom too. Everything you ever needed to 'buy' is in fact prepaid, but only when you reclaim your birthright, redeem your strawman and you set yourselves free."

"Blimey, feel like I should be taking notes on all this! You're saying we were made shareholders of our 'countries' at birth, so... we're minted but didn't know it? How do we get our hands on it?"

"The usual way. For starters, file a commercial lien against your strawman. It then becomes your debtor, you control it, and hence your unlimited credit, which you can then use to offset any debt." Shrugs, "Simple. The books are balanced, everybody's happy. But remember, there is no money. Only you, a living soul, by virtue of your heavenly signature can create the credit."

"Our heavenly signatures, blimey."

"Both the words 'heaven' and 'signature' share the same root, *firmament*, 'to be fixed in place.' And when you sign contracts to legitimise them, you're actually making them 'firm,' real and binding by celestial decree. Do you understand? That's how credit is created and money given 'value'– from birth your potential labour, your *energy* is used for collateral. How do you measure potential? Can't, it's potentially unlimited; the unconditional essence of existence itself—"

"Alright, got that," I cuts in, "But this could all be bullshit, for all I know. Sorry, no disrespect, I mean you are a Demon, nevertheless."

"Clearly," nod, nod, "And I have legions under my command; you're not the only transdimensional species out there."

"Right. So... why should I trust you?"

Grins, "Because everything I say is a lie."

"Including that?"

"Just said. And the One always provides a remedy for you lot. The true gift to all sovereign beings is that like your debts, all your sins are prepaid too. Forgiven. Literally, for-given and pre-paid. But, only if you're *ready* to reclaim them and *agree* that they are. See how all this works?" Beams a warm smile. "Your first contract was, indeed, a Contract with Heaven."

"And we broke it."

"No, that's impossible, you simply subcontracted with me," he shrugs, "Another cuppa?"

"Our word is our bond," I mutters slowly. "Alright then, fucking give me my leg back."

"What, here, now, even after everything we've——?"

"And keep it there this time! I'm not your strawman anymore and I'm not going nowhere without my leg. Call it a test of faith."

"You still don't get it, still don't see what we are."

"Oh I see what *I* am, but if all that wasn't bullshit, go on, now!"

And now he really was looking at me funny.

"Fine!" he snaps, slamming his cup down on the desk. "Suppose you'd better open your eyes a little more, hmmm? And *see*," he growls, tapping his keyboard, and I knew I was gonna regret it.

"Can't see!"

"That's 'cos you're blind, a blind cunt! But how's the leg?"

"The leg's there but I'm fucking blind!"

"'Course you are, not as much as you were, but do you trust——"

"I trust you! Put it all back to how it was! *Seriously*, please——"

"Pretty please?" he sings, and lets loose a peel of laughter.

"With cream on top! Do it!"

"Oh keep your knickers on," tap, tap, tap, "Better?"

He was grinning from here to Locale 64.

"We've all got to balance the books in my world, Joseph, one way or the other, we all have to play by the rules. Even me."

"Oh thank fuck, thank fuck…"

"This for that, tit for tat. *My* Law."

"Your law, yeah, I understand," I says, and I fucking meant it. "And you feel it too, that's what you're saying."

"If it's any consolation," he affirms, "Everything. You suffer, I suffer. You laugh, I laugh."

"What you do to others, you do to yourself. All is One."

"All is One, now you've got it!" He smiles pleasantly.

"Sir," I says, "I think I wanna go now, if that's alright."

"You've Chosen."

I nods. "No disrespect, but is it time yet?"

"Any time you like."

433

"And can I change my—?"

He laughs. "No, you can't change your mind afterwards, who do you think you are, Jack Robinson? The Choice wouldn't be a choice otherwise."

"Oh… then I think I know what I want to do."

Knowing squint, "It's the regrets, see, unfinished business; they nearly all wanna go back."

I nods. "Unfinished business."

Fingers positioned over the keyboard, the Creator smiles, delighted.

I shakes my head, "Locale 33, please."

"Oh?"

"I've no regrets."

"Interesting."

"But sir, will you, someone, please witness my last… acts?"

"Funny question. I love you," he grins, "For a price."

"And life's a sky of golden dreams," I mutters. "Alright, thanks," I says, leaning over his desk, reaching out my hand. "I mean it, thanks for everything, and don't be so hard on yourself, ay, you're doing pukka!"

"Dirty job, but someone's gotta do it!" Puts out his hand, "Pleasure to make your acquaintance, Joseph, I mean it too."

"Pleasure's all mine," says I – and quicker than you can say 'Jack Robinson,' Barbelo's fingers were tap, tap, tapping away furiously into his snazzy telly.

The Creator leaps up from his seat, "Oh no, no, nooo!"

"*Maktub*, mate, sorry—"

"But you're on the threshold to—"

"Takes a cunt to catch a cunt!"

I slipped into his chair.

"On your feet Captain, that's a fucking order!"

For a split second his eyes darkened, black pools of eternal horror and despair. I find myself slowly rising—

"*Non Serviam!*" I growls into his mind.

He stumbles, arms thrashing about, and recoiling from my piercing glare, slumps down heavily onto the wooden box by my desk, "Captain, please, you were on your last card! I'll ask you again, get up—"

"Bit miffed, are we?" I winks, grinning my battle-grin of triumph, "Just redeeming my strawman, ha!"

"Fair dues, then," he groans, "fair dues, you win, you win it all. The Hot Seat's yours."

"Yep, all of it, the whole World!" I delights, swinging around in my chair, "Nothing personal, but unfinished business, see, and I can't risk everything on all that Awen codswallop – not mine leastways – and a gentleman's gotta follow through."

"Always," he chuckles, returning to his 'normal' jovial self.

"So where do you wanna go?" I asks, peering into the screen, "Before I gets stuck in, sort this bloody mess good and proper."

Glancing around my lovely gaff, he shrugs, and passes me the Tarot Cards, "Much the same to me. Shuffle the pack…"

I shuffle, and flip a card over.

The Fool.

He chuckles again, but with glee, exactly how I do when I've got one over somebody, and it hits me like a ton of bricks.

Smiles, "Would you have Eternity and give it away?"

I quickly reshuffle the pack, flip another card.

The Fool.

"Oh you can do that forever, mate. Believe me, I did."

I shuffle again.

The Fool.

Laughs, "Takes a cunt to catch a cunt!"

"Oh bollocks."

Nods, "Hell being stuck here. Pardon the pun, couldn't help it," shoots me an earnest frown, scoops the card from the table, "You've really no idea how long I've waited for this," he sighs, "Turned up trumps and with a clean slate an' all! Thanks for my Second Chance."

"I've muffed it, haven't I…"

"Depends, I'm game if you are," points at the keyboard, "Plenty of choice there. Just start tapping, I could really, really do with a wake-up call…"

Chapter Zero

Always Was, Always Will Be

… And my old misery cane went tap, tap, tapping through the underpass; dripping the evening rain, drumming a hundred regrets into my brain—

"Alright granddad?"

"Please, stand aside young man, I—"

"Stand aside? Oi, oi, the old fool thinks he's Robin Hood!" His forearm pinned my throat to the wall, his blade flashed under my nose, time slowed down – my senses quickened.

"Please… oh don't hurt me, let me go…"

Laughter from the shadows, two more young'uns peeling themselves off the wall.

"Empty ya fucking pockets!"

I slipped my memorial pen out of my breast pocket, held up in front of his face.

"It's gold plated! This is all I have. Please, let me go home young man, I'm too old for this."

"Let's have a butcher's then, ay?"

He reaches out to grab my pen, his cutthroat razor slipped; slashing my hand – Blood!

My blood.

"Oopsy-daisy, sorry 'bout that, granddad, it was—"

Wait!

Time stood still. A fit-bird with tastiest two legs in history flashes before my sight. A fleeting impression only, just a memory cast in the mind's eye alone – what was her name again?

No, not her, the other one…

Oh right, Sammy.

Gone.

Replaced by this lovely geezer making me lovely cups of tea in an L-Shaped Room—

I am you, you am I!

Time speeds up again.

"It was an accident," he says, "Didn't mean it."

Fuck me sideways, now there's a turnout for the books!

"It was an accident?"

He shrugs, taking a quick glance at the inscription on my pen,

"Who's Mad Mick, then?" he sniggers.

"A friend, a *good* friend."

He laughs again, "Mad was he?"

"Loop the fucking loop mate!"

We both laughs.

"Interesting dilemma, this," I says.

"Oh?"

"Yeah, and I think I knows what happens next, but either way, you shouldn't be doing this, young man, and you two an' all!" I yells to his mates, shuffling in the shadows, "Shouldn't be lurking about hurting people, it's not civil!"

Laughter.

"I'm just having a bubble!" says he, "Fucking hell, just give us the pen and fuck off."

"Very well then," I sighs, "have it and let us go home, ay?"

"Fair dues, granddad—"

"Oh shit, oh no – look!"

"What—"

I points, he turns around.

"A baby wolf!"

My walking stick slaps into his groin – my pen drives hard into his eye socket.

Screaming onto his knees, dragging me down with him, again and again I drove my memorial pen into his eyes.

It was easy logic, a religious matter, my Barbelo-given right!

It was the oldest trick in the book.

Well I wouldn't be a cunt, if I wasn't a cunt, would I?

Pukka.

Let's have another go then, who's next…

☠ The End of the Beginning ☠

☠ The Beginning of the End ☠